HEART
QUEST.

More to Love

HeartQuest brings you romantic fiction
with a foundation of biblical truth.
Adventure, mystery, intrigue, and suspense
mingle in these heartwarming stories of
men and women of faith striving to build
a love that will last a lifetime.

May HeartQuest books sweep you
into the arms of God, who longs for you
and pursues you always.

CAMP HOPE

Forgotten Justice

LOIS RICHER

Romance fiction from
Tyndale House Publishers, Inc., Wheaton, Illinois

www.heartquest.com

Visit Tyndale's exciting Web site at www.tyndale.com

Check out the latest about HeartQuest books at www.heartquest.com

Forgotten Justice

Copyright © 2004 by Lois Richer. All rights reserved.

Cover photograph © by Jerome Tisne/Getty Images. All rights reserved.

Cover image of forest © by Photos.com. All rights reserved.

HeartQuest is a registered trademark of Tyndale House Publishers, Inc.

Edited by Lorie Popp

Designed by Ron Kaufmann

Published in association with the literary agency of Janet Kobobel Grant, Books & Such, 4788 Carissa Ave., Santa Rosa, CA 95405.

This novel is a work of fiction. Names, characters, places, and incidents are either the product of the author's imagination or are used fictitiously. Any resemblance to actual events, locales, organizations, or persons, living or dead, is entirely coincidental and beyond the intent of either the author or publisher.

Library of Congress Cataloging-in-Publication Data

Richer, Lois.
  Forgotten justice / Lois Richer.
    p. cm. — (Camp Hope ; 2)
  ISBN 0-8423-6437-4 (sc)
  1. People with disabilities—Fiction. 2. Canada, Northern—Fiction. 3. Amnesia—Fiction. I. Title.
  PR9199.4.R53F67 2004
  813'.6—dc22   2004019186

Printed in the United States of America

09 08 07 06 05 04
9 8 7 6 5 4 3 2 1

*This book is dedicated
to the One who knew me before.*

ACKNOWLEDGMENTS

My grateful thanks and appreciation to Ken and Louise and all the staff at Torch Trail Bible Camp. Your labors of love may go unrewarded but not unnoticed. Thanks also to my local RCMP detachment for their generous assistance.

To Rhonda: My darling girl, that chair will never hold you back from anything God wants you to do.

A heartfelt thank you to Anne Goldsmith, Lorie Popp, and all the Tyndale staff for their persistence.

To Janet Grant for her wisdom and patience.

To the generous, wise, and always on-call e-mail friends who've supported me so much, I owe you.

To Barry and the boys—no more bologna sandwiches.

To the Father of Life—my questions will never stop, but You hold the answers.

PROLOGUE

Chicago
April

At first he'd thought it was a joke.

For two weeks the misguided e-mails had flooded his mailbox—strangely worded messages with grim directives for deeds so horrific he refused to give them credence.

Until this one. He couldn't ignore this one, not given what he'd already seen.

The sender put up all kinds of electronic impediments to cover his tracks, but none that couldn't be breached—if you knew what to do.

He knew.

Minutes later, the information he sought scrolled across his computer monitor. Hairs on the back of his neck rose as the implications hit home. The traitor had joined forces with those who sought only destruction. According to this latest missive, they now knew his intentions.

The order was unmistakable: He was to die.

How long did he have left? Moments? Hours?

He swallowed the coppery taste of fear and frantically punched buttons on the keyboard, knowing the next step could cost him greatly. Fine. He would deal with that.

But no one else would pay.

A noise in the hallway alerted him to the presence of an intruder. He held his breath and waited for his PC to finish its task. Two minutes later he had what he needed. After rendering the hard drive of his personal computer unreadable, he shut it down, reached for his laptop, and slid it into its leather case.

His gaze skimmed the room for an escape. An odor, pungent yet somehow familiar, carried through the air vent. If he could smell dynamite, they must be very near. The only light came from the hall-way.

He froze when he heard the elevator open, then observed a man in combat fatigues walk past his window, weapon drawn. The door-knob rattled. He slumped against the wall as the door swung open.

"Hurry!" One black-gloved hand beckoned him out.

No time for questions. He stepped over the would-be soldier now lying prone in the hallway.

"Take the stairs. Disappear."

Then he was alone, the piercing scream of the security alarm rattling his head as he silently descended the steps two at a time. To avoid the foyer, he stole onto a service elevator that slid him to the basement with barely a whisper.

Gray walls, gray floor, gray light—it was like walking into a cement coffin.

He took a step, remembered the e-mail.

Use any means.

Fifty feet away his car waited, but they knew that. They knew everything about him and they would be waiting.

He squeezed the handles of his laptop case tighter, eased past two delivery vans, and crept up the incline of the parking ramp. Outside he pasted himself against a wall as two men raced up the ramp toward an SUV, jumped inside, and tore down the street.

More noise ahead.

Like a statue, he paused in the gloom, sucking soundless breaths into his lungs while police cars rushed past. The metal doors of the garage rattled shut, sealing off that escape.

It came to him then that he was in over his head. This was not his business; he knew nothing about the covert games of intrigue and furtive machinations those e-mails had described.

Even though he was innocent of the crimes they'd planned, it didn't matter. By keeping their secret for even a minute, he'd become as involved as surely as if he'd signed their membership form with his blood.

But no longer.

Rain peppered him, soaking through his custom-made suit jacket to his silk shirt underneath, yet unable to penetrate the thick bubble wrap that covered a piece of evidence lying next to his heart. He brushed one hand across his eyes, scanning the panorama before him.

It was now or never. Confusion provided the cover he needed to escape, if he could only figure out how.

Two blocks away was a bus shelter, and another one waited across the street. In the distance he spotted a Chicago Transit Authority bus lumbering toward him. Getting to the shelter would put him in the open, but it was unlikely that anyone would notice one more businessman in the early-evening rain. He kept his head down, waited for traffic to abate, then sprinted across the glistening pavement. He bought a paper and pretended to study it.

The bus did not come. He leaned on one foot, then the other, forcing his mask of unconcern to remain in place, risking surreptitious glances down the street. At last the bus lurched away from the curb on the adjacent block, then jerked to a halt to admit a latecomer.

He recognized his foe—even from this distance.

Immediately he stepped back into the shadow of an elaborate awning, saw the man move slowly to the back of the bus, head rotating from side to side, searching the faces, looking for someone—him!

Using a signboard as cover, he prayed the bus would pass this stop without pausing. When its red taillights finally melted into a gaseous fog of diesel and water spray, he slipped out of his hiding place and strolled down the street into a bookstore. Walking to the back, he pretended to study the titles displayed, while retreating ever farther into the rows of shelves.

The laptop dragged on his arm, a constant reminder that he must pass on his knowledge before it was too late. He thrust one hand into his pocket, felt a card, pulled it out, read the number. The man outside his office?

He flipped open his cell phone, remembered the device he'd found under the edge of his desk this morning, thought twice. Of all people, he knew how easy wireless devices were to home in on. He eased the cell back into his jacket.

Frustration ate at him. Useless. It was all useless.

He'd been so focused, so determined to push himself to the top of the heap, to regain what had been stolen from him. But what did success matter if he disappeared without a trace?

Revenge no longer seemed so important.

He crumpled the card in his clenched fist. Turning, he saw the pay phone and approached it. Dial tones were replaced by a series of clicks and beeps. Finally a voice gave him instructions and a password, then a location.

Relief squeezed from his lungs, then caught in a choke of surprise as a hand closed around his forearm.

"You'd better come with me." The steely barrel pressed against his spine demanded his cooperation. There was no escape.

So it was over.

Funny, he'd thought his life would amount to more. As he walked forward, he was reminded of all the things he hadn't done, the promises he hadn't kept. His worst regret was Sally.

An altercation at the door momentarily loosened the clutch of fingers. It was an opportunity he couldn't ignore. A push, a shove, and he was free, racing down the street, running away from the hate.

But for how long?

CHAPTER ONE

Northern Canadian Woods
September 1

They're not coming."

Despair reached down and blew out the last flicker of hope in Christa Anderson's heart. Drawing upon her newly found courage, she fought past the black cloud and infused her voice with an upbeat tone.

"You might as well take that gorgeous tray of goodies back and share them with Fred. It's almost his coffee time anyway." Christa swallowed the lump in her throat. "I don't think I'll be needing them."

"Try calling again, honey. Maybe there's a problem." Ever the optimist, Ralna Jones believed in giving second, third, even fourth chances.

Christa slid the cell phone from the side pocket of her wheelchair, dialed, and waited. On the ninth ring she accepted defeat. "No answer. Which is really a very clear answer." She tucked the phone away, then forced a smile. "Let's forget I ever thought of this, okay? But thanks for helping me."

"Anytime. You know that." Ralna hugged her tightly, like a grandmother trying to ease the hurt. She gathered up the picnic things, stuffed them into the basket, and left in the direction of the dining hall.

Only when Ralna's bustling figure disappeared did Christa finally accept what her head had already admitted. The six former high school friends she'd invited out here to Camp Hope for the afternoon had silently but effectively declined her invitation to forgive the past and move on.

Well, she deserved it. They'd come after the accident—the first day Christa had come home from the hospital—with books, flowers, cards, and tentative smiles, olive branches outstretched. But she'd pushed it all in their faces and demanded they leave her alone. So they had.

I'm sorry. Regret for what could have been overflowed. *I didn't realize how much I'd lost.* Forgiveness—easily asked for, warily given.

Though the empty afternoon loomed before her, Christa couldn't concentrate on camp crafts now. So she steered her chair inside the craft shack and slowly packed her dreams into a small wooden box, excitement leeched away by dashed hope. When everything was squashed inside the box, she pushed it under a stack of donated odds and ends. Maybe tomorrow she'd have the heart to turn them into a project for next summer's junior camp.

A noise outside drew her attention. "Kent, is that you?"

No one answered.

Christa moved to the door, expecting her brother's goofy grin. It wasn't there.

But someone had been. A muddy footprint in the center of the path hadn't been there when she'd arrived.

"Hello? Anybody?"

No response.

She urged her wheelchair outside, glanced both ways. To the south, the covered pool looked desolate without a squealing mass of excited kids cavorting in it. Nearby the camp horses placidly grazed, munching on whatever green sprouts they could find in the pasture. To the north, no familiar figure walked around the silent dining hall or camp office. In front of her the playground swings remained still. At the moment, the usually bustling campgrounds looked entirely deserted.

That's weird. She shrugged, turned her chair, prepared to close up the craft shack. *I'm sure I heard something.*

It took only a few moments to snap the padlock shut. She forced her wheelchair to turn in the clinging sand and headed for Camp Hope's main office. Her fingers eased off the control knob when she spied a wisp of smoke in a cavern of cleared forest behind the cluster of girls' cabins. Someone was burning something.

Hopefully the fire was under control and whoever was responsible for it would make sure it was out before leaving. The last thing anyone wanted in these dry conditions was a forest fire. The thick woodland blanket of spruce and pine needles provided perfect tinder for a blaze that would be hard to extinguish. She'd mention it at dinner. Someone would check.

That decided, she pressed the button that sent the motor whirring into action, carrying her chair to the office. Would the letter be there yet? Her dreams would live or die by that letter.

But what if—?

Lately whenever she got stuck on what-ifs, Christa sought out her friend John Riddle, Camp Hope's computer guru. He'd arrived a couple of months before via the Royal Canadian Mounted Police, who'd found him beaten, lying by the roadside. Aptly named by the RCMP, John Riddle was a complete enigma. He didn't know his name or where he came from. He had stayed because no one else could find out either.

The first time they'd met, John found Christa lying face-first in the dust, unable to get back into her wheelchair. From that moment on, John ignored her demands to be left alone. Eventually Christa found herself looking forward to their verbal duels. After a while, she'd simply accepted his friendship.

It was because of John that Christa had decided to initiate her plan. She wouldn't leave until after Kent was married, but she could take the first step by figuring out how to get the house in shape. Unfortunately housekeeping had never been Christa's strength. She preferred not to ask Ralna to help, especially after the busy summer Camp Hope had enjoyed. With a new grandchild, Ralna's spare moments were devoted to her family, which was as it should be.

Maybe if I hire someone . . . The motor on Christa's wheelchair matched the whir of her brain as she mulled over a solution. She could ask the Murdock sisters, members of the small church in the nearby community. Those two gentle souls had their fingers on the pulse of the community so they would know of someone suitable.

Solving that dilemma seemed doable. Now if only the letter was there. *This waiting is killing me.* She nudged the knob, upping her speed. Patience was an attribute she still needed to work on. If the letter had arrived, Christa didn't want anyone to see it before she knew its contents. The project was her secret, and for now she intended to keep it that way.

She paused in front of the office, savoring the freshness of the air. Even the giant sunflowers nodding their heads beside the dining hall seemed to perk up with the cooler days that signaled autumn's arrival at Camp Hope.

Autumn, her favorite season. A time to relax and regroup. A time to harvest what had been sown.

Please, God?

To her utter delight and nervous trepidation, she spotted an envelope on the corner of Ralna's desk as soon as she entered the office. Plain. Ordinary. Except for the logo in the top left-hand corner. An answer.

Christa snatched the envelope up, slipped it under her left thigh, and arranged her sweater to cover it. Guilt kicked her heartbeat into high. That was the problem with secrets; you had to keep covering your tracks.

Glancing around to see if anyone had noticed, Christa saw the man she sought sitting silently before the camp's computer screen across the room. She approached him. "John?"

He seemed not to hear. His chest expanded as he took a deep breath before opening his eyes. He began typing in rapid sequences. Mere seconds elapsed before a Web page burst upon the screen, a page whose words filled her with apprehension, and yet she couldn't look away from it.

John, too, seemed mesmerized. "There's something I was supposed to do. Something that means life or death to someone. But I can't remember what it was."

She reached out to touch his shoulder, to offer a scrap of comfort that might relieve that tortured note in his voice. But before her fingers made contact, a deep sense of foreboding filled the room. Christa froze, her arm hanging in midair while a voice inside her head warned her to wait and watch what happened next.

John stabbed at the bottom of the screen with one finger. "Look." *October 29.*

"Today's the first of September. That means it's almost two months away." He grated the words out. "Two months until the deadline."

"What deadline?" Christa huddled in her chair, a tickle of fear enhancing her already active sense of dread. Though the office was stuffy, she shivered as if winter had moved into the room. A prayer for protection trembled on her lips as she surveyed the man before her.

"I don't know," John whispered in a ragged voice, his navy eyes wide with confusion. "I have no idea how to stop it."

"Stop what? John, what are you talking about?"

"I only know that it will happen," he repeated, his voice one notch above a whisper. "On October 29 it will happen."

"Unless you stop it?"

He nodded.

Her eyes tracked his, focused on the screen. "But what is it, and how can you stop it?"

"I don't know," he groaned. His tormented gaze held hers. "I can't remember."

CHAPTER TWO

Y ou really outdid yourself with this dinner." Kent Anderson grinned at his bride-to-be.

"Thank you, darling." Georgia MacGregor leaned across the table to brush her lips against his cheek. "Gallant, as always. But I think the delights of this meal have more to do with the loads of fresh garden produce people have been bringing us than with my culinary expertise. Everything tastes great when it's fresh."

John Riddle shifted, discomfited by the affection between the camp director and his fiancée. Something in him yearned to share the kind of tenderness these two showered on each other.

Though they'd allowed only a scant two weeks between the last day of summer camp and their wedding, neither Kent nor Georgia appeared bothered by a wealth of prenuptial details or by John's presence in their lives.

"We want a simple wedding ceremony in the chapel here, with a small reception to follow in the dining hall, and we want you to be an usher." Kent's face had beamed when he shared their plans with John.

"Then Georgia and I are going to disappear for a week. Think you can keep Ralna, Fred, and Christa busy?"

"I'll try."

Busy . . . until October 29. That date burned in his mind while the feeling of impending doom after looking at that Web site this afternoon returned in double portions.

"Kent, I noticed someone had lit a fire." Christa looked troubled. "There was smoke behind the girls' cabins earlier. You might want to check it out during your rounds tonight. It's getting awfully dry out there."

"I'll do that," Kent promised, his smile drooping. "I wish these trespassers would find another place to intrude. I've posted enough signs. But with open season, I suppose the hunters are bound to show up. This afternoon I found some candy wrappers out behind the barn. Maybe it was the same person." Sighing, he rubbed the back of his neck. "Everything is like tinder, just waiting for a spark."

"It would be nice to get some rain without the lightning. That would help. We'll have to keep praying." Georgia seemed to share Kent's worry with a gentle smile.

"So who do you think was eating candy out there? Kids, hunters, or vagrants?" Christa glanced around for a consensus. "All of the above?"

"Kids would explain the candy," Kent muttered. "But Fred said he noticed a pile of stubbed-out cigarettes at the corner of the chapel when he was mowing just before supper. From the way the grass was packed, he guessed someone had been standing there for a while. That doesn't sound like a kid or a hunter."

John frowned. Someone had come to the camp and he hadn't noticed. But he'd been outside, working along the road all afternoon.

Except when I was at the computer.

His hands fisted at his sides and his eyes closed. How could a machine have the same effect as an opiate? How could a screen no more than fifteen inches across hypnotize him so he forgot everything else?

"Somebody poke John. He's falling asleep." Georgia's soft voice drew him from his introspection. "Is Kent working you too hard?"

"Far from it. In fact, I can't imagine he's getting his money's worth when you consider what I'm costing this place in meals." He grinned. "I eat an awful lot."

"Not as much as Kent. If he doesn't stop, he won't fit in his suit for the wedding," Christa teased, grinning when her brother responded by puffing out his cheeks like a chipmunk.

"Please don't worry about that, John. You've saved us a lot of money with all the work you've done on our computer. I don't think a few meals would equal the bill we'd have if we hired someone." Georgia held up a pie plate. "More?"

John shook his head. "No, thanks. You spoil us, Georgia."

"After all you do, you can use a little spoiling."

He smiled at her, but inside he felt like a cheat. He did very little. What was worse, his attention was never fully on his work. He constantly planned enhancements to computer programs Camp Hope didn't have and dreamed up new ways to do things that had nothing to do with camp operations. He'd have to correct that.

He made a mental note to watch for intruders.

Christa turned away from the soft chuckles and teasing that her brother and Georgia indulged in regularly these days. She winked at John. "Let's shoo them away while we do the dishes," she whispered.

He nodded, rose, and began stacking plates, the memory of that Web page burning behind his eyes. The Society for Order.

"You've been staring at those plates for ages, John. Is something wrong?"

He blinked, turned to face Christa. "No."

Her forehead furrowed, but finally she looked away and began filling the sink with hot sudsy water. John carried the dishes to the counter, pretending everything was normal.

"Something's bothering you. I know because you've gone all quiet."

Christa always noticed details. Though she had always refused to leave her yard during summer camps—except for those times after dark when no one could see her legs—she'd still manage to spot a kid who didn't fit in, a kid who needed someone to talk to, a kid who was up to no good. Then she'd send John to intervene, which was kind of funny when you thought about it. Camp Hope was all about God, one subject about which John was completely illiterate. He'd tried to tell her that, but Christa had trouble with the word *no*.

He'd done as she asked, partly because even though Christa had begun to come to grips with her disability, she remained ultrasensitive about anyone staring at her useless legs. But mostly he'd done her bidding because he wanted to make that flash of joy dance through her pale blue eyes.

"If you're certain we can't help, then I guess we'll go for a walk." Georgia touched John's arm, her smile gentle, understanding. "Are you really all right?"

"How can you ask after such a delicious meal? It must be hard for the campers to go home after a week of eating at your table. Kent's very lucky you agreed to stay."

"Not luck, John. God. And, yes, God did me a very big favor when He sent this woman to Camp Hope." Kent's arm wove around Georgia's waist. "Come on, honey. Let's leave them to it. You know Christa sprays the entire kitchen when she washes dishes."

Christa aimed the sprayer at her brother. "Take that back, you slanderer!"

Kent ducked behind John, who wasn't fast enough to dodge the stream of water she directed his way. She soaked his shirt.

"You might have noticed that *I* didn't say a word." John lifted the sprayer from her fingers and replaced it. He looked down at himself and rolled his eyes at Kent's grin. "You owe me."

"For a lot more than that. I'll clean this up." Georgia dabbed at John's wet shirt with a cloth, raised one eyebrow. "Do you ever feel like a referee between these two overgrown kids?" she whispered loud enough for Kent and Christa to hear.

"Every so often. We'll have to discipline them." John took the cloth from her with a smile. "I'll handle Christa. You go ahead and straighten him out."

"I think it's too late." Georgia shook her head when Kent tossed a spoon into the sink in front of Christa, deliberately splashing her. "Come with me," she ordered, threading her arm through Kent's. Of course, Kent didn't argue. In fact, neither one appeared unhappy to leave the kitchen.

Yesterday the couple had barely waved good-bye to the last of the summer staff before buckling down to prepare for three new groups who'd rented the facilities. John figured the least he could do was help with the dinner dishes. He hadn't done dishes since . . .

He picked up a plate and began rubbing, his gaze fixed on something he couldn't quite see.

"John, you've looked out the window six times since dinner began. Are you expecting someone?" Christa squeezed a few more drops of lemon-scented detergent into the sink, then started washing the cutlery.

"Not necessarily expecting."

"What does that mean?"

He debated the wisdom of telling her and decided it didn't matter. Everyone probably figured he was a little off his rocker anyway. "While I was cutting grass this afternoon, the same car drove past three times."

"Maybe they were lost." She flicked soapsuds at him and giggled when they backfired and landed on her nose. "Since the car didn't stop, don't worry about it. You don't have to look for problems. We've got enough on our plates with the wedding coming up."

"You sound as if you're the wedding planner or something." He added a stack of plates to her water.

He liked it that Christa confided in him. Only tonight there was something different about her. He couldn't put his finger on it . . . yet.

"In a way, I guess I am planning it—or parts of it." She made a face. "Georgia is worried about making a fuss. She insists on keeping everything so plain. I'm worried that she'll be sorry later, so I'm adding a few teensy tiny details."

"Teensy. Uh-huh." Christa loved planning surprises and he knew it. "You look small and defenseless. That chair even makes you look frail. But I know the truth about you."

"What truth?" She blinked her innocent baby blues.

John wasn't fooled. Christa Anderson was no delicate flower. He'd seen her grit her teeth and push past the pain. He'd watched her face her mistakes head-on. She had spunk, ingenuity, determination, but she also tended to hide her fears behind a mask of capability that made everyone think she'd fully recovered from her depression. He knew it wasn't true. She was free enough in camp, but he wasn't sure she'd really addressed her fears about appearing in public.

"I know you're tough. Once you make up your mind about something, nothing short of an earthquake could change it."

"That doesn't sound very flattering." Christa spun around to the sink once more, the curve of her shiny brown hair shielding her face, but he knew she was smiling.

Though Christa was lovely to look at, it was her heart John admired most—her big, open heart that, once released from her own hurt, couldn't help making other people's worlds all right, even though hers was still a little rocky. As Sally would say, she was a born buttinski.

Sally?

"It wasn't supposed to be flattering. It was supposed to be the truth. But just because you're gaining confidence doesn't mean you have to pretend everything is all right. It's okay to ask for help, you know."

"I know." Christa sighed, then grinned. "I want Kent and Georgia's wedding to be something they'll cherish, so I'm working on a couple of really special things. You could help me with them."

"That wasn't what I meant and you know it; but I'll help with whatever you want." John waited, but when she didn't explain, he let it go. Christa did things in her own time. She'd explain when she was ready. "I feel awful for disrupting your peace of mind with that ugly Web site."

"It was just a Web site. I'm fine."

"Sure you are." John had learned to catalog every nuance of her voice in his otherwise useless brain. He had firsthand knowledge of her innate curiosity, so he figured she'd been wondering about the Web site ever since he'd clicked on it. And despite her protest, he'd seen her shiver when she read the horrid words.

"You're going to have to stop worrying about me."

"Okay, *I'm* not fine." He met her gaze. "All the Web site talked about was revenge. It's . . . unsettling."

"I didn't get to see a lot because you clicked off too soon. But what I did read bugs me too," she admitted quietly. "Everything was so negative, so miserable. I'd like to take a second look sometime, see if there's some way to change their opinion."

Over his dead body! No way was John going to let her get to that site again. "Stop pretending and tell me the truth. Are you feeling miserable about something, Chris?"

He saw Christa's frown that dissipated when she looked at him. "Not miserable." Her contemplative tone sounded faraway. "But sometimes I feel in the way."

"Why? You belong here. Camp Hope is your home."

She gave him an arch look. "Newlyweds want time alone together, private romantic moments that only the two of them should share. I'm a fifth wheel, stuck in the middle."

Her words stunned him. Christa had changed so much from the sad, defeated woman he'd first met. She was making a lot of progress toward accepting her limitations, and he hoped she'd continue to work toward becoming less self-conscious. But tonight she sounded dissatisfied, as if she wanted to get away. "Has anyone made you feel as if you're in the way?"

"Of course not!" She started filling the sink with clean water for the pots and pans. "I don't mean it's anyone's fault. I'm only trying to tell you how I feel. Can't you imagine what it's like?"

He couldn't suppress a grin. "You're trying to explain to me about being in the way?"

"Yes." Her head tipped to one side. "What's so funny about that?"

"Everything. How do you think I've felt ever since I arrived at Camp Hope? I have no idea what I'm doing here; I'm interrupting everyone else's life; and I have no concept of when I'll leave or where I'll go when I do. In fact, I don't know anything for sure. Trust me, the one thing I completely grasp is the feeling of being in the way."

"I'm sorry." Christa patted his arm, leaving a wet spot on his sleeve. "Oops! Anyway, I shouldn't be complaining. Compared to yours, my problems must seem small."

He hated it that he'd made her feel guilty. "Listen to me." John hunkered down in front of her chair, grasped one of her wet hands, and held it between his.

He lowered his voice, hoping to reassure her. "You're not in the way. Everyone knows that there are adjustments to be made, and we all understand that no one has to make more of them than you. You're dealing with your world in your own way. Don't get side-tracked by maybes, and don't be so impatient. Just keep pushing ahead. One day at a time, remember?"

She nodded but didn't look at him. That was noteworthy. Christa was earnest about everything. But she also worried about being a burden. Over the past few days he'd glimpsed the shadows dancing at the back of her eyes and knew they held a secret.

"There's something you're not saying. Do you want to keep tiptoeing around what's really bothering you, or do you want to tell me the truth?"

"The truth." Christa drew a deep breath. "I'm planning to leave Camp Hope."

The words threw him. His confidante, the one person he'd been able to really talk to, would be gone. Questions raged inside him, but he knew he couldn't ask them. It was none of his business, and besides, he had no right to question her decisions.

"You're not saying anything."

"I'm surprised, I guess." That was an understatement. Without Christa, Camp Hope would be an empty place.

"You're surprised because I've spent so long hiding out and

suddenly I want to fly the coop? Or because even after all this time it still bugs me when people stare at my legs or my chair, and you're wondering how I'll handle that in the real world?" She shrugged. "I guess I'll have to take your oft-repeated advice and face reality."

John nodded, stalling.

"Maybe it sounds crazy, but leaving is something I need to do. It's the only way I can get on with my life and start working toward a future."

"You have to go away to do that?" He swallowed, fighting the lump lodged in his throat.

"Yes, I think maybe I do."

He didn't want her to go. Christa had shared so many of his self-doubts, his nebulous memories, his frustrations. Her constant assurances had helped him through many haunting uncertainties. Without her, he would be alone again.

John straightened his shoulders, trying to find a mantle of bravado he didn't feel. An obstinate wave of sandy hair flopped over one eyebrow. Georgia's styling now rendered his hair neat and tidy, but according to Christa, it didn't come close to the perfectly snipped haircut he'd had the day he arrived at camp. He'd laughed at her description. No belongings but an expensive haircut. Yet another piece of the puzzle that made up John Nobody Riddle's blank past.

"When will you go?" John choked the question out. His fingers tightened around hers, as if he could hold her there and make her reconsider.

"I'm not sure. There are some things I have to do first. I just wanted you to know."

"I see." But he didn't see. Because of Christa, he'd found a measure of peace in days spent doing odd jobs around the camp. He'd looked forward to evenings and weekends chatting with her, teaching her chess, encouraging her to forget her handicap and focus on what she *could* do. Sure, he'd suggested she think beyond the boundaries of the camp—but not yet!

Now she'd taken him at his word. She would move and build herself a new life. And he would stay here . . . forever?

October 29.

He had to figure things out before then, but even if he did remember why that date was so important, Christa would be long gone. The loss of her accentuated the ache he'd tried so hard to bury. Alone again.

With one decision Christa Anderson had bumped John's entire world off kilter.

And he felt utterly powerless to right it.

⸺⬖⬗⸺

Washington, D.C.

He submitted to the security scans just like the others. Eyeballs, fingerprints, weapons check—all conducted by faceless robots who never spoke.

The check complete, a series of corridors and elevators carried him to a small steel room below the main level of a security building, where shadows lay so thick no one's face was identifiable, a protective measure to ensure that no single individual could be targeted for the outcome of today's vote.

They didn't realize the decision was his and his alone—or that he'd already made it.

He let them think they were in control by implementing this elementary procedure. Black marble for *no*, white marble for *yes*. The marbles waited in contrasting pairs—round glass balls that they believed would bring a conclusion to weeks of debate. Not that there had ever been any doubt.

From his vantage point, he watched the council members take their places at a polished steel table, saw the red Chinese bowl pass before each of the others with catlike stealth. His fingers rested on his worsted-wool pants as each member chose a marble to put in the bowl.

Every vote cast into the porcelain container echoed across the room in a stab of noise, drawing everyone's eyes though they couldn't see through the gloom. Seven reports in all—sharp, distinct, like gunshots. Fatal. Irrevocable.

Silence as the bowl disappeared.

No one spoke; no one moved. Not yet.

After accepting the bowl, he tallied the vote. No dissenters. Good. He'd taught them well. He leaned near the microphone to issue his verdict through invisible speakers behind their chairs. "Gentlemen, we have a decision. White wins—the decision is yes. Our plan will proceed as discussed. You will be escorted out. Good day."

Our plan? It was his and his alone! And it was pure genius.

The members filed from the room silently, each choosing the same separate path he had entered on.

Only one was barred from exiting the building, only one received an eight-by-ten glossy photo. Only one heard his faceless instructions. "This has gone on too long. He must be found. Immediately. You have been assigned this task. The success of our plan now rests on your shoulders. Do not fail."

No further explanation was given. None was needed.

He'd chosen his followers with foresight, then provided the appropriate training and knowledge for each level to perform as needed. His plan was infallible.

It would succeed.

No one could stop it.

CHAPTER THREE

Y ou're so quiet. Are you angry, John?" The painful silence in the small kitchen had stretched to gargantuan proportions. Christa felt uneasy. John's stony acceptance wasn't the response to her announcement she'd expected.

"Of course not," he insisted in a quiet voice. "Why should I be angry?"

"You're not saying anything."

"You're leaving. What is there to say?"

A *lot*, Christa thought. So many details to think of, unexpected challenges that she'd have to evaluate. Sometimes she was tempted to reconsider and forget about this crazy plan. But then the yearning to break free and find out what life held for her grew stronger. The need to prove she was going to be fine ate at her, and the knowledge that she owed Kent rested heavily on her conscience. She couldn't back down now.

The words from an old song reverberated quietly around the room. "It's my turn."

Whoever had written that couldn't have known how well it

applied to her. It *was* her turn. God had sent this opportunity—it was up to her to open the door no matter how difficult it would be to leave.

"I'll stay for a couple of weeks after the wedding." To make sure Kent didn't need her. Then she'd leave the newlyweds alone and get on with her own life. If everything worked out.

"So you're making a new start. That's great."

"You act as if you can't see that I'm in the way."

"Sometimes you are." He pointed to her chair blocking the cutlery drawer, eyes flickering with amusement at her groan. "Seriously? Don't be silly. You're less in the way than I am."

As if he suddenly realized that he still held her hand in his, he let it go and stood to peek out the kitchen window.

"What now?" Christa used the opportunity to study him. John Riddle would age wonderfully. His aristocratic nose and firm jaw gave him distinction. Over six feet tall, lean, and muscular, he had a certain unconscious authority, an assurance in his attitude that translated to the way he carried himself, as if he knew exactly where he was going and how to get there. His navy eyes only emphasized that confidence. To look at him no one would guess his mind withheld the secrets of his past.

"I thought I saw a shadow. Maybe it was someone walking past. Our newest intruder." John shrugged and turned to dry another pan.

"Doubtful. Trespassers don't often show themselves." She frowned, thinking about her plans. "You know, it's harder than I realized to make decisions about the future."

"Start with what you don't want," he suggested.

"I don't want to stay here." She resumed washing.

"Yes, you've already said you're leaving." He set the pan down, picked up another, and subjected it to the same torturous rubbing. "Would it be so terrible to stay?" A hint of rancor edged his usually smooth tone.

"Not terrible. But staying at Camp Hope forever is impossible. Leaving is something I have to do."

"Of course it is."

Christa bit her lip. So nonchalant. After the first few days he probably wouldn't even notice she was gone. Funny how that stung. "It's not that I don't want to stay. I *can't*. I don't belong here. This is Kent's milieu. I have to find my own place in the world. Anyway, it's not as though I'm going tomorrow." She frowned when he walked to the screen door and looked through it into the night. "What are you doing?"

"Looking outside." He faced her, eyes intense with thoughts he didn't share.

"You did that already. For anything in particular this time?"

"Just looking," he mumbled.

Christa had a hunch he was thinking about the Society for Order. "Forget that Web site. You are not part of that miserable group."

"You don't know that."

"Yes I do, John. The Society for Order has nothing to do with you." His lips tightened, but he simply returned to his task.

"If I can move on, so can you. It's taken me long enough." She grimaced at the memories. "After the accident happened, I gave up. It seemed like my life was over, and all I could do was put in time."

"Completely natural, I imagine. A time of grieving for what you'd lost." He kept his face averted. "But it's not the same for me, Christa. I haven't given up, but neither can I move ahead."

"You mean not until you remember your past?"

He touched her nose with his fingertip and trailed it down to her chin. "Don't look so sad. I'm fine. But our situations aren't the same. Your future looks bright, so go for it. But remember you don't have to do it alone." He glanced out the window again. "There. Did you hear something?"

She shook her head.

"Sounded like a car." He obviously saw her skepticism because he insisted, "It did!"

"Sure it did." His pained look made her sigh. "Fine. Maybe we'll have a real visitor, one who will come to the door and knock." Was he hoping someone would stop by to take his mind off things?

Christa kept working as she searched for a new topic, but nothing came to mind. Which was odd. She and John had always been able to discuss anything. There had never been enough hours to say all the things they'd wanted to, yet now awkward silence yawned between them like a chasm that couldn't be crossed.

John began drying the pot she'd left draining. Every so often his gaze shifted to the window. "Nobody there," he admitted when he caught her staring.

"It's that Web site that has you so nervous. Relax." She shifted in her chair, reaching to rinse the roaster. A crackle reminded her of the letter. One finger surreptitiously touched the envelope still under her leg. She longed to rip it open and find out if her dreams were feasible, but she'd wait until later after everyone had gone to bed to learn the answer. And if it was no—

"There! You had to hear that. I know that was something," John interrupted her thoughts.

"John, give it up." Exasperated, she glared at him. "Georgia and Kent are out there. Maybe Fred's working on the van or something. You're jumpy tonight."

"I'm not the type to get jumpy."

"Really?" She let her expression do the talking. "Anyway, I was thinking. The Society for Order sounds decent, like something ordinary people would want to belong to. But when you start reading the stuff they've posted, you realize they're nothing more than a hate group. At least, that's what I'd call it."

"I thought you didn't see much."

"I saw enough to notice they'd taken great pains to malign someone." She searched his face for some flicker of recognition. "They made a lot of threats against this man called Kane Connors. You kept looking at his picture so I wondered if his name rang a bell."

His forehead pleated in concentration as he hung his damp dish towel to dry, then lifted the plates onto their shelf. Christa pulled the stopper and spritzed water into the sink to wash away the suds.

"Connors. Kane Connors." John said it over and over, his voice growing progressively quieter. "The name is familiar, but I don't know it. Does that make any sense?" He waved his hand toward the door, one eyebrow raised. He was asking if she wanted to sit outside again tonight.

"We have to," she reminded him glumly, rolling out the door. "Solar flares, remember? Kent prompted us about six times during dinner. He's relentless when it comes to astronomy. Tomorrow he'll probably give us a pop quiz, so you'd better pay attention."

Minutes later John was busily building a campfire, as he had almost every night since he'd arrived.

Christa snuggled into the cowl neck of the sweater she'd just finished knitting, feeling a little like a caterpillar in a too-warm cocoon. "We won't see many solar flares with that going."

"I'll put it out later. According to Dr. Kent, the big event doesn't start till after nine." He glanced over his shoulder and winked. "Weren't you paying attention?"

"I heard every word. I just didn't absorb them all. Kent gets way too technical about his hobby. I'm glad he has Georgia to share it with."

She watched how carefully he built the fire in the enclosed pit, the way he filled a water bucket and set it nearby in case the wind blew the flames too high. He was methodical, conscientious, and organized in everything he did, which always made her speculate about his past.

In the three months she'd known John they'd shared a lot, usually beside a campfire. Strange that a few bits of wood snapping and glowing in the dark could create an intimacy not found in broad daylight. The anonymity of that darkness had eased Christa through many hard times and made sharing confidences so much easier.

But tonight she'd keep the letter to herself.

"What are you contemplating so deeply?" John asked.

"You." The answer slipped easily from her lips. "You've been such a good friend to me, listening whenever I need a shoulder to cry on."

He stopped shaving tinder from a log and stared at her, the axe by his side. "Has something happened that I don't know about?"

"Not that I know of. But as you've often reminded me, things change, sometimes quickly. I-I wanted to say that I've enjoyed knowing you, John." A lump of emotion clutched her throat, but Christa pressed on. "You dragged—even shoved—me through some very difficult days. I'll never be able to explain how much it means to me that you keep encouraging me to break free of this nagging depression."

"That's ridiculous." He shrugged off her words, his tone brusque. "I do less than what you, Kent, and Georgia do for me."

He was downplaying her desperate straits of a few months ago, and Christa was grateful. But one day soon she would leave this place and his friendship behind. When John remembered his past and returned to his own life, she didn't want regrets.

Of course a tiny part of her wished that their friendship could remain unchanged, but she was learning that a real friend wanted the best for the other. John needed to know who he was. He'd proven his friendship. She owed him the same loyalty.

Silence stretched between them. The longer autumn evenings meant the stars came out earlier. A streak of white shot through the sky.

"Oh, look!"

But by the time John followed her pointing finger there was nothing to see.

"You missed it. A shooting star." Feeling like a child, she squeezed her eyes closed, then made her wish. When she opened them, she met John's steady stare.

"I hope you get what you wished for." He hesitated. "Why did you thank me? Why now? I thought you said you weren't leaving immediately."

"I'm not. I'd appreciate it if you didn't mention it to my brother. I'll tell him," she explained hurriedly when his brows drew together, "but not yet. Not until my plans are firm. And I don't want to talk about the future anymore tonight. I'd rather enjoy the evening."

"Fine. Short conversation for me anyway. I haven't got a future. Or a past." He poked at the pile of wood with a long stick, his rough motions telegraphing his frustration.

"Of course you do! You have both. One day everything will click into place and you'll remember it all. You'll go back home and rejoin your world, and these days will seem like a bad dream." Christa forced a lilt into her voice. "I'm sure the police will find something new any day now."

"They haven't found anything in all these weeks. I doubt they'll turn up much now." When he looked at her, his expression was inscrutable. "I think it's time to resign myself to giving up on the past and focus on whatever future I can make. Maybe I should look for a job."

"Kent would give you one."

John snorted at her suggestion. "The camp director can't offer work to every stray who comes along. Besides, Camp Hope shouldn't have to pay me to make blunders on its property. It's bad enough they have to feed and house me. This place needs someone with experience who knows what he's doing. I have to learn everything about carpentry and maintenance the hard way."

"Well, where would you go? What would you do?"

"I don't know." He began chopping wood.

"I'll miss you very much if you go," she whispered. But she'd get over it. She had to. Their paths had crossed at Camp Hope, but they would part because finding her independence and building her own life was the only way to give Kent the freedom he deserved.

"I'll miss you too." Though he didn't turn to look at her, his voice grabbed her heart and squeezed.

Christa gulped. As she reached in her pocket for a tissue, her fingertips grazed the corner of the letter she'd taken from the office. "Before you do anything, you have to check with the police. But there's no rush. I know everyone wants you to stay."

"Since my mind is as blank as it ever was, looks like you'll get your wish, so don't plan a farewell party just yet." John split two birch logs into kindling, his movements swift and economical and a touch more forceful than necessary as he built a small tent around the tinder.

Christa caught the look on his face in the flare of the match he used to light the fire. She suspected John's harsh response was his way of brushing off thoughts of a future he couldn't envision. Instead of soothing, she'd made things worse. She had a knack for doing that.

"I could die happily sitting right here," she murmured, her senses actively absorbing her surroundings. "No matter where I go or what I do, I'll always think of our campfire nights as perfect little moments in time."

If he thought so too, he didn't say it. John remained silent for several moments, then resumed chopping.

Once the flames had grown into a steady flicker, casting a soft golden glow that chased away the evening's coolness, and there was nothing left to do, he pulled a chair near hers and sank into it. "Are you warm enough?"

"Yes, thank you." As she lifted her face into the breeze, she caught a faint shimmer of white through the trees across the road. A new intruder?

Christa glanced at John, intending to point it out, but he was concentrating on something else, his face turned away from her. His index finger and thumb played with the metal button on his jean jacket the way she'd seen Middle Eastern men fiddle with their worry beads.

Pop. Pop! Pop, pop!

"There it is again. I knew I heard something earlier." He jumped up and went striding into the darkness. "I'll be back in a minute," he called over one shoulder. The sound of his footsteps crunching across the gravel road faded. After a moment Christa saw a flicker of light and assumed it was his flashlight, which he always carried in his pocket.

She wondered if her words had made him feel like he should leave the camp. Perhaps he needed space away from her. Her heart ached for his situation, and she tried to remember when John's welfare had become so significant to her.

Moments later John came back.

"Find anything?"

"These." He held up thin slivers of wood about fifteen inches long with burned tips. "Kids and matches. I wonder why their parents don't keep them at home." He threw the wood into the fire.

"Kids need to explore. Besides, all the best stories take place in the woods. And that's what we're surrounded by. You can't blame them for wanting to share our forest." She scoured the darkness beyond him, trying to catch sight of someone.

"I'll look again in the daylight. There were lots of tracks and what looked like a pile of ashes." John flopped into his chair. "Good thing school's started. Give these kids something else to do."

Christa shook her head, remembering. "They'll be back when it snows or gets very cold. We have a built-in attraction beyond camp property by the creek. Kids have been going there for ages. There's a great big rock that soaks up the sun during the day, and if you sit on it at night, it keeps you warm for a while."

If she imagined hard enough, she could almost feel the heat from that rock penetrating to her legs. Her useless legs.

No going back. Push forward. Gulping down the sting of pain, she rushed into speech. "I kissed Thomas Tunney on the cheek when I was in third grade. We were sitting on that rock. Only it wasn't at night. It was the middle of the afternoon. He ran away bawling." With the tip of her finger she pressed away a single tear and forced a smile.

If only she'd known then what she knew now about hurting people. You could never take it back, never. Poor Thomas.

"A terror in grade three, hmm?" One eyebrow arched in reproof, though John grinned at her blush of embarrassment. "Kissing probably scared the daylights out of him."

"Maybe. It was my first time at camp. I just wanted a friend."

The aroma of freshly cut alfalfa wafted over from a nearby field. She turned her head and saw a bit of white fabric disappear in the bushes to the right of where she'd seen it before. The same glossy blond head topped it.

Another pop surprised Christa until she remembered Georgia and

Kent. The noise could have been a branch they stepped on, and Kent could have had a flashlight. Surely they'd soon run into whoever was out there.

"I didn't know you'd attended camp here as a child."

"Oh yes. Camp Hope and I have a history." She lapsed into those happier memories.

A giggle broke the silence of the evening.

John nudged her, his eyes wide with an unasked question.

She shook her head. "Leave the kids alone," she whispered. "Kent will find them." In a louder voice she continued. "I love this season. When autumn comes, it's like life is letting you draw a second breath so you can take stock of things and prepare before winter hits."

There was a sudden scramble in the bushes, then Kent's low rumble as he called out the names of two local teens.

"Don't take this the wrong way, but I told you so." Christa laughed at John's look of disgust.

"You were talking about autumn," he reminded her grumpily.

"I thought I was talking about Kent." She hid her smile. "Anyway, did you notice a few leaves have already started to change color? I used to love walking by the creek after the first frost. If I sat on my rock and waited long enough, deer would come to drink."

She would never walk there again. Christa swallowed the hurt, got past it, and realized it was getting easier to let go of what could have been. Thanks to John.

This time the giggles came from a totally different place. Christa tried to catch sight of who might be hiding there. The laughter grew louder.

"I don't think those kids are up to anything good. I'm going to chase them away." John disappeared into the gloom for a second time.

Sighing, Christa closed her eyes. She was pretending to enjoy this evening for John's sake, but at the moment her body was so tense her neck caused pain halfway down her back. The canceled party, that Web site, worrying about the letter—all of it combined into a painful squeeze of her neck muscles.

She'd never been great at tricking her mind into relaxation in rehab, but why not try now? While a seascape scene expanded in her mind, her other senses picked up on the liquid patter of water dribbling over brook stones in the creek beyond, the leftover aroma of vinegar and dill from Georgia's newly preserved pickles, and the whisper of wind telling secrets in the tops of the wavering pine trees.

A loud bang killed the mood. Christa flinched, stared into the night sky, and saw puffs of smoke that fireworks left behind.

"Get a grip," she muttered, disgusted with herself for not recognizing the sound earlier. "It's the annual back-to-school fireworks." She waited a moment, then nodded. Just one. Good. Less danger of starting a fire.

Her pulse rate was almost normal when the sharp metal ping of something hitting the wheel of her chair jacked her pulse up again. She looked down. Firecrackers. A quick glance and she spotted a figure running across the grounds. Christa called out. But the runner didn't turn around, didn't even stop.

The short hairs on her arms prickled as Christa searched the shadows. Who was it? She'd caught kids out here before, but they usually stopped to sheepishly admit they were trespassing.

Twinkling light showers reappeared in the distance, this time without sound; then they were gone.

"That was not fireworks," she whispered.

"No, of course not. Somebody set off a rocket upwind of us. That's why we didn't hear anything. They left this." Panting from his impromptu jog, John held up a backpack. "When they come back for it, we'll find out who it was."

"There's no name?"

"Not that I can see. I'll look more thoroughly when we go inside."

"Can I see it?"

He dropped the pack in her lap.

Christa ran her fingers over the material, opening each zipper to search the cavities. "It doesn't look like a kid's backpack."

"How do you know?"

"For one thing, it's expensive. This material is the kind mountain hikers use to keep out the elements. It's stronger. But also there's a waist belt. Those are put on the serious climbers' packs to evenly distribute the load, hold it so it doesn't shift around when they need to keep their balance." She worked her way through all the pockets. "I can't find anything in it. Doesn't that seem odd?"

"Not if they only used it to carry their fireworks and rocket," John replied. "If it's expensive, it's more likely the owner will return for it. Then we'll know who our trespasser is. I'll leave it in the office."

"Maybe we already know."

"Okay, what's going on?" John leaned down and searched her eyes. "You've got that look on your face again."

He was getting far too adept at reading her. Christa countered his question with another. "What look?"

"The one that says you're not telling me what's going on in your busy little brain. Spill it, Anderson."

"I thought I recognized one of the trespassers. I'm not sure though; I just got a glimpse. But I might know him." She frowned. Maybe it was wrong to say anything until she was positive. But only one person she knew had that hair . . .

"I don't suppose it would be easy to say for sure since you saw him in this twilight, but you might mention it to Kent so he could be on the lookout. I wouldn't know him, of course." John tilted back in his chair and dug his heels into the ground.

Christa stared into the fire. If it was *him*, it meant trouble.

"I thought this place would be peaceful once the kids went back to school, but tonight it's humming. It's sure different than when I was a kid. The autumns I remember were the end of things like swimming, picnics, freedom." Leaning his head back, he gazed at the stars. "When September rolled around, all our house rules were back in place. Early to bed, early to rise, homework, football."

Though he offered nothing more, Christa wanted to cheer. For once John was allowing his memory free rein without even realizing it. When he didn't speak again, she decided to prod him by painting a word picture of autumn's slide into winter, hoping he'd be drawn in enough to recall more details from his past.

"Don't you love autumn's slow progression? First that intense heat seeps away as the days get cooler; the nights crisper, fresher. The machines slink back into their sheds when the crops are all harvested, and the land looks almost barren." *Hmm, he doesn't look interested in machines.*

"The wind undresses the trees until they are only sticks jammed into hard black dirt. Days shrink; nights stretch. Sun-dried leaves create a thick multitoned carpet that crackles when I run down the hill. Ran, I mean." She ignored the stab of regret for a past she could never recapture.

"I remember big gold oak leaves," he whispered.

Delighted with this small sign, Christa continued. "Have you ever seen autumn leaves dance a jig when the wind picks up?"

His eyebrows rose, but he humored her. "A jig? I don't think so."

Running through piles of leaves, tossing them all over Kent when they were children, dashing through their father's apple orchard—the memories grew so strong that Christa had to gulp back the tears. So much joy and happiness seemed wrapped up in her early life, so much pain in the latter. Would she ever again know that sweet rush of having everything right in her world?

Please, Father, show me how to be truly happy in this life You've given me.

"So what's it like, your leaf-dancing jig?" John's words drew her back.

Christa closed her eyes. For his sake she recalled a past in which anything seemed possible and any dream attainable. "Like feeling your spirit soar," she said, allowing herself to sink into that dream-world. "Vibrant orange and gold leaves skipping to an Irish tune played on a flute in the moonlight."

"You're very whimsical tonight."

"I suppose I am." Christa drew her hands inside her sleeves. She'd never thought of herself as whimsical, not recently anyway. People in wheelchairs were forced to deal with restrictions. Dreaming of something else could be terribly frustrating. But tonight seemed a time for possibilities.

She continued describing the changing countryside. "The garden is all picked; its bounty stored away. The carrots and potatoes are in the root cellar, preserves and jams are in the cupboard, and the freezer is filled. Though the land looks bare, its abundance is safely stockpiled in shiny granaries. Even the moon swells orange and round and fat in the autumn, as if it's gorged on too much carrot cake."

An owl hooted in the distance; then the night mellowed until all was quiet. Christa stuffed her hands in her pockets. "It's like now—the whole earth holds its breath. Everything's waiting." She paused, loath to disrupt the reverent hush that had fallen.

"Finally winter arrives and the sky exhales, blowing down fat fluffy snowflakes that kiss the earth, then embrace it. Spruce and pine trees don white velvet robes to celebrate; frost decorates everything in shimmering crystal glitter." Smiling, she glanced at John.

"And?"

"You look around and suddenly you realize you're prepared for whatever happens next. That's when you feel that deep-down certainty that you can make it through whatever blizzard comes along."

"You're a born storyteller, Chris." John used his sneaker-covered toe to push one of the cement blocks surrounding the fire pit back into position. A burst of sparks rushed upward. "Too bad we can't prepare for real life like that. You know, expect the unexpected."

"In a way, I think we can. I'm starting to understand that God gives us experiences to train us for what is to come. Not that they make it easier or that we'll have all the answers, but they do give us something to measure our response against. Our lives are like seasons, and each season changes us and shapes us into who we are becoming."

Christa twisted to get a better look at John's face, unable to decipher his expression. "Do you understand what I'm trying to say?"

"Sort of." He prodded the burning logs with a stick. "You're paraphrasing that old saying—something like 'God never gives us more than we can handle.'"

"No, I wouldn't say that." Her hand automatically brushed a bit of ash from his shoulder.

He smiled his thanks.

She chose her next words carefully. "I think He often gives us more than we can handle. That's what living is all about—to see if we've learned enough to trust and rely on Him for what we need to get through it or to show us that we need a few more lessons and a bit more practice." She made a face. "Not that I'm claiming divine wisdom or anything. This is only my view on my current situation."

"Maybe you're right." He didn't sound convinced.

"Tell me what you're thinking." She didn't know if John would respond, because he often used silence to avoid saying what he thought she wouldn't like to hear, or what he believed might hurt her feelings.

"I don't know if I can explain it in a way that won't irritate you."

"So I'll be irritated. Go ahead," she encouraged.

"Okay—" he took a deep breath—"you painted a good picture with your pretty words, Chris. You made everything seem all nice and cozy in the world, a natural progression of the seasons changing that is beautiful to behold. But that's not parallel to reality." He snapped a twig between his fingers and tossed it on the fire with unnecessary force. "Not my reality or yours. We aren't living those picture-perfect lives you described."

"No, but—"

"I don't understand how you can rationalize God that way." His voice changed, hardened. "Either He's good, in which case He wouldn't have allowed you to be paralyzed; or He allows bad things to happen that He could have stopped, in which case I don't think He's so chock-full of goodness."

"John, I didn't mean—"

"How could a good God allow people to spread hate like we saw on that Web site?" A stiff note of strain exposed his confusion, as if saying the words pained him.

He sounded exactly like Christa had only a few months ago—ranting at God for not living up to her expectations. Now that she faced a future on her own that would tax her every resource, she was learning that she had to rely on God more than she ever had. In her quiet times she'd begun to probe the real meaning of hope.

"God's way of doing things is hard for us to comprehend. Can you imagine sending your only son to people who would kill him? That kind of love is unfathomable to us with our little minds. We don't see the whole picture, so it's impossible for us to understand God's actions." She gnawed on a fingernail. "If He was easy to understand, He wouldn't be God. He'd be like you and me."

Christa struggled to find words that would clarify. Crafts she was good at. Words were so much harder. "I'm not saying I know everything about God. But I did spend a long time blaming Him for what happened to me—my winter of discontent, if you like."

"So you see what I mean?" The tension in John's face eased a fraction.

"I know exactly what you mean, believe me. People always say God is love, but goodness can't be all there is to God. He has to have many sides to His character if only because He created humans who are so different. The Bible says God goes far beyond what we can even imagine."

"Saying God is unknowable doesn't bring understanding."

"No, it doesn't." She thought a moment. "Okay, let me put it this way. I see God's position similar to that of a parent's."

"I thought your parents died years ago."

"They did," she said. "But I remember enough of them to know they loved me, even though there were times when they didn't do what I wanted or expected them to, and I didn't understand why. I've rethought my accident from Kent's perspective as my protector, my surrogate parent, as someone who was forced to stand back and watch me make my own choices. It's made me see things in a new way. Kent loves me and wants the very best for me."

"Naturally."

As if she'd ever been anything but lovable—a lot John knew! "Kent was smart enough to realize that forcing me to do his will would be slavery, not love. He agreed to my speed swimming because he thought it would make me happy. And it did. I loved the rush of pulling through the water and being the first one to finish. I took chances I shouldn't have, just to feel the adrenaline kick in. The exhilaration was like a drug, pumping me to push harder."

"I know the feeling. But if he'd stopped you, then the accident—" John winced—"sorry."

"No, it's okay." She thought of that time and her need to exceed the limit. "Kent could have stopped me that night, and maybe I wouldn't be paralyzed now. Maybe. But who knows what else I would have done that would have led to exactly the same result? I was into rebellion big time." Christa felt the familiar swell of guilt rising and fought it. God had forgiven her. That's what counted. "I did a lot of things I'm not very proud of, played some mean and nasty tricks on people I called friends. What if I'd been driving too fast and had hit someone else, paralyzed them? How would that have been better?"

"I hear what you're saying." John shook his head, a tightened muscle in his cheek testifying to his frustration. "But it seems too harsh that you have to pay so much for one youthful mistake."

"Sometimes I think like that," she agreed quietly. "It hurts a lot to know I'll never accomplish the things I'd planned, never achieve certain goals, and never manage the simplest things, like a walk through the field. But honestly I have to admit it isn't God's fault. He gave me the freedom to choose, and I chose badly. He didn't make the mistake; I did. And now I'm paying for it."

"I hate that." His jaw was white with strain.

"I know." He was sweet to feel so bad for her. As she touched his arm, a spurt of affection gushed up inside her heart. "I hate it too. But I didn't die, John. I'm still here. I got a second chance. You're the one who keeps reminding me that there are things that I *can* do." She forced herself to smile, to break the tension that hung between them.

"And now you're turning the tables on me, I suppose."

"I'm trying. Which brings us back to the future."

"The future?" He looked up. "You have some ideas about what you're going to do?"

"I always have ideas. You know that." She laughed, pretended it was a huge joke, and drew a breath of relief when he smiled with her.

"Do I ever! Christa's ideas. Watch out."

John was her friend and he wanted to help her, but she had to be careful. During those long months at the rehab center, Christa had studied disabled people like herself who could barely manage to scrape through life on their own. Families showed up and helped out of a sense of duty or charity or even love. It was so easy to get used to leaning on someone else. But that constant stress was a drain on the relationship. She'd seen paraplegics grow so dependent that even their loved ones began to resent always being tied to a wheelchair.

Christa had already made Kent feel guilty, responsible, and ashamed because of something that wasn't even his fault. She would not ruin his marriage to Georgia by getting in the way, being too needy, and demanding moments the couple should spend on each other.

It was time to cut herself free. She couldn't do that by transferring her dependence from Kent to John, by leaning on him, sapping his strength. It wouldn't be fair. John deserved his own dreams.

"We've shared a lot these past months." He frowned. "Now I'm getting this feeling that you're pushing me away. Is there something else you're not telling me?"

"Probably a lot," she answered, stunned by the perception of his question. "A thousand things go through my head when I envision what's next. It's been a while since I let myself think, *what if?* It's overwhelming sometimes but also kind of exhilarating."

"But you'll still leave?"

"I hope to, yes," she admitted. "It's part of my growth process. It's very comfortable for me at Camp Hope. I don't have to exert myself if I don't want to. I get enough income to pay for whatever I need. I can avoid all the pitying, patronizing looks by remaining right here. I can spend my time reading or watching television. I don't have to venture out in the real world at all. In among these pines I'm protected."

"That's bad?" John asked, as if he already knew the answer.

"You showed me that for me it is." The words that slid from her lips were deeper truths she'd once refused to acknowledge in her heart of hearts. It felt good to let them out. "I think one reason I sank so low into my depression was because there were no highs and no lows in my life. I'd lost that thrill of accomplishment when I put my head on my pillow every night. I had no purpose. One day was the same as the next, empty hours waiting to be filled. All I could think about was what I'd lost and ruined by being so selfish." The waste of past months brought tears to her eyes, and there was no one to blame but herself.

"Christa—"

"You've forgotten your past. Did you ever think that might be a blessing?"

"No!" The color drained from his face.

"I do. Some days I wish I could forget the things I've done, then start over with a clean slate. But I can't change the past. I messed up, and it cost me friendships I wish I still had. All I can do now is work on the future."

He opened his mouth, but she held up a hand. "You can't fix this for me, and you can't protect me from what could happen. I know that's what you and Kent would like to do, but you showed me that I need to live outside the bubble. You said it yourself, remember? I've got to get a handle on facing the curious stares and the whispers. You were right. I can't choose the easiest route anymore and wait for life to come to me."

"What are you going to do?" He sounded worried.

Christa smiled as the freedom of finally letting go simmered in a battle against fear and hesitation. "I'm going to prepare for the next step God tells me to take. I'm going to stop living in the land of 'I wish' and get on with my life."

"You can only do that away from here?"

"I believe leaving is what God wants me to do."

"God again." He sighed, then nodded. "If leaving Camp Hope is your ticket to a full and happy future, go for it. But there's no rush. You're young."

A ping of hurt that he'd accepted her departure so easily lingered in the depths of her heart. It was silly and childish, but she'd wanted him to say that he'd miss her and that they'd shared something special. "I'm twenty, John. Not all that young."

"Twenty seems awfully young to me sometimes. Especially when I realize thirty is next on my horizon."

"John! You've just told me your age." She giggled at his surprised look and waggled a finger. "My, you are an old-timer."

"I'm not thirty until next month," he blurted out. "Hey! Maybe that's it."

"Maybe that's what?" She waited, watching his face as he computed something in his brain. "John?"

"I'm not thirty until next month," he repeated, glancing at her. "Maybe my birth date is October 29. But then—"

Christa didn't have to ask; she knew how that sentence ended. If October 29 was simply his birthday, why would he think someone was going to die on that day if he didn't stop it?

From the corner of her eye she caught a flash of white clothing as someone moved around the side of the house. "Did you see that? There, by the hedge."

He followed the direction of her finger, frowned, and shook his head. "I don't see anything, Chris. Maybe it was the reflection from one of those solar flares," he teased.

"Yeah, maybe." *A solar flare with blond hair?*

"Do you think I should put out our campfire so we can watch?"

"Sure."

They sat for over an hour staring intently at the elegant dance of light in the sky. But Christa spent at least half of that time scanning the trees and bushes, trying to decide if she'd really seen him or just another person with the same hair color.

If it was him, what was he doing out here?

CHAPTER FOUR

Later that night, with the house quiet around her, Christa closed the door to her room and lifted the wrinkled white envelope from its hiding place.

For a moment it was enough to sit there and hold it. But when she couldn't bear the suspense any longer, she slit open one end and drew out a single sheet of paper. Her hand shook, blurring the words, so she had to read them two or three times to be sure she understood. They wanted more information, of course, and a lot more samples. But based on what they'd seen, they found no reason to repudiate her plan.

She let out a pent-up breath. It wasn't an ironclad guarantee or a promise, but it was a start. Phase one of her life-rebuilding campaign had begun.

She flicked off the light, content to sit in the dark and revel in the wonder of it. One baby step. But she'd taken it.

A ribbon of light in the night sky drew her attention. The solar flares were still going strong. Kent had watched them for a long time after she'd said good night to John. In fact, she had heard him come into the house just moments ago.

A movement in the yard to the right caught her eye. She had to readjust her chair to get a better look. Peering through the darkness, Christa spotted someone creeping across the compound, trying to open doors. Her window offered a panoramic view of the backyard, enabling her to follow his progress for several moments before realizing she should alert Kent.

Once she'd done that, Christa returned to her room. Soon Kent appeared outside, flashlight in hand. He walked through the camp and stopped at the RV where John had stayed ever since he arrived. She couldn't see the other person now. He had disappeared.

No one. Nothing. She'd stared so long her eyes were watering.

Reluctantly, Christa gave up, then readied herself for bed. The letter crackled as she crushed it with her elbow when she lay down. She picked it up and held it to her chest. The birth of a dream.

"Thank You for the hope, Father," she whispered. The verse she'd read this morning returned as a gentle reminder: *"Without faith it is impossible to please God."* Faith, hope, trust. That's what she had to cling to. God would show her the next step.

The headache she'd pushed back for so long now returned with a vengeance, throbbing loud and hard inside her head. She leaned back against her pillow and forced herself to relax, though the stabbing behind her eyes sent her stomach churning. It was getting worse.

"There is some damage to the optic nerve, though we don't know how extensive it will be. It may accelerate into something more serious, or you may never have a problem again. If you experience unusual symptoms, you should consult a doctor."

The words uttered in those black days in the hospital returned like a thundercloud. To lose her sight, to never see a sunrise again, to never watch children run through the camp—how could she bear that? Paralysis was one thing. But her plan would be impossible for a blind girl in a wheelchair.

No! She wasn't going to think negatively. It was just a headache, nothing more. She closed her eyes and began to silently commune with Someone who knew all about suffering.

Christa had almost drifted off when something hit the foot of her bed with a soft thud. She bolted upright, flicked on a light, and glanced at the window. It had no screen. With mosquito season over, Fred had taken the mesh off several days ago for repair and hadn't yet replaced it. How had someone known that?

"I saw your light on. What's wrong?" Kent stuck his head around the door.

"Someone was at my window. They left this." Christa willed her frozen fingers to reach out and grasp the square white card attached to a rock on her bed. Hands shaking, she read the words scrawled across the paper: *Give it back.*

"What does it mean? Give what back?" Kent asked.

"I have no idea." But the memory of a glossy golden head would not leave her.

<hr />

"You're probably wondering why I asked to speak to you, Corporal Mercer." John motioned the RCMP officer inside the RV. He'd taken particular care to keep it immaculate and left out only one or two personal items that would even show his presence. As impersonal as it was, he'd still come to think of this place as home.

"Call me Rick. I was going to stop to see you anyway."

"Fred said Christa called Constable Grant out last night. What was that about?" John asked.

Rick glanced around the RV. "Angie checked the grounds because an intruder tossed a note through Christa's window. It told her to return something. I guess Christa didn't want to bother you with it."

"Bother me?" John clamped his jaws together. He'd deal with Christa later. "Have a seat."

"Thanks." Rick balanced on the edge of a narrow bench. "I know I haven't been out here for a while. You're probably wondering if we've learned any more about you since I brought you out here."

"Yes I am." Christa was getting on with her life. So would he.

"I'm afraid we haven't learned a thing that would tell us who you are. It's not for want of trying, you understand. But we always seem to hit a blank wall in our investigations." Rick's smile looked forced. "I don't know where else to try. If we had a name, an address—anything to go on."

John cleared his throat. "I may have something that would help you."

"You've remembered your past?" Rick frowned. "It's odd that Kent never mentioned anything. I saw him on the way here and—"

"Kent doesn't know. No one does." John stopped himself. "Well, technically Christa does; she saw what I saw. But it's not what you think. I haven't remembered anything. Not yet."

Rick took off his hat, thrust it under one arm, and stared at him. "I have no idea what you're talking about, John. Want to clue me in?"

"It might make more sense if I showed you."

"Okay." Rick looked skeptical.

"This is Christa's laptop. She and I were looking at something on the office computer yesterday. I didn't want to worry her so I borrowed her computer and did a little of my own investigating last night. Which is probably why I didn't notice Angie arrive." He felt the taut muscle in his cheek twitch and told himself to relax. "Something about computers makes me forget everything else."

"I'm the opposite. I go the long way around them. We have to use them for work, of course, but other than that, I can't be bothered. Maybe you'd better show me what you found."

John clicked the icon that linked them to the Web and connected to the Society for Order's site, thankful that the person who had loaned the camp this RV had requested a phone line connected to it. Though he didn't have a phone, the jack was handy for a dial-up connection. He'd been able to take a second look at the site without alerting anyone.

Rick scanned the screen. "This is something you're connected with?"

John watched confusion fill the police officer's normally unread-able countenance as he read the vituperative comments and vile denigration of the helpless. "I don't think I'm part of it, but the thing is, I can't say for sure. There's a date I keep remembering."

"You're concerned your date has to do with these people?"

"Wouldn't you be? They want to add to the pain of people who are already suffering. Not something anyone would be proud to belong to. Read this part." He pointed. "You'll see what I mean." John held his tongue, watching as Rick obeyed.

"I want copies of this. I'll run a check later."

John nodded. It was time to share what had been swirling through his brain for weeks now. He had no answers. Maybe Rick could find some. "I need to explain something to you. I don't know what it means, but . . . well, take it for what it's worth." He took a deep breath. "I get these pictures in my head sometimes."

"Pictures?"

John clicked print and waited until the printer began spewing out the documents, then broke the Internet connection. "Sort of like dreams but more vivid. Flashbacks, the doctors called them. For a while now something has been spinning round and round in my mind. Yesterday I tapped a string of letters and numbers in and was connected to that Web site."

"So a flashback led you to this." Rick studied the sheets of paper, brow furrowed. "You know, I think a notification came through the office about the Society for Order a while back, but I can't recall what it said."

John was half afraid to ask, but it was impossible to continue living in limbo and fear of the unknown. He had to follow this one little lead, even though it might cost him. "Can you find out more? Something about this Society for Order seems familiar to me. I don't know why, but maybe more information will prod my memory." *And help me figure out what's so important about October 29.*

"Okay. I get that part." Rick rose, slipped the folded papers into his pants pocket, and paused. "What aren't you telling me?"

John expected that. From all he'd learned about the Mountie, he knew that Rick usually saw beyond what people said.

"If I am involved with them, there's a possibility I could bring harm to this camp. I don't want to be responsible for that. Everyone here has treated me decently. I want to make sure nothing ruins the work that Camp Hope does. I don't want to turn something wonderful into something ugly."

"From what I've seen, the Society for Order is certainly ugly." Rick glanced at the computer. "Is there a reason why you disconnected so quickly?"

John took his time, sorting through all the possible ways to explain. Not that it mattered. However he disguised his words, they would be unpleasant.

"I'm operating solely on some nebulous feeling so I don't know anything for certain. You're already aware that I have knowledge about computers. Trust me when I say that the more times I connect to the site, the higher the risk that this group will realize I'm accessing it." He closed the lid of the laptop. "I'm sure you know there are a thousand ways to track someone on the Internet."

"Actually I didn't. I told you, I'm not much on computers."

"Then take it from me, there are. From the sound of their rhetoric, these people are actively recruiting members. In their eyes someone who keeps hitting their Web site could be a potential member. I disconnected because I don't want to be tracked to Camp Hope. Call it another hunch, but it doesn't feel safe."

"Safe for who?"

"Anyone. But especially for Chris. Kent and Georgia are going on their honeymoon. I don't want her afraid to be alone in the camp."

"Alone? But Ralna and Fred will be here." Rick's face mirrored the confusion in his voice. "So will you."

"But how much help will I be? I can't even remember my own name, and since somebody we can't identify slipped a note through Christa's window last night, it bothers me." He exhaled. "I don't think these society people are the type to march in and confront anyone openly. They sound like a bunch of bottom-feeders, the kind who blab a lot of empty words and are propelled by hotheads. I doubt they'd come up here to spread their propaganda, but still . . ."

Rick leaned against the wall, obviously mulling it over.

"I'm guessing from the look on your face that there's something *you* need to tell *me*." John sat down. "What is it?"

"Kent phoned me twice this week about two separate incidents. He's sure someone has been trespassing, but he wants to keep it quiet and doesn't want to accuse anyone until there's concrete proof." Rick leaned forward, his voice quiet. "Last night one of our officers was called out to the old Morris campground. It's just down the road from here. The Department of Environment closed it a week or so ago because a tree fell over and almost hit a homeless fellow camped out there. After an inspection, we were told that many of the trees have been attacked by Dutch elm disease and that it wasn't safe for anyone to be there. The site was shut down until the environmental people decide what to do next. From what our officer saw there last night, he felt someone has been staying illegally."

"For how long?"

"There's no way of knowing. When Georgia was having all that trouble a while back, I made sure I stopped by there two or three times a week, but since it's been closed—" he shrugged—"I didn't see the point. We make a run past every so often naturally, but since the gate is still in place, we never even thought of going inside. Not until someone phoned in a report that there was smoke spotted in the campground."

John felt the familiar throbbing at the base of his skull take up a rhythmical thud. Would this finally lead to one solid clue to his identity? "You think this camper, Kent's trespasser, and Christa's visitor are one and the same?"

"I can't say that—yet," Rick admitted. "But these . . . coincidences do seem unusual given the proximity to Camp Hope, especially when things here generally slack off at the end of summer."

"I wouldn't dream of second-guessing anything Kent said; he

certainly knows his own turf. But from the other night, I got the impression that whoever's been hanging around Camp Hope fit into the teenage category. Last night there were fireworks and a rocket."

"Ah yes. The yearly rite of summer passage." Rick shook his head. "It's hard to make these kids think about things like land that's dry as tinder when they're in a group and excited. We've had problems with campfires all over the county. In some ways I hope we get an early winter so everyone will stay inside." He paused. "I don't think this camper is a teen though. Our officer found a tent pitched in the back, where no one from the road could possibly see it. One of those pricey jobs that mountain climbers use even in winter. That's noteworthy because kids usually go home to sleep. We've never found any of them sleeping in the campground."

"Then whoever was using that tent might have had to leave quickly and didn't have time to take it."

"Could be, I suppose."

"I found a backpack last night," John remarked. "Christa said it was a special pack that climbers use, not a normal school pack. Do you think it could be the same guy?"

"A possibility. But what was he doing here?"

"Maybe it has something to do with me."

"Not after all this time," Rick said. "Angie lives nearby. When Syd Grant, her father, used to live there he got some strange visitors. Perhaps he knew this camper/intruder."

"Then you don't think there's any connection between this intruder and the Society for Order?"

"Doesn't seem likely to me. But I'll do some checking, step up patrols. Maybe some of my guys can ask around and learn something new." He shrugged. "This is a small community. Strangers get noticed right away."

"I didn't," John reminded him, feeling somehow smug.

"You've been able to remain virtually unknown for several reasons. The camp is isolated and the groups here are constantly changing, so no one would know your history or that you weren't supposed to be here for the summer. Also, nobody in town is likely to discuss you, mostly because they didn't know we brought you here. Those who do know have kept it to themselves or forgotten."

"And?" There was more; John knew it. Excitement zipped through his veins. At last, something to go on.

"I'm not trying to be hurtful but . . . well, no one has come look-ing for you, John. There haven't been any missing persons bulletins posted that match your description. I can't imagine some obscure outfit from who knows where would hightail it here to spy on you." He sounded apologetic.

"It sounds far-fetched to me too." John's spirits took a nosedive. "I'm a nobody. Don't worry about my feelings. I realize no one seems anxious about my return. I guess if I was involved with this group, they'd expect to see me every so often."

"Good point."

"So we're back to lots of questions and no answers." When Rick didn't respond, John prodded him. "Just in case there is some problem I've brought, do you think I should leave?"

Rick frowned, obviously deep in thought.

"I could go tonight," John offered. "There's nothing to stop me from leaving Camp Hope, if you think it will help."

Nothing but Christa with her bubbling exuberance for life. Christa, whose mind was a cauldron of plans and ideas that only worked out half the time, but when they did—wow! Christa, who'd snuggled a place for herself into every day he spent here so that now he looked forward to seeing the twinkle in her soft blue eyes each morning. Christa, who made him think about a God who actually cared if he lived or died.

A keen rip of pain tore through John at the thought of walking away from the sense of belonging he'd found at Camp Hope, but he'd gladly suffer that and more if it would keep Christa safe.

"Slow down, John. Leaving is not the brightest idea." Rick's stare was intent. "Where would you go that you wouldn't stick out?"

"Well, I—"

"You haven't got any ID papers or money. You can't remember anyone to contact. What would you do?"

"I don't know. But I do know how to hide." John was shocked to hear the words from his own lips. He sounded like some kind of escaped criminal.

"Really?" Rick didn't react as John expected. Perhaps he hadn't heard him. Rick tapped his index finger against his leg. "Well, for the moment, don't bother leaving. If your worry is for Christa, she can manage a lot better than you think. I can't imagine anyone would think she's a threat. If your worry is for yourself, that's another thing entirely. I doubt running would solve anything though. You could probably leave tomorrow and it wouldn't matter."

It mattered to John. He'd hoped for reassurance. "If you're so anxious to have me go, I'll leave today."

"I didn't say I was anxious, so calm down." Rick stared at him. "In fact, I was arguing the opposite. You're familiar with everything here, you can find your way in the dark, and you'd know almost immediately if something's not right. If your concern for Christa is genuine, then your choice is easy."

"What do you mean?"

"You'll be better off watching her from here. If someone from your past is after you, let him come to us. We'll be on guard and prepared to deal with anybody who makes trouble."

"Maybe you're right."

"Yes, I am, but in case you're still harboring ideas, let me make this very clear. You go nowhere without getting permission from us first. Got it?"

"In other words, you're grounding me. Okay." He paused. "Who's us? You and your pretty titian-haired partner?"

To John's surprise, Rick flushed a dark red.

"Sorry. Guess I blew it, huh? What happened?"

"Nothing happened. Angie's working a different shift these days, that's all. And she's not my partner." Rick's terse comments signaled his disinclination to talk about his private life. "The one good thing about this mess is that Angie's fresh from a course involving task forces that track hate groups and their crimes. I'll ask her opinion on this Society for Order to see if she can help. Is that okay with you?"

John waited for the rush of sensation that would signal some unconscious worry about Angie Grant. When none came, he said, "From what I've seen, Constable Grant is very thorough. It would be great to have someone who understands how this kind of mind works." John clicked off the printer. "There's just one thing."

Rick's head jerked up and his eyes narrowed. "Something you left out?"

"No. But it occurs to me that this whole discussion may be pointless. The Society for Order could be nothing more than an ugly Web site I ran across sometime before I got here."

"It could be," Rick conceded.

"Maybe it bugged me so much it hung around in my mind, maybe I read an article, or maybe I know someone who belonged. The point is, I don't know! I can't give you anything concrete. I can't say for certain that I wasn't involved in this, and I can't reassure you that they won't come after me for things I might have done before." The vague nature of this nagging unease sent John's hand tugging through his hair. He wished he could ease the bands of strain in his neck as easily.

Rick merely nodded, watching him.

"The whole thing might be a hoax and I'm worrying you for nothing."

"Anything's possible. My job is to find the truth, John. For what it's worth, I'd rather hear what you think up front. I can only repeat: Be patient. And don't go running off or I'll chuck you in jail." He grinned. "Get my drift?"

"Yes, sir." John said with a mock salute.

"Respect. I like that." Rick opened the door, then stepped down. "Leave the investigations to us."

"Yeah, okay." As John followed him to the cruiser, he forced himself to ask one more question before Rick drove away. "Could you tell me everything you can find out about a man named Kane Connors?"

"Who is that?" Rick asked.

"He's the guy the society people didn't manage to kidnap. I realized when I read those comments on the Web site that his name is familiar. Don't ask me why."

"I'll do what I can. Let me know if you need anything else or if something around here seems strange to you. I'll keep my eyes peeled for a camper who might inquire about a backpack." Rick scratched his chin. "Come to think of it, the Murdock sisters—"

"What do the Murdock sisters have to do with this?" John pictured the two older ladies who stopped by Camp Hope from time to time, usually to see Kent.

"Maybe nothing. They've been complaining about someone using their summerhouse uninvited. Since their land is adjacent to the Morris campground, the two could be connected," Rick said. "Just trying to connect the dots."

"So it could be the same person."

"Well, you have to know the ladies to understand my skepticism about their complaint. Fiona Murdock's eyesight isn't anywhere near twenty-twenty, and Emily sometimes . . . uh . . . invents what she can't remember."

John smirked. "Not the best witnesses you've ever had?"

"Ha! Anyway, with all the hunters coming in, we've got our hands full checking licenses and gun registrations."

Guns? John blanched.

"So that's it for now. You okay?" Rick asked.

"I guess. I appreciate that you'll need to keep Kent apprised. I want him to have full knowledge of what might happen if I stay. But if you could keep Christa out of those discussions, I'd be grateful."

"I'll try. It might be a good idea to keep her busy with something."

"I don't think that's going to be a problem." John sighed at the Mountie's obvious curiosity. "Christa spends most of her time in the craft shack, but she refuses to tell me what she's up to."

"She's independent all right." Rick patted John's shoulder, then climbed into his car. "This society bunch aren't the type to bother with people who leave them alone. Not in my experience. I wouldn't worry too much."

"I just don't want anything to happen to Christa because of me."

"Neither do I, though I feel pretty confident that anyone who dares accost Christa would feel the lash of her tongue."

John bristled at the disparaging words. "Christa's not like that."

"She must have changed then." Rick gave him a pitying stare. "Gotta go."

When John turned, he saw the topic of their conversation whirring toward him. Christa's dark brown braid bobbed over one shoulder as she negotiated the ruts and rocks. Nothing caused her to deviate from her beeline toward him.

"What was Rick doing here?" She waved a hand at the retreating police car.

"He came to see if I remembered anything else." He grasped the handles of her wheelchair to help her, but one look from her snapping eyes and John let go. "Where are Kent and Fred? I need to find out what's on my list for today."

"They're going to try burning a fire wall around the perimeter of Camp Hope, just in case. It's hard for the fire department to get out here quickly, and with all the trees, we'd burn pretty fast with only a puny water hose and that one tank of water we keep ready."

John's foreboding inched a notch higher. He held her gaze. "So you probably came to tell me about last night, right?"

She blushed. "I didn't want to bother you."

"Yeah. Next time bother me," he ordered.

"I wasn't alone, you know. Kent was there." She sighed heavily at his intransigent glare. "Fine. Next time I'll tell you about it. Anyway, Angie checked it out last night. Since I had some free time, I thought I'd see what you and Rick were discussing." She eased her neck left, then right. "My shoulders are so tense, I had to get out of the craft shack for a break." She winked at him. "I have an idea."

"Oh no. Not another idea." Groaning, he patted a hand against his chest.

"You keep that up, I won't tell you."

"Okay, so don't tell." He started walking toward his RV, unable to suppress a smile at her silence.

"Hey!" She buzzed the wheelchair past him, whirled, and did a wheelie within half an inch of his toes. "I need to talk to you about that Web page."

So much for keeping her out of anything. "What about it?" John couldn't figure out what bothered him about that date, so he wanted to forget the Society for Order.

"Can you find it again? There's something I want to check."

There was little point in stonewalling her. Either he was there when she looked at the site, or he left her to spend hours scanning the contents, maybe leaving behind a link that would lead directly to the camp. But he'd already accessed the site a number of times. It would be prudent to run a little interference that would slow down anyone interested in tracking him. If there was anyone. He was beginning to wonder if it was all in his mind.

"So?" Christa frowned at him.

"Okay." He motioned ahead. "If Ralna is off the office computer, let's use it. It's got a bigger screen, and it's easier to get your chair in there."

She agreed with a shrug, and they moved toward the office. Ralna was out, but she'd left a cache of mail for the Andersons. Christa grabbed the letters, then shoved them all into the side of her chair next to her thigh. It was a strange move, almost as if she didn't want him to see who was corresponding. But that didn't make sense. John didn't know anyone who would be writing her.

For the moment he ignored her weird actions and concentrated on the computer, punching in the last of the routing sequences that would hide their identity—for a little while. Then he pulled up each page and printed off whatever Christa asked for, encouraging her to hurry when she would have dawdled.

"I don't want to stay on here too long," he explained. "Organizations track visitors through cookies and start harassing them to join."

"Cookies?" she repeated. "How do you know what these people do?"

"I just do." Suddenly a picture appeared inside his mind—the leaflet was mostly black with Gothic writing that proclaimed North America a haven for those who believed they were too smart to get embroiled in the problems of the rest of the world. He could even read the slogan across the bottom: *Keep America's products here.*

"The Society for Order is against giving aid to foreign nations who've experienced catastrophe or war or famine," he recited as if he held the pamphlet in his hand. "They're especially against helping the impoverished. They say it encourages other nations to think of us as benefactors, to believe that we owe them. They don't want immigration from third-world countries to be allowed. They don't want any but the educated elite from specific nations to cross our borders. If they can't benefit us, we shouldn't let them in."

"Uh . . . okay," Christa said. "What else?"

He continued, allowing the words to spill out, not knowing where they came from. "They employ radical means to force North Americans who don't agree with their isolationist policies or who believe in reaching out to those less fortunate out of office. They'll go to extreme lengths to stop—"

Christa's fingertips turned white where she clutched her chair. He caught sight of the fear in her eyes and his mind blanked, the words cut off with no way to recall them. In his heart, John knew that what he'd said was true, but how he'd gained that knowledge was another matter entirely.

He should have shut up.

"I'm probably stressing for nothing. Even Rick doesn't think they would go to the trouble of tracking us here." He didn't believe that, but he wasn't going to admit it to Christa. Instead he made a joke, then disconnected.

John almost removed the sequences but hesitated. Christa might be tempted to check the Web site again without him. Some protection was better than none. He'd also do a few things to her laptop when he got the chance. Just in case.

"Did you get the wedding-dress situation resolved?" he asked, hoping she'd put the ugly literature away where neither Kent nor Georgia would see it. He didn't want it to mar their happiness.

"Not quite." When Christa shifted her heart-shaped face, John noticed lines of strain.

"Why not?"

"The dress is fine. I can make the finishing touches with no problem. But Georgia wants me to be her bridesmaid."

"And?"

"Me, John. Crippled Christa. In a wheelchair. Rolling down the aisle." She choked up, her voice shrinking to a pathetic wobble. "Everybody staring."

"Why wouldn't they stare? You're a very lovely young woman. I imagine you'll stun them in your bridesmaid dress." His tactics weren't working, so he changed his argument. "Besides, usually at a wedding, people focus on the bride and groom and their future happiness. Not on the attendants."

"That's true. Georgia feels it will be more like a family affair if I'm part of the ceremony." Christa's small capable fingers knotted together in her lap, as they often did when she was distressed. "I wish them both the very best—you know that. But I'm not sure I'm ready for that much exposure. Not yet."

"Then when?" He didn't like saying it, but if she was going to survive in the world outside Camp Hope, she had to toughen up. "Realistically, this is how it's going to be when you leave here. You can't pick and choose who will see you or when."

"You're right." She summoned a faint smile. "Sorry. I guess I lost it there for a moment. But still, it scares the daylights out of me."

"Aren't you being a little selfish?"

"Wh-what do you mean, selfish?" Her eyes lost their teary look, darkened, and narrowed until he saw his reflection pinpointed in her pupils.

Rick's comments about her returned to John's mind, and all at once he realized she'd probably used her tongue to keep others from seeing her insecurities. A wave of sympathy deluged his heart for the pain she endured long after her accident wounds had healed.

"I'm just thinking that this is Kent and Georgia's day, their special time. The wedding isn't about you, Chris." Her lips pinched together, but she stayed silent. He admired the quick way she forced herself to regroup. "They obviously want to include you and have you share their joy."

"And I need to get over myself and go with the flow?"

"Something like that." He nodded, snuggled her hand in his, hoping to infuse whatever courage she needed. "Maybe it's the only thing that really matters to them. I know they don't want to ask anyone else. If you don't do it, they might worry that you don't want them to be married or that you believe they've made a mistake."

"I don't believe that!"

"I know. So can you do it? Can you focus on your brother and his fiancée and support them during this special event?"

"As usual, you're right on target. That *was* pretty selfish of me, wasn't it? I hate that being paralyzed has that effect—makes everybody kowtow to me. Gross!" She shuddered. "What was I thinking?"

He shrugged. "It'll be a memory they'll have for many years."

"True. So will I." She appeared to ruminate on his comments for several moments, then looked up at him, lips twitching as she spoke. "You're a fine one to talk about memories, John Riddle."

"I know." He grimaced. "I don't have many. But if I did, I'd want them to be happy ones. They'd make up for a lot of bad ones." *I think.*

No one knew better than he that whatever was locked up inside his brain could turn around to bite him when he least expected it. Rick had said that nobody was looking for him. Maybe John didn't even have a family waiting for his return.

Like a mirage, the picture of a little girl with shiny blonde hair, sitting in a wheelchair, danced in his mind. *Sally.*

Maybe he was a member of the society and so totally detestable that those who'd once cared about him were simply relieved that he was no longer around. Maybe Christa would end up hating him too.

Christa had been his beacon of light through these blank weeks, a true friend. But until he knew exactly what secrets were in his past, friends were all they would be. He'd had proof of his burgeoning feelings when they'd gone to the creek to test her sailboat prototype for next year's preteen camp. She'd had to accept his help to get there. She held her precious craft securely as he fought to steer her chair past the thousand and ten rocks, roots, and other obstacles that denied her access to the spot. Out of sheer frustration, he'd finally lifted her free and carried her to the edge of the water. She'd felt right in his arms.

That evening he'd cleared a regular path to the creek. But it wasn't the need for efficiency that drove him; it was the memory of Christa's quiet murmur one summer night not so long ago when she'd longed for facilities that would allow disabled campers to attend Camp Hope.

The simple truth was, if Christa wanted it, he wanted to give it to her.

Now she wanted freedom from Camp Hope, the only place he could call home right now. But freedom was one thing John couldn't offer, not to her and not to himself.

⟫◈⟪

John sat outside long after the others had retired and the night had grown black, pretending he wasn't standing guard against some faceless enemy. Tonight the sounds of the camp were different from those he'd heard all through the summer. He could almost hear nature move through the cycles of life, counting off time on her clock of seasons.

Chilled by the night air, he was finally forced to return to the confines of the RV. Though he wasn't tired, John stretched out on his bed and remembered Christa's description of autumn. What he wouldn't give for the assurances she'd spoken of—to relax and know that his future was secure, that someone was in charge and would help him handle whatever came. But the same smothering fog of dread crept through him on a misty belly of unspoken worry. He could not relax.

A flickering breeze moved the stuffed red heart someone had hung on an overhead light. The heart made him smile. Yesterday Christa had worked on a mobile of wooden hearts, trying to find the right balance for the painted red pendants.

She'd caught him staring. "If you're so interested in them, you could drill holes in the tops."

"I guess I could." He'd worked alongside her on the picnic table in the sun until she grew tired, but the memory of hearts stayed stuck in his mind.

The Society for Order wasn't a hearts-and-flowers kind of organization. They despised and persecuted the sick, the injured, and the underprivileged.

They'd done it to Sally. That's why she'd ended up in a wheelchair.

The amorphous memory collapsed, leaving him baffled. This Sally—was she his daughter?

No answer.

John turned on his side and resolutely shut his eyes. Drawing in a deep breath, he willed sleep to come. But his brain wasn't ready to shut down. It conjured up hearts.

He stopped fighting it. *Okay, hearts.* The specialists had told him to try free association. *Makes me think of . . . what? Valentine's Day. Mail.*

Why mail? Cards about love. The word pictures and accompanying questions rippled across his mind in rapid sequence and he let them, hoping something would kick-start his memory.

Love. He kept going back to that word. Maybe he'd run away from love—to the society. Or was running from the society. The answers eluded him.

"If I knew how to pray, I'd ask You for some help," he mumbled aloud, feeling foolish as the words slipped from his lips. "But I have a hunch that You'd tell me I got into it myself, and I can find my own way out. So I won't ask for me, but could You please keep Christa safe? She's got enough to deal with, and Kent and Georgia too. I don't want my problems to ruin their lives."

It wasn't a satisfactory conversation. In fact it was probably the least effective prayer in the history of modern religion. The problem was that his concept of God came only from the bits and pieces he'd overheard while working at Camp Hope. People talked about God and having a relationship with His Son, but John couldn't remember exactly how you were supposed to do that. It had something to do with being what they called a child of God. Maybe he'd ask Christa about it.

For the rest of his problems there was nothing to do but wait it out.

And hope.

His eyes had barely closed when a deafening crack broke the still-ness of the night. In seconds he had tugged on his shoes and was hurrying out the door.

He met Kent a minute later. "You heard it too?"

Kent nodded, his face tight. "I heard it. And I called Rick."

"The cops? Why? You think—?"

Only when they'd reached the barn did Kent slow down enough to answer. "Because when I hear a gunshot, I think the police should be involved."

John froze, recalling Rick's earlier words. He'd said there were a lot of people with guns. Hunting. "Is Christa all right?"

"She's fine."

A mewling broke through the darkness. A moment later Kent dropped to the ground.

"But Maggie isn't. You'd better call the vet. Somebody shot Christa's dog."

CHAPTER FIVE

Though his phone listed the caller as anonymous, he knew exactly who was on the other end.

"It is done?"

"Not yet."

A pause.

"But you found what we were looking for?"

"No."

The tone grew icy. "You jeopardize your position on the council with this delay."

"It will be done. The problem will be resolved. Soon." He picked up the binoculars to scan the area he'd been assigned and watched the rush of activity. "Has someone else been delegated?"

"No. Why?"

"An unexpected occurrence. Nothing more."

"We will not permit the plan to be thwarted. Not by him, not by you."

"I understand." And he did. Too well.

The council didn't issue second chances.
Not ever.

———◆———

"I really appreciate the ride into town, ladies." Christa waited until the frail, white-haired driver had pushed her wheelchair near before she shifted herself from the backseat into it. Her body wasn't as tense as it had been, but her ears rang. She'd been late again. The Murdock sisters did not tolerate tardiness quietly.

"That camp van is getting less reliable by the day." Christa bent and lifted each foot onto its lift. "Today it wouldn't even start, though it worked fine last night. Kent is trying to find a used one that we can afford."

"We don't mind driving you. It's no trouble at all, dear." Emily Murdock patted Christa's shoulder daintily. "Especially since we had to stop at camp to meet with dear Georgia about the wedding."

"It's so sad about Maggie," Fiona said. "Will she be all right?"

"Yes. She's staying with the vet for a couple of days so she can rest and heal. Then she'll come back home."

"Who would do such a thing?"

"Rick Mercer said they caught two hunters using night lights to hunt. One of them thought Maggie was a fox."

"It's very careless. What if it had been a person they'd injured?" Fiona's indignation echoed in the faint red spots on her cheeks. "Not that Maggie isn't almost human. I hope they are severely punished."

"Well, I don't think they'll be allowed to hunt again for quite a long time."

Settled in her chair at last, Christa placed her hand over the knob to engage the motor.

"Shall we wait for you, dear?"

Christa glanced at the Van Meters' ramshackle house in front of her.

"I'll meet you at the drugstore," she offered, stuffing down panicked thoughts of riding the street with everyone watching. Good practice before the wedding, she told herself. "Would that be all right?"

"Of course. I need some new hand lotion." Fiona's myopic gaze wandered to the children hollering in the front yard. "I wonder where Abigail is. Her children seem to run wild. Why, our neighbor said he saw the boy—what's his name, Emily? Anyway, he saw him out walking long past midnight. I expect he slipped out to meet a girl. He's of the age."

"Abby will be with Penny, I imagine."

Something in Emily's tone caused Christa to look at her, to try to read the odd expression on her face. "Is something wrong with Penny?"

"I don't think there's been much change." Emily's narrow shoulders straightened; her tone turned brisk. "How long will you need, Christa?"

"Shall we say half an hour?"

"Perfect." Emily slammed the back door of their old boat shut, tiptoed around to her side, adjusted the black feather on her hat, and climbed into the driver's seat. "See you later." One black-gloved hand offered a queenly farewell.

Christa hid her smile as the car choked and sputtered before it turned the corner. She told herself to ignore her self-consciousness as three pairs of eyes watched her approach the broken-down gate. This was one of the hardest things she'd ever had to do.

She fought with the gate for several minutes, fully aware that a tall, lanky boy standing in the shadows saw her struggling. He didn't even look up, let alone offer to help.

Finally one of the other children walked over and yanked the gate back, allowing her free passage up the cracked and broken walk.

"Thank you. Is your mother home?"

The child nodded.

Christa pushed the knob that impelled her forward, trying to avoid the worst of the dips. "Good. I need to speak with her."

"What do you want with Ma?" The boy stepped away from the wall, placing himself in front of Christa. He jerked his head at his sisters. "Get lost."

They gave him a mulish look before walking away.

Christa waited until they were far enough not to overhear, then spoke softly. "I need to speak to her about something, but I was hoping to speak to you too, Braydon." She realized he was trying to intimidate her. "You've been at the camp, haven't you?"

"Why do you think that?" He sneered, his lips curling. But the flaxen gleam of his hair in the afternoon sun couldn't be diminished.

"I saw you. You were warned not to trespass on camp property before. You promised you'd stay off."

"You might have got me kicked out of that camp, lady, but that was then. You don't have any say about what I do now, so turn that thing around and get out of here."

"If I tell the police, you'll be in trouble. I don't want to do that. But we can't afford to have you lighting matches near the camp. The ground is too dry and once a fire starts, it'll burn everything." She leaned forward. "I'm not trying to hurt you. I'm trying to help."

"Like you 'helped' me two years ago, right?"

"Yes."

The menace in Braydon Van Meter's voice shocked her, but not as much as the malevolence on his face. He was desperately, furiously angry.

"You were stealing," she hissed. "I couldn't just ignore that and then finish my shopping!"

"Of course not. So you did your civic duty. Rah, rah, rah! For your information, I paid off that debt. I don't owe you anything. Now leave me and my family alone!"

He pushed past her, knocking against her chair so that one wheel slipped off the sidewalk and she had to work hard to get it on again.

"I told my mom you were here," said the young girl. Christa remembered Tara from junior camp. She was in dire need of a brush and some barrettes. Christa wished she'd brought along the package of combs she'd bought but never used.

The other girl was Micah, a wisp of a girl who'd once come to camp on a scholarship. She'd matured into a lovely teen, if one could disregard her angry frown. Her clothes were so ill-fitting it was obvious she'd hit a growth spurt.

"Thank you, Tara."

"What are you doing here?"

Startled, Christa glanced up and found Abigail Van Meter staring at her from inside the screen door. Her face did not encourage visitors.

"Hi, Abby. I don't know if you remember me. I'm Christa—"

"Oh, I know you well enough. You embarrassed my sister so badly she had to leave town."

"I'm sorry."

"Really? You're sorry for telling the whole town that she had to get married? You're sorry for taunting her publicly? Or you're sorry you didn't drive me away too?" Abby crossed her arms over her chest, her face hardening into lines that a woman her age shouldn't have.

"I'm sorry for all of it. If you'll give me her address, I'll write and tell her that. I know she must hate me. I can only say it again. I'm very sorry."

"Huh!" Abby glared. "Like that will help her now. She lost that baby, you know. Lost her second one a couple weeks ago. We had her down for a few days, but she still thinks people are talking about her. She's so depressed, even the kids couldn't cheer her up."

Christa closed her eyes, the sting of those words biting deep. More hurt and she'd been the cause of it. If only . . .

"Well, if you're here about that camp, the girls can't come to whatever it is you're having now. We can't afford it."

Relieved to have the subject changed, Christa shook her head. "That's not why I'm here. Fiona Murdock told me you were looking for some work. I have a few odd jobs that need doing. I hoped you'd be available."

"What kind of jobs?" *Belligerence* didn't begin to describe her attitude. "I'm busy. It costs money to go traipsing out to that camp, and I've got four kids to feed."

Briefly Christa wondered where Penny was.

Abby cleared her throat, indicating that she wasn't prepared to stand around and chat.

"I understand you're busy." Christa smiled to show she'd meant no harm. "I thought that maybe while your children were in school, you'd have a few free hours. My brother's getting married and . . ."

The face looking back at her didn't soften at all.

"I'm sorry. I guess it was a mistake coming here." As Christa moved the knob to turn her chair, she heard the screen door slam behind her.

A moment later Abby stood in front of her. "You look like you're doing all right now."

Christa smiled. "I'm dealing with it. It's easier with this chair. I found it pretty difficult to move around camp—all that sand, you know. The doctors felt a motorized wheelchair would be appropriate."

Abby and the three kids were all staring at Christa as if she'd lost her mind while she babbled.

Finally Abby touched the power knob with one rough red hand, then pulled back. "What's that?"

"It's my hope stone." Christa let her fingers close over the big blue stone she'd glued onto the top of the knob.

"Hope," Abby murmured, her eyes dark with unspoken thoughts. "I think I've almost lost hope."

"When we stop hoping we get into trouble. That's why I made myself a hope reminder, so I'd see it and realize that as bad as things look, God is still in control and I can put my hope in Him."

"I see."

With no idea what was going on in Abby's mind, Christa remained where she was while Abby looked at the fake sapphire. At least her legs weren't the object of that stare. For the moment.

"I have to meet the Murdock sisters for a ride back to the camp," Christa said at last. "Our van isn't working. I hope I didn't bother you."

"It's no bother." Abby blinked, then straightened. "With school starting there are some things the kids need. I guess I could use extra work. Why don't we talk about it? I apologize for being so rude. What's done is done." She sighed. "I got fired from the supermarket today so I'm a little testy. I had to leave early again, and they didn't like it." She stopped, as if it would cost her too much to say more.

What lousy timing. *Please, God, let something I say encourage her.* "C'mon inside."

Christa eyed the steps and noticed a ramp to the right. Without a word, she rolled up to the door. Abby held it open while she maneuvered herself over the frame and inside.

"Thank you. Doors are hard sometimes. I never know—" The rest of her words got stuck in her throat when she noticed the room's only inhabitant. "Penny?"

"Hi, Miss Anderson." The little girl in the wheelchair pushed herself forward until she was directly in front of Christa. Her grin spread from ear to ear as she patted her chair. "You and I are twins!"

"We sure are." Christa smiled back but glanced at Abby for an explanation.

The last time she'd seen Penny was over two years ago when the sunny eight-year-old had laughed and jumped on the camp trampoline so long the staff had to bribe her off. What happened? Christa wanted to ask, but good manners forbade it. "Good grief, you're getting big. What grade are you in?"

"Four." Penny giggled as a small gray cat jumped from the windowsill into her lap. "I got a hundred in spelling today."

Stop staring, Christa ordered herself. She knew exactly how that felt, had endured it enough times to vow she'd never do it to another person no matter what they looked like. But this was such a shock.

"A hundred? Wow! I don't think I ever got a hundred in spelling. You must study very hard."

"She does. And she's got some work to do now, don't you, honey?" Abby tenderly smoothed Penny's brown tumble of curls.

"Aw, Mom!"

"Off you go."

"See you later, Miss Anderson."

"Not if you don't call me Christa. When you say Miss Anderson, I always look around for somebody very old and feeble."

Penny's round face wreathed into a huge smile. She laughed, the sound a delightful tinkle in the tired room. "You're not old or feeble. See you later, Christa."

"See you, Penny."

Penny's thin little arms pressed hard to roll the chair across the threadbare carpet. Once she was free of the living room, she moved much more quickly, disappearing around a corner moments later.

"I'm truly sorry, Abby. I didn't know . . . I hadn't heard anything."

"A car hit her when she got off the bus after camp," Abby explained bitterly. "Didn't even stop."

"I'm so sorry." Christa felt helpless and angry and stupid. "I shouldn't have come here."

"I don't blame the camp. Besides, you had your own problems that year." Her eyes were hard as marbles, glints of silver fierceness lighting their depths as she stared at Christa.

Now what? Make excuses and leave or continue with the offer? Christa prayed for guidance while she waited for some sign from Abby. She couldn't help but notice the shabby condition of the furniture, the windows that needed caulking before winter, and the door that let in light and probably cold air as well.

"What's the job?"

"Kent's getting married in less than two weeks. I've been trying to keep up with the housework, but some of it is beyond my ability. I want to make sure the place has a thorough cleaning before Georgia moves in."

"That's a fair-sized house. It'll take some time."

"It'll take a lot of time." Christa made a face. "Kent has probably doubled the junk he started out with when we moved in, but he's been so busy he hasn't had time to clean. If we can get done before the wedding I'll be surprised."

"So the job lasts two weeks; is that it?"

"Well, that's the thing. I'm not sure." Here at last was someone not personally involved with her or the camp. If she told Abby about her plan, would she understand?

Hope, she reminded herself as her idea ballooned.

"I'm working on an idea that will eventually take me away from Camp Hope to my own life. I could offer you some extra hours help-ing with that." Christa launched into the bare bones of her idea, hoping Abby would agree.

"Wow." Abby's eyes were huge.

"I thought I could do it all myself, but I see now that I can't. I need to hire someone. I don't know the hours yet, but you could work on some projects at home if you wanted."

"I don't know." Abby visibly stuffed down the intrigue that had lit her thin face mere moments ago. "It would mean an awful lot of driv-ing, and with the kids and Penny—" She shook her head. "I can't see how it would work out. I can do the housework and stuff while they're in school; that's no problem. But at night I have to help Penny do her exercises. That takes a lot of time. The other kids have homework. I don't think I could add on any more."

It was obvious that Abby longed for something new and different in her life. It certainly couldn't be easy being a widow and managing four children on her own, one of them handicapped. And now she'd lost her job.

Christa reached out and covered Abby's worn hands with her own. She'd spent so long feeling sorry for herself, but the truth was, there were worse things than being paralyzed. "What if we start with the cleaning and see how it goes after that? The kids could come out to the camp on Saturday and play while you and I spend the day going over my ideas." *Braydon at the camp?* Christa gulped. "There are lots of things for them to do and space to do it in. Kent and John and Fred are always working on something, of course. They'd watch them."

"John?" Abby pulled her hands away. "I didn't know you'd hired someone else."

"He's not exactly hired. Look, I can't explain it all now. It's almost time for me to meet the Murdock sisters. But if you want to come out tomorrow after the kids have left for school, you can meet John for yourself. And let's plan on Saturday too. Ralna loves the chance to play grandmother to any child she meets, and Georgia's been complaining that there's no one to eat her cookies." She explained how much she would pay for the housecleaning, and they discussed a few other details.

"All right. I guess it wouldn't hurt to drive out tomorrow morning." Abby still looked skeptical. "I'll have to leave early enough to pick up Penny."

"That's fine. There's just one thing I didn't mention, Abby. It's imperative that you agree to keep my plan private. If you feel you can't, I'll understand, but our agreement will have to end with the housecleaning."

"That doesn't sound good," Abby admitted. "I can't see you involved in something shady."

"It's not shady. It's personal and I don't want anyone to know about my plans. No one. You can't say a word about it—not to your friends, not in passing at the grocery store, not to anyone. It has to be my secret until I tell it."

"Even from Kent?" Abby's worried gaze begged for reassurance. Christa nodded.

"But he's your brother. He should know what you're up to."

"He will but not yet." She saw Abby open her lips to protest. "He'll worry and try to talk me out of it. I can't let him douse my dream before I've even got it lit. Kent's big on being practical."

"Shouldn't you be?"

"Probably." Christa glanced at her chair, grinned, then sobered. "Maybe you'll understand better when I show you tomorrow. Okay?"

Abby was silent a very long time. Finally she agreed.

"I knew you were an answer to prayer!" Christa touched her shoulder in excitement. "I have to go. I'm late and Fiona already lectured me once today. I'll see you tomorrow."

As Christa motored down the sidewalk, she glanced back at Abby standing on the steps, staring after her. The look on her face was hard to decipher, but it was not one of joy. Well, why would it be? Worries about her family must be overwhelming.

Braydon leaned against a corner of the house. He gave Christa the once-over before he returned to lighting long skinny fireplace matches and dropping them to the ground. His expression hadn't changed; he still looked furious. At her.

The question was, had her words to Braydon helped or merely added fuel to the fire that seemed to burn inside him?

CHAPTER SIX

Christa stretched wearily, then pushed away the last piece of the foam visors she'd been working on. She was shocked when she checked her watch. It was one in the morning. Why wasn't she in bed where she belonged instead of here in the craft shop?

It was Maggie's last night at the vet's. Maggie was a terror if she got hold of foam, which was why Christa had decided to work late. Without the dog around, she'd lost track of time and spent hours perfecting a new craft. Kent had paged her twice. Both times she'd reassured him she'd be right there. He probably thought she was in bed by now.

After Christa flicked off the light and locked the door, she rolled over the path, breathing deeply of the fresh air. Muffled laughter in the bushes beyond drew her attention and she veered toward them. There were three or four voices, but Christa recognized just one. "Braydon?"

Utter silence.

"You can come out here. I know you're there."

"You guys go ahead. This won't take long. I'll meet up with you later. You know where." Braydon emerged from the shadows, his black shirt and jeans invisible in the darkness. But his blond head gave him away.

"What are you doing here? It's way past your bedtime."

"Who made you my boss?"

She almost chuckled at the sullen words so reminiscent of her own youth but managed to cough into her hand in time. "I'm not trying to boss you. But I happen to know there's a curfew in place. For 11:00 P.M. It's well after that."

"The curfew's in town. This isn't town." He glanced over one shoulder. "Go on, guys. I'll be there." He waited till the sound of footsteps ceased, then raised one eyebrow. "Seems I'm not the only one who's wandering around here."

Meaning her? Christa ignored the jibe. "Were you and your friends lighting matches again?" she asked, looking around for the telltale signs of smoke.

"None of your business."

"Yes it is." She sighed. Teenagers were so hard to talk to. "I live here. The danger of fire worries me." She paused, stared into his face. "You're acting as if I'm your enemy, but I'm not. I'd like to help you."

"I don't think I can take any more of your *help*. Thanks anyway." He turned to leave, then spun back around. "Maybe you should think more about helping yourself."

There was no time to ask him what he meant before he disappeared into the forest, his footsteps crunching over the dried leaves littering the ground.

He's mad and his emotions are rolling up and down like a ship on a billowing ocean. Please draw near him, Father.

She eased her way onto firmer ground and noticed a flicker of light inside one of the deserted sheds that was waiting for Kent's ministrations to its floor. The flicker of light was hard to define. A flame?

It seemed best to check it out. If the boys had been doing something wrong, maybe she could put out any flames before the boys did real damage and got in deeper trouble.

As she whirred over the ground, she cast her mind over the problem of Braydon. Should she tell Abby? But that would add to the poor woman's problems. Maybe she should try to reach him herself. After all, she had no real evidence that he'd done anything, and she didn't want to turn him in just for coming out here. There was no sense in alienating him further.

Maybe she could find a way to talk about Braydon with Abby while she worked. A whiz at cleaning, Abby had almost caught up with the housework and had elected to spend only mornings on it. In the afternoons they worked on Christa's ideas. It was during those times when Abby sometimes opened up about her husband's death several months before, her dire straits, and the lien against her home.

"We've got to do what we can to help without being obvious," Georgia had insisted. "You encourage her to use the Handivan to take Penny around, and I'll make sure they stay for dinner."

Maybe Georgia could think of a way to help Braydon. Between Georgia and Christa they should be able to come up with something, though at this point Christa had no clue how to get through to him. Abby believed his surly outlook on life had to do with his father's death and his need to be responsible. Privately Christa felt his anger was directed mostly at her.

John's reaction to the Van Meters confused Christa. After one look at Penny, he'd turned ashen and disappeared. He refused to speak about it later, but Christa knew it had to do with the child he said he half remembered—Sally.

Please, God, keep Your hand on John. Bits and pieces of memory aren't much to work with. So many hurting people. I wonder why it took me so long to see them all.

Finished with her prayer, she looked up, thinking of John. If he could only see how these stars sparkled in the night sky, a vibrant and living testament to the reality of someone bigger than either of them, maybe she'd be able to witness to him more effectively.

Yesterday John had gone with Rick to the city for a medical checkup. He was supposed to return tonight, but Christa expected him to be late. Kent had told her that Rick intended to take John to a rodeo, which was another reason she'd chosen tonight to work late.

John was worried about something that he refused to discuss. Every day he reminded her that October 29 wasn't that far off.

I don't understand what's going on, God. But You do. You know everything. You know what tomorrow will bring. You had it all firmly established in Your plan long before I was born.

The soft whisper of wind through the towering pines soothed her spirit as she remembered Scripture:

"If you need wisdom—if you want to know what God wants you to do—ask Him, and He will gladly tell you. He will not resent your asking. But when you ask Him, be sure that you really expect Him to answer, for a doubtful mind is as unsettled as a wave of the sea that is driven and tossed by the wind. People like that should not expect to receive anything from the Lord. They can't make up their minds. They waver back and forth in everything they do."

I do need help, God. My world seems to be growing. I need wisdom to help Abby and her kids. I especially need wisdom to talk to John. There are so many things to think about. I ask for Your help. I promise to wait for Your answer.

It came to her then that it didn't matter what the Society for Order or anyone else had planned. If she made herself available, God's will would prevail. He'd set His own plan in motion long ago. He even knew she'd be paralyzed.

That thought shocked her into immobility for several minutes.

"God knew I wouldn't walk again," she whispered in awe. "He knew I'd go through this." Her mind stretched to comprehend it.

Because He knew, He'd made allowances, not given up on her. Her being paralyzed was not a barrier to Him. It allowed her the opportunity to make a difference in her own unique way. She didn't have to agonize about the future or what decisions to make. She simply had to expect an answer from God and wait to find out what that was.

Peace settled over her like shawl. *Thank You, Father.*

She glanced at the shed. There was no light now.

Stop fussing, she told herself when a niggle of worry started to form. God could take care of things better than she could. It was time to go home. Christa took one last look at the stars tossed into the sky by the same hand that guided her days, then closed her fingers around the hope stone.

At that moment a shape appeared in front of the cabin called Girls A. She sucked in a breath. The figure froze, looked around. Christa remained where she was, praying she was hidden by the shadows. After a moment, the intruder lifted something, and Christa heard the snap of metal breaking. Then the person disappeared into the cabin.

Terrified, Christa couldn't decide what to do. To get to the house, she had to pass the cabin, so whoever was skulking through the dark would see her. The shed she'd been going to check out was nearest and it was unlocked. She'd hide there and wait.

The wheels of her chair got caught on the threshold of the shed, and she had to move back and forth to gain enough momentum to get across.

Suddenly someone grasped the handles and shoved her inside the shed.

Christa gasped and pressed the knob to get away. The battery seemed dead. She tried to twist around to see who was behind her, but strong gloved hands pressed against her neck, holding her in place.

"I want it back." It wasn't Braydon's voice. The tone was too low and hinted at an Eastern accent.

"I don't k-know what you're talking about," she stammered. Tension knotted like a band around her forehead, making her eyes water. "I don't have whatever it is you want."

"But you know who does. He's the one who led you to us."

"Nobody led me anywhere. I don't know what this is about. Please, you're hurting me."

The fingers loosened their tight grip but just a fraction. Christa was so scared she could barely draw breath into her lungs.

Her pager! She slid her fingers down the edge of her chair and into the pocket. Not there. Like a nightmare she pictured the interior of the craft shack, the small device sitting beside the pattern she'd been using, her cell phone next to it. She was alone and couldn't get help!

Desperately afraid of what would happen next, Christa tried to come up with some way to get free of this person. But all that echoed through her mind was one word: *Help!*

"Perhaps you need to think about it a little longer. I'll be back."

The wind fluffed her hair as the door slammed shut and she was enclosed in the dark. Footsteps crunched on leaves, then silence.

Even though Christa's hands were icy, she forced her fingers around the hope stone and pressed on it. Nothing. The battery!

She urged the wheels forward manually. Her cold stiff fingers ached with the effort but she could not give up, not when he'd given her this chance to get away. It was so dark in here.

After feeling the door, she finally found the handle and pulled on it with all her strength. It wouldn't open! Using all the force she could muster, she pulled and turned the handle again, but the solid wooden door still wouldn't budge.

Could her situation get any worse? She was alone in the dead of night, with no way to summon help, at the mercy of whoever was out there, the person who probably intended to come back. What could she do?

Christa forced her breathing into an even pattern. *Think!* How could she describe him? He had strong fingers, he wore gloves, and his voice hinted at an Eastern accent. It wasn't much to go on.

This had to be about her past—something she'd done or said or allowed—and would now have to pay for. Maybe inviting her former friends to that party she'd intended as a peace offering had brought it all back again. Maybe someone wanted revenge.

One of those people had moved back here from somewhere near Boston, she remembered. Another from Maine. But they were perfectly normal people, not prowlers. She tossed that idea away and tried to come up with something else.

"He's the one who led you to us."

Did the man mean John? But he hadn't led her to anything. Except that Web site.

Round and round, back and forth, the unanswered questions flew through her mind until she could remain silent no longer. If he came back, fine. But she wouldn't go quietly.

Christa began alternately pounding on the door and calling for help. After a while her voice grew hoarse and her hands ached. She leaned back, trying to reduce the throbbing pain in her head. She thought she heard a sound, but it was gone as quickly as it had come.

When dawn finally crept into camp Christa had barely enough energy to hold herself upright.

Surely someone would come looking for her soon.

———⟫⬧⟪———

"Christa?" John touched the pale blue scarf snagged on a splinter in the door of the shed, fingering the softness of it against his hand. "How in the world did this get here?"

He had to force the door open in order to free it. The gossamer silk fell to the floor, so he bent to retrieve it. He stared at the sight of Christa huddled in her chair. In a flash he reached her, touched her shoulder, and called her name.

She jerked awake, eyes wide with terror.

He cradled her hands, surprised by their chilliness. "Are you all right?"

"John? Oh, thank God."

Her raspy voice did nothing to ease his concern. "Yes, it's me." He rubbed her fingers vigorously, their icy tips frigid against his skin. "What are you doing out here, Chris? What's wrong?"

Her eyes remained on him as her mouth worked without producing sound. When he knelt to the left of her, her gaze slipped past his shoulder and slid to the door. She winced as the sun's rays caught her full in the face.

"How long have you been in here? You must have risen with the birds," he teased. "Did the door get stuck? I'd have come earlier if I'd known, but I stayed with Rick last night because we got back so late. He took me to a rodeo."

"That's nice. I, uh . . ." Her voice emerged cracked and broken, dry sounding. She swallowed, licked her lips, and tried again. "I guess I fell asleep."

"Got up too early, huh?" John chafed her fingers, but she jerked them away. He touched her cheek. "You're frozen."

She held her cool cheek against his hand for a moment, closed her eyes, and drew in a deep breath. She pulled away to peer at her watch; then her fist nudged the blue knob. "I need to get home but my chair won't go."

"What happened to your hands?" He met her surprised look evenly, trailing one finger over the scratches that covered her palms. "What are you doing out here, anyway?"

"I was here most of the night. Someone locked me in. A man. I don't know who. I was trying to get out, but I guess the door jammed when he slammed it." Her eyes pleaded with him. "Please, just help me get out of here. Something's wrong with the battery." The hiccuped sob was stifled by the hand she pressed against her mouth.

John leaned over, jiggled the cable to the battery, and waited for her to try again.

The chair purred to life, and Christa negotiated her way out of the shed and onto the path.

He stepped outside. "Are you all right?"

"I'm fine, I think." She glanced at the door.

"Don't worry. I'll fix it later." He pulled the door shut.

"Leave it until I call Angie. Maybe she can get some fingerprints." She motioned to the cars in the parking lot. "What's going on?"

"Someone plastered graffiti on some of the cabins last night. Your brother put out a call, and volunteers started showing up to help remove it."

She looked away from him, hiding her expression. "Did the police come yet?"

"They were here earlier. Apparently Angie and another officer did a routine check around three. They saw nothing unusual, but I don't expect they examined every cabin."

"No," she muttered. "Of course they couldn't. And because there's no camp running at the moment, Kent wouldn't have done a night check, especially since he and Georgia got home late from the fall supper."

John followed her toward the house. He had a thousand questions that he didn't ask, unwilling to press her right now. Christa seemed fragile, shaky, not at all her usual self. His hands fisted at his sides when he thought of someone deliberately terrorizing her. If he ever found out who—

All at once her wheelchair took off with a high-pitched whine. John half jogged to keep up. Christa revved up the ramp of the house and snatched a small brown box lying by the door.

"What's that?" He frowned when she tucked the box under her jacket, hiding the label.

"Just some stuff I ordered. Nothing important."

But it *was* important. He knew it by looking at her. She was keeping more secrets, excluding him from her life bit by bit. The knowledge stabbed deep.

"Christa, what happened in that shed?" He waited on the bottom step.

She paused in the act of opening the screen door and shuddered.

"Can I talk to you about it later? I need to get inside, and I have to phone Angie right away. Then I promise I'll tell you." Her gaze shifted from him to the box.

Her lapel slipped and he saw the small round logo on the corner of the box. The hairs on his arms bristled.

Even though John was frustrated by the wait, he understood that she preferred to hide inside the house until her equilibrium returned. Noticing how pale she was and the cuts on her hands, his heart welled with longing to soothe her pain.

He swallowed hard, then nodded. "Of course. Take all the time you need. I'll be here."

"Thanks. And thanks for finding me. I appreciate it." She dragged open the door, wedged it with her chair, her impatience to get away obvious. She moved inside.

He was about to turn away when the creak of the door stopped him.

"John? Can you get the keys from the office and my cell phone and pager from the craft shack? I'll collect them from you later."

"Sure."

"Thanks." The door slammed shut behind her with a bang of finality.

John retrieved the items from the craft shack, left them at the office, then walked back toward the work crews. Within minutes he'd been handed a brush and shown where to scrub.

As he labored, the even rhythmic strokes calmed his mind and allowed him to think. He spent a long time remembering Christa's ashen face and her shaking hands. The angry bubble inside him swelled a little bigger as he thought about her being so frightened and so alone.

He couldn't dwell on that, so he turned his thoughts to the package that sat on her doorstep. His reaction to the logo on it didn't make sense. The little box tied with a ribbon was nothing special. Simple Gifts used it on all their paperwork. He'd seen it many times before.

He replayed that thought. When had he seen it? And where?

Somehow John was certain that Simple Gifts wasn't what it claimed to be, but he had no idea why he believed that to be so.

He only knew that something about Simple Gifts was terribly wrong.

And now it had come to Camp Hope.

<hr/>

"Thanks for helping us out."

"No problem." The man kept his face turned away as he slapped rust-colored stain onto the log-faced building. He pretended to join in the hearty singsongs as if he were one of their group, though he knew neither words nor tune. No matter. He was here to do a job and he would do it.

Finally lunch was announced. He spent an extra long time sudsing his hands under a steady stream of warm water, scrubbing at invisible spots. After the others were finally inside the dining hall, he slipped outside and to the back of the buildings, took a circular path around the camp, noting pertinent details as he went. He paused only once for twenty minutes, searching a certain RV for something that had been missing since April.

Nothing.

His fruitless search completed, he left the RV and bypassed a cop dusting a door handle for fingerprints. So silent was his step that she never even looked up. She wouldn't find any prints—he always wore gloves.

He returned to his vehicle and quietly drove away, smiling wryly as he passed the huge entrance sign: *Camp Hope—Where nothing is impossible with God.* If things didn't pick up pretty soon, he might have to resort to asking for some heavenly intervention.

He hadn't quite believed it when he'd been sent here. Finding his man holed up in a Bible camp was a surprise, but it also made locating the item exceedingly difficult. It seemed like someone was always wandering around. He'd looked in most of the usual places without success. Giving up wasn't an option. He'd wait a few days, then search the more unusual places.

The council teetered on the cusp of a rout. If successful, the ripples of their actions would be felt from Washington, D.C., all across America. But they'd get only one chance.

The level of their success all depended on the man in that camp.

——————>=◆=<——————

"So you don't know who this guy is or what he wanted?" Kent's fury was obvious to anyone who'd experienced his usually easygoing manner.

"She already told you that. Ease up, Kent." Angie placed her hand over Christa's. "You're sure you don't need a doctor?"

"Don't you start. John's been asking me that every five minutes. I'm fine. He didn't hurt me; he just scared me."

John felt Angie's scrutiny even though his own gaze was locked on Christa. "Please tell us again what he said," he insisted quietly.

She sighed. "He said, 'I want it back.' I said I didn't have anything. He said, 'But you know who does. He's the one who led you to us.' Then he said he was going to leave me there to think about it and he took off. The door slammed, and I figured he'd be back any moment so I tried to open it. After a while I thought maybe he meant he'd be back later on. I yelled and pounded and tried to get the door open, but it was stuck. I heard a noise after that. I thought maybe it was him, but even if it wasn't, my voice was too hoarse to call out."

"It was probably us, doing our check." Angie looked chagrined.

"Then what happened?" John frowned at the flicker of something he saw pass through Christa's eyes. "Do you think this guy was the one who did the graffiti?"

"I don't know. I don't understand anything that's going on around here anymore." Christa slumped in her chair.

Georgia rose. "I think that's enough. Christa needs to rest. Come on, sweetie. You look bushed."

"Just one thing first." Kent's jaw was firm, his eyes dark and intent. "From now on you girls don't go out at night unless one of us is with you. If this guy thinks he can accost us on our own property, he's got another think coming."

"Don't worry, bro." Christa brushed his sleeve with her hand. "I'm strictly a daylight traveler now." She raised an eyebrow at Angie, silently asking permission. When the cop nodded, she pushed the big blue stone that directed her chair down the hallway to her room.

"Let's step outside, shall we?" Angie led the way, waited until John and Kent stood beside her patrol car. "Anyone have anything to add?"

"I think this guy—whoever he is— is after me." John knew with an unshakable certainty that it was his fault. "I used Christa's laptop to check out that Society for Order Web site one night. I guess I wasn't as careful as I should have been, and they tracked me to Christa's computer."

"Several things about that don't make sense," Angie said. "This guy creeps into the camp, sneaks up on Christa, then leaves her to paint graffiti? It doesn't seem logical. Graffiti is usually something kids do."

Once again John recalled his feeling that Christa had withheld something from them, that she hadn't told everything she knew. "Did you find fingerprints?"

"None." Angie shook her head. "But then Christa said he wore gloves."

"I'm getting concerned about leaving here after the wedding," Kent confessed.

"We'll handle Camp Hope. You deserve a break, and Georgia deserves your undivided attention for a few days." Angie glanced at John. "We'll all pitch in and make sure Christa and the rest of the place are still safe when you get back, Kent. So if this is your attempt at wiggling out of the wedding, think again."

"Wiggling out? Are you kidding me? I can hardly wait."

John tuned them out, his gaze snagged on some bits of silver he saw glittering on the ground. He picked them up.

"Gum wrappers. Something significant about them?" Kent stood beside him as Angie drove away.

"Nothing really. Except they're the same brand I picked up the night I found that backpack. The night of your solar flares."

"Kids again. For the first time in my life I'm actually looking forward to winter and long weeks of peace and solitude." Kent walked away, his voice carrying as he talked to Fred on his radio.

John remained still for a few minutes while he made up his mind, then went to the office. He took down the backpack and began to methodically search each and every pocket and crevice again. This time, at the very bottom under a piece of cardboard, he found a key.

But a key to what?

John tried every cabin lock in Camp Hope. The key fit none of them.

But it fit something and it had been hidden.

As he mounted the steps to the main house, John slipped the silver key onto his ring, determined to keep looking. Somehow, some-way, he was going to find an answer to whatever was going on.

It was just a matter of time.

CHAPTER SEVEN

Dearly beloved, we are gathered here in the sight of God . . ."

A reverent hush filled the room as Pastor Ben recited the timeless words for Georgia and Kent's wedding. Christa sat to one side of the bride, deeply cognizant of the serenity that pervaded the camp's rustic chapel and the couple who stood at the front. As she listened, she dreamed of another bride, another groom, another wedding.

Hers.

What would it be like to be forever tied to someone you loved more than any other, to know that your sorrows would be lessened because he shared them and your joy magnified because he'd laugh with you? How glorious to share all the solemn and secret moments of life that stretched into years, to be confident that no matter what, you would always be first in his eyes, esteemed and valued simply because love made it so. It was a dream she never thought she'd long to live, to feel, to share. She'd been wrong.

Christa scanned the chapel, finding John standing at the back. He was the closest she'd come to thinking of a man in terms of a future together. Given her sharp tongue and the tricks she'd played, the only guys who had hung around her in high school were not the sort one married. Couple that with her accident and . . . well, romantic love was something foreign.

In many ways, getting to know John had opened Christa's eyes to what relationships were all about. As he helped her ease out of the depression that had held her captive, he'd modeled the give-and-take of cutting some slack when it was needed, of encouraging without badgering, of simply being there to listen. Now she found herself wanting to hear his doubts and fears and cheer him up.

Today in the black suit he'd rented, he looked strong, tall, almost a stranger. His smile was pleasant, but it didn't light sparks in his eyes as he escorted guests to their seats. He hadn't chuckled out loud with the others when Maggie escaped the house and squeezed through the chapel door to follow Christa up the aisle. He'd kept his focus on Christa, silently building her courage to face the stares at her chair.

Now he grinned at her, and suddenly the world grew brighter. Christa drew a deep breath to steady her fluttering stomach. No matter what clothes he wore, he was still John, best and dearest friend she'd ever had. She would miss him terribly when she left.

"I now pronounce you man and wife. You may kiss your bride."

Christa blinked back to reality and to her wheelchair and almost wept at the loss of the dream. She would never be a bride, never know the joy she saw radiated on Georgia's face when Kent's lips touched hers. Her heart ached at the loss, but she was determined not to let it spoil the event.

Christa held her smile in place, felt it turn into the real thing when her brother, careworn from early spring, now beamed with happiness. For a moment she envied him; then she chided herself for being selfish. She'd almost wrecked his life once. She wasn't going to do it again.

"Ladies and gentlemen, may I present to you Mr. and Mrs. Kent Anderson."

Everyone rose and clapped as the bride and groom moved down the aisle. Since Georgia's dress had no train to straighten, Christa's duties were simple. She turned her chair, waited for Rick, then rode down the aisle beside him, glad that Maggie had disappeared. Not that it mattered. John had been right. Everyone's eyes were on Kent and Georgia.

After the ceremony, guests poured out of the chapel, waiting to congratulate the couple. Waiting, Christa suddenly realized, for her to go first. She shoved back the rush of inhibitions and pressed the knob that would roll her chair over to Kent.

She reached up to hug him and whispered, "Congratulations. Be happy, brother."

"I am." He hugged her tightly, cupped her cheeks in his palms. "Thank you. For everything. We didn't expect this to be so much work for you."

"But we love it," Georgia assured her.

"You deserve it. And it was fun. John helped a lot."

"I'll make sure to tell him how much we appreciate his help." Georgia bent and embraced her. "I don't know how we can ever repay you."

"If you can keep my brother from getting too smug with himself, I'll be very happy," Christa teased, needing the release their laughter provided.

"I promise I'll do my best. But, of course, you'll be there to make sure." Georgia winked. "We'll have him so dazed and confused he'll never realize what we're up to."

"Kent's already dazed and confused. I was hoping you could clear things up." Christa grinned, ignoring his burble of protest.

Remembering the others behind her who waited for a chance to speak to the couple, Christa let go of Georgia's hand and tried to move out of the way.

But Rick prevented her from going very far by gripping the handles of her chair.

"You have to stay here, Christa," he whispered, his eyes dancing with mischief as he manipulated her into place. "We're part of their receiving line. Besides, as faithful attendants at this shindig, we need to plan something for their getaway. I've got a string of cans all ready to tie on Georgia's car, and I've filled her trunk with scads of confetti. Did I forget anything?"

It was the one aspect of the wedding Christa hadn't even considered, so she was glad he'd brought it up. Now she didn't have to dwell on how strange it felt to laugh at the teasing and applaud the well wishes of everyone she'd deliberately hid from for the past year. Some of the guests were the same friends who'd refused her invitation two weeks ago; she found herself scrutinizing each one.

John offered quiet congratulations to Kent and Georgia, then leaned down to brush his lips against Christa's cheek. "You're scowling," he whispered. "Try to look happy."

"I am happy." Christa visually dared John to say another word as she bared her teeth in a wolflike smile. It was a good cover for her racing heartbeat. "Very happy."

"Sorry." He didn't look it. "It must be hard to greet people you haven't seen since before . . . actually you're doing great." His dark blue eyes met hers and began to twinkle. "Are you tired?"

"Not at all." She grinned at his quick turnaround. "How are we going to get all these chattering people inside the dining hall?"

"Just watch." He lifted one hand to smother his chuckle as the Murdock sisters appeared.

They'd shed their elaborate headdresses made especially for the wedding and were now swathed from head to ankle in pristine white aprons. Each woman carried a set of chimes and tapped out a pretty wedding tune that was popular many years before. The sweet harmony echoed through the camp on a soft breeze that swirled the ladies' fancy dresses and ruffled the men's hair. At the finish of their musical number, spontaneous applause drew curtsies from the sisters.

"They're good," Rick commented.

"Thank you very much. Now please, everyone, come into the dining hall. Have a seat." The ladies hung their chimes beside the door, then beckoned.

"I'm glad you hired a photographer." John strolled beside Christa to the reception. "Kent and Georgia will cherish the memories of this day even more when they look at the pictures ten years from now."

Christa was delighted that the photographer she'd hired remained in the background, unobtrusively choosing his shots. She hadn't realized he worked with an assistant, but that must be who the man behind him was.

"I hope so." She giggled. "I also hope the Murdocks will leave their hats off until after the reception. Feathers and wedding cake don't mix."

"Stop worrying. Everything is perfect. You've thought of every detail." John's face softened as he stared down at her. He took her hand and squeezed her fingers. Suddenly his voice altered. "Of course, it would be even more perfect if Ralna managed to prod Fred into recording the sisters' musical rendition on his video camera."

John inclined his head at Ralna, who had walked up beside them. The older woman's gaze was locked on their entwined hands.

Immediately Christa broke the connection. She kept her head down, pretending her cheeks weren't on fire.

"I made sure he taped it." Ralna matched her pace to John's, her tone conspiratorial. "The sisters wanted to leave on their hats. But I convinced them that their complete focus should be on the food. Abby Van Meter backed me up with a few horror stories of weddings where there was food poisoning. That seemed to do the trick." She looked Christa square in the eye. "You're sure you're doing okay?"

"I'm perfectly fine. How could I be otherwise on a day like this?" Christa couldn't be mad at the unasked question she saw lurking in that stare. Ralna's gentle concern had seen her through some very rough times. "Now stop mothering me and go sit beside Fred while he does the honors as master of ceremonies."

"My word, yes! He refused to tell me his jokes ahead of time. Said I'd give away his punch lines. I hope he doesn't end up with cake on his face." She gave them one last assessing look before she hurried away, her white curls bouncing with every step.

"You've got to love that woman, don't you? She's got a heart big enough for everyone," said Christa.

Without a word John pushed Christa's wheelchair over the bump of the threshold, smoothing her progress inside. He seemed to know ahead of time when she'd need him. He was always there. Christa couldn't imagine daily life without him. But when she turned to thank him, John had already slipped away, as if he were avoiding her. Or embarrassed to be seen with her in public.

Maybe he saw her as damaged and deformed. Maybe John wanted to hang around with her only when no one else saw, but in public . . . The intense pain those thoughts caused her shocked her. Before the accident she'd never really cared what people thought. But now she didn't want pity, not from John. She wanted—

"Here you are." Rick helped her take her place at the head table. "I was wondering if you'd deserted me."

"Not yet. Where did Angie go?" She scanned the room, unable to find Angie's bright auburn hair.

"Abby gave her a message that arrived during the ceremony. Angie had to make a phone call. She'll be back. I hope." He tilted his head to one side. "Abby's kids are certainly well-behaved. Look at their eyes."

The girls sat like statues, their saucer eyes absorbing everything. Braydon wasn't there. Abby claimed that his boss needed him, but Christa had overheard her chiding him for refusing to come. That was fine with her. The longer Braydon stayed away from Camp Hope, the less likely he was to cause problems.

Since the latecomers were still finding their places, Christa focused on Rick. "Did you find out anything about John's Internet friends?"

"Not a lot." He leaned toward her and kept his voice low. "Angie did some digging and learned that the Society for Order is more than a hate group. Crime units suspect they are behind the recent targeting of several shipping companies that are involved with overseas humanitarian aid."

"Humanitarian aid has become a target?" Christa shook her head. "This society should see some of the literature I've received depicting children with missing limbs who have to forage in the streets for food. They have no clothes, no homes, no parents. Nothing. Now that's sad. I hope the society is being charged."

"So far they can't prove one iota of these suspicions. Whoever the society's leader is, he's hidden himself well. Information about him and the society's exact location is sketchy, but the group's actions indicate they're out to destroy more than the reputations of these companies. They divert the funds and render their own coffers richer at the same time as shipments destined for third-world relief are lost, damaged, or rerouted."

"So their Save America's Products slogan doesn't include generosity toward anyone but themselves. That's pretty scary." She tucked away the information to be chewed on later, when the hubbub was over and she was alone.

"After checking their Web site, I'd say the Society for Order is far from generous. Someone claiming affiliation with this society is crediting them with kidnapping Evan Julian and Nicolas Petrov, both in charge of overseas operations for food shipments and missing for several months. A third kidnapping of a man named Kane Connors failed, and now he is under extreme security."

"John recognized Kane Connors's name," she murmured. "But he can't remember why. Are the other two okay?"

"Hard to say. Large sums have been paid out in ransom for them, but the men were not returned. There's no way of knowing whether either one is still alive." Rick paused and watched as Angie moved around the edge of the hall directly toward him, while John arrived from the other side. "I think she's learned something." He stood, waiting until Angie joined them.

After Angie glanced from John to Christa, she raised one eyebrow at Rick.

"Why not?" he told her with a shrug. "It concerns them."

"Well, I think we found out something about our mysterious camper. A man from the environmental department was out there and saw a car come in via a back road. He got a partial license number. I've had the office tracking it down. Took a few days, but we backtracked to the lessee, right back to who paid for it."

Christa's fingers automatically curled over the metal arms of her chair, eager for just one little clue.

"The renter of that car apparently carried a driver's license from Washington," Angie continued.

"State?" Rick's eyes moved to John and narrowed to speculative slits.

A pause. "D.C."

Rick's whistle of surprise was quickly muted.

Angie scrutinized John, then glanced at Rick.

Rick had a far-off look in his eyes. "So whatever's going on has a long reach. What's your best guess?"

"That we'll never see the car again, or if we do it will have been abandoned or in an accident," Angie replied promptly. "Naturally, the name on the driver's license didn't check out."

"Back to square one," Rick said. "That makes me more determined to get to the bottom of whatever's going on. I think I'll phone Pastor Ben and get the prayer group working on this."

"You do that. And while you're waiting for answers from God, I'll do more of my own investigating." Angie's brusque tone softened. "There was a trespasser in that field behind Parsons' again last night."

"Did anyone get a look at him this time?"

"Uh-uh. Mrs. Parson saw him when she was out harvesting moss for her latest sculptures. That woman can sneak up on you like nobody I know. She claims he appeared, dug something out of a hay bale, then a few minutes later was gone. She checked the bales after he left but found nothing."

"So is it the same guy, or have we got two of them out there?" Rick asked Angie. "I'm beginning to understand John's frustration."

"I asked the office to send somebody out, have them look around."

"Thanks." Rick turned to greet a friend, who then asked John to help him find his place.

Angie grabbed the opportunity, leaned down, and whispered in

Christa's ear, "I checked the shed. No fingerprints. Nothing. Thanks for phoning me first and letting me investigate. I'm just sorry I couldn't help."

"You're welcome." Christa debated asking her whether Braydon had been in trouble lately, then nixed the idea. Her suspicions weren't strong enough to warrant accusations. She wouldn't damage anyone else's reputation. Never again.

"What are you two whispering about?"

"Girl stuff, Rick. You wouldn't understand." Angie winked at Christa. "You look pretty high-class beside old sourpuss here."

"Enough dissing me. Off you go now." Rick ushered Angie to her place at a nearby table and seated her. She answered her cell phone, dug a piece of paper out of her handbag, scribbled a note, and handed it to him. Rick spent several moments scanning it. They discussed something that made Angie blush; then he returned to the table and sat down beside Christa.

"What's wrong?"

"Nothing for you to worry about. Angie received an update from one of her sources. According to their current information, John doesn't fit the description of the two missing men or any of the known members of the Society for Order. The Kane Connors connection bothers me, but I'm not sure where to go with it."

"I'm glad John's not involved, but still—another dead end. It's discouraging." Half of Christa's heart stung with deep disappointment that John would find no answers today. The other half rejoiced that he'd still be around tomorrow.

"For now it's a dead end. But we'll keep looking."

The photographer appeared in front of them to take a shot of the head table.

"You and your assistant will stop for something to eat, won't you?" Christa glanced around. "Wherever he is."

"I don't have an assistant. I work alone. Once in a while my wife helps out but not today." He snapped several shots of the crowd. "I'll get something later, thanks."

Christa frowned. "But earlier I saw a man with you outside."

"I don't think so." He shook his head, then nodded. "Oh yeah, there was a guy hanging around. Figured he didn't like having his picture taken. He was asking about one of the guests. Not that I was much help."

"Which guest?" Christa noticed Rick was all ears.

"That one. The usher." He inclined his head toward John, who had just taken his place at a table.

Christa was so taken aback, she didn't know what to say.

"What did this guy want to know?" Rick asked.

"A whole bunch of stuff. Where the usher came from. Where he's staying. His name. Like I'd know. I never met the fellow," he replied. "Funny, all that curiosity."

"Yes, it is strange. I'd like to talk to you a bit later, if you don't mind."

"No problem." The photographer handed him a card, then continued snapping. "Call me anytime."

Christa had her own questions to pose to Rick. But as Fred Jones rose and rapped his spoon against his glass, she knew she'd have to wait.

"Ladies and gentlemen, welcome to Camp Hope. This place has seen many changes over the years. Campers have come and gone, learned about God and each other, and hopefully taken something with them to help them in later life. We've built, rebuilt, added on, and altered almost everything in the place. But this is the first time we've ever held a wedding. Congratulations, Kent and Georgia."

A tinkling sound filled the room, led primarily by Doug Henderson, Georgia's childhood friend whom she had chosen to walk her down the aisle.

"Your wish is my command." Kent laughed. "I have no trouble kissing this gorgeous woman." And he proceeded to do exactly that to the delight of the assembled guests.

Fred offered a few droll jokes that soon had the audience hooting with laughter. Then he nodded to Doug, who stood and held up his glass. "I would like to propose a toast to the bride, my very best friend and play buddy for many years. To Georgia, a woman who's known rich joy and deepest sorrow and has emerged from it with a kinder heart, a gentler soul, and a purer spirit so that she can share all three with those who need her. I'm so proud of you for all you've accomplished, so glad you found a man who is worthy of your love, and so delighted to offer this toast to your happiness. May your blessings multiply until your heart can hardly contain them. To Georgia."

Everyone rose, raising their glasses of punch. "To Georgia."

While the others drank their toast to the bride, Kent quietly offered his own salute to his wife, his voice so soft that only those seated very near heard his words. "To the woman who brought hope back to this camp and to my life. I love you."

After Kent ably responded to Doug's toast, platters of food filled the tables. Many toasts, much tinkling, and a few very romantic embraces followed. The Murdock sisters moved quietly around the tables, refilling beverages and platters of endless food in the relaxed atmosphere that prevailed. Abby ensured that the guests lacked nothing, though she lingered longest beside Doug.

"Kent said most of these frills were your idea." Rick grinned at Christa. "You did a good job. I'm a little concerned you're not eating anything, but I don't suppose you'd poison all of us now, would you?"

"Very funny." She didn't need food. It was enough to feel that soft swell of contentment rise inside as she watched others enjoy themselves.

"If you don't need 'em, I could take down those white and gold balloons you used to decorate outside. The seniors' home would love them for their harvest festival tomorrow."

"Good idea. Can you think of a use for all this tulle?"

"What's tulle?" She pointed and he nodded. "Oh, the fluffy stuff. Nah, that's not up my alley. Ask Angie."

Christa passed him a platter.

Rick hesitated. "Uh . . . what are these things?"

"Frogs."

"Oh." He pulled his hand back.

"They're veggies, silly." Christa giggled as he picked one up, then gingerly tasted it. Abby's little crudités were ingenious. If she could copy them, maybe use cork and some green felt . . . the ideas spun through her mind, one after the other, filling her head with possibilities for another craft.

"Not bad," Rick said, reaching for a second helping, "for frogs."

Relaxed for the first time in ages, Christa almost sighed, then swallowed when Georgia leaned over to whisper something in her husband's ear.

A moment later, Kent rose and tapped his spoon on a plate. "My wife and I have one more toast to make." He helped Georgia to her feet and turned toward Christa, his grin widening as he took in her surprise. "Our toast is to Christa."

Georgia's lovely brown eyes welled with tears as she stood in the circle of Kent's arm and began to speak. "I never had a sister, but if I had, I'd want her to be you, Christa. You go above and beyond anything we could ever expect.

"Today, our ceremony, this reception—it's all a tribute to you and your thoughtfulness. Our wedding day is doubly precious, much more treasured because of you. We love you, Christa."

Kent held his glass aloft. "To Christa."

"Hear! Hear! To Christa."

Christa sat front and center in the limelight, stunned by the words of love they'd heaped upon her. Georgia's hug was tight, precious, and sweet, and she clung to that slim body for a moment, loath to let go and face the ogling group whose focus was now turned on her.

Georgia transmitted her understanding with a squeeze of her hand. "Sisters of the heart, okay, Christa?"

Christa reached up to straighten the bride's tilting hat. "Sisters of the heart, Georgia," she agreed on a broken whisper.

"What about me?" Kent towered over her, his smile broad.

Christa detected a glimmer of worry at the back of his gaze. She knew that look and itched to dispel it. He didn't have to be afraid for her—ever again. She intended to make certain of that, one way or another.

"You're my big brother, Kent. I'd do anything for you." She couldn't stop the flow of tears. "You should know that by now."

He enveloped her in a bear hug. "Same here," he whispered.

When he finally pulled away, Christa took a few moments to regain her composure. Only then did she realize that a hush had fallen over the entire hall, that all eyes were on her. It was up to her. Either break the tension that had crept in or let them all watch her bawl— and bawling at this wedding was not an option she was prepared to consider.

Glaring at the guests, she shook her head in dismay. "Don't you people know this is a wedding? You're supposed to look happy."

As she'd hoped, the room erupted in laughter.

"Well done, Christa." Rick brushed his lips over her knuckles.

"Thanks—" she grinned—"but I think there's someone else you'd rather be kissing. Isn't there?" She raised her eyebrows at him, relenting only when his cheeks colored a dark shade of ruby. That suspicion confirmed, she turned to the bridal couple. "You two need to cut that cake and pass it out. Time's a-wasting."

Kent rolled his eyes. "Give her an inch and she thinks she's in charge." He picked up the cake knife and drew Georgia's hand under his. "There's no point in arguing with my sister, you know."

"No point at all when she's right." Georgia winked at Christa, then posed with Ken as the photographer took several shots of the cake Georgia herself had decorated yesterday. "Come on, darling, try to look happy."

"That I can do, Mrs. Anderson—" he kissed her cheek—"with no effort at all."

"They look the picture of bliss—something we all dream about and hope we'll get to experience." Rick's quiet words echoed Christa's thoughts.

Christa watched with satisfaction as Kent and Georgia handed out pieces of wedding cake to all those who'd gathered to celebrate their happiness. This union was blessed.

"Now if I can only get some heavenly help with John and his memory, I'll feel as if I've done something to earn all those kind words." She hadn't meant for anyone to overhear her musing.

But Rick twisted, frowning at her. "As far as helping John goes, I'm not sure there's a lot you should be doing right now. Let us look into it. It might be a good idea to stay away from that Web site too. We don't know exactly who we're dealing with." His eyes darkened, pinpointed hers. "And don't forget to report anything unusual. I'll be checking on you."

"Define *unusual*."

"Out of place, odd. Anything that doesn't fit." His gaze drifted to the tall, silent man at the back of the room who didn't know his own name. "I have this nagging feeling that we've rattled someone's cage, and it won't be much longer before we find out how hard they can bite. Nothing concrete, just . . . a hunch. You be careful."

The words sent a ripple of uneasiness down her spine that she tried to cover by joking with Ralna and teasing Doug. But the tension built as the guests left and she was finally alone in the house with only a pager and her dog for company. The gnawing disquiet made her hang on to Maggie's collar and draw her near, grateful for the animal's silent companionship.

"It's your own fault you're nervous, Christa Anderson. Everyone thinks you want to be alone here because you made them believe it."

That had been phase one of her independence campaign.

"Anyway, what's the big deal? You're hardly alone. John is about five hundred feet away in his trailer with a matching pager. One click on the radio reaches Ralna and Fred, who will take about two minutes to rush over here and coddle you as if you're five. Independence— isn't that what you wanted?"

The pep talk had Maggie confused. She quirked her head in a way that Christa had long ago decided meant she thought humans were nuts. The dog set one paw on Christa's leg as if to share in the discussion. Spunky Maggie was healing quickly despite the bare spot on her flank.

"It's a good thing you can't speak, Mags." She ruffled her fur and giggled when Maggie woofed a response. "Well, speak English, I mean."

Maggie turned round and round on the mat in front of the fireplace. When she had exactly the right amount of twists and folds in it, she curled into a ball and flopped one paw over her head.

"Meaning lights out?" Christa chuckled. "Not yet, girl. First I want to go over the details of this wedding, remember them."

A knock made Maggie perk up.

Christa moved to the kitchen, glanced out the window, then unlatched the door.

"Hi." After John stepped through the door, he closed and locked it. Only then did he lean back against its solid barrier and allow his breath to burst out in deep gasps as if he'd been running.

His white face shocked her. "What's wrong?"

"I need to use the phone."

"Sure. But why?" Shadows wavered through his eyes, adding to the fear that was growing inside Christa.

"Someone broke into the RV." He grabbed the phone and began dialing.

Christa remained frozen in place as she listened to him relay the entire story to the police.

———◆◆———

"We'll be making regular patrols out here from now on. If you have any more problems, call. I'll bring Rick up to speed tomorrow."

John thanked the officer before closing the door behind him. "I should go too."

"There's no rush." Christa didn't want to be alone.

"I'm sure you don't want to babysit me." John raked a hand through his hair and faked a smile.

"It's already way after one, and we don't have to get up early tomorrow." She noticed his color was almost normal. "It was a nice wedding though, wasn't it?"

"I don't think I know all that much about weddings, but this one seemed fine. The guests stayed long enough." The lines of worry shifted to frame his eyes.

"Did having so many people around bother you?"

"A little. I kept watching them, wishing one would jump up and admit he knew me. It's a funny feeling to be among so many people and not know who you are."

"I'm sorry. I didn't think of that."

"Why should you? It's my problem."

"But I'd like to help. I think it's about my turn to give." She mulled over what he'd said about the break-in. "If you left the CDs on the table, why would someone move them to the bed?"

"Who knows? Maybe they were looking through them, wanted to take one, and realized it was in the wrong case."

"Awfully choosy thief. More likely they were looking for something specific. What's under the table?"

"Nothing. There are benches on either side. One holds the water tank; the other is for storage."

"Is there anything in the storage compartment?"

"I don't know." His face regained the same tight, tense look it had when he arrived. "This is so frustrating. Every time there's a question, I have the same answer. I don't know. *Why* don't I know? What's holding me back?"

The strain was getting to him. Christa wanted so badly to help, but she had no answers to his questions. All she could do was listen. She urged him into a chair, set the kettle to boil, and pulled out the makings for hot chocolate.

"This might not be what you want to hear, John, but there is a reason for all of this. I'm beginning to realize that simply because I don't understand doesn't mean God isn't working. But His timing is different than ours. We see the short term, but He looks at the big picture."

"You think God is behind this?" His shock might have been laughable if the whole situation wasn't so serious.

"Well, I'm not suggesting He sent someone to break into your place, but I do think He knows why they did. And I believe that when the time comes, He'll show us."

"Blind faith," he mumbled.

"Maybe not so blind," she countered. "Why would God create people in His image only to abandon them? If you read the Old Testament, you can see how closely God watched what His people did. Only this morning I was struck by how detailed His orders were in so many things. Both Noah's ark and the tabernacle had very specific plans that the builders were to follow."

John seemed to be listening so she continued. "That isn't disinterest. That's making yourself an intricate part of someone else's life. He cares. He knows what you're going through better than anyone."

"You really believe what you read in the Bible, don't you?" John smiled at her energetic nod. "And you, Kent, and Georgia—all of you here at this camp—live by it. I don't think I ever knew anyone else who does that."

Please, God, give me something that will encourage him.

She looked around, noticing the verse she'd stuck to the fridge that quoted Ecclesiastes. Perfect.

"I'm not all that different from you. I just put my faith in a different place." Christa picked up her Bible. "When I came home from the hospital, my former pastor came to see me. I didn't want to talk to him, so he didn't press me. He'd sit beside the bed and read. This is what he read the first day." She flipped through the pages.

"'There is a time for everything, a season for every activity under heaven. A time to be born and a time to die. A time to plant and a time to harvest. A time to kill and a time to heal.'"

His face changed from quiet contemplation to something darker. "A time to kill."

"I was thinking more in terms of a time to heal. The secrets in men's hearts are not hidden from God. He sees; He knows."

"You're very good to me." John leaned forward to cup her cheek in his palm. His thumb seared a path against her skin. "I don't know how to thank you."

The caress surprised her with its intimacy. *Be careful.* Christa licked her dry lips, seeking the right words. "It's not as though you haven't done the same for me many times."

"I'm not sure I can ever believe like you do, but I do realize there's nothing I can do right now but carry on." He smiled, but the shadows lingered in his eyes.

"You have to let go, John. Admit you're not in control; God is. I think that's the hardest step." She kept silent as he appeared to think about her words. But the ticking clock, the warmth of the furnace air bursting from the vent behind her, and the lateness of the hour all conspired against her. She tried to stifle a yawn but couldn't.

Seeing it, John trailed one hand over her hair, now loose from its earlier upswept style. "You're tired. No wonder. You've been on the go since first light, and here I am drowning you with my sorrows. Go to bed. I've stayed far longer than I meant to." He stood, but his gaze remained on her. "Thank you doesn't seem enough."

"No thanks needed between friends." She watched him rinse out their cups and walk to the door. "Good night, John. Please try and get some sleep." She couldn't stop herself from moving closer, grasping his hand, and squeezing it. "Things will look better in the morning."

"Is that a promise?" His fingers tightened around hers.

"Yes."

He stared down at her for a moment. Finally he bent. His lips hovered above hers, then descended.

Realizing his intent, Christa tilted her head slightly so the featherlight caress brushed her cheek.

He smiled as if he understood her reticence to take their relationship to the next step. "Good night, Chris. Page me if you need something. Anything." His mouth was inches from hers, and his hand still held hers in a firm, sure grip.

"I have the pager and the radio," she reminded him, forcing her breathing to remain even. "I'll be fine. Don't let your mind magnify this. Trust in God."

He studied her a long time before he straightened and left, the lock clicking behind him. Knowing he would wait until he heard her chain the door, she did so.

"Good night," she whispered, though he couldn't hear.

She switched off the lights but remained in front of the window, watching until John disappeared from sight. The burst of feeling still simmered inside and scared her with its intensity. They shared a lot but not the most important thing. There was no way around that.

Please don't let me lose sight of who I belong to, of the path You're leading me on.

Christa didn't need electric illumination to find her way to her bedroom. The moon was full and flooded in through the now-repaired screen. She lay in bed, considering the work she and Abby had done on her secret project. It was good. It was very good. As enthused as Christa, Abby was eager to help however she was asked and constantly suggested alternatives that enhanced the products. They were almost finished with phase one.

"Thanks for a very cool day, God," she said softly as her body sagged into the mattress, waiting for the sandman to take her away.

A creak from outside drew Christa back to reality immediately.

A tree teetering in the wind? Someone opening the machine-shed door? She couldn't tell. As it had that afternoon John had pulled up the Web site, she felt a cloud of oppression move into the room. Maybe the person who had broken into John's RV was back. Panic choked her.

Another squeak.

Through her open window she heard footsteps on the gravel road. They came closer and climbed the steps. The hairs on the back of her neck stood to attention. Christa gulped and reached for the phone, realizing she'd left it in the kitchen.

Maggie was awake, head cocked, listening. She rumbled a warning. Christa held on to Maggie's collar, her heart in her throat as she waited for the sound of the door opening. It didn't come.

Instead a soft thump from outside shifted her heart rate into high. Her shoulders knotted with tension, and her head throbbed. Fear clenched her muscles.

Desperately she grabbed the radio and punched a button with fingers that barely worked.

"Fred! Someone's outside my window!"

"On the way."

"Hurry! Please hurry."

The words had barely slipped past her lips when the quiet hiss of danger spoke from the darkness. "You cannot hide. Return it before the council exacts revenge."

A burst of anger billowed inside Christa. She was scared, but she would not be rendered totally helpless!

She eased herself from the bed into her chair, mentally searching the house for the best place to hide.

She'd made it to the doorway before the second threat slipped into the room. "Return it or be warned."

She gasped. It was the same voice from the other night.

Peril lay behind those words, as tangible as she'd ever felt it.

CHAPTER EIGHT

Christa, why didn't you page me? Why did you wait till now to tell me about the intruder?"

It galled John that he'd been asleep while the police made a second trip to the camp to search for someone who shouldn't have been there.

Christa looked like a piece of fragile glass about to shatter. She sat slumped in her chair, her face drained of all color, as if she hadn't slept a wink, and there were dark circles under her eyes.

"I called Fred. He got the police back, and he and Ralna stayed with me. You've done so much already and you'd had a shock and—" She swallowed, then looked down.

"And what? Tell me," he demanded, fed up with trying to guess what was going on in her mind.

"I guess I didn't want you to get the wrong idea," she whispered.

"The wrong idea about helping you? I thought we were friends."

"We are, John. But that's all we can be." She turned away.

She meant the kiss. He'd known that was a mistake. She didn't have those feelings for him. "You're certain you're all right? He didn't hurt you?"

"Nobody came inside. He only whispered stuff about me returning something, revenge, and to be warned." She shivered.

Her voice was thready when next she spoke. "The police didn't have any answers and neither do I. I don't know who it was or what he wanted." Christa paused, squinting into the distance. "Maybe it was someone from my past. But I can't imagine what he thinks I took. Anyway, he's gone now, and I don't want to talk about it anymore. Not right now."

John let it go. But later he intended to hash it out with Fred. He wasn't an outsider; he was part of this place. If Christa was in danger, he wanted to be the one who protected her. "I'm sorry I snapped at you. I'm glad you're all right."

"I'm fine." A crooked smile lifted her lips. "It was a little scary at the time."

And probably every time she closed her eyes. He'd seen her earlier, sitting on her porch, watching the sunrise. He'd almost interrupted until he caught the sheen of tears and realized that she was sharing a private moment with the God she spoke of more and more frequently these days, a God he didn't understand. That's why she'd pulled away from him when he'd tried to kiss her. She was different than he.

"What are you doing?" Christa asked.

John followed her glance and realized he'd been tracing his fingers over the words written on the camp van. "Good question." How could he explain the familiar niggle of uncertainty he felt inside whenever he looked at this vehicle?

"We've got to get rid of it. It doesn't work as it should."

"Christa, is Kent selling the van?"

"I know he was thinking about it. Why do you ask?"

"I'm not sure. There's something about this van . . ." Unable to say exactly what that was, John shoved his hands in his pockets, felt the cold metal of the key, and remembered he was going to try every lock in camp. Later. When he was alone.

As usual, Christa seemed to understand.

"I brought some coffee and cookies," she murmured. "Why don't you take a break? I want to tell you something."

"Good timing." He sat down on a nearby stump. "I just finished building the boardwalk."

Christa rolled nearer and pivoted her chair so she had a view of both directions. "So you have." Her face suddenly came alive. Silver flecks danced through her eyes before she whirred off over the new boardwalk toward the pool and back again, her chair making a rhythmical thud at each joint.

She looked too vibrant, too full of life to be confined to a wheelchair. That familiar sting of regret burned John's throat as he wished yet again that he had the power to change things for her. He would do almost anything to give her back the use of her legs.

Just as quickly he tamped the feelings down. Christa had her whole life before her, a life she'd begun to look forward to. She didn't need his regrets to drag her down.

"So you like my boardwalk?"

"Very much. I want to thank you for doing this, John. I know carpentry isn't easy for you, but this means a lot to me. Do you know how freeing this is?" Crystal teardrops sparkled on the tips of her thick brown lashes. "It's so liberating. The simple things that God gives us mean so much."

God. How did God come into this?

"It doesn't matter if it's pouring buckets or snowing. Whenever I come to visit, I'll be able to get outside into the world He created."

When I come to visit. For a little while he'd let himself forget that she wouldn't be staying.

"I'm glad you like it." The way her fingers curled around his sent a strange rush of warmth to flood his insides. He was pretty sure this blossoming burst inside him hadn't happened with anyone else—he'd have remembered *that*.

He studied her with fresh eyes. To him, Christa had always been beautiful, but this radiance came from something more than her glossy hair or those flashing eyes. The vitality that spilled out of her was part and parcel of who she was becoming. Every day he saw her growing, changing.

"You're staring at me." She took her hand from his, her expression quizzical.

"Just wondering."

"About what?"

"Why you credited God with this walk. I built it." Great. Now he sounded like a little boy boasting about his accomplishments.

Apparently Christa thought so too. She patted his hand as if he were six years old. "Yes, I know you built it, but God sent you here to do it." Her forefinger flicked his cheek. "Don't make that face. I don't believe in accidents or random events in my life. God is in control and He cares for His children. I'm one of them, so He cares for me."

God cared for her by letting an intruder get near? John let it go and concentrated on the other part of her words. Curiosity plagued him.

"How did you get to be one of His children?"

She studied him as if she thought he was teasing.

He held her gaze.

After a moment, she nodded slightly. "Well, Christianity is pretty simple. It starts with the mind, by making a conscious decision to believe in God. Then we look inside our hearts and admit that we need Him. After that, it's a matter of accepting Jesus, God's Son, and the sacrifice He made for us. As we surrender our lives to Him day by day, He shows us how to serve Him."

"You sort of take God on trust?"

"On faith, yes. That's the first step."

She made it sound so simple that a part of him yearned to lean on someone else. The more he heard about her God, the more the empty space inside him grew into a potent ache that never went away. He craved the inner serenity that Christa possessed. But how could he trust and put his faith in someone he couldn't see or hear and . . . what? Ignore the past and hope for the best? It didn't make sense.

If he asked her more about this Christianity thing, he was pretty sure Christa wouldn't laugh. But she might be hurt if he didn't accept her beliefs, and John knew he wasn't ready to do that. Not yet.

There were too many unanswered questions in his life, too much that he didn't understand, too few certainties to trust anyone. He wouldn't ask any more questions right now. He needed space and time to think about what she'd said.

John shifted, uncomfortable under her steady gaze. "Did you say you brought coffee?"

"Yes." Christa had slung a backpack she'd constructed from the top half of a pair of worn blue jeans across the handles of her chair. Now she lifted it off, then unzipped it. Out came a thermos and a cup.

"This is service." He took the steaming coffee she held out, sipped it, and fought to conceal his reaction.

"It's no good, is it?" Christa frowned. "Rats! I hoped maybe I'd gotten it right this time."

"It's fine. Just fine." He took another sip, as if that would prove its goodness, and immediately tasted coffee grounds.

"Don't try to lie," Christa said, lips twitching. "You're not good at it. Besides, I know all about my coffee. Kent's ordered me to leave the machine alone, but I thought if I followed Georgia's directions . . ." She let the sentence trail away, then shrugged. "I only wanted to have a coffee break with you, to get rid of the mem—"

"I appreciate your effort." He didn't know what to do with the cup or the dregs in it.

Obviously Christa observed his hesitation, because she took the cup, tossed out the contents, and filled it with two inches of water from her bottle.

"That's water, and these are Georgia's cookies so you don't have to worry. I didn't bake them, and I couldn't do much to mess them up just putting them in the bag, could I?"

He took one of the cookies, bit into it appreciatively, taste buds tingling as the gingersnap melted on his tongue. "She certainly can bake."

"I know." Christa waved one hand airily, her voice matter-of-fact. "She does everything well and looks like a dream doing it. It's disgusting."

Searching her face, he saw a glimmer of banked excitement and remembered the reason she'd come. "What did you want to talk to me about?"

Christa fiddled with the wheels of her chair, rocking back and forth with that barely leashed impatience so typical of her. "This morning I spoke with the administrator of a rehab center I went to after my accident."

"And she convinced you to take up golf . . . or no, let me think . . . choreograph the annual Camp Hope potato races?" He was at a loss to figure out what made the blue in her eyes deepen, like a shield hiding secrets.

"Golf? Me? No, silly." Christa's laugh reminded him of youth and energy, like a lamb frolicking in springtime. She pushed the long, spiky bangs out of her eyes. "My friend gave me the idea for a fund-raiser for Camp Hope."

"Christa, I know all about your ideas," he teased. "My short-term memory is very good. Remember that sailboat? It would never float."

"So? Some of my ideas have been great. You just won't admit it." She bit down hard on a cookie. "Anyway, this is an excellent idea."

"Uh-huh. That's what I'm afraid of. Another excellent idea."

Christa rolled her eyes.

Once again, John noted how much she'd changed. When he'd first met Christa, she reminded him of a little wren who'd been hiding. But once she began breaking free of her depression, everything about her had changed.

Now her hair glowed and shimmered with highlights of rusty red, burnished copper, and beaten gold. Her face, tanned a soft peach color, added to that healthy lambency and increased the depth of her radiant eyes. Except for the chair, she didn't look like Sally at all.

"Are you going to listen to me, or have you disappeared into your never-never land again?"

Blinking, he jerked back to awareness, thoughts of Sally evaporating. "My what?"

"Your never-never land. Peter Pan. You know?" She bent forward and squinted at him. "Surely you haven't forgotten Peter Pan?"

Her words brought only one thing to John's mind: green tights. He gulped.

"I'd be Tinkerbell. Only I can't fly." She lifted her arm, pinched two fingers together, and waved her hand toward him. "There, I've given you some pixie dust. Now will you listen to my idea?"

"Of course. Pixie dust always works on me."

"I think you mean sawdust, and it's in your hair, but that's okay. At least you don't mind joking around with me." She swiped her hand over his head, dislodging some of the golden dust. "I suppose my sense of humor is a little strange. Quite often people look at me with one eyebrow raised and let me babble on."

He made a face, hoping to hear her laugh.

"Anyway . . ." Christa dragged the word out. "Every year in October we do a big fund-raiser for Camp Hope, kind of a launch to get working on next year's major projects. Usually it's something staid and boring like a fowl supper with door prizes and local entertainment."

John knew staid and boring wasn't part of her idea when she took a deep breath and pinned him with her gaze.

"Kent hasn't mentioned his plans yet, but this year I think we should make it into a weekend—a mystery weekend."

Though his stump seat was growing increasingly uncomfortable, John stayed put while he tried to fathom her meaning. Sometimes understanding Christa was like trying to catch a lightning bug—a lot of expended effort without much illumination. Better to just ask her to explain.

"How's a mystery going to work?"

"First of all, we announce that we have only so many invitations available, so there will be a rush to buy them. Then we put together a puzzle that the guests have to solve with the clues we give them over the weekend. The final night at the banquet is when the mystery is revealed. The next day, after giving them a taste of life at Camp Hope and sharing some of our vision, we bid everyone a fond farewell."

"Uh-huh." This was one of those times when John ardently wished he had some past experience to guide him. He had no idea what Kent would think of Christa's plan nor any memory to gauge the effectiveness of her idea.

"Well?" she prompted, the gleam in her eyes dimming a fraction when he didn't immediately applaud.

"Well, what? I don't know anything about this kind of thing. In fact, I don't know anything about anything." He didn't want to discourage her when she was obviously excited, so he lifted his hands, palms up. "My brain is a blank, remember?"

She fixed him with one of her disdainful looks that scoffed at his excuse. "Your brain is not a blank. It simply isn't sending out any impulses at the moment." No sooner had she spoken the words than she clapped a hand over her mouth. "I didn't mean that the way it sounded! I meant that it isn't . . . uh, receiving the impulses—"

Her ruby cheeks were enchanting, but after another moment of stumbling, John took pity on her. "I know what you mean, Chris. But though I'm not brain-dead, I really am clueless when it comes to theater stuff." *Among other things.*

"Not theater. It's a mystery, a game. My friend has one she used and she says it went over wonderfully well for them, though they did it all in one night. Of course, we'd have to decorate around the camp, get some clues planted—that kind of thing."

The way she explained made it sound all right, but with Christa he'd learned to look for what she wasn't saying. "What about the . . . uh . . . actors?"

She shook her head. "I told you, it's a game. No actors. No lines."

He heaved a sigh of relief. A flash from the past—a Christmas concert at school, stuttering, the shame he'd endured—fluttered through his head, then dissipated without releasing anything else.

"John?" She stared at him, a frown tipping down the corners of her mouth. That look told him several moments had elapsed.

"What is the mystery about?" Maybe he could forestall any questions.

"I don't have all the details yet, but the gist of it is that a woman and a man plan to get married and someone stalls their plans by creating problems that get out of control." She offered a tentative smile. "Love and all its attendant issues."

Love. The word triggered an immediate reaction in John that surprised him.

"Now what's wrong?" She pushed her hair out of her eyes to glare at him. "Honestly, talking to you is hard sometimes. You're like some kind of mental shape-shifter—here one minute, gone the next." She sighed. "It's a good idea. Admit it."

"It is a good idea," he repeated while visions of hearts danced through his mind.

"Off to never-never land again?" She snapped her fingers in front of his nose. "John!"

He groped for the threads of conversation he'd dropped.

Christa's eyes narrowed. "Every so often you get this look on your face and kind of blank out. I think you remembered something just now. Out with it, buddy."

"Nothing new, really." He shrugged away the image of those hearts. "I keep recalling the same old thing. It's not important."

"You don't know that. Tell me."

John shook his head, but when she insisted he found himself explaining.

"Love? That's it?"

"Love and hearts. I tried some word associations, but the only thing that brought to mind were Valentines. That led me to mail. But beyond that, I'm stymied."

"Mail?" Her whole face lit up. "As in a post office?"

"I guess. I don't really know." He spread his arms. "I told you. It's all a confused jumble of images. Love and mail. Nothing makes sense."

"It might." She nibbled on her bottom lip, staring past him toward the pool. "It very well might. I need to phone Rick."

"Something about the mail means you need the police?"

She ignored his question, fingers flying as she closed the thermos and stored it in her pack. "Can you drive?"

"I guess. I drove the lawn tractor to cut the grass. Why?"

"We're not going to be cutting any grass. Not today."

"I know. Fred and I are going to mend a couple of the canoes."

"That will have to wait." She unclipped her radio from her belt and spoke into it. "Ralna, it's Christa. Is Fred there?"

"Just finishing his coffee. Do you need to speak with him?"

"Ask him if he'll meet me at the house in five minutes. Oh, and would you ask him to bring over the van? It's running, isn't it?"

"For now." Ralna's surprise was evident. "Is everything okay, honey?"

"Yes. Fine. I need the van."

John stared at the tired vehicle, wondering what she needed it for.

"Okay—" a pause—"Fred says he's on his way."

"Thanks." Christa pressed the lever on her chair that sent the motor humming and rolled over the boardwalk.

John stared at her retreating figure, opened and closed his mouth a couple of times, then decided to follow. Something besides that fund-raiser was going on in that complex brain of hers, and he intended to find out what it was.

<hr />

"Let's see if I've got this right. You think that John's dreams about hearts are somehow tied in with the post office?" Fred's dubious tone conveyed his feelings about Christa's latest idea.

Judging by Fred's confusion, he was beginning to share John's doubts.

Christa offered him a reassuring smile and pressed on. "I'm sure of it. Hear me out." She waited until they'd taken a seat. All except John. He kept watching her. Every so often his glance moved to the van and rested there.

"John remembers hearts. He connects them to love and to mail." She waited for understanding to dawn, then rushed back into speech when it didn't. "Don't you get it? Maybe he was in Love, as in the town of Love."

"Okay, I see where you're going with this." Fred nodded, his thin face thoughtful. "The hamlet of Love is known for what?" He tilted his head toward Ralna. "Their postmark, right? Which is?"

"Of course!" Ralna clasped her hands. "A fancy heart with a cupid superimposed on it. Christa, you are quick."

"Well, I think John needs to look around the post office in Love and see if anybody remembers him."

"And you think he should take the van." Fred was up to speed now. "But we don't know if he has a license."

"This is too important to wait." Christa shrugged. "Besides, who doesn't drive these days?"

They were onto something. She knew it. Maybe she was impatient, but after all these months, if there was even a chance . . . "I tried to get hold of Rick, but he's investigating some hunter types who've been using the Parsons' land. The department is short of staff, and Angie's in court today. So it's up to us." She looked at Ralna.

"I can't leave," Ralna responded. "Not today. I promised the accountants I'd be available to answer any questions they had about my figures. I need those numbers for head office."

"I'd like to help too, honey, but Kent ordered a couple of loads of sand." Fred checked his watch. "They deliver at two if they're on time. I have to be here to show them where we want it dumped, but before that I have to do some prep work."

"That leaves John and me. If I'd taken those driving lessons and ordered the vehicle I was supposed to, I could have taken us without bothering anyone." Disgusted with her own shortsightedness, Christa pinched her lips together. "But I didn't think of it till last week. So for now that leaves us with the camp van and John to drive it."

Fred and Ralna didn't like it; she could see that. But perhaps they sensed, as she did, that this could be the clue they'd prayed for.

"Please be careful," Ralna said. "If Kent knew—"

"He'd understand. Come on." The words died as she saw John half turn toward the vehicle. He remained frozen in that position, sandy hair ruffled by the wind, his tall frame angled in an awkward position. "John? What's wrong?"

"Hmm?" He faced her. "Nothing."

"The last time you said that, it led us here," she reminded him softly. "Just tell us what you're thinking. We want to help."

He pushed back the droop of hair that partially blocked his vision. Once more he focused on the van. "I'm not sure," he told her, his voice fading. "There's something about this vehicle—people inside, the back door . . . never mind." He tossed back his head. "It's nothing. Just a mess of mixed-up pictures. Let's go."

Sensing a car ride in her future, Maggie came dashing across the drive. She sat with her tail feathering the sand as she politely waited for someone to offer her entrance.

Three things happened simultaneously. Ralna's portable phone rang. John began tracing the lettering on the back window that spelled Camp Hope. Fred pointed to the stairs of her and Kent's house and asked, "What's that?"

Christa followed the direction of his finger. A small, brown package had fallen off the front doorstep into the mass of wilting red petunias below.

"I . . . er . . . I don't know." Christa gulped. It was hers, left by the postal worker. It had to be. Who else got little brown packages? This had to be step two in her independence plan. But she wasn't going to tell them that and be stuck with explaining.

"A late wedding gift maybe? I hope it hasn't broken."

Fred retrieved the parcel. "I don't think it's a wedding gift," he said, stepping out of the flower bed.

"Oh. Why's that?" *Don't let him see my name on there.*

"There's no card. Look at the wrapping."

She did. Plain brown paper tied with ordinary string. No return address, no one indicated as the recipient. Well, that was different.

Now she couldn't tell if it was what she'd been waiting for or not. But she didn't want anyone else knowing her secret—yet. Maybe she'd look first, then, if she was wrong and it was a wedding gift—but wedding gifts didn't come in brown paper packages.

"Want me to put it inside for the happy couple to look at when they return?" Fred asked.

"You know me too well for that." Christa held out one hand. "I'll open it now. It might not be theirs. It might be something important for the camp." Well, it *could* be. She'd just take a peek.

"That curiosity of yours is getting worse," Fred joked, watching as she slid off the string and dragged one fingernail across the tape holding the seams of paper together. "You're going to feel really silly if it's a wedding gift."

"I know it. Can't be helped." Perhaps it was wrong to check it out first, she speculated, pushing aside layer after layer of tissue paper inside the box. But if it was hers, she had to get it out of sight fast. If it was a wedding gift, well, she'd apologize later. She pressed away the final sheet.

The uncontrollable scream formed in her chest, slid up her throat, and pushed through her lips in a gasp as she recoiled from the horrifying contents. Inside the box, a dead rat lay spread-eagled, its glassy eyes peering up at her, claws clenched into the paper.

Christa's entire body felt frozen in that moment. She couldn't look away from the ugliness, couldn't mobilize her fingers to push it off her lap and get free of the terror that gripped her. For the first time she was glad the paralysis had left her legs with no sensation. That way she didn't have to feel its weight lying on her, rucking her jeans.

Then suddenly the repulsive thing was gone, lifted away by unseen hands. She could breathe again.

Through the mist of tears she hadn't known was there until now, she saw John staring into the open box. He yelped.

Seconds later Fred was by his side. Both faces tightened, mirroring their revulsion at such an appalling deed.

"There is a card after all," Fred stated.

Christa hiccuped a sob behind her hand when John reached inside the box and picked up a small white rectangle. "What does it say? Surely no one meant that for Kent and Georgia." Christa could hardly believe anyone would have sent it.

"Not for them." John stared at the card and shook his head, his face blanching. "I think it was meant for me. Someone is trying to send me a message."

"What message? What does the card say?" Fred asked.

John handed Fred the box before walking toward Christa, the card dangling from his fingertips. He held it so she could see the spidery words scrawled in black ink against the pristine white: *From one rat to another.*

She grimaced. "What does that mean?"

"At a guess, I'd say somebody thinks I've told something I shouldn't have. Or they're warning me to shut up. Either way, they want me to know that they're aware I'm here."

"Why you? And told what?"

John looked directly into Christa's eyes, clasped her shoulder, and squeezed it reassuringly as if to encourage.

"You think it has something to do with that Web site and the date you keep remembering," she said.

"I think so."

"You cannot hide. Return it before the council exacts revenge."

Tentacles of ice spread from the cords of tension in her neck, across her shoulders, and down her spine as she recalled the specific moment when she'd heard a thump on the step. Without a doubt, Christa knew that the rat had been left then. Because she always used the ramp, she hadn't noticed the package on the stairs. Maybe the door swinging open had sent it into the flowers. Regardless, someone had come to *her* house to leave it.

Because she hadn't obeyed the warning that night.

She glanced up. Ralna had her eyes closed, her lips moving silently in prayer. Fred and John gathered the paper and string, no doubt so Rick would be able to examine everything.

"I . . . uh . . . I think it arrived the night of the wedding," Christa explained. "That night I called Ralna and Fred."

"All the more reason for the cops to check it out."

"Can you call them, Fred? Maybe there are fingerprints or something."

He nodded, took Ralna's phone, and dialed. After a brief conversation, he said, "Someone will be out later."

"Fine. Right now I want to get to the post office." And away from the lingering thoughts of that night, of someone deliberately leaving that—

"The police want to talk to you."

"I'll be back by the time they get here." For a moment Christa asked herself if it was worth leaving the security of the camp, then remembered that the intruder already knew where to find her. She rolled her chair up the ramp, checked that the house door was locked, and redirected herself toward the van. "You can't go, Maggie. Not this time." The dog whined but Christa ignored her. They needed answers now, before this council did something else. "Come on, John. Let's get me loaded."

He stood looking at her.

"What?" she demanded, impatient to be on the road. She refused to think about the rat.

"I'm not sure it's a good idea for you to be involved in this," he said. "Whatever 'this' is."

"I'm already involved," she insisted. "I live here. For the moment, Camp Hope is my home. Yours too. But we need answers, so let's see if we can follow up on the only clue we've got." She kept her face expressionless, her hands relaxed on her legs. She would not show the trepidation that tiptoed over her taut nerves. This time she'd be strong.

As John drove them toward Love, Christa prayed for a break. She'd never felt more helpless. She was a paraplegic, a cripple, who was only beginning to find her way. She'd told John to trust that God would send the answers he needed, but now she needed to remind herself of that too.

Maybe in Love they'd find the answers to a host of questions and to two in particular.

What dangerous secret did John Riddle know that someone was afraid he'd tell? And what had she stolen that someone was determined to retrieve?

CHAPTER NINE

Thirty times over John told himself to expect nothing.

Thirty times over he couldn't quite tamp down the fizzle of excitement of knowing that perhaps there would be an answer today, that maybe he and Christa would come across some clue that would break open the seal of his mind.

In the passenger seat, Christa directed her attention steadfastly forward. From the jut of her chin and the way she kept fiddling with the seat belt, John could tell that something was on her mind and she wasn't yet ready to share it with him. That was okay. He was content to simply have her here with him.

"Is that bothering you?"

"What?" She followed his stare down, then unclenched her fingers from the webbing of the belt. "Sorry."

"This could be nothing," he warned, reminding himself of the same thing. "Another of my crazy dreams." *If You're there, God, please let it be more than a dream.*

"You're right." She nodded, brown hair swinging an arc toward her chin. "It could be. But I don't think so. Turn here. The post office is over there. It's angle parking."

John pulled up to the curb, shifted into park, and turned off the engine. Even though he knew he should get out, walk in there, and ask his questions, he didn't move. *Get it over with*, he thought. Why was he hesitating?

Because of the butterflies dancing in his midsection.

"John?" Christa was looking at him. "Do you mind if I pray before you go in?"

He shook his head, closed his eyes, and waited. He'd never really prayed about anything before. He didn't think so anyway. But Christa believed, and because of that, he was willing to try. He could use all the help he could get today.

"Father, thank You for leading us here. Please be with John. Direct him to the right person, give him the right words. We need Your help, God. Thank You."

The words were simple and direct, and they touched him deeply. That she would be so concerned for him, a virtual stranger who'd long since overstayed any welcome he might have expected, was amazing. Dear Christa—the woman with a heart big enough to include everybody. He touched her hand as his feelings exploded in a starburst of happiness. At least he still had her. For now. "Thank you."

"You're welcome." She clutched his fingers briefly, then released them. Her regard was unwavering as it met his. "I'll attract too much attention if I go in with you. It's better if you go alone."

Her smile encouraged him to leave, but John still couldn't move. He'd expected her to be there beside him. Though she harped about him always offering her his physical help, she'd returned the favor time and again by giving him a sounding board, a perspective on his situation that he hadn't found with anyone else.

Now she was pushing him away. With piercing clarity, John realized that Christa had accepted that whatever he learned today would eventually lead him away from her. In some intrinsic way she already understood what he'd only begun to assimilate—he didn't belong in her world and he never would.

"Why are you waiting?"

"Second thoughts. Maybe remembering the past isn't the best thing." Maybe he didn't want to know the truth anymore—not if it took him away from Christa. "No, forget I said that."

He was no use to her without the ability to understand what had made him who he was, where he came from, and where he was going. She needed someone who was strong, not a man who preferred to be lost in the caverns of a memory on which he couldn't depend.

Christa said Christianity began with faith. Hope in God. He considered the idea, then forced it away. God couldn't help now. Better to learn the truth and face whatever he found, rather than worry about secrets that could hurt Christa.

He opened the door. "Here I go," he announced, keeping his voice low as several people walked past the van. "Wish me well."

"I can do better than that. I'll be praying."

He climbed out and walked into the post office.

A woman stood behind the counter, rimless glasses perched on the end of her nose. She examined him as he strode toward her. "Can I help you, sir?"

"I know this will sound strange, but I'm wondering if you recognize me."

She did a double take, then stepped back. "I beg your pardon?"

John scrambled to find a reason to explain his unusual inquiry. "I was in several months ago, and I believe I forgot my credit card on the counter. Since this is such a small town, I was hoping you might remember me." As a last-minute thought, he added, "And that you'd hung on to it."

"Oh, we never do that. Always send lost cards right back to the credit-card company. Don't want to be liable." The woman squinted. "You sure don't look familiar. Maybe you left it somewhere else."

"No, I'm fairly certain I was here last. So you don't recognize anything about me?" he pressed, aware by the whoosh of warm air against his back that someone else had entered the building and he'd soon have to give up.

"Nope. Sorry. I've never seen you before. And I'm good with faces."

His heart dropped to his shoes. All that buildup of hope for nothing. "Well, thanks anyway."

As John turned, he found himself directly in the path of a young woman and tried to sidestep her. For some reason she didn't move. He glanced at her and knew immediately that she recognized him.

"Hello." He smiled, but she stepped backward, making it patently obvious that she didn't want to speak to him. "I don't mean to bother you, but I was wondering if you recognize me."

She frowned and shook her head.

"Really? Because I noticed that when you saw me, you seemed surprised."

"I said no."

"She said no, mister." The postmistress cleared her throat as if to emphasize her words. Her tone changed to a warm welcome. "Hello, Sally. What are you doing home?"

John's mind filled with the picture of a girl in a wheelchair, flaxen hair glowing like a halo around her pinched sad face. *A daughter?*

"Sally? Is that your name?" he asked, touching her arm.

"Let go of me!" She jerked away from him.

"Maybe you'd better leave, mister. She said she doesn't know you."

John saw the terror filling Sally's eyes and knew then that he'd lost any chance of learning whatever she knew. He'd probably frightened the poor girl to death. One thing was certain—this girl was not the Sally of his dream.

"I'm sorry. Please forgive me. I never meant to scare you. I only—" How could he possibly explain this? "Never mind. Sorry." He yanked open the door, walked outside to the van, and wordlessly climbed inside.

"What's wrong?" Christa listened avidly as he started to explain, then stopped him with one uplifted hand. "Sally Barrett, I imagine. I saw her go in. She used to be in my high school class." She didn't elaborate because Sally had emerged from the post office.

"Hey, Sally! How are you?" Christa beckoned the girl closer to her side of the van.

"Hi, Christa." Her voice was cool. "I . . . um, I'm sorry about your accident. I tried to see you but—"

"I know. Thank you." Christa's smile looked shaky. "I'm getting better every day."

Sally had been listening, up until the point she saw John. She glanced from Christa back to him.

"This is my friend, John Riddle. John, this is Sally."

"We met," he said, wondering if she'd race away screaming.

"He was asking me questions."

"I know. John can't remember some things. He's trying to find clues that will help him figure out who he is."

"Really?" Sally's eyes brightened with interest. "We talked about that in psychology, but I never knew anybody who couldn't remember. I've finished my first year of college, you know. Now I'm into second year." She said it triumphantly, as if to prove something.

"I'm glad." Christa's sincerity shone through the words. "Did you see him before today, Sally?"

Meeting Christa's direct stare, Sally finally nodded.

"Can you take a couple of minutes and tell us about it?"

Sally shrugged. "I guess. The day I saw him, I was helping out at the post office, like I used to do in high school. It was my summer job this year. I was filling in at the counter when he came in." She leaned into the van, looking at John's face. "He was hurt."

"Hurt? What do you mean?"

Though John itched to hurry the answers out of her, for now he let Christa do the talking. He'd already frightened Sally once. Better to allow Christa to find out what he wanted to know than risk alienating the only source he'd come across. Though Christa and Sally didn't exactly sound like friends. Their conversation had a wary edge to it that piqued his interest.

"His face was bruised, like somebody hit him or he ran into something. And he was bleeding. He acted like he was in a big hurry, looking out the window every three seconds as if he was checking for something."

Christa glanced at John and winked. She was enjoying this?

"So he was in a hurry. But why did he come in? Was he trying to mail something?"

"Uh-huh. A package. It was small and real light. One of those bubble envelopes. I said he should send it airmail, that it would get there faster." Sally laughed. "He had a wad of cash in his hand, and he could have paid for it easily."

"But he didn't," Christa guessed.

Sally looked perplexed. "No. He said it had to go regular mail. I asked why and he got kind of mad. Said he needed the extra time. Sounds funny, don't you think? Most people want the stuff they send to get there earlier, not later." She risked another peek at John.

Now Christa was staring at him too. He shifted uncomfortably. "You're sure that's what he said? That he needed the extra time?"

"I'm sure. I kind of teased him about it. Next thing I knew he told me to forget it and went rushing out the door. He dropped some money too. I picked it up," she said half defiantly.

"Oh?" Christa prompted.

"I would have returned it, but he never came back." Sally's cheeks reddened as she dug in her pocket. "I haven't got enough on me, but if you want to stop by my house, I can get it for you. It's in my desk."

"How much money did he drop?" Christa asked, her curiosity evident.

"Two hundred and fifty-five dollars." Sally looked worried now, her attention on John. "I wasn't trying to steal it, truly. I tried to follow you, but by the time I got outside, you were gone."

"The money doesn't matter," he told Sally quietly. "You can keep it."

She narrowed her eyes. "You're sure about the money?"

"I'm positive. You probably need it if you're going to college. I'm sorry if I frightened you. But I would like to ask you a couple more questions." He thought for a moment. "What was I wearing?"

"A suit," she answered promptly. "Black, really nice, but it had a couple of tears in it. And a white shirt, silky, I think. Like those marionettes we made for drama class that year." She paused, began again. "Anyway, it looked expensive. There was a blob of mud on the front and, I think, some blood. You were kind of a mess."

"Anything else?" Christa prodded.

"A red tie. And polished shoes. I remember I thought it was funny because you had dust on your clothes, but your shoes were very shiny."

"And I didn't mail the package." John puzzled over that. "So what did I do with it?"

"You took it. I remember you were holding it in one hand and a briefcase in the other when you left."

"A briefcase?" John felt his pulse inch upward. Rick had said nothing about finding a briefcase. "What did it look like?"

"Fish scales."

"Pardon me?"

"It was black and it had this pattern, like fish scales," Sally explained. "Maybe it wasn't a briefcase. I don't know much about them. I thought it seemed a little small for that, but I guess they come in all sizes. That's the best description I can give of it. Except . . ." She paused.

"What else do you remember, Sally?" Christa encouraged.

"I remember thinking it must have been heavy 'cause you were sort of leaning a bit, but maybe you were hurt or something." She shrugged. "I don't know what was inside. I didn't see anything. In fact, you never even put it down. You hung on to it tightly the whole time."

"Did I drive away?"

"I don't know. I didn't see you arrive either. I figured that's why you were so messed up, because you had a car accident. Anyway, by

the time I got outside, it was like I said. You were already gone."
Sally's dark eyes lit up. "You were in town that day, Christa. You and
Kent. I remember I saw this van parked over there."

"Physiotherapy," Christa whispered in answer to John's puzzled
look.

"Do you remember what day this was?" John asked Sally.

"Not really. My university classes were out because I came back
here to start work in late April after exams, but that's about all I
remember. Oh yeah, they'd put down the new floor in the post office
already, because your black shiny shoes really showed up against that
white tile. That would make it late May at the earliest, but I don't
know a specific date for certain." Sally made a face. "I guess I'm not
really much help. Sorry."

"Don't be sorry," John said. "You've been very helpful." *Another
dead end.*

"Sally, if we tell what you've told us to the Mounties and they
want to talk to you, would you be willing to explain it all again to
them?"

"The Mounties? Why? I thought you said I could have the
money." Sally's face tightened, and her eyes flashed angrily. "It's just
like high school again. You're trying to trick me."

By the look on her face, Christa's tricks had been no happy experiences. John glanced from one to the other and wondered again
about the history between them.

"No, I'm not trying to trick you. And please forgive me. That's
one reason I invited you and the others out to the camp a couple of
weeks ago. I wanted to apologize for my behavior back then. I didn't
understand how much I was hurting people, but I understand now and
I'm truly sorry."

"Yeah, sure."

"I mean it. I apologize to you. You have every right to be suspicious of me now, but I'm not playing a trick. Really. You can keep the
money. That's not the issue."

"What is?"

Christa waved a hand toward John. "He's had a really tough summer trying to figure things out. The police need every piece of the puzzle they can get to help him. It's important, and we'd appreciate it very much if you would talk to them."

"Okay, I guess I could talk to them. But it will have to be right away. I'm only home for the weekend to pick up some more of my stuff." She paused to glare at Christa. "I'm studying education, you know."

"That's so great! You always wanted to be a teacher. I'm sure you'll do very well." Christa's sincerity radiated from her smile.

John wondered why Sally didn't seem to believe Christa.

"Thanks. And thanks for the apology. It helps." Sally chewed her bottom lip for a moment, then frowned. "What about you? Are you going to stay at Camp Hope?"

"I'm not sure. I've been checking into some opportunities that look interesting." John heard Christa's voice drop and soften. "I was hoping to tell you guys about it when I asked you out, but I guess everyone was too busy." Though she tried to hide it, he heard sadness behind her words.

"Well, it was a hectic time right then with school gearing up." Sally's face turned a bright shade of hot pink as she rushed into speech. "Still is, actually. But maybe we could plan something for after exams. Maybe before Christmas. The others will probably be coming home then. We could all get together one afternoon and catch up."

"Sounds like fun." Christa's voice sounded tentative.

"I'll call you. Okay?"

"Sure."

He couldn't understand why Christa didn't sound more excited about the prospect; then he remembered that she'd been disappointed once. Maybe she didn't think they'd show up the second time either.

"This time I'll organize it myself. Wait till you see Jenny Wagner. You're not going to believe what she's done to her hair." With a wide grin, Sally tilted on her tiptoes, peering into the van to check out John's face. "It's nice to see you looking better."

"Thanks. And thank you for your help."

"It wasn't much." Sally made a comic face. "I better get home. I'm supposed to get my stuff packed so Mom can paint my room. My grandmother is coming for a visit." She waved. "See you, Christa."

"Thanks, Sally. Thanks a lot." After Sally disappeared around the corner, Christa said, "It just goes to show you." Sometimes Christa's thought processes were a complete mystery to everyone but her. John waited for her explanation.

"Remind me of the words on the big sign that leads to Camp Hope." Christa fidgeted as she always did when she was excited.

John scrutinized her expression but found no clue to unravel his confusion. *The words—what was written on that sign? Ah yes.* "'Camp Hope—Where nothing is impossible with God.'" The last part dragged out of him as he absorbed her meaning. "You think God sent Sally along to talk to me?"

"And to me." She arched her eyebrows. "Well, who else?"

On the drive back to the camp John mulled it over. Was it possible? Was God that concerned about him?

As he lifted Christa from the van, his eyes met hers. Her fingertips brushed his cheek, her voice gently chiding. "He's in charge, John. God knows things we can only dream of."

Maybe. But if He knew, why didn't He enlighten them? Christa might have an answer to that, but John didn't ask. He wanted time to think about what Sally's words meant.

Christa had other plans. Back in her chair, she beckoned him to follow as she led the way to her home with Maggie bouncing along beside her. "When Rick comes to talk to us about the rat, we'll tell him what we learned. This is the best lead we've ever had."

"It is?" Had he missed something?

"Yeah. The best."

John followed slowly, digesting what he'd learned. A package he didn't mail, a briefcase no one had found, torn clothes he hadn't woken up in. For the life of him, he couldn't see a lead in that mess.

A piece of rope lay on the ground, one end frayed and the other twisted in a knot. He picked it up, turned it over.

Two men, tied together, lying on the ground, hands bound behind them. Someone stood over them with an automatic weapon pointed at their heads. The panoramic flash startled him with its intensity.

John heard Christa go inside the house, but he stayed where he was and sank down on the bottom step. As he searched his memory for more information, he begged, *Only a little bit more. A little more.*

But all he could see were the men—beaten, tied.

Waiting for death.

CHAPTER TEN

Garden-variety rat. Killed with ordinary rat poison. No fingerprints on the box, paper, or anything else. Label is self-sticking so no DNA. Could have been from anyone in the district. No clues there." Rick spread out his file of papers. "There is one thing you might be interested in, though. There are some reports that rats have been left on the doorsteps of people who have tried to leave the Society for Order."

"So it is them." Christa could hardly wait to tell John.

"I'm not saying that."

"But it could be?" She grinned at his nod. "What else?"

"I brought a copy of the police report with me, but you won't find much in it. The night John was found he carried nothing that Sally described. No bubble envelope, no briefcase."

After two frustrating days of waiting, Christa's hope deflated. "So no help here?"

"No suit, no shirt, no tie, no shiny shoes either."

Christa harrumphed.

"This is the nature of police work," Rick scoffed. "Questions lead to questions. Get used to it."

"But there's nothing here. Nothing!" She pushed the papers away, put her elbows on the table, and dropped her head into her hands with a moan of pure frustration. "I was hoping for something! We don't know one more thing than when we started."

"There might be more here than you think," Angie Grant said. Though not officially on duty, Angie had accompanied Rick to the camp. Christa still wasn't sure why she'd come—maybe just to be with Rick.

She glanced at Angie, puzzled by her comment. "What do you mean?"

Angie looked at Rick. When he nodded his consent, she continued. "I checked out Kane Connors yesterday. All I found was stuff about his humanitarianism, good deeds, etc. I asked Chicago PD about him because that's where his company is located, but they also clammed up. A source of mine suggested that the man is under federal protection. The moment I started asking questions about him, the FBI was on the phone."

Christa swallowed the lump that rose in her throat. She hadn't thought of that. Kane Connors was in so much danger from the society that he had to be kept hidden—maybe John was in danger too.

"I explained what I was looking into in reference to the kidnappings of those two men. The FBI told me there was no possibility that Mr. Connors was connected with my investigation, because he was working with them. Then I was told that Mr. Connors couldn't be reached. By anyone."

She'd barely finished speaking when there was a light rap on the door. It opened and John stepped inside. He seemed disoriented.

"Oh, sorry for interrupting. I'll come back." He turned to leave.

"Hey, don't go. Something wrong?" Rick inquired mildly, though anyone could see he was cataloging every nuance of John's troubled face.

"No, nothing." John shifted restlessly from one foot to the other. "That is, yes, there is something, but . . ."

"Come and sit down, John. Tell us what happened." Christa indicated the chair on her other side. "Go ahead."

"I was working in the office, you know, trying to fix the computer for Ralna when the phone rang. The answering machine never picked up and you didn't either, Christa. It rang for ages before whoever was calling hung up. A few minutes later someone tried again. The third time, I answered. It was the camp's head office."

Calm, unflappable John, who took everything in stride, seemed unnerved. The longer he spoke, the more concerned Christa became.

"Head office? But it's eight thirty and they're two hours ahead of us. Everyone should have left for the day."

"Apparently not." He sighed. "You do know Ralna sent some reports to them via an e-mail attachment."

"I know she was trying to send them," Christa answered, then explained for Rick and Angie. "Kent completed them before the wedding, but the head office was closed because of a flood and then for a couple more days while they moved to a new temporary location. Kent asked Ralna to e-mail them. They were supposed to go out yesterday, but the computer was acting up so she tried to send them today."

"They're gobbledygook."

"Pardon?" Christa shifted in her chair, focused on John. "Kent made a mistake on something?"

"No. The attachment went through, but when the head office opened it, all they could find was a bunch of unreadable scribbles with several vile words across the bottom. Their office person was so upset that she called in Harry Perkins, the head honcho guy who did the inspection of the camp last summer. He was the one on the phone a minute ago, and he wasn't happy." John stared at his feet.

"Vile words?" Christa repeated. "Something must have happened. Did you tell them we'd resend?"

"I tried."

"And?" Worry boiled inside her. "John?"

When he lifted his head, his face looked haggard. He licked his lips several times as if trying to summon up courage.

"You're scaring me. Tell me what's wrong."

"Mr. Perkins is furious. Something in our reports corrupted their system. They have data recovery experts trying to sort things out. But one thing appears sure: the problem came from our transmission."

"You mean you sent them a virus?" Angie leaned forward, her short auburn hair tumbling around her face.

"No, it would have been a worm." At Christa's and Angie's surprised expressions, Rick added, "John's been giving me the odd lesson."

"Worse than that." John rested his hands on the table as he explained computerese to them. "More like a Trojan horse, from what I gathered after talking to their techs. I did a scan of our system and found the Trojan horse buried in our accounting program. It gets into program files and alters them, then sends important information from them to all kinds of people on the address list. Sort of."

"We get the idea," Christa reassured him.

"Well, we've been receiving confidential data from head office by the truckload. Most of it should have never left their office. Our in-box is full. As soon as I empty it, it fills up again. We're fortunate that Ralna doesn't keep much on the hard drive, but I have no idea who else has received Camp Hope information."

"Information that comes back? So whatever they've got in their system from you is sending stuff back to you." Rick frowned. "How can someone do that?"

"It takes a certain talent. And it's not coming just to us. Or at least it wasn't; that's why Harry Perkins was so mad. The head office is shut down now." John stared helplessly at them. "The scope of this thing is massive."

"How massive?" Rick demanded.

John began to explain. After several moments Christa took a survey of the others and knew neither Rick nor Angie understood any more than she did.

She touched John's arm. "You're miles beyond us," she told him, inordinately proud of his wealth of knowledge. "Pretend we're little kids. Because when it comes to this stuff, we are."

"Sorry. Sometimes I forget—"

Rick slapped John on the shoulder. "We understand, man. You forget stuff. Tell us what you think happened."

"We've been hacked."

The simplicity of the explanation shocked them all into silence.

"But . . . how?" Christa asked. "You did something to the computer the other day, didn't you? Something that would stop these society people from tracking us?"

"I tried to block them, but this is far more sophisticated than I'd given them credit for. At least I think it's them. Who else would be behind an attack like this?"

"You're the computer expert. You tell us," Rick said.

"It sounds like the society, given the verbiage in that e-mail message." John sighed. "But it's more sophisticated than some rednecks talking big. Whoever rigged this knows how to hit where it hurts. He's made it look like we're to blame for several very ugly Internet crimes. If it wasn't head office that had been targeted first, we could be charged. As it is, Harry thinks they'll be able to contain the damage before it goes any further. But they're completely shut down right now. Because of me." His voice dropped. "I'm sorry. I should have left well enough alone."

"It's not your fault," Christa assured him staunchly. "It's this horrible group. They're like a bug on your back that you can't swat and you can't brush away. A bloodsucker," she cried, finally lighting on a word that seemed most appropriate. "They want to draw all the vital, life-giving force out of everything. Now they're trying to attack Camp Hope."

"How do you know it's the Society for Order? Couldn't it be a virus you contracted from someone or somewhere else?" Angie asked. "Trojan horse," she amended when John opened his mouth to correct her.

John remained silent for a moment, apparently contemplating her words. "Perhaps I have jumped the gun. It may be that the Society for Order is not associated with this at all—" he shrugged—"except that

I know of no one else to blame. Everything seemed to happen after I punched in those numbers and their Web site came up."

"I'm not sure the society has ever been implicated in Internet crimes." Rick's brown eyes glowed almost black in his tanned face. "Unless you can trace this horse or whatever it is directly back to them and track the perpetrator, it will be difficult to find out who sent it."

"I can try to follow it," John offered.

"Just tell me what you need." Rick shoved his little notebook and a pen across the table.

John began writing. "A clean computer would be best to do this on. One that has nothing on it for them to find."

"You can wipe my laptop and use it. There's nothing on it that I need, except my e-mail addresses." Christa caught Angie's curious look and smiled. "Kent asked John to set up a chat room on our Web site; we call it Dear Hope. Kids who came to summer camp can keep in touch, ask questions, or encourage each other after they've returned to their normal world. 'Hope' is the moderator, and she answers whatever they ask or points them in the right direction."

"Great idea."

"Sometimes I feel like I'm in way over my head, but the kids are fun and it seems to work well because so far I'm anonymous."

"Anonymous. He's the one behind all of it."

They all turned to stare at John. He was very pale, his gaze focused on some distant point.

Christa touched John's hand. "What do you mean?"

"I don't know." He faced her, his trancelike state finally broken. "It was just there in my mind. Anonymous. He's behind it."

His confusion touched something deep inside her. Christa rushed to cover the silence. "Is anonymous a person?"

"Yes. I think so. He's the one in charge." He lifted his head, gulped, and sought out Christa. "He's the ringleader. He's planning . . . I don't know!"

"Anonymous. Okay, I'll do some hunting. And I'll get a modem out here that's through our office. If they want to trace it, fine. We'll be waiting." Rick frowned. "Maybe wireless would be better."

"That won't stop someone from pirating your network or using your e-mail." John explained how anyone could use someone else's signal. "I don't know why I know that," he added.

Christa lifted the coffeepot and poured several cups of coffee, which Angie handed around. "Ralna made it before you arrived. It should still be okay; don't you think?"

"Sure." Angie pulled the cream out of the fridge, then stood staring into it, her eyes on the burgeoning shelves. "What is all this?"

"Stuff the Murdock sisters brought over today. They were worried I'd run out of food before Georgia got back. As if!" She grimaced. "It's mostly sweet stuff. I didn't know what to do with it, so I stuck it in there. Interested?"

"Yes. I'm starving." Angie pulled out a lemon jelly roll, a platter of iced cupcakes, and a blueberry pie. "Rick, there's pie. Do you want some?"

He gave her a look.

Angie winked at Christa. "Now that was a no-brainer." She cut a huge piece of pie and slid it onto a plate, adding a slice of jelly roll, a cupcake, and a fork. Then she leaned over to set it in front of Rick, one hand on his shoulder.

Covering her fingers with his, Rick whispered his thanks.

Though Angie smiled as she set a cup of coffee in front of Rick, she was quick to move away, as if the contact had singed her. The gold in her hazel eyes glinted brighter, swirling into the green and masking some unspoken emotion.

When John was suitably served, Christa motioned to Angie. "Let's take ours and sit outside. It was so warm today that the evening still hasn't cooled off."

"Sounds good. You go ahead. I'll carry our things." Angie grabbed a tray and began loading it. "It won't be long before it's too cold outside to do this."

Angie eased through the door, set the tray down on the small patio table to one side of the fire pit, and grinned, hitching a thumb over one shoulder at the smoldering coals. "I see John already built his usual campfire."

Angie propped her feet up on a stool and sipped her coffee. "Even though it's gorgeous out here in the boonies, I don't know how you can hack it every day. Don't you get sick of the solitude and the quiet now that there are no camps?"

"I used to." Christa sipped the lemonade she'd poured earlier. "Before the accident."

"And now you don't? You're staying put; is that it?"

"To tell you the truth, I don't know what the future holds. I'm making plans to leave, but God hasn't shown me exactly where He wants me to be yet, so I guess I wait."

"Well, good for you. But I'm not going to wait." Angie's voice hardened. "I don't intend to hang around in this back of beyond for any longer than it takes to get a transfer out."

"A transfer to where?" Christa kept her voice mild, interested. Anger or maybe frustration simmered beneath the surface of Angie's picture-perfect face. Something was obviously eating at her, but Christa had a hunch it had nothing to do with the flora and fauna surrounding Camp Hope.

"Anywhere there's something happening. The work here bores me. Kids write on store windows with soap. A senior citizen misses a stop sign. Mr. Brown took a candy bar that he didn't pay for."

She threw her hand out in exasperation. "Georgia's stalker and John's case are the most exciting things that have happened around here in ages, and I missed most of the stuff with Georgia because I was away."

"Be glad." Christa shuddered at the memory. "Anyway, now you've got a new problem to work on."

"You mean what's happened to you," Angie confirmed. "I still have questions about that night you got stuck in the shed. I had a feeling then—and it hasn't gone away—that you knew more than you were telling about the graffiti."

Christa bit her lip, then met Angie's curious gaze. "You have the inquisition glare down perfectly, you know."

Angie kept staring.

"Fine. I'll tell. I have a hunch. It's nothing certain and I can't possibly accuse him with any degree of truth, but—" she huffed out a sigh—"Abby's son, Braydon, was out here that night. I spoke to him. He was with some other kids, and he left right after I talked to him. But it was absolutely not him in the shed."

"I see. And you're sure he's not the one who left the rat?"

"That's about the only thing I am sure of. The voice was different, and I don't think Braydon is that good of an actor." She forced herself to speak the truth. "I have a lot of horrible things from the past on my conscience. Braydon and his friends were here, but I didn't see them do that graffiti. I don't want to make another mistake by accusing someone of something I didn't see. I won't accuse him, Angie. I've hurt that family enough. I don't want you saying anything about it either. Do you understand?"

"All right. But you tell me if you see anything else. No more secrets."

"Agreed."

Silence reigned for several moments.

"I know it's not very exciting here. Is excitement what you're after?" The question popped out before Christa saw Rick standing in the doorway. She cringed, knowing he would hear every word.

"Life is what I'm after. I want to do something important, something that matters."

"I'm sure your work matters very much to the community and to keeping the peace."

"Keeping the peace. Huh! That's all there ever is here. Give me a bank robbery, a car chase. Something!" She was immediately apologetic. "I know it's wrong to wish for that. Someone could get hurt. But can you understand? I need to get away from here."

Rick turned, walked back to the table, and sunk into a chair, defeat dragging at his usually upright form. Christa sensed in him a sadness she'd seen in Angie. She whispered a prayer for these two unhappy people.

"A new perspective is good," Christa agreed quietly. "But sometimes what we really want is right in front of us, even though we don't always know it. I hope you find what you're looking for, Angie."

"Yeah. Me too. And I hope it's soon." She poked her fork into the jelly roll, pushing away the cake part to eat the filling. "Enough about me. At least tonight there's nothing happening."

"No." Christa glanced around the darkened grounds. "It's been quiet around here lately."

"Good. That's what we want, lots of peace and quiet."

There was nothing to add, so Christa looked up, admiring the diamond-studded black velvet sky, thankful that—for now—she belonged right here.

A sudden crash broke her serenity.

Angie surged to her feet. "Did you hear that? Sounded like a tree fell." She covered her nervousness with a grin. "Guess the peace is getting to me. I'm a little jumpy. But why would a tree fall now?"

"I don't know." Christa grinned at her. "Maybe you're about to get your wish."

"Investigating dead trees doesn't begin to cover Angie's wish list." Rick walked forward, his eyes speculative as he scanned the woods around them. "No wind. Seems funny a tree chose this precise time to fall, especially when Fred told me he's finished cutting out the dead ones. Think I'll take a look." He hiked down the steps, paused, and looked back. "Don't you want to come?" he asked Angie.

"Check the woods for falling trees? Oh, sure. Why not? It'll be a highlight of my law-enforcement career." She carried her dishes inside, then hurried down the steps to catch up with Rick. "If I'd known we'd be risking life and limb to probe the perils of Camp Hope, I would have brought my gu—"

It happened so fast, Christa had no time to react. One moment the two Mounties were walking toward the road. The next a motor gunned and a car burst out of a grove of trees, racing toward them. She saw Rick grab Angie's arm and yank her with him in a flying leap to the side of the road. The car sped past, spraying them with gravel as it disappeared into the night.

"John, come here. Quick!" Christa gripped the knob of her wheelchair, paused, unsure of her next move. "Are either of you hurt? Angie? Rick?" she called as John thundered down the steps.

"We're fine. See ya." Angie, hot on Rick's heels as they raced toward his SUV, tossed a grin over one shoulder and called, "Thanks for coffee and dessert."

Inside the SUV, Rick revved the motor while Angie fastened her seat belt. Soon they'd spun out of the driveway and were barreling down the gravel road chasing the car that had so nearly hit them.

Christa noticed John standing at the bottom of the stairs, staring into the shadows. "What on earth was that about?" She blinked as the dust from the gravel settled and took a second look at John. The troubled glower marring his features confused her. "John?"

"Something's wrong. Can you feel it?" He rubbed his left temple with one finger. "I sense this dreadful heaviness, as if something sinister is at work." He swallowed. "Am I crazy? Do you feel it?"

"Yes, John. I feel it."

Until a few moments ago, she hadn't. But now Christa risked a peek into the gloom and shivered. No matter how she scoffed at herself, she could not dislodge what her nerves transmitted to her pulse rate. A foolish misreading of tension perhaps. More absurd still to admit to it, but it was there. Oppressive. Lowering. Evil. It hung in the atmosphere like a tangible presence, waiting for the perfect moment to accost them.

She prayed for protection, then zipped her sweater up to her chin. "What are you looking at?" she whispered, the hair on her neck rising.

"A dream. Actually a nightmare."

John was silent for so long she was afraid he'd fallen into some kind of trance. But then he turned, and she gasped at his haggard face.

"Please tell me what's wrong."

"Call Rick. Get him here right away." He blurted out the command, hands clenching into fists.

Sensing John needed someone to help chase away the bad memories, she touched his sleeve and tried to slip her hand into his to comfort him. It wasn't the right response.

John dropped to his knees in front of her, wrapped his arms around her, and held her tightly. As he pressed his chin against her head, his heartbeat thudded with the fierceness of a hammer. "Oh, God, why me?" His despair sounded soul deep.

"Please tell me what's going on." She didn't have the right words to comfort him.

"No. No!"

His arms tightened around her until she felt crushed by his grip. She worked her arms free, cupped his face, and stared into his eyes. "What's wrong? You can tell me."

"Can I?" His eyes glittered like black ice, his face loomed so close she could feel his breath feathering over her lips. "You're going to hate me."

"Of course I won't." Her fingers grazed the bristle on his jaw to the corner of his mouth as she tried to fathom his thoughts. "I could never hate you."

The magnetic draw of his gaze made her yearn to lean a little closer, to let her heart carry her where her mind said no. It would be so easy . . . She jerked away, frightened by the intensity of her own response, feeling the guilt well up inside. This could not happen between them! Especially not now. She drew in a ragged breath of composure. "Tell me."

He closed his eyes, and a huge sigh dragged his shoulders down. Finally he looked at her. "I'm sorry," he said quietly, regret washing over his face. "I'm so sorry."

"For what?" Christa glimpsed shadows of sorrow on his face, but she held her focus on him and waited.

"I'm not who you thought I was."

The words slammed into her, igniting a nebulous flicker of worry. "Then who are you? I'm your friend, John. I'll help however I can."

The words seemed to trip some switch inside him.

"You can't be my friend! Don't you understand?" He grabbed her hands to pull them away. His eyes blazed as they stared into hers. "Stay away from me. Don't try to be my friend or help me. You don't know who you're dealing with."

"I know exactly who you are, John Riddle. You're a man who cares about people, who tries hard to do the right thing, who goes out of his way to keep from hurting someone."

With every word his navy eyes darkened until they were almost black.

Squelching down her misgivings, Christa strove to infuse her voice with confidence, though John's glowering look inches from her face did not abate. "You are my friend."

"Really? Then shame on you for choosing your friends so unwisely." John's fingers tightened on her arms, his face loomed closer, the mocking light in his eyes too evident to ignore. "I've remembered something. Do you want to hear what it is?"

His eyes were wild, tortured. She knew he was deliberately scaring her because he himself was afraid. She swallowed. "Of course I want to hear. What have you remembered?"

"What would you think of John Riddle, this so-called friend of yours whom you think is so wonderful, if I told you I'm a member of the society?" He laughed—a hard, scraping noise that wound her jittery nerves an inch tighter.

"You're not. I know that for certain." Christa shook her head, then put both hands over his.

He recoiled from her touch and backed up until she couldn't reach him. "Do you know for certain?" His voice dropped, grating on her nerves. "Well, you're wrong. I am one of them."

She'd never seen him so out of control. That he was furious was evident, but behind that she sensed a profound pain that wrenched and tore at his spirit. It was like watching a noble statue crack under invisible strain.

"I'll prove it to you." He crossed his arms over his chest, his voice harsh, a ferocious storm barely contained. "Remember those two men the society supposedly kidnapped?"

She nodded.

"I know where they're being held."

CHAPTER ELEVEN

John's words shattered Christa's world so that there was no way she could conceal her shock.

"How?" she gasped. "How could you possibly know that?"

"Because I'm one of them, of course. I know exactly where to find Nicolas Petrov and Evan Julian." His entire body sagged. He rubbed his temple as if to ease the pain. "I'm the one who's caused all the problems here. I *am* the problem."

"I don't believe you."

"It doesn't matter what you believe." He tried to laugh, but it emerged as a painful wheeze. "I know."

"And Kane Connors. Do you know about his kidnapping?"

"Connors. He's . . ." John shook his head. "No, I don't know about him. But I do know where the others are." The sardonic tilt of his lips held no mirth.

"I don't understand," she admitted, surprised her voice emerged at all.

"Neither do I. Your God must be enjoying this. To think that I actually prayed and asked Him to help me remember. Is this your idea of an answer to prayer?" His hoarse voice testified to the depths of his pain.

"God isn't laughing, John. He's still here with us."

"Yeah. Sure. 'Trust,' you said. 'Hope. Have faith.' Wasn't that it? 'Just believe.'" His whole body slumped. "I can't."

"But—"

"Call Rick now. Before it's too late for those two poor souls." With that one whispered appeal, John sank down on the bottom step, a lonely man tortured by secrets he could neither understand nor explain.

Christa tipped up her chin and let the tears roll from the corners of her eyes as she focused on the heavens. *My trust is in You, Lord. Please help us now.*

————⟫◆⟪————

Nobody ignored Anonymous and lived to talk about it.

He picked up the phone, held it to his ear, and gritted his teeth, waiting until the diatribe ended.

"It's not that simple. He never leaves, never goes beyond the camp boundaries." Except once, in that funny little town, and he'd missed his opportunity. Better not mention that.

"Excuses!"

"Extenuating circumstances." He wouldn't mention the computer problems he'd arranged either. It should have made the man persona non grata. But like his other plans, it hadn't worked.

"Do you realize what's at stake? If that information falls into the wrong hands, there will be severe repercussions for you."

The disconnect signal hummed in his ear. After he put the phone away, he trained his binoculars on the office. The backpack was there. He'd seen it and even rifled through it when he tampered with the computer. The key was gone though. He wanted—needed—to get it back. Maybe then he'd find his answers.

The man slumped on the bottom step, staring at the ground, waiting. *She* sat framed by the window. Watching him?

Suddenly the answer was clear. The girl! From the beginning she'd been the answer. John followed her around like a puppy, was clearly attracted to her.

It had been a mistake to leave the card and the rat at the house, to assume the girl was in on everything. Maybe John had kept his secret. If she didn't know, she couldn't tell. John Riddle might not care about himself, but if his girl was threatened, wouldn't he give up information to spare her?

Assembling his thoughts into a mental map, he made his plans.

He'd felt sorry for her, hoped to spare her, but this was an all-or-nothing game. He had to use whatever means he could find. Besides, Anonymous would be very grateful.

⟫⟩◆⟨⟪

"Two men were freed today after months of captivity at the hands of an extremist group headquartered in the backwoods of Colorado." The news anchor's voice cut across the silence of the living room.

"A spokesman for the FBI will not discuss the source of information that led to the arrest of seventeen members of a group called the Society for Order, implicated in the theft of overseas aid shipments. We do know that the leader of this group has not been identified or arrested."

John couldn't tear his eyes away from the screen as the two men whose faces still haunted him were freed of their shackles and helped to a waiting ambulance. Deaf to the rest of the reporter's words, he searched his brain for something that would provide the answers he sought.

But there was nothing save the usual blank wall.

"I don't recognize anything about the place. Sorry." John couldn't look at Rick, couldn't watch hope fade away again.

"Didn't think you would. I faxed pictures of you to the Colorado state police. Neither Mr. Julian nor Mr. Petrov identified you as a member of the society. In fact, both men claim they have never even met you. Preliminary investigations of the society's camp have uncovered no traces of you on their membership lists, and no one in their group named you as one of their comrades."

Obviously Rick wanted answers as badly as he did, but John had none to offer. "I don't know what more I can tell you. I must be part of that disgusting society. Otherwise how would I have known where to find the kidnapped men?" He raked a hand through his hair, trying to slow the whirring of his thoughts into some kind of decipherable order.

In spite of his determination not to, John couldn't help but glance at Christa. She'd surprised him with her handling of his latest revelation, even shocked him by her repeated and calm assurances that he did not belong to the Society for Order.

A new maturity filled her eyes, a peaceful certainty that had not wobbled once in the forty-eight hours since he'd told Rick of his knowledge. He knew she drew her serenity from those quiet times spent sitting in the sunlight, reading her Bible, praying to the God she claimed knew what He was doing.

John envied her tranquility, but she was too young to know it couldn't last. She was also too trusting. Sooner or later the truth would come out, and she'd have to admit she'd been wrong to believe in him. His gut clenched at the thought of what his betrayal would do to the fragile bonds they'd begun to build.

"You both have too narrow a view of this. There is one other possibility," Christa stated. "Don't you see, Rick? John might have been in law enforcement. Maybe he knows all this stuff because he was part of some inner circle." She looked delighted by this new postulation.

"You are talking about me?" John blinked when she nodded.

"Then why hasn't anyone claimed him?" Rick seemed to be taking Christa's idea seriously. "We've sent his picture across the country. No one knows him."

"Look, I don't know a lot of things. But this I know—" John was emphatic—"I'm no cop. I know nothing about guns, I don't understand your police speak when that radio blasts, and I'm almost certain I've never worn a uniform." As John looked at Christa and Rick, he realized neither was listening to him.

"What made you think that, Christa?" Rick demanded.

"It's the only thing that makes sense."

"Is anyone listening to me? I am not a cop. I'm probably some kind of terrorist. You should get me away from here before I do something to ruin Camp Hope."

"Uh-huh—" Rick scratched his chin—"or we should leave you here where no one has bothered to come after you. Yet."

"You're forgetting that car from the other night, aren't you? What was that about? Probably one of my goon buddies trying to renew acquaintances." John rose and paced across the room.

"Angie found it abandoned in town. One of the local kids admitted he stole it to go for a joyride. The reason he almost hit us is because he pressed the gas too hard and couldn't control the car. He'd been hiding in the trees waiting for us to leave, and when we came looking, he decided to make a run for it."

"The graffiti?"

"I'm pretty sure that was pranksters. It's not the Society for Order's style. Besides, why would they come all the way up here to write on some cabins?" Rick's raised eyebrows emphasized his skepticism. "If someone is after you—and I'm not discounting that—they'll make their move soon. And we'll have them."

"I think you're right. John knows his way around the camp and senses when something's out of place. It would be easier for him to spot a problem here." Christa rolled her wheelchair in front of John, forcing him to stop pacing. She chuckled at his glare. "You don't scare me, John Riddle. I know who you are inside and *goon* doesn't fit. Anyway, what kind of a terrorist tells the police where his victims are?"

John kept his objections to himself and thought about that for a minute.

"Remember the rat?" she persisted. "The society must have realized you knew about those men and they were warning you to be quiet."

"I hate to say it, but this time Christa's ideas make sense." Rick ducked the paper ball she tossed his way, then picked up his hat. "At the moment, John, I'd prefer it if you stayed here. At least until Kent and Georgia get back. There aren't too many certainties about this case. But one thing I know is that you'll keep Christa safe. That has to be my major concern right now."

"Hey! I don't need protecting. I don't need anyone. I can pray about this and rely on my faith in God—"

John hid his smile at Christa's bristle of disgust. She didn't mind standing up for him, but she didn't want the same for herself. One of these days he was going to remind her of the inequality of that stance. "You're always harping about God. Maybe He sent me here to watch out for *you*." John waited to see how she'd take that.

"I do not harp. And God knows I don't need watching out for." She led the way out of the house to Rick's patrol car, her nose lifted in disdain. "I can handle things myself."

The Mountie followed, speaking only when he'd reached his car. "That's not what Angie told me. What about Braydon?"

"Angie worries too much. Nothing else happened recently." Her body was rigid in the chair, her narrowed stare on the cop. "Besides, I have no foundation for an accusation. It could have been anyone having fun."

"That's your idea of fun?"

John glanced from one to the other. "What are you two talking about?"

Rick ignored him. "You're not facing the truth about him, Christa."

"But I am. I won't cause damage to a reputation again. Not without absolute proof. The old wounds have barely begun to heal."

"Sorry to interrupt," John said, "but I tracked that Trojan horse to an Internet service provider. Here." He handed Rick a piece of paper. "Maybe you can find out more." He scratched his head. "What you said before—why would they leave the rat at the main house? Someone already searched the RV. Don't you think they know that's where I live?"

"Maybe there's more than one person looking for you."

"I'm right here. What stops them from finding me?"

"That's the sixty-four-thousand-dollar question." Rick's attention returned to Christa. "Tell me next time. Don't leave it to Angie," he growled.

"I'm fine, Rick."

"Let's keep it that way." The Mountie didn't look convinced.

"Clearly this is a private conversation, so I'll go. I'm glad those men are still alive." John turned to leave.

Rick's hand stopped him. "You helped with more than that. It seems the Society for Order has suffered a huge dent in their organization. We got word this morning that the Feds seized a couple of their accounts that will eventually be turned over to the aid agencies they were stolen from."

"Good."

"A major amount will go back to Kane Connors's company, allowing it to continue its work."

"Kane Connors owns—"

"Some kind of charity. I didn't get all the specifics."

John looked at Christa as the hairs on the back of his neck rose. "You're saying Kane Connors gets the money?"

Rick nodded. "A lot of it."

"That can't be right. Not him," he muttered. A sickening feeling crept into his stomach, but he had nothing concrete to share, only that bad feeling. "Never mind."

Rick opened the cruiser door, then slapped the hood. "Man, am I an idiot."

"Now what?" John asked the cop who'd become a friend.

"I forgot all about this. The postal delivery van broke down on the way here. I said I'd deliver the mail. The carrier was pretty specific that this be given directly to you, Christa."

John couldn't decipher the strange rush of emotions washing over Christa's face, but he did take note of her quick grab for the small package in Rick's hands. "Do you want me to carry that?"

Christa flipped the box facedown in her lap but not before John saw the logo: *Simple Gifts*. His stomach lurched. *Not right. Not right.*

"I can manage. But you can take the rest of the mail to the office if you want." She kept her eyes down, her expression blank.

"Okay." *More secrets.* A twitch of pain squeezed John's heart. *Outsider.*

"Well, it's been a very busy day. I suggest you both get some rest. Kent and Georgia should be back next week. And then there's a camp, right?" Rick grinned at Christa's nod. "Never a dull moment around this place. I'm fairly sure nobody will come hunting for John now that the Society for Order has been accounted for. Things are shaping up pretty good."

Did the infinitesimal detail that John still didn't know his own name count for nothing? He tamped down his disgust and watched the cruiser drive away. A wind had risen, lifting leaves, twigs, and any other debris it could toss around. Dust burned his eyes. A campfire would be out of the question tonight.

"I wish Kent hadn't drained the pool. This is one evening when I'd like to work off some extra energy," Christa said.

"It's too cold to swim." John couldn't help staring at the box she was so poor at concealing. "Anyway, it's late. Come on. I'll race you home."

She gave him a funny look, then clicked her wheelchair forward.

Once she was over the threshold, he murmured good night and turned to leave.

"John, don't be discouraged. The pieces will start to come together; you'll see."

"Will they? How do you know? Did you ask your God?"

"Yes."

"Why didn't I hear His answer?"

Her gaze was steady, unrelenting. "You know why."

Because he couldn't believe. Anger threaded through his bloodstream but before he could give voice to it, Christa spoke again. "Something you said earlier makes a lot of sense. I think God did send you here. I think there's a reason for everything—why you wrote the camp's name on your arm before you lost your memory, why you stayed here instead of someplace else, and why God has used your skills to help the camp."

"Really?"

Christa nodded. "I don't know what that reason is, but I do know that God didn't bring us this far only to dump us. You can trust Him." She brushed her fingers over his arm. "You have to have hope."

He wanted so badly to believe her, to relax, to just let go. But there were too many questions and too few answers. "We still haven't solved the mystery of October 29."

"No, I guess we haven't." The box began a downward slide over her silky skirt. He caught it, fingers tightening as they brushed the return label. "Do you know how many times Simple Gifts has been investigated?"

"What do you know about them?"

"Never mind." No proof. Nothing tangible. He handed back the package.

"Thank you." Christa met his look with her own intense scrutiny.

"Good night." He walked back to his quarters, knowing with heartfelt certainty that all was not right in his world no matter how badly he wanted it to be.

Simple Gifts was not what it claimed to be. And Christa didn't even know it.

So how did John?

⟫━◆━⟪

He pasted himself against the chapel wall, only semiconfident the shadows would conceal him while he digested the latest information.

Someone had searched John's RV. That meant there was another player, someone else after the reward.

Beads of sweat formed along his upper lip as he considered the implications of that knowledge. Anonymous had undoubtedly sent someone else, someone higher up. That could only mean he'd lost confidence in him. He silently screamed a protest. It couldn't be!

A noise across the compound startled him. After moving quietly across the back of the building, he focused on a shadow slipping from building to building. His opposition? He'd seen this one before and rated him not worth his time. He heard the hissing laughter, the whispered remonstrances to be quiet, and the soft clink of bottles. No, he didn't have to worry about him. He was not a serious threat. His breath whooshed out in a sigh of relief.

But the other . . .

Carefully he worked his way through the trees, passing the horses who'd grown used to his stealthy trips. Using the cover of the roadside trees, he walked back toward the campsite, then slipped under the barrier and deep into the bush. The gazebo was empty, of course. It was long past the old ladies' bedtime. He wrapped himself in the quilt they'd left hanging on the line and lay down on the wooden floor. The slatted half walls provided little protection against the brisk wind, and he longed for his luxury tent. It had been a mistake leaving it—one he hadn't made again.

But maybe in his urgency to remove all traces of his presence he'd been too careful. Now someone else had come to take over for him. He decided to lie low for a few days, listen, and watch for the new player.

Maybe he'd figure a way out of this yet.

⇒◆⇐

"You really think it's a good idea?" Christa searched Kent's face for some sign that he was simply pandering to her, but all she found was genuine interest.

"I think it's the best idea I've heard in a long time. But I'm not sure how your mystery weekend will work. Today's the twenty-second. That's giving yourself a little more than a month to get everything done. Can you do it?"

"Of course she can if we all help." Georgia scanned the list Christa had given her. "This is a fantastic idea for a fund-raiser. You've put a lot of time into organizing the details." She glanced up at her new husband. "So it's okay with you if Christa does some advertising and sends out the invitations? You can clear it with the board? That should be the first step."

"You're sure you want to do this, Chris?" Kent's eyes asked a question she tried to answer without words. After a moment he said, "Okay. The board will be delighted with anything that renews our coffers, but to make sure I'll do a phone blitz. I say go for it. Just tell me what you need from me."

"To start with I need computer time. John's working on some scheme with Rick. They've got my laptop tied up, so it'll have to be the office one. Since John's already got a brochure designed, all we have to do is print it, mail it, and send e-mails to those we correspond with regularly. We'll take registrations online."

"Whew!" Kent swiped a hand across his forehead. "You didn't waste any time."

"Nope—" she grinned—"John's also going to make some more changes to our Web site to advertise. What's the maximum we can accommodate for a weekend like this?"

They discussed logistics for several minutes before Ralna's radio page summoned Kent to the office.

Christa was so excited about explaining her plan to Georgia that she barely noticed he'd left.

"It's great, sweetie, and I think it's going to be a terrific success." Georgia's face mirrored her doubts.

"But?"

"I'm concerned about the things that have been happening around here. John hasn't remembered anything more?"

"Not since those two men were freed. And there haven't been any more incidents. We're in a rut these days. The Society for Order is busy elsewhere."

"I hope so."

"We can't sit and wait for the worst to happen, Georgia. I've been telling John that we have to move on and trust that God will take care of things for us." She smiled at her sister-in-law's look of surprise. "I know. It doesn't sound like the old doom-and-gloom Christa, does it? That's your fault."

"Me? What did I do?"

"You started me thinking about goals. Life goals." Christa shrugged. "I realized I didn't have any and that I was waiting for my life to change. But I didn't know how or when or where I wanted it to go."

"And now you've figured out what you want?" Georgia asked.

Christa understood her doubtful tone. That so much in her life had changed in just a few weeks seemed implausible, even to herself! "Let's just say I don't have the long-term plan . . . yet, but I am working on some short-term goals. One of those is the mystery weekend. I want to see this camp forge ahead, and to do that it needs funds. Something like this could help rebuild our reputation."

"Is that why you're doing it? Because you feel responsible for past problems the camp has had?"

"I *am* responsible. My accident in the pool and paralysis sparked a lot of fear in parents who send their kids here. The camp and Kent still suffer because of that. But, no, that isn't the only reason." She wasn't sure exactly how to express herself. "This is something I need to do. Not only for the camp, but for me too. Call it my first baby step. If I can be in public, with all those people milling past and staring at me, and keep the weekend moving, then I'll have made my goal."

"And then you can begin looking further into the future." Georgia squeezed her hand. "I understand, honey, and I know you'll do it. I'll help however I can, and we'll both pray about it."

Christa heaved a sigh of relief. "Then you don't think I'm crazy?"

"Crazy like a fox! I think you're the bravest, smartest woman I know."

There was something she wasn't saying. Christa could see the cloud of worry darkening her sister-in-law's beautiful brown eyes until they glowed almost black.

"What's really bothering you? You can tell me."

"The date. It's very close to John's . . ." Georgia let the words die away.

"To October 29, the date he says something is going to happen. Is that what you mean?"

Georgia nodded.

"I know it is. Truth to tell, I thought preparing for this mystery weekend might help take his mind off that. But John wasn't my only reason for choosing that particular weekend and getting him involved."

"Oh, right—" Georgia winked—"that's your story and you're sticking to it. Okay by me."

Christa wished she could have controlled the heat burning her cheeks. Though she'd prayed many times, her feelings for John had not disappeared. She'd heard the admonitions a hundred times during her Sunday school and youth days about not marrying someone with different beliefs. She had no intention of allowing that to happen, but in the depths of her heart, something had taken root.

Perhaps God was testing her to see if she would stay true to her first love or allow something—or someone—to come between them. Christa knew she could not allow that. So she'd keep praying while trying to remain John's friend.

"You're not denying it."

"Hmm?" She blinked and found Georgia's gaze on her.

"You said John wasn't the only reason you'd chosen that weekend."

"It's not. By then the camps will be finished till after the New Year and we won't have to rush to clean up. I'm hoping the weather will still be good enough for us to plant some of the clues outside. I didn't dare go any later. We usually get snow in November. It won't be nearly as much fun if everyone's stuck inside."

"True." Georgia tapped her forefinger against the tabletop. "What are you hoping to see as a result of this? What's your tangible goal?"

"Fund-raising, of course," Christa answered. "Publicity for the camp. Maybe people will begin to see the facility as more than a kids' summer camp. John was talking the other day. He opened my eyes to the possibilities for this place. I'm hoping we can intersperse part of the quest for clues with ideas we have for the future, and that whoever comes will get on board and carry the vision back to their own churches."

"You are so clever." Georgia looked up as her husband stepped through the doorway. "This woman is a genius. She's thought of everything."

"Not quite, though I agree she's awesome." Kent leaned down and brushed his lips against Georgia's forehead. "I've been on the phone."

"What's wrong now?" No sooner had the words left her lips than Christa clamped her mouth closed.

They'd given the newlyweds only a sketchy outline of the problems they'd experienced. "Informed but not worried" was how Fred put it. Besides, now that the Society for Order was in jail and no connection to John had been found, their problems seemed to be over.

"Nothing's wrong. Why would you think that?" Kent stared at her for a moment, then urged by his wife, explained his call. "So the deal is, this family, the Eversons, wants to rent our entire facility for a combined family reunion and their parents' fiftieth anniversary right before your mystery party. They have a number of events already planned, so we don't have to be responsible for entertainment, only food and lodging."

"Well, that's a blessing." Christa gulped. "I don't know if I could handle the party and the mystery weekend and do justice to both of them."

"It's more of a blessing than you know. One of the Everson children owns a hot tub company, and he's bringing out three tubs for the time they're here. He said he'd be happy to leave them if we had a booking after theirs and wanted to use them."

"Hot tubs—they're going to make our fund-raiser even better." Christa knew now that the idea hadn't been hers alone. God had His hand in it and He was working through the details.

"Yes, it will, but I'm not finished." Kent's smug smile warned them he had something else up his sleeve.

"Oh, stop preening and tell us," Georgia scolded with a little grin.

"Yes, dear. Two of the Everson daughters own a floral-supply store and would like permission to come out a day ahead of time and decorate the camp and the buildings in a harvest theme."

"We won't even have to buy the decorations for our mystery weekend if they don't mind leaving them!" Amazed, Christa could only stare, her heart filling with praise.

"Oh, they don't mind. And not just leaving them. Actually they wondered if we'd mind taking the decorations down. Most of the family have jobs they need to get back to after their reunion. Since the ladies don't want to sell used stock, they're willing to donate everything for crafts next year or for whatever use we want."

"It's perfect. God's really nudging you along on this one, Christa." Georgia grabbed a piece of paper and a pen. "If we plan it right, we can order enough supplies for both events to get a better price on groceries. How many Eversons will there be?" she asked Kent.

Christa left them discussing financial details. She needed to see John. The sooner they got that invitation out, the better. But first she had to stop by the craft shack and see if she could find the exact shade of green paper she wanted. There were only a few days left until she and Abby would send off the final package to Simple Gifts. No way was she going to let this opportunity slip through her fingers.

Christa hurried outside, grateful for John's boardwalk that made her travel so much easier. She had barely turned the corner beyond the infirmary when a man burst out of the door, knocking her chair over.

He didn't apologize, offer to help, or even stop. All Christa could see was a pair of once-white sneakers disappearing in the dust. In a matter of seconds his footsteps died away and she was left alone, lying on the ground. Who was it? She was afraid to ask herself that question—afraid she already knew the answer.

Christa struggled to right herself, but with nothing to hold on to and no leverage, she couldn't manage it. Her pager lay five feet away. Cold, breathless, and feeling more powerless by the moment, she forced herself to lie still and think of another way.

Helpless. She'd fought against that feeling for so long, but the word echoed through her mind with stinging clarity. She *was* helpless, and she was alone, which only proved how futile her pretense of independence really was. Except she was supposed to rely on God.

Father? Help me.

Christa waited a moment, then bit her lip as she dug deep for a morsel of courage. Okay, this was a challenge. But if she could coordinate a fund-raiser, surely she could reach that pager to call for help.

She dug her fingers into the ground, and using every muscle in her arms, dragged herself forward inch by grueling inch.

"If this is a test of my grit and determination, God, I intend to pass," she warned with a grunt.

Christa was sweaty and drained, but she pressed on until her arms ached and she could summon not one more ounce of strength. No matter how far she stretched her fingers, the pager still lay five inches away.

"Okay," she huffed, leaning her head on her arms, "now what?"

"I can do all things through Christ who strengthens me."

Was it only a few hours ago she'd stuck the little card containing that verse on her bathroom mirror with smug self-assurance? John was right to question her. How easily she prattled out the words and pretended she had all the answers. How much harder to put them into practice.

Well, Lord, this is going to take some of Your strength.

Christa inhaled several deep breaths. The sun's warmth on her back chased away the chill. She dug her fingernails into the sandy soil and pulled for all she was worth, ignoring the little voice inside that said the pager was too far away and she was too tired.

At last her fingers touched the plastic, enclosed the smoothness of it in her palm. She pulled it near, rolled onto her back, and held it against her heart like a lifeline. She forced herself to a calm, even breathing pattern and waited for some of the heat to leave her face.

When she'd recouped as well as possible, Christa pressed the button. "Fred, are you there?"

"Sure am, honey. Need me?"

"I wonder if you could meet me. I'll wait by the infirmary."

"On my way. Anything wrong?"

"Not a thing," she answered, trying to suppress her victorious feelings. She clicked the button and watched the billowy white clouds scurry past in the sky.

That problem was resolved. But the other one would be more difficult. Somehow she'd have to try to reach Braydon again. She needed to warn him and keep him from making a big mistake. Until she'd done her best to make him see that trespassing on camp property was wrong, she wouldn't mention her suspicion that he was involved in today's incident.

But if that didn't work, she'd have to tell Abby and Angie and let them deal with it. It was not something she looked forward to.

CHAPTER TWELVE

This is going to be the best fund-raiser we've ever had."

John smiled and nodded, but he couldn't share Christa's enthusiasm for the event. Not after what he'd just learned. Imagining what could have happened made his blood run cold.

"I know what you're doing," he muttered.

"What's that?" She glanced up from the papers she'd been studying.

"You're trying to pretend it was nothing, that you weren't afraid when you were lying there." The rage burned anew. "You can pretend you're not angry, but I won't. You should have told Fred immediately that someone knocked you over; then we could have searched the grounds for this person."

"Maybe I should have. But I chose not to." She looked at him steadily. "I have to handle this the way I think best. I'm sorry if that bothers you, but I wasn't really in any danger."

John reassessed her confident look. "You don't know that." An overwhelming sense of guilt filled him. It had to be tied to him. Christa had simply been in their way. Whoever *they* were.

"I do know it. I wasn't in danger of anything but getting dirty."

"Rick must wish I'd regain my memory and get out of town. I'm beginning to wish the same thing."

"Stop trying to take on all the guilt. It happened; I'm fine. Now let's leave it to the police and get on with what we can control—our mystery weekend." She held up a hand. "I know what you're going to say and you can forget it. I'm not canceling."

"You haven't thought this through."

"Oh, yes I have." Christa sighed. "Look, a kid stole a car and took a joyride out to Camp Hope. He or some others wrote on a few cabins. It's nothing I haven't seen before." She shrugged. "I absolutely refuse to live my life worrying about what could happen. Lying out there on the ground taught me something about myself, about the reserves of strength I have. If they aren't enough, I'll call on God. I will not be afraid. Not anymore."

He looked dubious. "Then I'm afraid for you."

"Don't be. I'll be as careful as I can. But apart from that, I have God watching over me. Nothing He doesn't allow can happen to me."

"Your God *allowed* you to be paralyzed!" He bit his lip, wishing he hadn't said it.

Christa nodded. "Yes, He did."

"But—"

"I'm His child, John. I can yield to His control and believe His words that He will never leave or forsake me, or I can fight it. What does fighting it get me? Can I change anything? Can I know the heart of the person who knocked me over? No. But God does and I believe He'll work things out."

"It sounds too easy."

"Easy?" she scoffed. "Total surrender is never easy. I work on it every day. I don't have all the answers, but my Father does. In a way, that's a huge relief."

"Huh?"

"It's hard to explain." She paused. "When I first found out I was paralyzed, the doctors said there was little hope I would walk again. I interpreted that as a chance I would and I clung to that, forced myself to try so hard I injured my arm. I wanted it so badly I kept pushing and trying and straining. I tried anything and everything. And I only made matters worse."

"But maybe—"

She shook her head and touched his shoulder gently, her beautiful eyes soft. "There are no maybes, no miracles waiting to lift me out of this chair and set me on my feet. I am a paraplegic. I will not walk again."

The words hit his heart like a hammer, crushing and cold. He stared at the floor, tried to understand how she could accept that.

"I'm not saying God couldn't heal me," Christa continued. "I'm saying that right now this is the life He has given me. Am I going to waste it on wishing, on being afraid something might happen to me? Or am I going to use the hours and days God has granted me to make a difference? I choose the latter because I know He wants the best for me."

From the first time he'd met her, he'd had questions about this God she believed in. To think of Him as personal, as someone who was always present, always listening, always caring, seemed somehow childish and yet so attractive. The yearning inside him gaped a little wider. *Why can't I understand?*

You have to believe. The voice shocked him to his core. He had so many questions for that voice, so many things he didn't understand. How did one believe?

"John? Are you all right?"

"Yes."

"Then let's get busy. Camp Hope needs a cash infusion, and this fund-raiser could do it. It's my way of saying thank you."

"I know it's important for you to give back when you feel you've accepted for so long." But with so many people expected to arrive at camp his dread magnified.

Believe. Hope. Trust.

He wanted to so badly. But something wasn't right. He could feel it in the pit of his stomach. It wasn't just the computer problems—he'd fixed them, repaired the damage the Trojan horse had inflicted. The feeling went deeper, and it was tied to the society. It was supposed to be contained, yet a man was still skulking around the camp and he could have hurt Christa so easily.

A constant foreboding hung over him, a gnawing perception that he'd missed some important clue, that if he could remember only one detail, it would put an end to all of his questions. And always in the back of his mind October 29 blazed its warning. Maybe if he asked the right way, the voice would tell him what he needed to know.

"We need to get the invitations out quickly, especially since we've got a limit as to how many can come. I was hoping you could set it up so we could have them register online. That way we'd know exactly who was going to show up and when."

"Okay. Rick said he'd run a check on anyone we weren't sure of. Just to make sure there aren't any surprises."

Christa skimmed the list of names she held. "If we don't know someone, we can ask who referred them. We don't want to be too blatant about it though. A contest would make asking for information seem plausible; don't you think?"

John didn't know what to think. Recurring dreams of linked computers and secrets passed between them plagued his sleep so he never felt truly rested. Lately the image of the little girl named Sally had returned to haunt him in the wee hours of the morning. Sometimes Sally had Christa's face and openly wept. Those were the worst dreams.

Other times the face was that of young Penny Van Meter; sometimes it was of an older woman he felt he knew. She often reached out one hand, repeating the same request over and over: *Help me.* He wanted to. No one knew how desperately he wanted to free her from whatever held her prisoner. But no matter how heroically he tried, he couldn't do it.

And then there was Kane Connors. He'd tried to explain his concerns to Rick, who'd run some kind of check before assuring him that everything about Simple Gifts was legitimate. CEO Kane Connors remained a mysterious figure and was seldom seen in public. A rich recluse. Nothing more.

"John?"

Suddenly he was aware that he'd missed the rest of whatever Christa had been saying.

Now she wore a frown of concern. "Is everything all right?"

He smothered his snort of disgust.

"All right? No, but it's no different than it was yesterday. I finished the invitation. I hope you'll like it." He pulled his sample from the desk, handed it to her, and caught himself holding his breath as he waited for her reaction. He'd spent hours fine-tuning every detail from the graphics to the tear-away information section—all because he craved Christa Anderson's approval.

Veering away from the inner knowledge his actions revealed, John concentrated on Christa. Today's office appearance was rare. Christa usually locked herself in the craft shack. In the afternoons, Abby helped her. John wanted to know why, but since nobody had volunteered the information and he was a guest of the camp, he could hardly browbeat Christa into telling him what she was up to.

"You've really done it this time." Her fingers curled around his, zapping a spark of electricity from her fingers all the way up his arm to squeeze his heart in sweet pain, reminding him of that near kiss. "You've done a marvelous job. This is exactly the mood I wanted." She smiled up at him, her joy touching his heart. "How can I ever thank you?"

He didn't want her thanks. He wanted her to care about him, to share with him, to make him part of her world. But that was impossible.

John pulled back to lean against the desk, away from her magnetic allure. "I'm glad you like it," he said, struggling to keep his voice even. "Shall I print some? Ralna has the address labels all ready."

"Please tell me what's wrong." Christa's honeyed voice compelled him to look at her. "Maybe if we pray about it—"

"You'd be wasting your breath."

"You think the God of the universe is too small to solve your problems?" Gentle teasing underlay her words, a chiding chuckle that irritated him with its certainty.

"I'm not sure there is a God of the universe," he blurted out, afraid to look at her and see the hurt in her eyes.

"I think you're lying to yourself." Strangely enough, she didn't look upset or angry, merely saddened by his denial. "You're a smart man. You can't seriously believe that all this—" she waved a hand around her—"just happened. *Bang*—there it was, a thousand different species of fish, perfectly managed ecosystems, humans with enough intelligence to survive and prosper. There's no way someone with your IQ would accept such a feeble theory."

"You don't know my IQ. Besides, you're talking about religion."

"I'm talking about faith. Hope in something bigger than me, in someone who knows me for what I am and loves me enough to—"

"To what? Paralyze you? Put you in the path of someone who would push you over without a second thought? Is that what you mean?" Anger chewed at him. He would have walked away to spare her his emotions, but he wanted to hear her explain it. Something deep inside him ached to understand why she was so adamant about this God of hers.

"You refuse to understand. God gave me strength to push through the pain and heal, to live again. It's God who is with me all the time, shielding me with His love." Christa's eyes brushed over him, darkened. "But because I believe in God doesn't make me immune to problems. Even if I'd died after the accident, He would have still loved me. That's the basis of my hope."

"Hope for heaven, you mean? Isn't that what those speakers were touting all summer?" John was pushing her and he knew it, but the anger, the frustration, the desperation emanating from that empty space inside drove him. "There's no evidence about an afterlife to corroborate your belief."

"There's not a whole lot of evidence about the Internet either. You can't show me where it's housed or how to drive there, but you don't doubt it's there. You have faith that you will find what you seek on it."

He shook his head. "I'm a computer geek. I understand how and why the Internet works. I don't understand your God." He watched emotions flicker across her face. "I'm sorry, Chris. I didn't mean to offend you. If it works for you, I'm glad. I want you to be happy."

"I want you to be happy too. But if I've learned anything since I got in this wheelchair, I've learned that true happiness apart from God doesn't exist." She sighed, but her gaze never left his face. "I wish I could explain it better. I wish you could trust a little bit, that we could share this."

The chasm yawning between them had never been so evident or so uncrossable. He leaned forward, trailed his knuckles down her cheek. "We can share other things. Like those little parcels you keep getting. You share them with Abby. Why not share them with me?" The words slipped out in spite of his resolve not to demand answers.

Christa's face turned a bright pink while she looked away from him and focused on her hands.

"It's just something I've been working on. I promise I'll tell you sometime soon but not yet. Not until I'm sure."

"Sure of what?" He rose, paced back and forth across the room. "I'm beginning to wonder if I'll ever be sure of anything again."

A motion outside the window drew his attention. Kent and Fred were standing by while a man inspected the camp van.

"What are they doing with the van?" he asked, unable to tear his eyes away.

"Kent's finally had an offer to buy it. Isn't that wonderful? It's way past time to get rid of that tired old thing."

Rid of it? The words stabbed him so hard he lost his breath for a moment. Then some inner force compelled him to put a stop to it.

"No!" John ripped the door open and raced across the campgrounds. "You can't sell it, Kent," he panted. "You can't."

"Why?" Kent stared at him as if he'd gone crazy; so did Fred.

"I don't know." John fidgeted under their scrutiny. "I don't know why it has to stay. I can't give you any definite reasons. I only know that if that van leaves camp property, I have no hope of stopping a murder."

Behind him Christa gasped.

John knew exactly how she felt. He had no idea where the words had come from, but he believed they were true.

Was that faith?

⊰⊹⊱

"Why did you need this eye exam today?" John lifted Christa into the van seat with the same gentle care he'd always employed, but this time his touch lingered—his fingers brushed a wayward curl from her eyes and eased her collar up around her neck.

Christa reprimanded herself for acting like a schoolgirl with a crush, but she truly enjoyed feeling John's arms around her. She felt *cherished*—an old-fashioned word perhaps, yet it applied. But she couldn't let this feeling overtake her commitments to another.

Facing the gap that separated them hadn't stopped the longing, but it had shown her how little she'd changed from the spoiled brat of two years ago. She wanted what she wanted—now. But God was in control and His ways were different.

Whenever she spoke to John about God, she was forced to reexamine her own motives. Did she think that because she prayed for John often and counted out his good qualities to the one who had created him that God would change His rules? No matter how strong her feelings, it wasn't enough to erase what she knew—they were not on equal footing. And without that they could not have a future. Which meant she would have to let John go.

"Well?" John prodded. Somehow Rick had managed to get John a temporary license after he passed a road test. Now John stood in the space between the passenger door and the vehicle, arms akimbo, waiting for her response. "Why today?"

"Today is October 6. Emily Murdock's birthday," she added when he looked confused.

"So?"

"Emily doesn't do appointments on her birthday, so the office phoned me to come in and take her canceled appointment." Just thinking about the sisters' eccentricities made her smile.

"And you had to take it?"

"Yes. I keep getting these horrible headaches. You know I've been doing a lot of crafts. Well, I thought maybe the close work was causing some kind of eyestrain, so I've been avoiding the tiny stuff, trying to work on bigger projects. When Georgia pointed out how much medication I was downing for those headaches, I realized that it was past time to find out if something else is going on. Funny how you put things like that off, isn't it? Anyway, I took Emily's appointment. I also needed to come into town for some supplies."

"And you learned what?" A muscle flicked at the corner of his mouth. It only appeared when he was angry or upset.

"You're very sweet to worry about me." Christa touched John's shoulder. "I'm okay. There's been a change in my eyesight, that's all."

He took her hand and pressed it between his warm palms. "So what happens now?"

"I ordered a pair of glasses. Next week we'll be coming back to pick them up. You can call me Four Eyes." Relief made her giggle as her heart sang a song of praise. "I owe Georgia for pushing me. I don't know why I waited."

She knew. So did he. But John was kind enough not to tell her that she was afraid. Without a word, he rounded the van and slid into the driver's seat. Christa watched him shift into gear, his movements smooth, practiced, as if he'd done it a thousand times before.

She frowned. "Where did you get that van key?"

"From Kent. Why?" About to back up, he paused, looked at her closely. "What's wrong with it?"

"Nothing. But Kent didn't give you that one." She reached into the glove box and pulled out a keychain with Camp Hope's insignia on it. "These are ours. Did you have another set made?"

John slipped the gearshift back into park. "I wouldn't know where to go to have that done." His jaw flexed. "Then where—oh!"

"What?" she demanded.

"The backpack. The one I found. Remember? You said it was a special kind for mountain climbers."

"Oh yes. The one in the office."

He nodded. "I went through it."

"I know. I was with you. But we didn't find anything."

John switched off the engine, pulled out the key, and held it up.

"I looked in it again later and found this. I tried it on a whole bunch of locks all over the camp, but it never fit. It didn't occur to me to try the van." His eyes brimmed with questions. "I wasn't intending to try it today. I guess it was an automatic response."

"Why would this person who's camping out have a key to our van?" she asked. "Was he going to steal it? Why? It's not worth very much."

"Maybe he wasn't going to steal anything. Maybe he wanted to look inside."

"For what?" Christa surveyed the well-used seats, the carpet that lay threadbare and worn. "It's not as if we hide stacks of gold in here."

"Good question. Unfortunately, I don't have an answer. Again." He slid the key back in the ignition, and soon they were traveling the familiar road back to Camp Hope.

As they drove, she kept tossing out possible scenarios for the key.

John snickered when her theories grew too wild to take seriously. "Tramps who find a way to get a key made for a van so they can live in it instead of camping out? That's crazy, even for you. It's not as if people wouldn't notice this behemoth tooling around."

"Are you calling me crazy?"

"Aren't you? And I don't just mean about this tramp theory you dreamed up." One corner of his mouth lifted when he said it. "You have this way of bullying through life, Christa, of refusing to back down or lay off."

"That doesn't sound very nice." She wrinkled her nose. "You make me sound like an overbearing, pushy control freak."

"Yes. And your point is?" He burst out laughing at her outraged yelp. "Kidding, just kidding. Truth to tell, I admire your tenacity. You go all out for what you believe in. It's refreshing, though a little risky."

"Don't you do the same thing?"

He took a long time to answer. Finally he shook his head and said, "I don't think I do. I think I'm the type that takes the easy way out."

"Not from what I've seen." She refused to accept that John Riddle wouldn't be as committed to his goals as she was to hers.

He peered through the windshield. "I wish this road wasn't so slippery. All the rain in the past two days has washed the gravel to the side."

"What's your hurry? Am I boring you?" Faintly irritated by his rush to get back to the camp, Christa wished it were warm and sunny, that he'd suggested they stop in the little park in town and sip a latte while the leaves tumbled down. Instead it was cool, wet, and rather miserable.

She'd worried a little about this public foray as she scooted up the ramp to the optometrist's office. Waiting in his office along with a bunch of other patients was a test, and withstanding the curious stares of three children was even more difficult. But Christa had managed it and a little shopping besides. Victory was sweet. Maybe she was beginning to get the hang of moving around in public. Good thing. The fund-raiser was less than three weeks off.

And after that she would leave.

"No hurry, really. But I promised your brother I'd spell him off with that bunch of teenagers he's got at camp. Their questions are nonstop, like their energy." He yanked the wheel to one side to avoid a gaping pothole, then struggled to keep the van on the road.

"That's the way teenagers are supposed to be—inquisitive."

Clutching the armrest, Christa held herself steady as the van fish-tailed. "Why don't you slow down? What's wrong?"

"The brakes aren't working. I can't keep it—"

Christa needed no explanation for the loud pop. She'd been in the van once before when it had blown a tire. That time Kent had eased his way off the road and into the ditch with no problem, but John wasn't as successful.

The sheer length of the van made it less maneuverable even on a good road. This was not a good road. The gravel stretch toward Camp Hope looked as if it had been chewed up by a dinosaur in search of lunch. One wheel sunk into a rut too deep to maintain traction. John pressed the gas to push out of it, but the van's motor overcompensated and they slid across the road in a slurry of mud.

Christa closed her eyes and prayed as the van lurched, then tilted and rolled over. Once. Twice. She lost count, felt herself fall forward against the dashboard. Though she tried to brace herself, the stabbing pain radiating in her temple told her she'd hit it. She saw stars and wondered if she'd blacked out.

The van finally shuddered to a stop. After a few calming breaths, she knew she was all right. No permanent injuries sustained. But, oh, her head!

Christa dabbed her fingers against the throbbing lump on her head as she assessed their situation. The van lay on its side, her side. Around them rain poured from a leaden sky quickly growing dimmer in the late afternoon. She couldn't move.

She was a prisoner, helpless to both John and herself.

CHAPTER THIRTEEN

When Christa glanced around the van, she realized that she was still buckled in and the seat belt was causing the pain in her neck. She undid it, freed herself, and using her arms, wedged into a better position to look around.

"Practice makes perfect," she grunted, remembering her efforts after her wheelchair had been knocked over. "Maybe I should consider weight lifting."

Then she saw John. Blood trickled from a cut she couldn't locate. His eyes were closed; he appeared to be sleeping. The armrests and his seat belt held him in place, though his head drooped sideways. John was suspended. If she undid his belt he would fall directly onto her, which would be bad enough, but it might also exacerbate internal injuries if he had them.

"John?"

He didn't respond.

Oh, Father, how do I deal with this?

Cold air whooshed inside from the rear where a back door had swung open sometime during their rollover. The motor was still running. She switched it off. "John?"

He didn't move.

She tried the cell phone Kent kept in the van. No service. That was no help. *God, we're in a fix here. Please help us.*

John moaned, but his eyes remained shut. The throbbing in her head had increased a hundredfold, bringing tears to her eyes. Christa huddled into the warmth of her jacket, glad she'd chosen it for this trip. All around them rain still pelted the countryside. Every so often a gust of wind carried the moisture-laden particles into the van, their chilly fingers cooling what little heat was left.

She kept up her litany of prayer, bolstering her courage with the reassurance that the gravel road was well traveled. Soon someone would come along and help them.

Useless. Helpless. Cripple.

"Fine," she responded to the unseen voice in her head. "I *am* helpless here. I'm a cripple. But I am *not* useless. I can pray. I can help John."

"Help me do what?" John stared at her in confusion. "Who are you talking to? Why did you say those awful things about yourself?"

"Never mind me. How do you feel?" Joy and praise raced through her. She watched him move his head back and forth. "Is anything broken? Do you think you have internal injuries? Can you move?"

"My head hurts. I don't think so. I don't know. Yes." He frowned. "What a lot of questions."

"You cut your head." She tugged out a length of white cotton she'd purchased in town and handed it to him. "Here. Maybe you can wind it around your head."

"I've never been any good at first aid." John grunted with the effort of swathing the yardage around his head like a turban. "I'm all thumbs. I flunked the test three times. My instructor offered to pay me if I went somewhere else to retake the course."

Christa said nothing as he continued to speak, but her heart soared. John was remembering things! Then her stomach dropped to her toes. If his mind finally cleared, if he completely recovered, he would leave Camp Hope far behind.

You are my strength.

"You know those rhythmical presses you're supposed to do to keep the breathing going?" John barely glanced at her as his fingers searched to find a place to tuck in the end of his bandage. "I broke the dummy doing that."

Christa spread her fingers over her lips to stifle the laughter. "Really?"

"Really." He checked his reflection in the rearview mirror. "I finally got my certification though. Fat lot of good that did me. A woman went into labor on the 'L' one day. I tried to help her, but she wanted to charge me with assault."

What was the "L"? Christa wondered.

He turned his head to glare at her. "She grabbed some guy's umbrella and hit me with it. I had to have ten stitches. Right there." He pushed up his sleeve to show her the faint white puckering of an injury long since healed. "You can still see the scar."

"Did you study medicine then?" Christa decided to sit quietly and wait. Obviously John hadn't noticed that his memory was flowing back. Maybe he'd let something else slip.

"Medicine? Me? No way. Can't stand the sight of blood." He twisted in his seat. "I feel like I'm strapped into a parachute."

"Have you ever jumped?"

"Oh yeah. Once. Thought for sure I was a goner. Now I can barely get into a plane without getting sick. It's horrible to be in free fall. Hot-air balloons aren't much better." He poked and prodded the steering wheel. "No air bag. Too bad."

"You went up in a hot-air balloon?" *Keep him talking,* she told herself. *Drag out every single memory he's got tucked away.*

"In Napa Valley. When I was a kid my dad thought it would be a great way to learn about wind currents and aerodynamics. I got the rapid descent part down real well." He gazed through the cracked windshield. "That was before . . . ," he whispered at last.

"Before?" Christa asked, watching his expression change.

"Before they took everything." His voice was so soft she barely heard what he'd said.

"They took everything?"

"Mm-hm." He nodded, but his eyes were focused on something far in the distance, something she couldn't see. "It was never the same after that. He killed my dream."

When John didn't elaborate, she prodded again. "Who did?"

He froze, then faced her. "Pardon?"

"Who stole everything? Who killed your dream?"

His whole body underwent a change, as if he physically withdrew from something too painful to explore. "I don't know what you're talking about. How long do I have to hang trussed up like this before we can get out of here?" he snapped.

"I don't suppose you have to wait at all—if you can get yourself free, that is. Are you sure you're not hurt?"

"Yes, I'm sure." By easing one foot against the dash and the other against the floorboards, John managed to work himself free of his constraints, though his face was pale and he favored one arm. "I think it's broken."

Christa offered him her scarf for a sling, and he tied it across his chest.

"We're quite a pair," she said. "What do we do now?"

"I could walk to camp, but I'm not going to."

She frowned, prepared to argue.

"Don't even start. With all the weirdness that's been happening, I refuse to leave you here by yourself, so you might as well get comfortable. Together we're safe." He managed to wiggle past her to the back of the van.

"What are you doing?"

"Trying to get this door closed." John groaned as he pulled on the handle. "It's stuck."

"Maybe I could—"

"Don't worry. I've got it." A second later the door thudded closed with a clang. "It's not latched, but it'll keep the wind out."

"And the rain," she added. "Aren't you frozen?"

"I'm fine, but your chair's a little worse for wear. Kind of like this van."

"So in a way you got your wish. I don't think the insurance company will fix the van, but nobody will buy it either."

He stared at her. "I didn't want to crack it up. I hope Kent gets enough money to buy another one."

Christa looked out the window. Nobody. "Since we seem to be staying for a while, I wish I'd brought my CD player. This van is so old it only takes cassettes." There was a sudden movement in the back. She turned, saw him slide one hand along the back door. "John?"

"CD. That's what you said. Of course. A CD."

Christa watched him skim his palms over the door until he stopped at a place on one side.

"I need a screwdriver. Do you have one?" His voice was hushed.

"No. I don't usually carry one. I bought a new pair of scissors though. They were in with that cloth—"

He scrabbled around until he found the scissors.

"Those are the ones." She tilted her head to her shoulder to ease the crimp, then gasped at the sound of tearing cloth. "What are you doing?"

"Retrieving something I put here." John was calmly feeling his way under the upholstery fabric. Maybe too calmly. After a moment he held up a brown bubble-wrapped envelope.

"What is that?"

"A package. I was going to mail it. But then I decided it might get damaged, so I opened it to . . ." He paused, peered into the envelope. "Nothing. But it should be here. I know it should be."

"What should be there?"

John began to speak as if he were watching a movie inside his head and relaying the action to her. "That day, when I was at the post office, you and your brother went into a building. I needed a place to hide, so I crawled into the back of your van. There was enough space where the glue had worn out to slip this in."

The truth dawned on Christa. "That's what Sally saw, what you were going to mail!"

He nodded, turning the envelope over. "But I didn't. I wonder why."

"What was inside it?"

"A CD. But it's not here now."

"Look in the pocket of the side door behind me," Christa suggested. She turned around, watched his fingers work their way down, and held her breath when he paused. "Is it there?"

"Yes." He held up a silver disk.

"I opened the back door to put some things inside. A CD fell out. I stuck it in the side pocket, thinking I'd get it later. But I forgot about it."

Christa gulped. "Do you think it's yours?"

"I don't know."

Christa's back ached like fire. If she didn't get more comfortable soon, she knew she'd start to spasm. "Can you pull that bench seat cushion off? I'd rather sit on it than on this armrest." She wobbled on her precarious perch.

"Yes, of course. I should have thought of it before."

He tucked the CD back in the pocket, then set to work. When he had everything ready, he helped her into the back of the van, where he'd rearranged a place for her to sit and lean against. His foot caught in the handle of a shopping bag. "What on earth is in all of these bags?"

"Wool. Abby got it at a garage sale."

"Why do you need so much?"

"We're working on a project."

"Is this the project you can't tell me about?"

She bit her lip. "She's helping me."

"With what?" He pinpointed her in his sights and didn't shift.

Christa swallowed. Simple Gifts was making her an offer, and everything was almost settled. "If I tell you, will you please stop nagging me about it?"

"No promises." He laid his good arm across her shoulder and hugged her close. "For warmth, okay? I can tell you're shivering even if it is a little dark in here."

She closed her eyes, trembling at the sensations that rocketed through her. *Lord, he's not one of Yours. I can't have these feelings.*

His voice brushed against her ear. "Is that better?"

Better but worse because it couldn't last.

Christa cleared her throat. "I had an idea to form a company that would supply kits of projects to summer camps, kids' camps, clubs—that kind of thing. Figuring out crafts is one of the hardest things a camp director faces every year and is very time-consuming, so I figured that if kits were already packaged, ready to go, and offered at a reasonable price, someone would buy them."

"Very clever."

After taking a deep breath, she continued. "I found an ad from Simple Gifts offering start-up funding for people with a great idea but no capital behind them."

"I thought—"

"I have some money, but not enough to get this off the ground. I sent samples of a few ideas to Simple Gifts, and they asked for more. Abby and I have made up three displays in all. So far they like all of them. Now we're working on number crunching—costing out each craft, time, age-group, materials. After we get that done, the company says they will help us get a catalog printed. It looks like they're going to lend us the money. They've even offered to find some office space for us in Chicago. Once the deal is finalized, we can begin looking for customers."

When Christa finished, she cocked her head to stare at John.

He was glowering. His fingers snapped around her forearm like tentacles. "Did you sign anything with them, Christa?"

"Not yet. Why?" She tore her arm free and watched him exhale. "What's wrong?"

"How well did you research Simple Gifts before you began this?"

"Research it?" She frowned, trying to fathom his expression. "I didn't. I found the name of the company online, read about their loan offer, and proceeded from there."

"Tell me what you've sent them so far."

"Why?"

"Tell me!" he yelled.

"All right. You don't have to shout." Christa briefly explained the initial package containing her ideas. "Then Abby and I did a small sampling of possibilities. Simple Gifts returned it and said they needed something more like a portfolio. They sent information from other projects they'd funded, ideas for packaging samples, and start-up cost projections. We've been going back and forth for a while now."

"So they've seen all your ideas?" His chin thrust out. "They have samples of every craft you want to sell?"

"No. I did only six initially. A few more after that. I told you, they returned those."

"Returned them in the small brown boxes?"

She nodded. "John, you're making me nervous."

"And the rest—you said Simple Gifts wanted a portfolio."

"Yes. I made one. I thought it was ready to go, but then Abby showed my work to her sister, who suggested we tweak things for a more professional look. We've changed almost every craft from the original. We've got three more to go before we're ready to send the portfolio out."

"Thank God." He heaved a sigh of relief.

"I thought you didn't believe in Him." She opened her eyes wide when he scowled. "Well, that is what you said."

"Christa, I'm prepared to concede that in regard to you, I may have been wrong. Somebody is certainly protecting you."

"Why do you say that?"

"Kane Connors is not what he seems to be and his company Simple Gifts is not a kind, benevolent charity that backs loans and helps people get back on their feet." John held up a hand as her lips opened to protest. "Don't ask me how I know; I just do. I know it as surely as I know my own—" He stopped, swallowed. "As I know what day of the week it is."

"You're wrong!" She stared at him, aghast. "You have to be."

He shook his head, his face tight.

"This is my future. All my plans and dreams have gone into refining my work into building a company I can be proud of. I've developed a name, researched suppliers, and built a list of contacts. And with every step, Simple Gifts has helped me."

"Kane Connors—"

"Has had no input in this. I've never spoken or corresponded with him. For all I know he's never even heard of His Creations."

"That's what you're calling this company of yours?"

"Yes." Couldn't he see how much of herself she'd poured into making this happen? The hours, the hopes, the dreams. Her future was all tied up. "What exactly is it you expect me to do?"

"Find someone else to back your dream."

Christa's temper inched higher, fueled by the careless way he said it. As if she hadn't thought it through a thousand times, planned and replanned every step. "Like who? Any suggestions?" Fury blazed, tossing caution to the wind. "Why don't you dip into your trust fund and set us up in business, John? Or suggest another agency who'd help us get started the way Simple Gifts is doing."

"I don't know anyone. I only know this is wrong." His eyes glowed with anger. "It's wrong."

"Tell me why. Simple Gifts hasn't charged Abby and me a fee. They haven't sold us anything, haven't demanded we give them anything. They're doing exactly what they said they would—lending us their expertise and their knowledge. And we're accepting it."

"But you can't—"

"Christa?" Kent's voice calling from outside the van was ragged with fear.

"I'm here. I'm fine. So is John, though he's hurt his arm."

After the back door wrenched open, Kent's head poked in. "What happened?"

"Slippery road, blown tire, and a little twist life handed us," Christa informed him. "Just get me out please, Kent. I'm cold, my head aches, and I want to go home." Frustration still chewed at her, but she thrust it down.

"Okay, hang on." It took him several minutes to reach her, then several more to ease her out of the van. His lips brushed the top of her head. "You scared the daylights out of me, kiddo."

"Me too. How did you know where to find us?"

"I didn't. Fred took a call from a neighbor who saw the van lying in the ditch." Kent set her in Georgia's car. "Wait here while I help John."

It took Kent and John a while to approach the car, and she knew why when she saw John clutching the bubble-wrapped envelope. He and Kent engaged in conversation on the way home. Christa had nothing to say. She was too upset. Even though John had been right about where the two kidnapped men were being held, Christa wasn't ready to believe him now. It meant giving up on her dream.

The moment they arrived back at the camp, John disappeared into the office. It wasn't long until Rick's patrol car arrived and he went inside too.

Christa fumed. John was getting on with his life, discovering whatever secrets that CD held. But he wanted her to put her life on hold. Well, it wasn't going to happen.

Kent left Christa sitting in the kitchen, where Georgia fussed over her, and later returned with Christa's chair. "It had a few kinks, so I did a bit of tinkering. I think it will run okay now. Your hope stone was knocked loose, but you can glue that back on." He handed it to Christa, then said, "I peeked in the office. Looks like the CD John found suffered from the summer heat and he's trying to restore it."

Christa didn't comment. She exchanged her coat for one that would repel the rain and had a hood, shoved the stone into her pocket, then tried out the chair. It worked. She opened the door.

Kent held the screen door for her. "Where are you going?"

"To the craft shack. I have work to do." She glanced at the office.

"John can tell you about it. He's got all the answers." It was exactly the kind of nasty remark the old Christa would have shot out. She regretted it as soon as she'd said it, but tears clogged her throat, blocking any words of apology.

She pushed the knob that felt funny without its hope stone, then rode down the ramp and over the boardwalk to what she'd come to think of as her office. Abby stood in the doorway, her back to Christa.

"All done for the day?" Christa called.

Like a robot operated by some remote control, Abby turned.

Christa sucked in her breath. The woman looked as if she'd been struck by lightning.

Abby pointed into the shack, eyes wide. "All done permanently, I'm afraid. Oh, Christa, I'm so sorry." She stepped back.

Christa rolled through the doorway. The room had been thoroughly ransacked. Everything was destroyed. Each craft was crushed, torn apart, damaged. Obviously not content with the mess he'd created, the perpetrator had plastered paint in spatters and pools throughout the room.

"Everything's ruined," Abby whispered. "The samples for the catalog, the templates, the supplies—they're all useless. All of that work spoiled by some vandal too stupid to know what he's done."

Christa moved forward, touching the layers of tulle that should have formed a centerpiece and were now stuck together with red paint. The marionettes—her pride and joy inspired from her high school days—had been ripped from the ceiling, their porcelain faces smashed into the floorboards. Even the wooden Popsicle sticks to make the boats she'd finally designed so they'd float had been snapped in two.

"Someone took his time," Christa murmured. "He was very thorough, left nothing to salvage."

When Christa poked the nylon kite triangles, she spotted a rock wrapped in white paper amidst the hacked-up, neon-colored strings. The unseen fingers of hate seemed to reach out toward her and she backed away. *Oh, God. Must You take all of my dreams?*

"Abby, please go home to your kids. You deserve a break. I'm going to get Rick."

"I'm really sorry about this."

"I know. It's become your dream as much as mine. I just need a minute to absorb it all."

"I'll leave you alone then. Shall I phone tomorrow morning?"

"Thanks." She waited until Abby had left, then closed the door, using the corner of a piece of sail to preserve the vandal's fingerprints. With no one's prying eyes to see her, she retrieved the rock from its hiding place and unwrapped the paper around it. The scribbled word sent her reeling. *Payback!*

She grabbed her pager. "Rick? It's Christa. Could you please come to the craft shack—now?"

———◆———

"We had sixteen reservations today alone. The spaces for your fund-raiser are filling fast." John kept on speaking, trying to draw Christa's attention away from the craft shack, but to no avail.

Christa nodded, but her eyes remained glued to the office window and the scene beyond.

Though it ached abominably, John's arm wasn't broken. He'd removed it from the sling several times while helping Kent clean out the craft shack last night long after Rick and the fingerprint experts had covered the scene. The damage appalled him, but the note infuriated him.

"Rick phoned this morning." John hated saying this. "Most of the fingerprints they found have been eliminated. He did have one piece of news. The Internet provider that our Trojan horse came through is in Washington, D.C."

"Oh." She closed her fingers around the blue stone that lay in her lap.

"I'm sorry for what I said. I wasn't trying to hurt you."

"It's over now, isn't it? You don't have to worry about me and

Simple Gifts anymore. We'll miss our deadline. The funds will go to someone else. Life goes on."

He gulped, distressed by the utter hopelessness in those words. He hadn't wanted to kill her dreams, only to keep her safe. "Leaving here—it was that important to you?"

"Is remembering the past important to you?" A flicker of the old Christa emerged in the steely glimmer lighting her eyes. "That business was my ticket out of here . . . to independence. It would have let me get out of Kent's way so he could stop worrying about poor little Christa." Her eyes spit daggers. "Now it's ruined. What do you think?"

John thought he should shut up.

Christa was quiet for a very long time. Eventually she asked, "What did the CD tell you?"

"It was damaged, probably because of the interior heat of the van during the summer. I managed to pull off images of those two men the society was holding, which is what I remembered, but not much else. I'll keep working on it, but—"

"So if the society's behind things lately, we have no way to tell if it's no longer a threat because we don't know who the leader is." The frustration of it echoed in her voice. "Round and round we go." She snatched up the mystery-weekend registrations he'd organized into alphabetical order.

John seized the chance to change the subject. "Those at the back are still question marks."

Christa pulled up the folders and glanced at the tabs. "I know these two personally. But not these four." She held out the forms he'd printed from the Web site.

"Kent mentioned this one, I think. Or maybe it wasn't. Some of these names are so similar." He couldn't sit here any longer; he had something else to do. "Your brother's supervising some archery students. I think I'll go over and ask him. If we don't want someone here, it's better to decline their registration early."

"Declining people for a fund-raiser." She shook her head. "It's crazy."

Cautious was a better word, but he didn't argue with her. "Will you be here when I get back?"

"Or in the dining hall. I told Georgia I'd help her peel potatoes for dinner tonight. The kids love her wedges."

"The kids aren't the only ones." He licked his lips. "See you later."

Christa offered only the most desultory of responses, but it was more than he'd expected. She was still dealing with the destruction of her dream and that would take a while. Beyond the controlled mask she presented, she was in pain. He simmered with anger at a God who would trick her so.

He'd gone about six paces across the compound when someone grabbed his arm. "Don't say anything. Don't try anything. Just walk."

CHAPTER FOURTEEN

Something cold, hard, and lethal pressed against John's back—
a familiar sensation, which made no sense at all. How could he be
familiar with a gun against his spine?

"Where is it?"

John turned his head to stare at his attacker. A youngish man,
late twenties, maybe. Long, stringy hair that hid everything but beady
eyes behind tinted glasses so large they almost covered his face.
Except for the snarl, he didn't look threatening. Or familiar.

"What are you talking about? Where is what?"

"Games, John? You didn't like to play our games before." The gun
dug in a little deeper. "Tell me where it is. Or should I go after the girl?"

Christa? John's heart nearly stopped. "You mean the CD," he said.
"It's useless, unreadable. By the way, she didn't know anything about
it, so you can stop asking her for it."

"Ah. So your trick failed. And the item?"

"Item? I don't know what you're talking about. The police found
me by the side of the road and—"

"Right where I left you."

Complete shock gripped John. This man knew who he was and where he'd come from. He had all the answers John had craved for so long. The words slipped out before he could stop them. "Look, I'll make you a deal. You tell me something; I'll get you something." He had nothing at all to barter with, but his captor didn't know that. Yet.

"You'll get me what?"

"An . . . item," John responded, using the same word. Since he didn't know what they were after, how could he get it? From the corner of his eye he could see Christa in the office watching him. He spun around, trying to give her a glimpse of the man's gun. "There is more than one, you know."

"You're supposed to be so clever, but you're stupid!" The steel muzzle bruised his backbone. "Betray us and you won't live long enough to regret it."

The rest of his rant froze on his lips as fifty noisy teenagers burst around the corner of the dining hall, trailed by Kent.

When they saw John, they clustered around him in a circle, their demands loud and insistent. "Are you going to give us another lesson on the Internet tonight?"

A rush of relief washed over John as the pressure against his back disappeared. At least his attacker had put the gun away. He caught a second look at him, but it was impossible to judge the man's size given the bulky sweater and huge jeans he wore. The hair and big glasses hid most of his face too.

"Hey, dude, did you come for lessons?" One of the teens grabbed the man's arm. "John's great. He can make the computer do all kinds of neat things."

"I'm sure he can." The man's smile was neither genuine nor long lasting, but it did display perfectly even white teeth. "He's a regular computer whiz."

John fought to keep himself between the interloper and the kids. No way would anyone be injured because of him.

His attacker ripped his arm from the boy's grasp and stepped away from the group.

John tried to follow, but the kids clung to him, blocking his way. "Wait!" he yelled.

The man sneered. "Thank you so much, Mr.—er . . . Riddle. I'll be seeing you."

"Good." Desperate to know something—anything—about his past, John grasped at this last chance. "Bring the information I requested. I'll have something for you too."

"Make sure you do." The man wheeled around and sped away.

If only John could get free, but there were too many kids around and he was worried about scaring them.

At last Kent blew a whistle and some of the teens turned their attention to him.

Seizing his chance, John sidestepped the last two kids, focusing on the man who was now hurrying toward the barn. Free at last, he broke into a run as a motor gunned. Minutes later a dirt bike accelerated out of the trees and zipped down the road, leaving nothing but a dust trail.

Noticing Georgia's car, John thought to follow, but he reconsidered as the bike took off across a newly harvested field. He raked a hand through his hair in pure frustration and sized up the horses.

"You are not going after him," Kent insisted from behind him, his voice low enough so only John would hear.

"Why not?"

"Because for one thing, you'd never catch him. Secondly, the horse could stumble in a gopher hole and send you flying. Besides, what would you do if you got him?"

"Get some answers."

"Would that be before or after he hurt you?"

John stared into the distance, feeling hope drain away. The man had disappeared and with him all the information that would clear up the mysteries that plagued John.

When John and Kent returned to the kids, someone tugged on John's sleeve. "Can we talk to you about the Internet now?"

"Yeah, my mom never lets me go on there without her watching. She says there are people who use the Internet to do bad things."

A picture of a satellite dish sitting on a balcony fluttered through John's mind. *Wi-fi. They couldn't track her through that.* Track who?

"The Internet is full of danger," he said, digging for a memory. "Even when you're very, very careful."

"Go call Rick. We have to report this," Kent told John before ordering everyone to be seated at the picnic tables beside the dining hall. "Since it's so gorgeous today, my wife thought we'd have our snack out here. Computers come later."

Defeated, John went to the office.

"Who was that man?" Christa demanded.

"Someone who knows me and wants something he claims I have. I told him about the CD, Chris, so you should be safe. He's after something else. 'An item,' he called it. I've got to get ahold of Rick. Maybe I can give him a description of the guy."

"I can do better than that." She held out a Polaroid picture. "I snapped it just as the kids showed up. I promised one of the girls I'd take some candid shots. Your friend turned at just the right time."

"It might help identify him, but I doubt it. His disguise is pretty good. Thanks, anyway." He dialed Rick's number from memory. "It's John. I need help again."

He was so tired of saying those words.

>>>•<<<

"Maybe having his face plastered all over the television will keep him from coming back. Your ingenuity in taking that picture was brilliant," Rick said.

"It wasn't exactly ingenuity, though I accept the compliment. It was more of an accident than anything." Christa tapped one finger against her chin. "At least it served one purpose."

"It did?" John stared at her.

"What purpose?" Rick asked.

"We know somebody wants something they think John has. The guy said, 'So your trick failed.' Meaning the CD. But he didn't leave when he found out. He kept asking, even said he'd be back. He's after something else so he has to keep John alive until he gets it. That means he'll leave me alone." She glanced around the room. "Right?"

"Maybe." Kent didn't look convinced.

Given this new twist, John wasn't heartbroken that Christa wouldn't be contacting Simple Gifts again, though he wished it had happened differently. Something about that company was bad news.

"The thing is, we don't know enough. Our Washington connection turns out to be a user with a fake name and an address that doesn't exist. I feel like I've missed out on something important, but I can't figure out what." Rick shook his head, brows lowered. "In the meantime we'll pull over strangers, do steady patrols here and in the area, and try and keep an eye on any newcomers who move through town. It's not great, but with our small force, it's the best I can do. If this continues, I'll call for more help."

John had a nagging feeling in his gut that it would continue, but he pushed it away. He watched Christa answer her cell phone. The shimmer that returned to her blue eyes told him something important was happening. When her skin flushed and her voice rose, he knew it was good news.

"Really? And you're sure this is what you both want to do?"

His heart did double time at the smile of pure joy that lifted the last cloud from her gorgeous face.

"If you're sure, I'm sure. This afternoon is perfect. Bye."

"Good news?" he asked, wanting to share her happiness.

"The best." She met his eyes with a grin. "Abby told me that all our paperwork was not destroyed. We'd both forgotten that she took copies of it home so her sister could double-check our figures and design a logo and folder. It's all sitting in the back of Abby's car in her craft bag. We're going to try again. She's already got donations of fabric and notions piling up at her house."

"What if the vandal comes back?" Rick asked.

"This time we'll be prepared. Fred boarded up the windows from the inside and bought a brand-new lock." She turned toward the door.

"I'm going to the craft shack. Don't worry about me. I'll lock myself in."

In spite of the angst he felt, John wanted to cheer her on. Determination and grit were two of Christa's strongest assets. Too bad he wouldn't be here to see her dream come alive.

"Gotta get back to those kids. Thanks, Rick." Kent stepped outside.

"You're welcome. I'm going too." Rick waved and left.

Christa moved toward the door.

John stood in front of her so she couldn't get out. "Can I talk to you for a minute?"

"Sure." She frowned. "You look . . . funny. Is something wrong?"

"No." He inhaled a breath of courage. "Christa, once the fund-raiser is finished, I intend to leave here." He sank down on Ralna's chair, his sudden burst of energy draining away.

"Leave? But why? This is your home. This is where you belong."

"Except it isn't. I've stayed here for many reasons—because it was easy, because you were all so welcoming, because Rick felt it was best."

"It was."

"Well, I've stayed too long. My mind hasn't released its secrets. In fact, all I've done is bring more problems to the camp."

"That's not all you've done and you know it." Christa's face was red, her mouth pinched. "That's not all by a long shot. The whole fund-raiser wouldn't be happening without you."

"Yes, it would. You're the brains and the power behind that. All I've done is make a brochure."

"That's not all," she insisted.

"You're trying to make me feel better about mooching here for so long. It's kind of you but not necessary between friends, is it?" John grasped one of her small capable hands in his, letting the warmth of her fingers drive the chill from his heart. He noticed her hope stone was back in place on her chair. "I know you don't want to hear this, but I have to say it. The only reason I stayed this long was because of you."

"Me?"

He nodded. They'd skated around the issue long enough. It was time for the truth. "There's something between us. Surely you won't deny that."

She ducked her head, avoiding his eyes.

"That doesn't change what I feel. You're spunky and generous and warm and kind. You charge ahead into life. I wish with all my heart that I could be here with you and see things through your eyes, but it isn't going to happen."

"I know." Her agonized whisper cracked something inside him, and he had to grapple with the loss her words engendered.

"You deserve a man who is whole, who can offer you the world. I have nothing to offer. I don't know who I am or where I'm going." He cupped her cheek in his palm. "You have your future mapped out. You had a setback, but you're poised to take the next step. I'm still taking baby steps."

"Because I'm going, it doesn't mean you have to leave." Christa looked at him then, her sapphire eyes unguarded.

John saw tenderness, anger, frustration, and sadness. But he did not see love. His heart plunged to his feet. No matter what, he owed her the truth. "I couldn't stay here without you. It would be too hard to remember the way you giggled when the ducks snatched the bread from your fingers." His thumb brushed a pattern along the line of her jaw. "I'd look at the craft shack and see your worktable and remember. I'd walk to the creek and be reminded of the boat that wouldn't float."

She smiled at his silliness.

"The thing is, Chris, I care very much for you. But I have this feeling you're going to tell me we can't be together, and I don't want to hear it." He placed his finger against her lips in case she tried to interrupt. He needed to get this said. "Not remembering the past is bad enough, but staying around here, hearing that you've met some-one—" he gulped—"I can't do that."

Her eyebrows flew upward. "I don't think you have to worry; that

isn't going to happen. I care about you too. You're the best friend
I ever had."

"But?"

"But it can't be more than that."

His hand squeezed hers, then dropped away. "Because I don't
know the God you know."

"Yes," she whispered. "Our paths are going separate ways, John.
I have to do as my Lord commands. I must answer to Him. I believe
that ultimately He will work things out for good. That is my faith.
And you don't believe that."

"No, I don't," he admitted. "I can't wrap my mind around it, and I
don't understand why someone you think loves you would permit the
things that have happened to you. It's incomprehensible to me—" He
let it go, the empty cavern inside him widening as a wave of sadness
washed across her face.

"It's confusing for you because you have to take God on faith.
There isn't any way you can analyze what I believe or run some diag-
nostic check on it like you do on the computer. You can't devise a
program to work out percentages of how many times God will come
through with what you want and how many times He'll choose a
different path. Logic and statistics don't cut it with God."

John frowned.

"That's the whole point of faith. God's taken the first—the
biggest—step toward us, but we have to accept His gift. Everyone has to
experience Jesus Christ for themselves. Nobody can use someone else's
experience to prove what the Bible says is true. Nobody can take your
place, ask God the questions you want asked, find the answers you
need. You have to find those answers for yourself. God is personal. He
created you as an individual, so you could know Him in your own way."

"So I end up alone again." He let a wry smile lift his lips. "The
story of my life."

"You're not alone, John. Kent and Georgia, Ralna and Fred—
they're here for you. I'm here and I'm glad you're my friend," she
whispered, her eyes glossy with unshed tears. "We'll always try to be

there for you, but I can't promise we won't fail you. Jesus is the only one you can totally count on. And He's here, waiting for you to ask Him to be your friend." Her blue eyes were soft with compassion as she watched him waver.

"I can't," he finally sputtered. "I don't know why. I just can't find that faith you talk about." He swallowed. "For now I guess being friends is going to have to be enough."

Christa stared at her hands. When she finally looked up, there were tears in her eyes. "I'll live with that. It won't be easy because I care about you a lot, and I wish we could build a future together. But in the eternal scheme of things it's more important that you come to know God, that you follow Him. That matters more than anything I want."

She brushed the tears from her eyes before continuing. "Somewhere, somehow the God you don't believe in is going to work this out. He's going to show you that He can make evil turn into good, that He can turn pain into joy. I don't know how, but I know He'll do it."

"Sure." He smiled, nodded, and turned away. Let her have her fantasies. Maybe they would ease the rocky road ahead.

"You don't believe me. But you'll see, John. God will help you see. That's what I'm praying for."

She hadn't said she loved him, only that she cared about him. And she'd talked about God. Again. The bitter ache could not be appeased as he watched her ride away from him to the new world she was creating in the craft shack.

If only he could change it all. But that wasn't in his power. It was up to her God; He was supposed to manage those things.

In his mind he heard the words from Scripture he'd heard her quote: *"I know the plans I have for you. . . . Plans to prosper."*

Christa would prosper—she was that kind of person. She took defeat and reworked it into success.

But not if she connected with Kane Connors again. The man was walking disaster. Her God might not worry about Kane, but John did. At the moment searching for the truth was the only way he knew to keep Christa safe.

He flipped open her laptop and connected to the Internet to begin the most intensive search he'd undertaken since coming to the camp. Until the fund-raiser was over and for as long as he was here, whoever had wrecked Christa's work would have to get by him to get to her.

And he had no intention of making that easy.

"You abandoned her, God," he muttered, "but I won't."

<hr />

Christa pressed the cell phone to her ear. "Are you listening to me, Braydon?" she hissed after checking to be sure the door of the craft shack was still locked. "It has to stop."

"Or what?"

"I won't cover for you anymore."

"Like that's new. Anyway, you have no proof that I did anything," he shot back.

She grasped the paper Rick had returned to her that morning. *Payback!* For what? "Stay away from Camp Hope."

"How are you going to stop me?"

After snapping the phone closed, she slid it into the pocket on the side of her wheelchair. She'd gone as far as she would go. If Braydon came back, she'd let the police deal with everything.

"I tried. I really tried not to get him into trouble. Please let that be enough."

Forcing Braydon out of her mind, Christa picked up a skein of wool and began cutting pieces off it. Braydon would make his choice. She just hoped it would be the right one.

<hr />

He crept through the undergrowth, fully aware of the risks inherent in coming here again when he knew the police had been called out. They even had a picture, though he was almost certain no one would recognize him now.

Necessity drove him. Time was running out—soon another person would be dispatched, if he hadn't been already. He could not fail. If he didn't get the item soon, he would be removed from service. Anonymous's plan depended on recovering the incriminating evidence before October 29. The date was drawing close.

Last chance. Last chance. His brain screamed the reminder as he headed for the main house, the one place he had not searched yet. He knew they were all away. The two older ladies talked constantly, so he could always find out what he wanted to know by listening under their kitchen window.

He'd made up his mind. If he didn't locate the item in this house, he'd snatch the girl. Simple enough to stop someone in a wheelchair. The only ransom he'd ask for would be the item, and he knew he'd get it. With her safety at risk, Mr. John Riddle would cave in and the game would be over.

Footsteps.

He pasted himself against the wall of the house, waiting for them to pass. But they didn't. He risked a look around the corner, then swallowed the epithet that rose.

Amateur night again!

The shock of splintering glass sent him into action. Sometimes force became a necessity.

He called out, "Anybody home?"

The noise stopped immediately. He saw the shadow creep down the steps, seeking a swift retreat.

Closer. Come closer.

The shadow obeyed his silent command until it stood four feet in front of him.

He inched forward, fingering his gloves as he waited for the perfect moment.

The shadow paused beside a tree.

"Time out," the intruder whispered as he struck his victim, rendering him unconscious. Hurting people went against his grain, but when there was no choice—

The low beam of headlights wove shadows through the lane.

"They're back. Now you've spoiled everything." Drawing in deep, calming breaths, he stepped backward into the gloom.

The passengers got out, someone yelled, and then they all rushed toward the body lying on the ground.

The intruder used the noise as a cover to make his escape. He retrieved a bicycle from behind the camp sign and climbed on, pedaling hard.

Twenty minutes later he ditched it to cross a field, cursing his luck as he distanced himself from the place called Camp Hope.

Tonight's opportunity was lost, but he wouldn't give up.

There was always the girl.

CHAPTER FIFTEEN

H ow's the head?" John shifted the ice pack, teeth clenched as he brusquely applied first aid. He'd have liked to apply it on the teen's backside.

"I told you, I'm fine. I have to go home." Braydon's defiant glare could have melted stone.

John forced himself to remain calm and stepped back to resume his position beside Christa. "You're not going anywhere," he assured the petulant youth. "Georgia called your mother. She'll be here soon. In the meantime, why don't you tell us what you were doing here?"

"I don't have to tell you anything. You're not the police or my mother." A sneer curled Braydon's pierced bottom lip.

"I *am* the police. And I'd like some answers. Now." Angie Grant picked up one of his hands and held on by digging in her nails when he tried to tug away. "You've got some nasty cuts here. Got them smashing that window, did you?"

He made an obscene gesture with his other hand.

"Braydon!" Abby Van Meter marched through the door and clamped her hand on his shoulder. "We do not speak to police officers or anyone else in that manner." She glanced around the room. "Would someone explain, please?"

"Perhaps it would be better if Christa told you." Angie turned. "Can you do it, Christa?"

John squeezed her icy fingers, then let them go. Though Christa nodded at the request, he knew she was too calm. She'd remained silent and frozen ever since he'd carried Braydon inside.

"Mom, you can't listen to her."

"Be quiet, Braydon." Abby turned to Christa, her face white, her hands shaking. "Go ahead. Tell me what you think he's done."

Christa touched Abby's arm. Her voice quavered. "I-I think Braydon should tell you himself."

Abby frowned, then faced her son. When he didn't speak, she laid her hand on his head. "Bray, what is this about? Why are you out here?"

He simply stared back at her.

John empathized with the worried mother. What Christa had told them was shocking. The only question John had was why.

"Will someone please explain to me what's going on here? I can feel the tension in this room, and it's making me very nervous. What's wrong?" Abby scanned all their faces.

Christa cleared her voice and opened her mouth.

But Braydon beat her to it. "Penny's crippled because of her."

"Is that why you did it? Is that why—because you blame Christa for Penny's accident? Maybe you should tell us how you figure that." Angie leaned against the doorjamb. "Christa wasn't even there. She had nothing to do with Penny's accident."

"Didn't she?" Hate blazed from Braydon's eyes as they rested on Christa. "You're not going to hurt my family anymore. I fixed that."

Christa gasped. The others remained silent.

Abby recovered first. "What do you mean—you fixed it?" The whispered words seemed sucked from her.

"I'm afraid Braydon is to blame for the damage in the craft shack." Angie's jaw flexed, emphasizing her anger. "Christa suspected him of trespassing several times and tried to get him to stop, but it seems that his hate—or whatever it is—goes too deep."

"Oh no." Abby flopped down into a chair, her head sinking into her hands. "Please tell me you didn't do it. Please say you didn't ruin our weeks of work in some stupid, selfish, jealous fit of anger."

"Our?" Braydon asked. "What do you mean *our* work?"

"I mean this." Abby grabbed the satchel at her feet and began pulling out sheets of paper. "This was *our* business plan. These are the craft designs we were going to sell to summer camps, clubs—anyone who would buy the kits we prepared. This is *our* agreement. Christa offered to make your aunt and me partners if she could get the funding we needed. Partners, Bray. Something with a future, with possibilities . . ." Her voice shook and she had to pause.

"You were working on the crafts? I-I didn't know. I wouldn't have—"

"So you did do it." Abby's whole body seemed to shrink as the grotesque truth sank in. "My own son committed this offensive act against someone who couldn't even defend herself." Abby's eyes were a well of misery. "Take a good look at yourself, Braydon. Then look at these papers. This is what you destroyed—*my* dream for *our* future. I worked like a dog to get these things ready. Christa worked twice as hard as me. We were so excited."

"But I didn't know—"

"Exactly! Without even asking you laid waste to everything we've tried to create. And why? You don't even have a good excuse. Christa didn't hurt Penny—a car did. But you couldn't accept that so you let hate take over until you blamed a woman who's done nothing but help us."

Braydon blustered, no longer quite so cocky. But that didn't help anyone.

Christa was still white with shock. John moved closer, trying to impart comfort.

"You're under arrest, kid." Angie gripped his shoulder.

"I'm not the bad guy here," Braydon bellowed.

"Yeah? How do you figure? You broke into someone's private property and destroyed it. According to the law, that makes you the bad guy. A criminal," Angie stated.

Kent cleared his throat. "What I can't understand is how you could possibly blame Christa for your family's problems."

"I can," Christa said quietly.

John stared at her in disbelief, then sank onto a chair beside her. This he had to hear.

"I don't condone it, but I think I can understand it. You're the one who knocked me over that night, aren't you, Braydon? I recognized your sneakers."

"Knocked you over?" Abby rose, one hand at her throat. "What are you talking about?"

"Why don't you tell her, Braydon?" Angie's voice was hard. "Go ahead, explain leaving Christa lying on the ground, paralyzed, with no one to help her. Tell us how fun it was to keep coming back when she asked you over and over to stay away, when you *promised* you would not come to Camp Hope. Did you and your buddies lock her in that night too?"

Braydon glowered at her. "I didn't lock anything. I only—" He bit his lip.

"Yes, I think it's best you shut up. You should have done it long ago." Angie crossed her arms. "There are no excuses for what you did. I can't believe you could get so out of control. Maybe a youth facility will help you curb that."

"I only wanted to scare her a little bit, pay her back. Someone needed to teach her a lesson. Why are you blaming everything on me?" He pointed at Christa. "Blame her! She's done horrible things, like hurt people who never did anything to her."

"Kind of like you." Abby's face streamed with tears.

"No! I don't go around wrecking people's lives and then wait for them to come running back to me. She invited them to a party, did you know that? All those people she hurt—she invited them to a party, as if nothing was wrong!" He laughed, but it came out harsh and broken.

"To apologize." Christa's whisper was barely audible. "That's why I invited them. To apologize."

"What good would that do? Sally Barrett's old boyfriend still thinks she cheated on him. Do you imagine Emma Simms will ever live down your lies? And what about my aunt? She told me what you were like, the stories you told. How will your apology bring back her baby? You did that! You did all of it."

"Yes, I did."

John heard the pain behind Christa's words, but she offered no excuses.

"Christa knows what she did. Do you, Braydon?" Abby's hands clenched. "There's no one to blame for your hate. You're fifteen, old enough to figure out the facts. Christa's past didn't affect you. It's an excuse you used to justify your own actions. So tell me right now why you did this."

"Why?" Braydon stumbled over the explanation. "Can't you see why? The guys—"

"Hold it right there. Who are the guys? Those lovely gentlemen who helped you destroy your mother's work, maybe painted some graffiti on some cabins one night? Or have we yet to find more damage?" Angie was in his face, and she wasn't budging an inch. "I want names."

"I'm not talking." Apparently peer pressure prevailed as he refused to say more.

"This doesn't make sense. It's not the whole truth. What I did happened several years ago. Why did you wait till now?" Christa's voice wobbled.

As she faced the arrogant boy, John clasped her hand in his, a lump lodging in his throat. She clutched his fingers for a moment, then brushed a hand over her eyes, pushing away the strands of hair that clung to her wet lashes. "There's something more behind your actions, Braydon. Tell us. I'm only the excuse you used. So why me?"

"Because you cheat and lie, and you always get away with it." His face contorted.

"That isn't true." John had to defend her, though he had no idea what this was about.

Christa pressed his fingers in thanks, but her eyes were on Braydon. "What else did I lie about?"

He waited, then burst out, "Our horse!"

"What horse?"

"Like you don't know. Daisy. You can't ride anymore, right? So when she went up for sale in the spring, my dad said we'd buy her and pay you to board her. But you stole Daisy from us and gave her to someone else."

"No, Braydon, I didn't."

His eyes flashed as he surged to his feet. "Liar!" A lone tear squeezed out and rolled down his cheek. "My dad paid for her the day he d-died. We did all kinds of jobs so we could get the money to buy that horse. I kept waiting, wondering why you didn't come over and tell us we could ride her. But you never did and you never brought our money back so my mom could pay our bills."

"You don't understand."

Braydon laughed, a harsh shriek that hurt the ears. "Don't I?" He faced his mother. "I was real mad about her cheating us, but I wouldn't have done anything." He turned to Christa. "Except when I went back to school this fall I found out that you *gave* Daisy away to someone else. We paid for the horse; then you gave her away. So that makes you a thief. 'Thou shalt not steal.' Remember?"

"Your dad was out here." Kent rose and walked over to stand in front of the raging teen. "I spoke to him, not Christa. But he didn't give me any money."

"You're lying!"

"I don't lie," Kent responded, eyes level with Braydon's. "Your father said he had almost enough money to buy Daisy but an unexpected bill came in. He said I should go ahead and sell her because he couldn't afford her. I told him you guys were welcome to come out any time to ride the other horses. He said he'd tell you, but—" Kent's voice dropped—"I guess he didn't get a chance."

"You're trying to protect her." Braydon shook his head. "That's not true."

"Yes, it is, honey. Your father and I discussed it that very morning. Kent is telling the truth. What he didn't tell you is that Christa gave Daisy to a little girl who has cancer."

"Wait a minute," Christa said. "I watched you the couple of times you came to teen camp. You never seemed to like horses, and you sure didn't ride them when you had the chance. Why would you want Daisy?" Suddenly her blue eyes flickered, then widened. "It was for Penny, wasn't it? She's the one who loved that big old horse."

"So?" Braydon dashed a hand across his eyes and sniffed. "What's wrong with that?"

"It's not going to happen, Braydon. Owning Daisy won't make Penny walk again."

John flinched at Christa's direct statement, but his lips remained pinched together.

"That's what you thought, isn't it? That if she only wanted to bad enough, one day she'd get out of that wheelchair. Then she'd be able to go for those rides she always talked about."

"I'm working now. I'll find a way to pay for Daisy and her food. You can't stop me from buying her from those people." Braydon's fists clenched.

"No, I can't. But it won't matter. Even if you bought a thousand Daisys and lined them all up in a row, Penny wouldn't be able to walk again. With some help and some teaching she could ride again, but that's not what this is about, is it?" Rolling near him, Christa met his glare with a soft wistful smile. "With all my heart, I wish she could. I'd gladly give up everything I have if it would help Penny walk again."

"You would?" he asked.

"Of course," Christa answered. "Do you think it's easy for anyone to see her in a wheelchair and not feel compassion? Nobody is happy about Penny's paralysis, especially me. I know what she has to go through and the problems she faces. If I could, I'd turn back time, undo all the things I did, undo Penny's accident."

Braydon stared at Christa, obviously moved by her passionate tone.

"If only I could. But that isn't going to happen, and nothing you do will change it. Penny is paralyzed. We all hate that. But all we can do is try to help her."

"But I thought—"

"I think I understand what you thought. You thought you'd take charge, fix things. But there is no way you can make this go away, Braydon. Nothing can do that. Penny is crippled. Just like me."

He started sobbing. "Maybe if—"

Christa grasped his arm and shook it. "Do you love Penny?"

"Of course." He glared at her, his anger still evident. "What do you think all of this was about?" He waved a hand.

"That wasn't about love. That was about making you feel better, wasn't it?" Christa dared him to deny it.

"I thought—"

"You thought that if you punished someone, if you made them feel the way you've been feeling inside, that would help take away some of your pain. But it won't. I know because I tried to do exactly the same thing after my parents died, and I hurt a lot of people. I did it again after my accident; I blamed everybody but myself."

John glanced around the room. Georgia had tears in her eyes. Kent was beside her, one arm around her shoulders. Abby sat in her chair, her face showing her confusion and pain.

Christa spoke into the silence. "Braydon, were you supposed to meet Penny's bus that day?"

The question came out of nowhere. John studied Christa's face and wondered what he'd missed.

"It was late," Braydon whispered. "I checked twice; then we decided to—"

"Were you supposed to meet the bus and walk Penny home?" Christa interrupted.

"You don't—"

"Were you?" she insisted.

"Yes!" He met her compassionate gaze. Tears streamed down his face, but this time he made no effort to rub them away. "But you already know that. You're the one who kept me at the drugstore. If it hadn't been for you, I'd have been there and my sister wouldn't be crippled. You did it!"

Stark pain bleached all life from Christa's face. She seemed to wither in her chair, shrinking from his tirade. "No," she groaned. "That wasn't my fault. It wasn't."

"Yes, it was! Mr. Gentry told you some kids had stolen some things. You saw the chocolate bars in my hand and right away you figured I was one of them. He grabbed me and called Mr. Mercer, all because of you. If I'd been there to walk her home, Penny wouldn't be crippled now. So it's your fault."

The silence lay thick upon them, painfully heavy, while Kent stared at his sister and Angie chewed her bottom lip. John felt as helpless as all of them.

"It's not her fault." The boom of his own voice surprised John, but he could no longer remain silent and let this beautiful woman take on the burden of something for which she was not to blame. "It is *not* Christa's fault."

"Were you trying to steal the bars, Braydon?" Angie questioned.

"That doesn't matter. She had no proof." But the telltale tide of red suffused Braydon's cheeks. "Penny's crippled because of her."

His mother moved to grasp his chin between her fingers and force him to look at her. "The truth. For once let us have the truth from your lips. You owe your father's memory that much."

"Penny's crippled because of Christa." Braydon gulped and sniffed. "Because of her and because of me." He winced as his mother stepped backward. "I wasn't supposed to be downtown, because you told me to be waiting for Penny at exactly four. The bus was late, and I got tired of waiting. Some of my friends came, and we were going to make s'mores. I thought I could go with them to get the bars and be back before Penny got there." He paused, saw the look on his mother's face, and began to cry. "It's my fault she's like that."

John found himself riveted by Christa. She watched Braydon
weep for the innocence that had been lost that day, her own tears
pouring down her cheeks. Abby stepped forward to wrap her son in
her arms, but Christa touched her arm, shook her head, then reached
out and gripped Braydon's hands between hers.

When she finally spoke her voice was barely audible. "There's
enough guilt to go around, Braydon. You, me, the bus driver, the
driver who hit her. The fault lies with a lot of people. Nobody wants
to admit it because it hurts to think we could have been to blame for
something as terrible as injuring someone."

At least the kid was listening. So was John.

"Penny and I ended up in wheelchairs. Nobody knows why, and
all we can do is figure out how to go on." Christa leaned forward and
put an arm around Braydon's shoulders. "The only way I've been able
to go on after remembering the horrible things I did in high school is
to ask God to forgive me. And then I ask Him to help me not to make
more mistakes, to be a help for people instead of a problem. I can't
undo the past. I can only work on today and maybe tomorrow and
thank Him that He loves me enough to forgive me."

At last the dam broke and he began to sob.

Christa waited several moments, then continued speaking in a
low steady tone. "I need you to understand something, Braydon. You
didn't hurt me with your tricks or your talk or by pushing me over.
You scared me, but you didn't hurt me. And even if you had, I'd
forgive you." She smiled at his blink of surprise. "But you are hurting
Penny."

"Am not!" He jerked away from her.

"You are." She nodded. "Penny knows how you feel, that you hurt
inside, that you're mad and angry. But she thinks you're mad at her
for being crippled. She'd do anything to get out of that wheelchair
just so you wouldn't hate her anymore."

"I don't hate her!" Braydon yelled. "She's not mean and nasty like
you. She's my sister. I love her."

"Then tell her that. Let her know that her being in a wheelchair doesn't make any difference to you, that you love her exactly as she is, no matter what. And when she needs somebody to talk to, a shoulder to cry on, or help to get over a bump, you'll be there. If Penny has her big brother, she doesn't need Daisy or anything else. A big brother makes up for all of that."

John watched the interplay between Kent and Christa, noted the tremulous smile on her lips and the way her eyes softened. Kent's smile matched hers, and he nodded. John gulped. To belong to someone, to be loved for being yourself—he wanted that too.

Head bowed as he mulled over her words, Braydon remained silent for a long time. They all did. Waiting.

Finally he faced his mother. "I'm sorry I wrecked your craft plans, Mom. So sorry."

"I know." Abby hugged him.

"I don't know if you can forgive me." He looked at Christa. "I'm sorry I did it—" his voice grew hoarse—"really sorry."

"I forgive you."

No one seemed to know where to go from here.

Except Braydon. He frowned at Christa. "You know when you caused all those problems for the kids you didn't like, you were around my age."

"That's true, I was." She met his gaze squarely.

"Yeah. Well, maybe you can understand then. My dad and I— we talked a lot about getting that horse, made plans and stuff. When I heard about you giving it to someone else, I got so mad . . ." He let that trail away, scuffed his toe on the floor in shame.

"I understand, Braydon."

"And?" Abby was relentless in her pursuit of justice.

"I'm really sorry," Braydon finished.

"So am I. I wish you'd come and talked to me. Often nothing is what it seems. It's better to talk about it first than be sorry later," Christa admonished gently.

"Yeah—" he cringed—"I'm going to remember that for a long time."

"Good. I'll gladly forgive you if you'll forgive yourself. I did some very dumb things myself not so long ago. That's the thing about hate—it always leads us the wrong way. It eats away at you until you make the wrong decision and things get worse. That's why the Bible talks about love so often. It's a better way." Christa's lips lifted in a tiny smile. "Some of us take a little longer to learn that."

Braydon stood and moved in front of Angie. "I'm a criminal now, aren't I?"

"Trespassing, breaking and entering, vandalism, lighting a fire in a banned area, malicious mischief, theft." Angie's glower didn't change. "Yeah, kid, I'd say you qualify as a criminal."

"Will I go to jail?" His voice was a small squeak, all defiance gone.

"I don't know."

"I do." Christa looked at Angie. "I won't press charges. Neither will Kent. Penny needs her brother to be there for her, not learning new crimes in some juvenile offender facility."

"But he has to pay for what he's done, Chris." John couldn't believe anyone would forgive so easily. "What about justice?"

"Sometimes mercy is more important than justice," she told him quietly. "It's harder to offer but infinitely more fulfilling."

John didn't understand that. Justice had been important to him for too long. Justice for what?

"May I make a suggestion?"

John's admiration for the overworked mother inched up another notch as he watched Abby regroup.

"My son has caused a great deal of damage to Camp Hope, but mostly to Christa. He needs to make retribution. Tomorrow he will quit his job at the store and come out here to work at whatever job she gives him. No matter how long it takes, he will pay for his deeds." She saw him open his lips. "You will also give Constable Grant the names of those who helped you. They should not be allowed on this property again. Nor should you, if the truth were told."

Braydon met her eyes and nodded. "I know. I'll tell her. I'll help with the craft things too. If you want. Anything."

John was amazed as the details were arranged by the group. How could Christa let it go, even allow the kid to help her? He wanted to protest but decided not to. She'd bring God into it. At the moment he didn't want to hear any more about God.

Besides, there was something everyone was forgetting.

"Can I ask a question?" All eyes turned to John as he directed his attention to Braydon. "Do you know who hit you tonight?"

"No. Someone called out right after I'd broken that glass. I snuck out into the yard to look around and—*wham!*—something knocked me over. I knew you'd all be at the church supper tonight, so that's why I came." His face burned red with shame.

"Was it a man?" Angie probed.

"I dunno. I didn't see anything. Just felt this hand come down and that was it." He hung his head. "It wasn't the first time I saw some-body here. I broke the lock on the rocketry shed because I was going to steal something. I was in the corner when a guy came in. He looked straight at me. I was sure he saw me. I was trying to get away when I knocked over your wheelchair, Christa. I didn't mean to bump you, and I wanted to stop and help you, but . . . he had a knife and he scared me."

Christa frowned. "You didn't see his face?"

Braydon shook his head. "It was too dark."

"So we've still got somebody wandering around." Angie tapped her fingernail against the tabletop. "I wonder if *he* knew no one would be here tonight."

The time had come. John coughed.

"He knew. I think he was here to look for his item." He felt the intensity of the group's scrutiny. "But I don't know what that could be." *Or when the intruder would return to collect it.*

John was certain of only one thing: Whoever their visitor was, he would return before October 29.

CHAPTER SIXTEEN

"Can you believe how fast the last month has gone, John?" Christa asked as she rolled into the office. She listened for a moment, then sighed with relief. "Quiet. At last."

She fanned her hands over her hot cheeks and tilted her head back, trying to stretch the band of tension across her shoulders.

"Are you nervous about the fund-raiser? You only have a few more days."

"Who has time to be nervous? It's a zoo out there—Everson family everywhere." She peeked over John's shoulder. "What are you doing?"

"There are a couple of people I still can't track."

"We've had the police off- and on-site for ages. They've seen no one. That man hasn't returned. You've received no threats, have you?" She hated it when he turned away, as if he were hiding something. "Have you, John?"

"No."

"Well, then, why are you buried in here?" She tried to decipher the visual display of emotion he usually hid, but all she could read was concern. "Did you get something more off that CD?"

"No. It's ruined."

"So why—?"

"Because I have to!" He seemed to fight to control his emotions. "I don't care how quiet it's been around here, Chris. I'm more certain than ever that something will happen on October 29. I want you to promise me something."

The edge to his voice surprised her.

"Promise you what? I told you that Simple Gifts contacted us; we didn't contact them this time. But we are going to follow through. If they offer us some kind of start-up capital, Doug Henderson, Georgia's lawyer friend in Calgary, has agreed to check out their terms before we sign anything. Isn't that enough?"

John shook his head.

"What then?" His almost fanatical fixation with the date worried her. With only four days left till the twenty-ninth, Christa was beginning to doubt he would ever know why it bothered him so.

"I want you to promise me that you'll tell me if anything strange happens. Whatever happens."

"Whatever happens?" she repeated, confused by the thread of steel his words contained. "Like what?"

"It could be anything. You've been very determined to keep your plans secret." He held up a hand. "I understand why. I know you're eager to fly away on your own, to prove to Kent that you can manage. You're carrying this load of guilt about holding him back, and you think independence is the way to go."

"What's wrong with independence?"

"Nothing. If that's what it takes to appease your guilt, I guess that's what you have to do." John rubbed his eyes and rolled his shoulders. "The thing is, we're getting close to that date and I haven't been able to find the item. When he returns—"

"When?" Not *if*, but *when*. Christa frowned. "Maybe you'd better explain what you mean."

As he told her about the agreement he'd made with the man who'd held a gun to his back, she grappled with her frustration.

"You bartered this *item* for information about your past?" She couldn't believe he'd done it. "John, that's crazy! You don't even know what the thing is, and you've virtually guaranteed he'll come back for it."

"He would have come back anyway. He knows who I am and what happened to me. Whatever I can't remember, he can tell me." The tension lines around his lips deepened. "I've got to know what I can do to stop whatever is about to happen."

"At any cost?" she asked. "You think he's going to explain everything and then leave you to do your worst? You're not thinking clearly."

"He only wants the item."

"And once he has it, why would he leave you around on the off chance that you might remember something else—about him?" Christa bit her lip. "You're trying so hard to control everything that you've lost your perspective."

Christa looked into her heart and faced the truth she'd kept hidden from herself. She'd hoped for so much and imagined how wonderful life could be if things were only different—if John adopted her faith. She'd let herself believe that the feelings John had aroused in her could somehow be reciprocated. But it wasn't going to happen.

Oh, Father, I've clung to my hopes and dreams, expecting You to make Your plans fit mine. I thought—no, hoped—John was here because You'd sent him for me. I was looking for a way that I wouldn't have to give up this sweet gentle love, but I was wrong. That's not Your will. Help me now.

John touched her arm. "We're getting closer to the twenty-ninth with every hour. I can't stand by and wait for your God to act before someone dies. I have to do something."

She saw that it was pointless to try to reason with him.

When John hit a computer key, a chart appeared on the screen. "These four people have excellent references and good addresses— all the things we agreed attendees at the fund-raiser should have."

"So?" Christa didn't understand what he wasn't saying.

"They don't exist."

"But you just said—" She stopped.

John was a man obsessed. During the past week he'd spent so many hours on the Internet, Kent had voiced his concern about John's mental state. As she looked at John now, Christa understood what her brother meant. Fear and frustration had driven John to this. That date, the gaps in his memory, the constant nag of worry and frustration—all of it had combined to drain him.

"Listen to me." She took his hand off the keyboard and held it between hers. "You've got to stop. It's making you sick."

"I'm fine." After tugging his hand away, he turned back to the screen.

Disregarding his comment, she reached out and switched off the computer. He scrambled to reboot, but she put her hand over the power button. "John!"

"What?" He wouldn't look at her. He bore the signs of strain and no longer resembled the well-kempt man she was used to seeing. His hair straggled around his eyes, he hadn't shaved, and his clothes were wrinkled. Her heart ached for him, but she would not weaken.

He reached past her toward the computer.

Christa grabbed his wrist. "Stop it!"

"I have to stop them. There are only four days left. Four days and someone will die because I didn't do something. I can't live with that, Christa. I can't!"

For a moment she hesitated because his grief was real, but his panic was overwhelming reason. She'd have to deal with that first. Christa placed her palms against his cheeks, forcing his gaze to hers. "No one's going to die. Do you hear me?" She slipped her fingers through the strands of hair, brushed them back off his face. "God is in control, not men. So first of all, we're going to pray. Then you're going to get some rest."

"I can't rest. Don't you see?" John tried to pull away, but she wouldn't let go.

"Listen to me." Dropping her hand to his shoulder, she pressed her thumb against the stiff muscles. "Your brain is trying to help you. It wants to cooperate and give the answers you need, but if you won't relax it can't do its job."

She kept talking, her voice calm, quiet, soothing. Eventually John's tense shoulders sagged, though his eyes grew dark with inner turmoil.

Her heart went out to him, so she took the problem to the only help she knew. "God, I pray for John right now. He's worried about something we have no control over. None of us understands what's happening and we don't know where to turn, so we are looking to You to protect us. Please help John. Give him clarity and under-standing. We thank You that You care for us. We ask in Jesus' name. Amen."

When she opened her eyes, he was looking at her, his expression incomprehensible.

"You think your God heard?"

"I know it. Don't try to figure out how," she told him. "Don't argue; don't fight. Go to your trailer and lie down. God wants to help, but He needs you to take your hands off. You have to have faith in Him, in His wisdom, in His love. Can you do that?"

"I don't know." After a moment he leaned forward to rest his chin against her forehead. "I'm so tired," he whispered, his breath soft and warm against her ear.

"Let go. Surrender to God."

His forehead pleated. "But if they—"

"Hands off. It's God's way or nothing. You don't get to give Him suggestions." She cupped his hand with hers, then pressed a kiss into his palm. "There's no other way but to trust and wait on God's timing."

John's eyes widened at the caress.

"I have to go. Georgia needs help. We'll talk later. But for now—rest."

She knew he wanted to respond. His mouth worked uselessly for several moments, but exhaustion won and he finally capitulated. "All right. I'll go." He pulled a whistle from his pocket. "If you need help, promise you'll blow this."

"John, I'll be—"

"Promise." He pressed the cold metal into her hand.

Christa looked down at it, then at him. The shadows still clung to him; the terror hadn't left. John was a man desperately seeking answers. This one thing she could do for him.

A wash of love rushed over her, its intensity filling her soul with a deep, rich ache. *I don't care about walking, God. I don't need Simple Gifts or the career they promise. Take it all—take my dreams and aspirations—but give me John. Please let me have his love.*

She knew the answer was no even before the still small voice whispered in her ear, *I am the Way.*

Yes, You are, Lord. She squeezed her eyes closed and whispered a plea for strength to face the future alone.

"Take the whistle, Chris. I won't ask anything else."

"Okay." She stuck the whistle into the side of her chair. "Now go and rest."

He nodded, left the office. She watched him stumble across the uneven ground, then step inside his trailer as if he were an old man.

Letting him go would be as simple and as necessary as that. And she would do it no matter how much it cost her. Because John was not hers. John was in God's hands. A man like him didn't belong with someone as needy as she. John deserved to return to his normal life and live happily ever after. That was exactly what Christa wanted for him.

Christa pushed the laptop to the back of the desk and flicked on the office computer, intending to check her e-mail. Her eye caught a new icon on the screen titled simply *Files*. Clicking on it, she found that John had created a comprehensive system of recording the information he'd obtained about each guest. The ones he'd been concerned about were highlighted. She opened each of those files side by side.

Names, addresses, and telephone numbers. All in order. Work

numbers for two, not for the others. All had references with a tiny check beside them. So what was his concern?

On a whim she picked up the phone and dialed the first number. "Yes?"

A little surprised by the gruff response, Christa hesitated. "Who is this?"

"I'm sorry. I think I must have the wrong number. I'm looking for—" she stared at the file—"Edwin O'Shaughnessey."

"Nobody here by that name."

"I'm sorry I bothered you. Thank you." Christa hung up quickly while her mind sorted through what she'd learned. Should she put Mr. O'Shaughnessey down for cancellation or had the number simply been recorded incorrectly?

"Excuse me?"

Stifling a scream, Christa whirled around to stare into the narrow face of a tall man with the greenest eyes she'd ever seen. They had to be colored contacts. "Yes?" she whispered.

"My name is Hiram Deal. I'm with the FBI. I must speak to the man you have staying here." He looked at the computer screen.

"May I see your identification, please?" Christa pretended to reach for a tissue and in the process minimized the screen. "We've had some trouble recently and . . . well, I'll need to see your ID."

"Of course." He held up his badge so she could see it. "Good enough?" His hawklike stare scanned the desk and rested on the laptop.

She reached out to take the badge, but he wouldn't release it. "First rule in the bureau, ma'am. Don't let go of your gun or your badge."

"I see." A prickle of apprehension tap-danced down her spine. The man looked honest enough, but she couldn't ignore her senses. Her fingers went to the pager hanging from her chair and she pushed it hard. One, two, three. The signal for come quickly. "You certainly took long enough to show up," she muttered, stalling for time. "My brother called months ago." Kent hadn't called; Rick had.

"I've been on another case. No one told me he'd called until last week. I came as soon as I could."

Indeed. But came from where? Christa noted his intent scrutiny of the little office, always returning to her laptop. "Why are you here now?"

"To question this John fellow. We're trying to track down all leads in a case we've been working. I was hoping he might remember something."

"He doesn't." Kent stood in the doorway, with John directly behind him. Both were breathing fast, and both kept their eyes on Christa until she smiled and nodded.

The agent turned, his eyes narrowing as they appraised John. "You can't tell me anything?"

John studied him for a moment, then shook his head. "Nothing."

"You do have identification, of course." Kent waited until Agent Deal flashed his badge, then grasped the man's arm before he could take it away. "I'll need to check this out."

Surprise widened the agent's odd eyes. "Check me out? With who?"

"If you wouldn't mind waiting outside the door on that chair, we'll get to your questions as soon as we answer mine." Kent motioned to the chair, raised an eyebrow.

"Sure. Okay." Agent Deal turned. "I don't know why you're so suspicious. The FBI doesn't venture into foreign territory without good reason."

"I'm sure that's true. Excuse me?" After Kent closed the door behind him, he studied Christa. "Well?"

"I don't know. Calls himself Agent Hiram Deal. He gave me the creeps."

"Good enough reason for me." Kent grabbed the phone and dialed. "I'll see what Rick has to say." But the Mountie wasn't in the office and Angie was also out.

"I'm probably bothering you for nothing," Kent said into the receiver, "but some guy showed up here claiming to be an agent for the FBI—he did? . . . Oh, I see. Well, thanks." He hung up.

"What's wrong?"

"Nothing, for once. The dispatcher said Agent Deal stopped by the police station before heading out here to tell them he was going to question John. Seems like we've gone to a lot of fuss for nothing."

"He wears the wrong shoes."

From the look on Kent's face, he was as surprised by John's words as Christa was. "Pardon?"

"Agent Deal." John glanced out the window but seemed to look far beyond the camp. "He doesn't wear the right shoes." He shuddered. "I don't know why I said that. It just came into my head."

"I see. Well, from here it looks like he's wearing some kind of black shoe, but beyond that I can't tell you much more. If that matters." Kent looked at Christa. "Let's go outside and hear his questions."

But Agent Deal ran out of questions when the first two couldn't be answered. "You're telling me you have no idea why you're here and that you arrived with nothing. That is your statement?" Again the agent's flick of interest to the laptop.

"Yes." John met his disdain head-on. "That's exactly what I'm saying."

"You've recalled nothing in all this time?"

"He remembers Sally," Christa mumbled, then saw John shake his head.

"Who?" Agent Deal seemed interested.

"Just a name. Not a person, a name. And I don't know why."

A burst of laughter from the hot-tub area drew their attention. The Eversons were a large, happy family who loved talking but enjoyed laughing even more. Someone was always playing a trick on another. Their presence was helping to ease some of the strain the residents of Camp Hope had been feeling.

"Seems odd to see children out of school this time of year." Agent Deal frowned at the little boy who chased his ball over to the office. One glance at the agent's cranky face, and the boy wailed for his mama.

"It's only a few days for the parents' anniversary. I think it's wonderful." Georgia had joined them moments earlier, and now she beckoned to Kent.

They whispered together for a few moments; then Kent excused himself. "I'll be back shortly."

Agent Deal merely nodded as his fingers tapped against his thigh. "I understand that after this bunch leaves, another group will be arriving."

"Yes. We have a fund-raiser scheduled next. But most of our guests have already been cleared." Once more Christa had the funny feeling that John wanted her to be quiet. She resented that because she wanted to ask about the agent's unusual ring.

"Perhaps I can help. What are the names of those you're concerned about?"

"It's all right." John stepped forward. "The local police are handling it."

"Great. Well, then, I guess I'd better be off. I have a couple of things to check on. But I'll be back for the fund-raiser. I intend to make sure that nothing happens to our boy here." He slapped John on the shoulder in a hearty clap that echoed around the room in a flat tone.

John said nothing, but his mouth was tight.

"I'm sorry, but if you didn't prebook, we can't possibly accommodate you," Christa said, wishing they'd left some extra space and not been so concerned about filling every nook. It would be good to have the FBI on hand.

"Agent Deal, you're welcome to stay in the speaker's cabin next to our house. It's pretty old and needs a lot of work, but as long as it doesn't rain, you should be fine. If you really intend to stay, it's the best we can do." Kent was back, his manner composed.

"A bed is all I require. Thank you." After a few more platitudes, Agent Deal was soon driving out of the camp.

Kent turned to John, his manner now urgent. "Do you know the guy in the end cabin, nearest the fence?"

"I know who you mean. He's the only one of that Everson family who doesn't join in with the others. Keeps himself on the outside, watching. Why?"

"Earlier Georgia saw him prying open the old van. Why, is anyone's guess. I only had it towed here for the parts I could use on the new one I hope to get. And because you insisted."

John's face turned a pasty white. "Did he take anything?"

"Not that we know of. What would he take?"

"Since I already have the CD, I don't know." John grabbed his head between his hands. "But he must believe there's something else." He twisted around, stared at Christa. "Maybe he's the one who made the key."

"You mean the person whose backpack you found?" Christa drew in a breath. "But that would mean he's been around for about two months!"

John only nodded.

"The fellow Rick said might be camping out in a tent?" Kent's voice dropped. "The campgrounds are near the Murdock sisters, and they've reported a trespasser." He thought for a moment. "Christa, call Angie or Rick. Tell them what we know. John, you and I need to search the grounds. "

"Yes. And Fred. Let's get Fred to help." John glanced at Christa.

"I'll be fine. You guys go ahead. I'll lock up and head over to the dining hall. Georgia must be wondering why I'm not there helping. I feel a little safer with this Agent Deal around, especially since he checked in with the local police."

"Maybe he'll scare away whoever's been prowling around." Kent ushered John outside, then pulled the door closed.

After Christa made sure everything was turned off, she tucked John's notepad at the bottom of the in-basket. On a whim, she slid the laptop behind the filing cabinet. She flicked off the lights, locked the door, and started to turn her chair.

"Be quiet and you won't get hurt."

Across the way Christa could hear the hot tubbers talking and laughing. Through the dining-hall windows, Georgia was visible whipping something in a huge stainless bowl. The fall decorations wavered in the breeze over strategically placed bales that had transformed Camp Hope into a ranch. Everything was perfectly normal.

No one noticed that she was being kidnapped.

CHAPTER SEVENTEEN

Do exactly as I say. Understand?" The press of strong fingers against Christa's throat demanded a silent response.

She nodded.

"Good. Now make this thing move. You and I are going for a walk. Nice and easy, no sudden moves. We wouldn't want anyone to get hurt, would we?"

The thought of bringing more shame to Camp Hope made Christa cringe. It had been bad enough before. Who knew what would happen to Kent's reputation if one of the guests was injured?

Her abductor kept to the shadows, with his collar up and the bill of his cap down. There was something familiar about him. . . .

"I don't know what you're looking for, but I don't have it," she told him boldly.

"I know." He pointed. "Through here. Now. Good thing we have this path. Our boy built it, didn't he?" His low gravelly laugh had an ominous tone. "Never knew him to even hold a hammer in his lily-white hand before. You must be a miracle worker, lady."

They were almost at the entrance of camp.

"Nothing is impossible with God," she mumbled, her confidence shaken at the sight of the black minivan waiting less than two hundred feet away.

"Then He should be able to help Johnny-boy get his memory back, shouldn't He? Either way, I have to have what he stole."

Though she went as slowly as she could, Christa knew it was only a matter of time until she was forced into the van. *Oh, Lord, hear my prayer. Help me now, please. Show me a way out.*

The van was only five feet away.

There was no way out.

⇒◆⇐

John sat, hands on the keys of the office computer. But for the first time in many months he could think of nothing to type in.

He wanted to. He longed to lose himself in a project that would bring the answers he craved. If only he could punch in the real name of the man who'd occupied the last cabin, the same one who'd been searching the camp van. The man they'd searched for but couldn't find.

Steven Everson was a fake. The family had never heard of him and assumed the name was a coincidence, that he was there because he had some connection to the camp. John clamped his lips together as anger surged up like a geyser inside. For the past three days the interloper had free reign of the camp, and no one knew what he'd found.

"John?" Kent pushed open the office door. He nodded at Fred before his gaze settled on the blank blue screen. "What are you doing?"

"Nothing. That seems to be the only thing I'm good at." He clicked on the shut-down command. It was futile to sit here any longer. "Fred and I came back here after our check of the grounds, thought we'd wait for the cops. Did you find anything?"

Kent shook his head. "Nothing to find. The place is as clean as

230

a whistle. I got a message on my pager. Christa says Rick's on his way out."

"How long do you think this guy's been here?"

"Hard to tell. Since we don't know where he is now—" Kent shrugged. "That's why I asked Fred to stick with you. Whatever he wants, it obviously has to do with you. Is he the one who stopped you when those kids were here?"

John nodded. "I think so, though he looked different when he became an Everson."

"Why the frown?"

"We have preliminary stuff on almost everybody who's coming to the fund-raiser, so it shouldn't be too hard to watch the four or five we couldn't pin down." John stared at the huge wall calendar, trepidation tiptoeing down his spine. "It's after that I'm worried about."

"That date still bothering you?"

"More than ever."

"You haven't said much about it lately."

"What's to say?" John raked a hand through his hair. "October 29. Something is going to happen on that day. That's all I know."

"You know what Christa would tell you, don't you?" Kent's mossy green eyes narrowed. "God has a way, He's in charge, and He'll figure it out. And she's right." He glanced around. "Speaking of Christa, where is she, anyway? I was sure she'd be here going over some last-minute checks."

"She's helping Georgia in the kitchen. Tomorrow morning the Eversons are going to get a huge breakfast and—what?"

Kent's face drained of color.

"They're not going to get a huge breakfast?"

"Christa's not with Georgia. I was just there. Georgia thought she'd gone to bed, that maybe she was too tired to help." His brows lowered. "She'd hit her pager if she was in trouble, wouldn't she?"

John closed the folder that contained all the info they had on their fund-raiser guests. He bit his lip. "Climbing meekly into bed the day before her big event doesn't sound like your sister, Kent. She's been going flat out to get every detail in place. Do *you* think she would simply leave things to us, especially knowing that Steven Everson is an impostor?"

Kent said nothing, simply headed out the door.

"We're right behind you," John said.

They made short work of the distance between the office and the house. A light was on inside, but it was only the lamp Kent always left on. No matter how much they called, Christa did not appear.

"This isn't right." John's old fear crawled up his back. "Fred and I will go around this side of the camp; you go that way. Check every building. She's got to be here somewhere."

A moment later Kent disappeared into the trees on his second check of the grounds. John followed the access road that led into the camp, waving his flashlight back and forth across the ground. Fred did the same on the opposite side of the road.

A glint in the grass to his left caused John to reverse direction. Silver on straw. He bent over to pick up a pager from the spray of chaff. His heart hit his feet. "Fred!"

He waited until the other man was near, then held out his palm. "Christa must have dropped it. That's why she didn't use it. Keep looking."

Fred nodded, then returned to his side of the road.

John walked a few steps farther, scouring the ground. There was nothing. And why would there be? Christa had no reason to go to the road.

"Maybe she's working on something," Fred called. "Another of her famous Christa surprises. And apparently it has something to do with straw." He held up a few golden straws.

Fred's words did nothing to alleviate the dread that dragged at John's spirit. "You're her God," he muttered, glaring at the diamond-bright stars that looked as though they'd been tossed into the black velvet sky. "Why don't You do something? Why don't You help me find her?"

The lack of response was no surprise. He didn't really believe in

God, couldn't imagine that someone really cared what happened to him. But Christa believed. "For Christa's sake, please help me."

John thrust the pager into his pocket. As he turned to leave, his hand brushed a rosebush, and when he yanked it away the thorns pricked his thumb. Snagged on a tiny branch near the bottom was a bit of blue silk shot through with silver threads. Christa's scarf.

"My banner of courage."

He stared at it, too stunned to absorb what seeing it here meant.

"Faith, John. Faith and trust. That's what God is all about."

God had left him this clue? Ridiculous!

"What are you guys doing?" Braydon Van Meter appeared out of the bushes behind Fred, and they moved beside John. All three stared down at the silky swath in his hands. "She dropped it when she was going with that guy. I was going to pick it up, but I figured I'd tear it trying to get it off those thorns."

"What guy?"

"The guy in the black minivan. You know, he was part of that Everson bunch," Braydon explained. "I was getting some stuff for Georgia from the house and I saw them."

"The guy from the end cabin?" The words flew out of John in a rage. How could he have been so stupid? God hadn't sent a clue, because if there was a God, He would never have let Christa be involved in whatever was going on.

"Yeah, that's him. He was really pushing her hard. Her chair kind of got bogged down and he yanked it sideways, then lifted her and it into the van. I'm pretty sure he doesn't know much about paraplegics."

"The guy's not an Everson," Fred said solemnly.

"We think he's the one who's been causing all the problems here, probably the same one who knocked you out that night, Braydon." The words hissed out of John in a whisper of fury. "Where did they go?"

Braydon's eyes grew huge; he looked scared stiff. "I-I don't know. Down the road. I wasn't paying a lot of attention." He looked away from John. "I think they turned. Yeah, I remember they did, because I wasn't sure he'd make the corner. He was driving awfully fast."

"Where?"

"Stop yelling at me." Braydon closed his eyes. "Toward Parsons' corner, I think."

John scrambled for a solution, heaving a sigh of relief at the sight of the patrol car turning into the lane. He told Rick the story as he climbed into the car. "He'll stash her somewhere, then come and ask for the item."

Rick nodded. "We might need help. Fred, you tell Kent, and then you two stay here. Come on, Braydon."

"A rescue mission? Excellent." He'd barely closed the car door before they were spinning out of the camp and down the road.

John hoped they weren't too late.

He couldn't lose Christa.

<hr>

"In times of trouble, may the Lord respond to your cry. May the God of Israel keep you safe from all harm. May He send you help from His sanctuary and strengthen you from Jerusalem."

Over and over the words whispered through Christa's heart as she bounced along in the van. One of the seats had been removed, which told her that this abductor had been prepared. She gripped the armrest of the seat beside her to minimize the jostling, but no way could she reach the door. She concentrated on praying, on centering her mind on the one who'd cared so much He'd sent His only Son.

"Please give me the right words. Help me know what to say, how to get information from him."

"Stop whispering. No one can hear you."

"God can."

He ignored that.

"Where are we going?" she asked.

"Nowhere. That's all there is here—a whole lot of nothing."

How could anyone be so blind? "You have no idea what you're missing with that attitude."

"You think?" He glared at her through the rearview mirror, his face in shadow, his voice a growled whisper. "I listened to your soiree, lady. All that hokey singing wasn't real exciting. Give me the city any day."

"Which city?" Maybe he'd give her a clue to his identity, to why he'd taken her.

"Chicago. You ever go out on that harbor, sail around in the summer, let the breeze carry you across the water?" His voice changed, softened. "Now that's a rush."

"You own a sailboat?" Christa used both hands to grasp the armrest as they turned.

"Me?" He scoffed at that. "Not hardly. But I sure wouldn't mind. Me and my kid used to take the 'L' and ride down to the Gold Coast. Now that's a view."

The "L"? She'd heard that before. Christa closed her eyes, concentrating. John had mentioned it, so he knew Chicago.

They were slowing down.

"Where are we?" She folded her hands together on her lap, sending prayers heavenward as she tried to find a landmark—anything. Only then did she realize that dark shades covered all but the windshield and the two front side windows.

"We're in the middle of nowhere. I thought that's what you liked." His laugh held a sour undertone that spoke of his frustration. The van jounced for painful minutes before it finally jerked to a halt. He jumped out. For a moment Christa thought he'd leave her, but then the side door slid open. She could see they were in someone's field. Bales of straw were piled high, concealing them from anyone who happened to pass by on the road.

The man had put on something that hid his face. The moon pushed out from between some clouds. She could see a space in the bales barely big enough for her chair. When more bales were added, she'd be completely hidden.

"Come on. Time to get out." He half pulled, half dragged her chair to the opening of the van. After he wrenched her chair free, it smacked the ground with a thump that jarred her whole body and sent a thousand pains shooting up her neck.

"Hang on. This will be rough."

She cried out at the jolting route he shoved her over. "Please don't do this. I don't have whatever it is you want. I don't know how to get it."

"Our boy does," he said. "Don't worry. It's not you I want. Or him, actually. More what he has. Had." Her abductor continued to roll her forward until she was tucked in where he wanted. "You'll be fine. The bales should keep you warm. For a while."

She watched him pat the straw around her, thankful that at least she wasn't being tumbled around anymore. When he paused, she looked him directly in the eyes but saw nothing she would be able to use to identify him. If she ever got out of here. "Why are you doing this?"

"You're bait."

"For what? I don't know anything. John doesn't know anything. The CD he found is ruined, and it doesn't tell us anything we didn't already know about the Society for Order." Christa's bravado was slipping. She was totally immobilized, but she would not go quietly. Maybe if she could get his attention off her—

"You're not going anywhere, so don't get any ideas." He ripped the connections off the battery on her chair, then walked away.

A few minutes later he returned carrying rope. "The Society for Order doesn't exist anymore. Not that it matters. It was only a cover anyway. A ruse to draw attention away."

The man had the rope around her wrists before she could protest. Christa wanted to push him away, scream for help, anything to be free of his malevolence, but she also wanted more information. So she sat compliant, waiting while he tied knot after knot. *Oh, God, please help me. Please help me!* "A front for what?" she whispered, when he stood back to admire his handiwork.

"You'd be surprised." He shook his head. "Never mind."

"What's next?"

"Now I bait a trap and a certain man we both know will finally give me what I'm after. I have to be sure he hasn't leaked that information to anyone. The council is going to know they can trust me."

"What council?" She saw the gag in his hand and rushed into speech. "You won't get away with this."

"Sure I will. Who's going to stop me?"

"The FBI, for one. One of their agents showed up at camp this evening. He and the RCMP will stop you and put you in jail." She stopped because he looked like he'd been frozen in time.

His hand dropped to his side, the handkerchief he'd intended as a gag clenched in his fingers. "This . . . agent. What did he look like?"

"Why do you care?"

"Tell me," he ordered, his voice low, brimming with threat.

"Tall, big. Green eyes, really green. Kind of too green, if you know what I mean." She shrugged. "I guess he wears contacts."

"I guess." He seemed different, introspective. "What was this agent wearing?"

"What you'd expect an FBI agent to wear, I guess. A suit and tie. John was bothered by his shoes, though I don't know why. They were black." She shrugged. "He had a diamond ring to die for though."

"A ring." The kidnapper's body language changed. He seemed to slump a little, as if the stuffing had been knocked out of him. "So he came. He's here. That's it for me then. I have to go."

The words were so softly spoken that Christa could barely catch them. She wanted to find out what he meant, but it was too late. The gag was already in her mouth and he was tying it in place.

"The bales will keep you warm till someone finds you." He stacked them up around her until they were several inches above her head. Then he moved out beyond the bales.

There wasn't a lot of light, but what moonlight had shone down on them disappeared.

Christa sat in her cocoon and waited. What was she supposed to do now? A noise drew her attention. Her abductor was speaking—to himself? No, she heard a faint crackle, something like Rick's police radio. She nudged a bale with her shoulder. It moved only a fraction, but that was enough to let her overhear some of the conversation.

"I'm out. I don't care if the council has tripled the amount. I'm finished."

Another voice argued. "Not yet. You have to find out who else has that evidence, and he's the only one who knows. Someone leaks it down the road and . . . you know what could happen."

Static cut off the rest of the conversation.

So John was safe—for the moment. Which meant the item was the evidence they wanted.

The voice came back through the static. ". . . Simple Gifts . . . kill . . . Kane C—"

"Justice will be done the day after tomorrow. I know. I've heard it all before. He should have let me do it my way. Now there's another player so I'm out."

". . . get caught . . . anonymous . . . don't know you—"

"I'm a dead man. That's why I'm going."

Christa heard a rustling in the straw but no other voices. Then the sound of an engine starting cut through the night air. He was leaving! She twisted her head from side to side, trying to work the gag free, to no avail. A moment later the whine of the motor faded until she could hear nothing but silence.

The reality of her situation hit home. Even if she could somehow get her hands free, maybe push off some bales, she would still be stuck out here—alone. No one knew where she'd gone or even that she'd been taken.

No one but God.

Help!

※——◆◆◆——※

John's fingertips tingled from their death grip on the dashboard, but he didn't release them. At least he could feel the pain, knew it wasn't an illusion or some phantom memory that might disappear if he looked too hard.

"You'll have to tell me exactly where you saw them turn." Rick's calmness surprised John, but one glance at the other man's face told him Rick was totally focused. He'd already told his office to send Angie to the camp. Now to find Christa.

"I didn't. Braydon said he thought it was—" John whirled around—"where did you say?"

"Parsons' corner. Do you think this guy has a hideout on their place?"

"There was another trespasser on the Parsons place last night." John reminded Rick of that conversation.

"We never found anyone." Rick's lips tightened.

"Wow! You drive like a racer." Braydon waited till they'd made the curve, then wheezed out a laugh of admiration. "Ronnie Parsons is a friend of mine. Since his mom saw the trespasser, she could tell us what she saw and where. The guy wouldn't pull into their yard, would he?"

"No, he's not that stupid. He'd have a place he could hide her," Rick muttered. "But the Parsons own a lot of land. Unless we can pinpoint the exact area where this guy took her—"

"Maybe beside a field," John offered, then realized they were surrounded by fields. "I found a few bits of straw by her pager."

"The bales." Braydon's eyes glowed with excitement in the green luminosity of the dash as he leaned forward between John and Rick. "The Parsons have this big stack of bales. Ronnie and I jumped off them a few weeks ago when I came here after we lit those—" He avoided Rick's hard stare and continued. "Anyway, it would be the perfect place to park his van, don't you think? Drive in here. I'll get Ronnie to show us."

"If he's home." John's fist clenched.

"He's home. He's got a big history paper due tomorrow." As soon as the car stopped, Braydon was out and up the steps, pounding on the front door.

A minute later another boy followed Braydon back to the car and threw himself inside. "Hi. Go through the yard till you come to the first left. Take it." He waited until Rick had made the turn. "Now past those trees make a hard right. It's a little rough."

"It's fine. Make sure your belts are buckled." Rick followed the road that soon turned into ruts, picking his path with care but also with haste. "What now?"

"Now you go about half a mile. You can see it once we get past these granaries and that bluff of spruce. There. See it. Go left. Left!"

The earth had been recently worked, forcing Rick to fight to keep the car moving in the right direction as he peered through the windshield.

"There's where we jumped. Only it's been moved around. See, Ronnie?" Braydon's enthusiasm sent his voice up an octave.

"Yeah, I see. But there's nobody here."

"We'll take a look. Maybe we've got the wrong place." Rick slewed the car around.

As soon as it shuddered to a stop, John bailed out, listening in the sudden silence as Rick cut the engine.

"Christa? It's me. Where are you?" He scrutinized the darkness. Then he heard soft muffled sounds. "You hear that? She's here." He grinned at Rick, then yelled, "I'll find you, Chris. Keep making that noise."

Conscious of Rick on his radio, John paced alongside bale piled upon bale until he could clearly hear the sound. He called to the others and the four of them began lifting away the bales. John wanted to shout for joy when Christa's white face appeared at last. He shoved away the barriers, removed the gag from her mouth, and grabbed her shoulders, fully aware that his hands were shaking so badly he couldn't possibly untie the knots in the ropes binding her hands together.

"Christa Anderson, you scared me out of ten years." He gathered her into his arms, snuggling her face into his neck.

"Are you all right, Christa?" Rick scanned the area as he slid a knife from his belt and slashed the ropes.

"I'm fine. He left right before you arrived." Her breath fanned

John's neck as she told him what she knew. "He was talking to someone on a radio, I think. He said justice would be done the day after tomorrow." She lifted her head to stare at John. "They think you have some sort of evidence. The person on the radio said they needed to find out who else had it, that it could come back to haunt him. Something like that."

Rick turned to the boys. "Start looking for some kind of radio in these bales. If you see it, don't touch it. We might be able to trace a call or get fingerprints."

After the boys scurried away, Rick looked at Christa. "I've got officers following up on the minivan Braydon described." He closed his eyes and sighed. "I apologize, Christa. I should have had someone guarding you, but I figured that since John was the one—" He shook his head. "Stupid, stupid."

"You can't guess their every move, Rick," she whispered.

"From now on, I'm not even going to try. But I am going to get some help. You're sure you're okay?"

She nodded.

"Good. Now tell me everything, slowly this time."

John sat holding her, listening as that trembling husky wobble in her usually strong voice resonated straight to his heart. His arms tightened around her until every cell of his being recognized that Christa belonged with him.

"At first he said he had to get the evidence," she said. "He had it all planned. Exchange me for the item."

Because of him she'd danced with danger. They'd threatened this tiny woman who possessed the courage of a champion to get at him. John's heart burned with rage, but he stuffed it down. For now. "It's okay," he said quietly, the satin caress of her cheek beneath his lips. "He won't hurt you, I promise. He's gone."

"It's not me he wants to hurt!" She pushed her hands against his chest. "It's you, John!" Tears washed down her cheeks in black rivers of mascara that dripped off her chin onto his shirt. She choked back a sob. "He's after you."

"I'm fine, Chris. Everything is okay." John drew her back into his arms, slid one hand down her back, trying to comfort her while his mind tossed possibilities back and forth.

"Did he say anything else?" Rick prompted.

"The c-council," she hiccuped. "He talked about the council knowing it could trust him."

"You mean the Society for Order?" John murmured.

She shook her head, her hair draping over his arm when she tilted her head back to look at him. "He said it didn't matter that the Society for Order was finished. He said it was a cover."

"A cover?" John looked at Rick, who shrugged.

"Yes. Later he told the person on the radio that he didn't care if the council tripled the amount." She paused. "You know, the person who left the rat on the doorstep mentioned the council too. I know I should have told you about that and I was going to, but then things got busy and I forgot and . . ."

John barely heard the rest of what she said.

The council.

Shadows, threats, danger. The council wanted . . .

He cursed his blank memory. *Where are You, God of the universe? Why don't You help us?*

"I heard bits and pieces of stuff. Something about anonymous."

Anonymous. The ringleader. John's pulse rate increased, and droplets of perspiration formed on his brow, though the evening breeze was cool. His palms began to sweat. Anonymous knew that he—

"Steven Everson—or whatever his name is—got very strange after I mentioned Agent Deal. He was in a rush to go then."

"Good. At least he left you alone." Rick's mouth was a tight white line. "You both stay here. John, you hang on to my walkie-talkie. If you see anything, call in. I'm going to look around and see if this guy is still in the area. I've got my staff checking the highways. We should find him soon. Then we'll finally know what this is about." Rick stalked to his car, then drove across the field as he talked on the car radio.

Christa shivered. "I have never been so scared in my life."

John stared into the pale blue pools of her eyes and almost drowned before her icy fingers burrowed against his neck, dragging him back to reality.

Remorse brimmed over. All of this had happened because of him. "I'm so sorry, Christa. It's my fault he grabbed you, but he won't do it again. I promise I'll take care of you."

"You can't take care of me," she told him, her eyes tracing the features of his face as her thumb rubbed a spot on his jaw. "Thank you for offering, but this is bigger than both of us."

"What do you mean?" John rebelled against her words. He had to protect her. If he didn't . . .

"I believe this goes far beyond Camp Hope, even beyond you." Her quiet, controlled tone surprised him, until he looked into her eyes and saw the shadows lingering. That's when he realized she was clinging to her courage by a thread.

"He didn't want to be here; he said this land is a whole lot of nothing." A shuddering breath whooshed out from between her lips. "He said he was from Chicago," she whispered, "and that he and his child used to take the 'L' to the Silver Coast—something like that."

"Gold Coast," he corrected. "It's along Lake Shore Drive, has apartment buildings looking out over the lake. The 'L' is the elevated train, which is also a subway in some parts of Chicago." John frowned at the sudden flash of info.

"All he wants is the item." Christa pinned John with her stare. "Do you know what the item is?"

"No." The futility of raging against his defective memory struck him as foolish when Christa had just been kidnapped. "I don't know. But don't worry. Kent, Rick, and I won't let him hurt you or anyone else." He brushed the hair from her eyes and let his hand remain until the warmth of her skin penetrated his fear.

She snuggled her face against his palm as if starved for comfort. "He's . . . driven. I'm not sure we'll be able to stop him."

"Maybe we can—together. You're a very strong woman, Christa.

But if there is a God, He didn't intend for you to do this by yourself. You keep saying God sent me to Camp Hope, that He had a reason. I think this is that reason."

"You didn't hear Steven Everson. If *he's* scared and he *knows* what's going on, I think you need to be very careful." Her whispery tone was a mere ghost of the voice he'd fallen in love with. "He's desperate."

Desperate because of that date. In John's mind, the words were clearly printed. *The council chose October 29 as the first day of their new agenda.*

Christa wriggled next to him. "I wish we could leave."

"Rick will be back in a few minutes." John leaned his cheek against her forehead, unwilling to let her go so easily. "I know there can't be anything between us, that your faith won't allow it. I accept that. But for now, let me be here for you, hold you, protect you."

She said nothing, but neither did she move away. John closed his eyes and breathed in the soft delicate scent of her perfume. *If only*, his heart cried.

"We found it!"

He'd forgotten about the boys. When John opened his eyes, he saw them almost buried in bales. Braydon held a black box aloft.

"Don't touch it!" John called.

"We didn't. I used that bandanna."

"What's Braydon doing here?" Christa asked John.

"He saw you leave in the minivan. Without Braydon, we wouldn't have been able to find you so quickly."

Christa smiled, her eyes glassy with tears. "I owe you, Braydon. Big time."

"Nah." He risked a glance over one shoulder. "But I'm glad you're okay."

Rick's car swerved into the clearing. John gently set Christa away, then stood. "Our ride's here."

"John!"

He responded to the emotion in her voice and returned to her side immediately. "What's wrong?"

She grabbed his hand, holding on so tight his fingers ached. "I've just put it together. I didn't hear all of the conversation, but I did hear one specific part and I'm almost sure—" Her eyes glittered in the shaft of moonlight that illuminated her smooth cheekbones and small bow-shaped lips. She waited until Rick drew near. "Kane Connors was mentioned."

"Are you sure?"

She frowned. "Pretty sure."

"And you think—?"

"That Kane Connors is the one who is to be killed on October 29." She stared at the two men. "Think about it. The Society for Order tried to kidnap him, but that didn't work. So now they'll kill him. That's why they're after you, John. Somewhere, somehow, you must have evidence of their plans."

"I don't even know the man. How could I know about killing him?"

Rick stepped forward. "That's the big question, isn't it? And to answer it, all we have to figure out is who you are, Mr. John Riddle."

CHAPTER EIGHTEEN

I know you're all busy with details for the start of the fund-raiser this evening, but I wanted to update you. We have a lead on Christa's abductor." Heads jerked upward and eyes widened as Rick walked through the dining-hall door, flanked by two other officers.

"The van was located at the airport in the city. No usable finger-prints, but security video shows a man exiting the vehicle, entering the airport, and buying a ticket to Chicago. He paid with a credit card belonging to Mr. Steven Everson. The owner of that card is a Mr. Steven Everson who lives in a nursing home in Washington, D.C. He's eighty-four."

"Stolen. Well, whoever that guy was, at least he's gone." John heaved a sigh of relief.

"We think so. Several of the passengers say they saw a man simi-lar to the one in the video reading a paper in the gate area. A flight attendant remembers him on the flight."

"Thank You, God." Kent slapped Rick on the shoulder. "And thank you. Any other good news?"

"We tracked one call made on the satellite phone—which

Christa thought was a radio—that the boys found in the bales. Again to D.C. Receiver unknown." He studied Christa. "I spoke to an associate about Christa's idea that someone was planning to kill Kane Connors. As far as I can ascertain, he's still under protection and perfectly safe."

Christa's heart went out to the generous cop who'd done everything he could to help them. "Thank you, Rick," she said, trying to remember each word she'd heard that night in exact sequence. "Maybe I was wrong. Maybe I didn't remember quite right."

"I know you did your best. We have to go with that."

"So what now?"

"For the next two days you carry on as you'd planned," Rick told them, his voice firm. "With this man out of the picture, I think you'll be safe, but I'm not taking any chances." He glanced around the room. "I've assigned personal guards for John and Christa. John, this is Peter. Christa, this is Arden. These are men I'd trust with my life. They're going to stick to you like glue, so get used to it." He studied John. "The twenty-ninth is Sunday. You're still certain of that date?"

John nodded. "More certain than ever."

"So if they're coimng after you, they'll do it before then. We're going to play up Christa's mystery theme for this weekend by having guards at the entrance at all times. If someone isn't on our list, he'll be turned away. Your suppliers have come and gone, and the volunteers who are helping have all been checked out, so there shouldn't be anyone on the premises we can't identify. We've staked out a perimeter and are patrolling it."

"Wow!" Christa marveled at the detail Rick had put into his plan.

"I've called in help from two other detachments, arranged for several undercover officers. They should be able to sniff out any problems and stop them from escalating. I think your guests will be fine." Rick's jaw thrust upward. "Insomuch as I can prevent it, nothing is going to happen on my watch."

"Thank you." Kent shook his hand. "I know you went to bat for us with your superiors and I appreciate it."

"Just doing my job. We've set up a twenty-four-hour manned phone line that any one of you can call if you see or hear anything unusual." Rick dredged up a lopsided smile. "We can do this, people, but we have to work together."

They all agreed.

"Okay. Carry on. I've got things to do. I'll be back later."

The somber mood lasted all through breakfast. Christa knew she would never have a better opportunity to tell the whole camp staff of her plans for the future. "Can I have your attention, please?" She ignored Kent's tight lips and Ralna's surprise as she explained the details. "So, if everything runs smoothly, I'll be leaving Camp Hope in a few weeks."

Georgia was the first to respond. "I hate to see you go, Christa. But if this is where you believe God is calling you, I don't see how we can argue with your decision."

"Thank you." Christa hugged Georgia, delighted by her sister-in-law's support. "I know my timing isn't great, but Simple Gifts is willing to give us a start-up loan at very competitive rates if we locate in their Chicago building. Next week I'll be leaving to set things in place. Abby and her sister have some local recruits who are willing to start work assembling our craft kits whenever we say."

"Where will you stay? How will you manage?" John sounded angry.

Once Christa would have chafed at those words, but now she realized he said them not to hold her back but because he cared. It was comforting, but God's will for her did not involve John. That hurt, and she had to pray constantly to die to her own will.

"I'm going to be fine. The company understands my situation. They've located an apartment for me that's designed for someone with disabilities. It's apparently very near their office on Randolph Street. I'll have an assistant so if there are any difficulties, she'll help me." Christa saw her brother's concern, so she covered his hand with hers. "It's my dream, Kent. Something I've worked for and planned but hardly believed could be possible."

"And now it is possible thanks to this Simple Gifts," Kent stated. "It seems too good to be true."

"It's what I want." Christa hoped he'd never know she was doing this for his sake, to atone for the past she'd ruined.

"If it's what you want, then I'm delighted. I have only one stipulation."

"Kent!" she exclaimed.

"I mean it. I'm not letting my only sister wander off into the unknown without making sure everything is all right. I'm going to have Rick check things out and when you're ready to leave, I'll be right beside you."

"I'm hardly venturing out to darkest Africa. I can do this by myself," Christa insisted, but Kent would not be swayed.

Georgia backed him up. "He's going. He won't smother you, and he won't comment on anything to do with your business or he'll answer to me." She lost her pseudo-fierce look. "We only want to make sure you'll be all right, Christa. That you have everything you need. Because we love you."

Kent hunched down in front of Christa. "Call it my one last brotherly duty."

"I'll think about," she promised.

But if things worked out the way she'd planned, Christa intended to leave Camp Hope alone.

＊＊＊

"Welcome to Camp Hope, where nothing is impossible with God. My name is Christa Anderson, and we are going to be seeing a lot of each other as we attempt to solve a mystery." She explained a few rules of the camp.

"This evening is a time to relax, enjoy the facilities, and maybe even check out some of our future dreams for Camp Hope. At eight thirty we'll gather in the chapel. I'll explain how the mystery will work. After that we have a hayride planned. You'll want to be on it because it's there you'll receive your first clues to solving the puzzle."

Murmurs of excitement rippled through the group.

"Just one more thing, folks. The name tags on the table by the door are a necessary part of the weekend. Please put one on and keep it on. If you don't, our secret police will stop you and you'll be forced to explain to them." She raised one eyebrow and smiled. They laughed as if it were a big joke and began to leave.

John walked with her to the kitchen, their guards not ten feet away. "That went well, I think." He'd been quiet all day, as if he were mulling something over.

"It was fine."

She'd pretended she didn't have time to chat, but the truth was she was avoiding John. After her kidnapping she'd sat in her room and let herself remember how it felt to be wrapped in John's embrace, to know that with him her spirit felt whole, alive, confident, free of the chains her chair forced upon her. That's when she finally admitted to that secret part of her spirit that a future together wasn't to be. After much prayer she would accept whatever God had in store for her.

"Agent Deal has arrived, all smiles and affability."

"You don't like him?" Georgia glanced up from the cinnamon-bun dough she was mixing to assess John's meaning.

"I don't know."

Christa knew he was thinking about that date. Two more days, that's all he had. Secretly she worried that October 29 would come and go, leaving John none the wiser about his past or the future.

"What I do know is that I don't want to face any more of his unanswerable questions. At least Kent has a list of chores a mile long to keep me busy. That will help."

Christa's heart pinched with sympathy as she watched John leave. Suddenly she identified with Kent's need to go with her to Chicago. It was hard to care for someone and stand back while they suffered.

Georgia patted her shoulder. "God will do His will, Christa. We have to be faithful and keep trusting."

"I know." Christa huffed out a sigh, then straightened. "I've got a thousand things to do. See you." She waved, then rode down the ramp, her guard, Arden, following silently.

The sound of muffled ringing drew her attention to the flower bed, where sunflowers, cornstalks, and a couple of stuffed scarecrows had taken up residence.

"Beethoven's Fifth?" She grunted, bending over to reach the small black cell phone she could barely make out in the straw. By the time she'd managed to pick it up, the phone was well into the familiar tune.

Christa answered, but before she could say anything, a voice barked out at her. "Two more days. We're counting on you. If you can't get that computer, if D-day isn't going to happen, then it's all been a waste. We put up a lot of money and we don't like waste."

Christa closed the phone, her thoughts whirring. *Two days. October 29—D-day.*

Arden touched her shoulder.

She glanced up to see Agent Deal standing in front of her.

"Hello, miss. This is an awesome job you've done here." Agent Deal tipped back on his heels, peering up at the fairy lights strung through the trees.

"Thank you." Christa discreetly slid the cell phone into her sleeve, though she wasn't sure why.

"You have a very full camp, but I wouldn't worry too much. We've planted agents around the place in case anyone tries anything. Both of you are safe with our boys on-site. The FBI doesn't fool around when it comes to protection."

She didn't like the way he said it, as if to imply that Rick hadn't done his job properly. "We have an edge over the FBI here at Camp Hope," she stated, watching surprise wash across his face.

"Is that so? You've hired some sort of private security then?" Agent Deal glanced over his shoulder at John, who had come up behind him.

Christa smiled. "Oh no, nothing like a security firm. We have protection much more powerful than that." She turned to John. "I need to talk to you for a moment. Is now good?"

"I'll let you two get on with your work then. We'll talk later, John." Agent Deal meandered toward the hut where he would be staying.

"More protection than Rick?" John frowned. "How come I didn't know about it?"

"Oh, you know. I've been telling you all summer." She grinned at him. "I was talking about God."

"Oh. God again." He frowned, glanced around. "Deal said they had men in the area. His cronies must be good at hiding because I haven't seen even one of them lurking in the bushes."

Christa held out the phone. "I found this in the flower bed. It was ringing. When I answered, somebody said there were only two days left. Then he hung up. I've turned off the ringer."

John's guard, Peter, looked it over closely. "I'll let Rick know. He and Angie will be out later."

"We need to find out who owns this phone," Arden said.

"We could lock it in the office," John suggested. "Kent can make an announcement this evening in the chapel that someone has turned in a cell phone. Whoever claims it will be our man."

Christa saw the other men nod. "Okay, John, you and Peter put it in the drawer in Ralna's desk. But leave the lights off in case someone's watching. We'll wait here."

By the time the two had returned, she'd remembered. "There was something else he said. He said to get the computer."

"What computer?" John asked.

"I don't know. He just said, 'Get that computer.'"

"That computer." John shrugged. "Our computer? But it's clean. I'm sure of that." He glanced over his shoulder.

"What's bothering you, John?" Christa asked.

"That couple in the cabin by the pool. Have you noticed them?"

"What are their names?" She pulled her clipboard from the side pocket of her chair.

"O'Shaughnessey. Supposedly a married couple who farm in the South," John replied.

"Well? What's wrong with that?" Christa ran her finger down the list and nodded. "We cleared them. I have the mark here."

"I don't think they're farmers. I don't care how many checks you have, there's something wrong about them. At dinner the guy next to him was talking about haying. Mr. O'Shaughnessey had no clue."

"Arden, you call that number and mention it to Rick. Till he arrives we'll keep our eye on them." Christa stared at the paper. "You know, I kind of remember calling their number. There was something unusual about it. I thought I'd noted it but there's nothing here."

John frowned, then checked his watch. "I've got to go. I promised Georgia I'd fill those big coffeemakers with water for hot chocolate. Are you going to be okay?"

Christa didn't want him to go, but she sure wasn't going to say it. Her intent was to show her independence. This was as good a time as any. "Of course. I've got to get my stuff in the chapel organized for the first clue tonight." She tilted her head toward Arden. "We'll be fine."

"Okay. C'mon, Pete. Back to work." John left.

Christa rode across the compound and through the doors of the chapel. Arden waited at the back as she sorted out her notes and placed the little bundle of scrolls in a basket with the clues. She savored the silence of this special place. So many times she'd come here, running away from whatever God was trying to teach her. Tonight she wasn't running. Tonight she wanted God to speak to her spirit.

Oh, God. She had no words to express what her heart felt, so she let her spirit do the talking while she waited for that steadying peace to reach out and calm her.

I'm here.

Please look after John. He's special. And he's got so many questions. She yearned for his love, and yet God's will was clear. Tears welled and flowed down her cheeks. *I love him so much. But he's not the one, so please take this love away. Don't let me get closer, Lord. Don't let me be swayed by anything but Your will for me.*

"A time to keep and a time to throw away."

It's time for me to throw away those wasted years; is that it? Time to look ahead to whatever You have for me.

Peace washed through her, wiping away past hurts. "I promise to keep You first in my heart," she whispered. "But please don't ask me to throw out my memories of John. Not yet."

By the time Fiona Murdock slipped through the chapel doors and began playing softly on the electric piano, Christa's composure was in place. When the chapel was full, she watched the crowd as Kent made the announcement about the phone.

No one would suspect the O'Shaughnesseys because they never even blinked at her brother's announcement. But someone here owned that phone, and if he got the message he would be looking for a computer.

All she had to do was pay attention and the culprit would show himself.

⟫◆⟪

The picnic table was a perfect vantage point for watching the main compound. Kent shifted in his seat while he sipped the hot chocolate Georgia had left for them. "It's a little different than the kids' camps during the summer, isn't it?"

"Yeah," John said, "you can't tell them to get to bed!"

They smothered their laughter as a pair of senior lovebirds strolled past hand in hand.

"Those two have been married forty-five years, and they still act like newlyweds. Can you imagine it?"

"Reminds me of you and Georgia." John studied the couple. "I think you'll be the same."

"I intend to try. Come on, Peter, the three of us should do one last building check for the night." Kent tossed his cup in the garbage, then led the way, tugging on the doors of the various cabins that housed their supplies. John matched his step to Peter's as he too scanned the grounds for anything unusual.

"I'm sorry I had to stick those two boys in with you, John. I had nowhere else to bunk them, and I need them here early to prepare for the dirt-bike races tomorrow."

"They're fine. Don't worry about me. Concentrate on your sister."

"Is that what you're doing?"

John shifted uncomfortably beneath Kent's assessing gaze. The camp director saw way too much, and John knew his emotions were easily read.

"She cares about you too, if that helps."

"You're not happy about that." John noticed that Peter hung back to allow them some privacy.

"She's a Christian, John; she believes in God. You don't. In my opinion that's not a formula for success." Kent's voice revealed his concern as he plodded forward. "It's not easy for her."

John laid his hand on his friend's arm. "Don't worry. I won't be here much longer. Once this is over, I'm going to ask Rick to let me go. I can't hide forever, and I need to get on with my life."

"You're welcome to stay as long as you like." Kent's green eyes glowed with sincerity. "I've enjoyed having you here."

"Thank you. But I have to go."

Kent scrutinized him. "Want to tell me why?"

"As you pointed out, Christa and I are from two different worlds. I don't understand her faith and I don't want her to compromise, not that she would. It's better if I go." It felt good to say it.

"Is it so hard to share her beliefs?" Kent asked. "Do you think all of this is happenstance? that your showing up is some kind of cosmic mistake? I don't think so."

"What then?"

"God has a plan for each of us. He's got one for you, too, whether you recognize that or not. Do you think educated, handsome men come strolling into Camp Hope every day of the week and have the skills and knowledge to know exactly how to get my sister to deal with her depression?" Kent snorted. "Hardly. We call that God working right here on earth, John Riddle. If you'd open your eyes a little wider and forget about your own plans for a bit, you'd see Him as clearly as Christa does."

"I—"

"She prays for you, you know. We all do. God is here, waiting to help, but you have to let go of the controls, take a risk. You have to believe. That's what faith is all about."

There was nothing more to say so they completed their rounds in silence. John and Peter walked Kent home, then returned through the camp. Even though a protector was nearby, John knew he'd be unable to rest. There were too many unanswered questions.

Inside the RV, his roommates snored. He'd only disturb them with his pacing. Not that there was any room to pace. He stepped outside.

Peter approached. "Are you okay?"

"Yeah. Too crowded in there. I need a quiet place to sit and think."

Guests still milled around, slipping in and out of different cabins as they renewed acquaintances and shared a laugh or two.

"Nobody in there." Peter pointed to the chapel. "Do you want a light?"

"No." John waited at the door while Peter checked the building, feeling the hush of quiet surround him like a blanket. The lock clicked behind him, drawing his attention.

"Here's your quiet place," Peter murmured.

"Thanks. You can wait here if you want. I'll be nearer the front."

Peter nodded, tested the door, and took a seat.

John stepped slowly up the aisle. He lowered himself on a wooden bench, leaned back against the wall, and let the soft night air from the open window above him soothe his fractured nerves.

The chapel was an ordinary building, had no special finish inside its rough interior, and boasted no jeweled altar or golden emblems. The main wall at the front was panel board, and it held up a rough-hewn cross. It had nothing to distinguish it from any other building in the camp.

Deep inside the secret places of his mind scenes he'd witnessed in here from the past summer replayed in slow motion. Teens huddled together, arms around each other as they quietly prayed. Bible studies where hard questions got asked and answered only after a thorough study of Scripture. In this place he'd heard people openly discussing God as if He lived and breathed and walked among them.

God was in this chapel.

For so long John had told himself he couldn't get a handle on God. But maybe he didn't want to. Maybe he was afraid to let go, to put his faith in someone he couldn't see or hear. Maybe he was afraid of surrendering the only part of himself he could remember, the only part he had left.

A pamphlet lay on the floor at his feet. *You must be born again.* Intrigued by the curious phrase on the front of it, he leaned down, picked it up, and scanned past the Bible verses to the words at the bottom. *Birth and death—a beginning and an end. The most important birth in anyone's life is that time when we let go of what we were and become reborn as children of God, people with new values, purposes, and characters.*

Rebirth. New purposes.

John had spent so long trying to recapture his past. But according to this, the past didn't matter. What he'd been or done didn't count.

A flicker of something—hope?—wavered inside him. If the past didn't matter, if he could begin again—

There is only one way to be born again. You have to admit you were wrong. Confess that Jesus, God's only Son, died to atone for what you did and then rose again. Make a change, turn your back on your old ways, begin walking His route, and become reborn into the family of God.

Family. No longer an outsider. The yearning to be part of something bigger than himself had never been stronger. Reborn, a new person, whole, complete. Free.

"Take a risk," Kent had said.

"Show me." John's whisper hung in the air.

The words on the pamphlet seemed brighter, illuminated by the yard light's glow from outside. He tilted the paper. *Admit. Confess. Repent. Surrender.*

It seemed so easy. Suddenly truth dawned: The choice to remain an outsider was his. He could take what was offered now or turn his back on it once and for all.

Take it! his heart urged.

"I admit I've been wrong," he whispered. "I confess I've tried to do things my way and it hasn't worked. So tonight I'm turning my back on the past. Even if I never remember, I want to go on from here living the way You want me to in Your family, Jesus. God, take over my life now. Teach me what to do next." The words spilled out of him like a dam suddenly opened.

The relief he felt was like a cool, refreshing shower after long hours spent working in the hot, dusty bush. But there had to be more. Christa said God talked to people. "Can You talk to me?"

The deafening silence in the room scared him. Maybe he'd waited too long. Maybe he wasn't good enough. Maybe . . .

John shifted, knocking something to the floor. He picked up a small pink book with gold-embossed words—*New Testament and Psalms. Christa Anderson* was scrawled inside the front cover in girlish script.

When he flipped open the book, he noticed that much of it was underlined and dated. Psalms seemed to be her favorite.

"But in my distress I cried out to the Lord; yes, I prayed to my God for help. He heard me from His sanctuary; my cry reached His ears."

This was God's sanctuary. John had prayed to God and asked for help from this place where God lived—wouldn't He hear?

"I need answers." The yawning gap in his soul begged for a response. He'd felt a barrenness inside for a long time but foolishly attributed it to his identity issues. But he knew—he'd always known—that his questions went deeper than merely knowing his own name. "I need the truth, God."

The banner hanging above the table at the front answered him. *"I am the way, the truth, and the life."*

The pamphlet indicated four steps.

Surrender. That meant giving up control, letting Jesus inside, yielding. John understood that. He closed his eyes, trying to open his mind to understand whatever God would teach him. *Surrender.*

His fingers tightened. He heard the rattle of pages and realized he was still clutching Christa's little Bible. He glanced down. *"I will call on the Lord, who is worthy of praise, for He saves me from my enemies."* And further down: *"But in my distress I cried out to the Lord; yes, I prayed to my God for help. He heard me from His sanctuary; my cry reached His ears."*

No going back.

You have to believe.

This was forever, no matter what happened.

"I believe. I trust in You."

Surrender.

John had so little control over his life, but to accept this way of faith he had to surrender even what little he had. He didn't know all the ins and outs of it, but after months of listening to speakers talking to kids in this very building, he recognized that much. One God, one master.

"Okay," he said quietly, staring at the cross at the front of the chapel. "I give up." The breath whooshed out of him as he took the first step. "I surrender everything. I don't know who I am or where I'll go. I don't know anything. But I believe You're here, that You will keep us all safe."

There were no shooting stars, no bang of fireworks. In fact, as he looked around, John saw that nothing in the building had changed.

Except him. For the first time in many weeks, his entire body seemed lighter, less stressed, more relaxed. His problems were God's.

But what about tomorrow? What about the people who wanted to kidnap him? What about the twenty-ninth?

Trust in Me.

Trust. Would that be enough? No, he'd need faith. Lots of it.

He rose and walked with his protector back to the RV. But he could not sleep. Instead he sprawled on his bed, peering through the murky night beyond his window, watching the misty fingers of fog slide over Camp Hope like a cloak giving cover to someone who planned evil.

While he watched, he prayed.

CHAPTER NINETEEN

Good morning, folks. Today will be jam-packed with things to do, starting with our silent auction. You will have until one o'clock to bid on the items our sponsors have generously donated and while you're doing that, you can pick up your next clue." Christa smiled at the assembly. "We'll announce the successful bidders at lunch—that's one thirty. I'll be checking your sheets, so make sure you've filled in the riddles you've already solved. Have a great morning."

She rolled her chair outside into the brilliant sunlight and came face-to-face with the object of her thoughts.

"Good morning, Christa."

"John! I wondered when you'd wake up. Excuse me." She dealt with a question from one of the guests, directed someone to a pay phone, and accepted a donation before turning back to him. "You look tired."

"I feel great. Anything more from Rick?" He plucked the stray hair from her lips and settled it against her head.

She had to force herself not to lean into his touch. "No. He phoned to say they found a packet of matches from a hotel in Chicago among those bales of straw. There's been no sign of anyone going back to look for the satellite phone, so I guess our Steven Everson is gone."

"Nobody noticed anything strange last night?"

"All quiet." Christa shook her head. "You look . . . different."

"I feel different. And a little scared. Anything could happen."

"Don't say that!" She motioned him to a nearby bench, aware that their guards were near enough but not too close. "Sit down and tell me what's wrong."

"I don't need to sit down. Nothing's wrong." John's hands enclosed hers and held them tight. "For the first time in a very long time, everything is exactly right."

"You remembered." She tried to pull away, but he wouldn't let her go. Her heart plunged to her feet. He would go now. Back to a world she couldn't share.

"I didn't remember anything."

"Then what?"

"I couldn't sleep last night for thinking about all the things that didn't make sense, the problems we've had, and that date. I had to get out of the RV so I went to the chapel." His fingers threaded through hers. He bent near enough to whisper in her ear, "I decided to believe, Christa. No matter what happens, I've left it in God's hands."

"You . . . you did?" She couldn't take it in, couldn't absorb what he was saying. "You believe in God?"

John nodded. "In God, in His Son, in His ability to sort this thing out, in His wisdom in bringing me here, that I'm forgiven. All of it. And so much more. I believe." He held out her testament. "Thanks to you, I think I finally see."

"Keep it." She could see it in his eyes, now free of the shadows, wide open and brimming with . . . love? "I can hardly believe this." She wasn't aware that she was crying until the tears dribbled down her chin.

"What's wrong?" John whispered, standing in front of her to shield her from passersby. "I thought it would make you happy."

Christa pulled back and studied him. "You didn't do it for me, did you?" she asked fearfully.

Her pulse slowed when, with no hesitation, he shook his head. "I did it for me. Because I need God in my life, and I want Him to be in charge. I need His forgiveness, His wisdom, and His direction. But most of all because I need His love."

"You have it, John. Forever."

"I know—" he grinned—"isn't it great?"

What now, Lord? Christa had a ton of things to do, but nothing else mattered at the moment. Nothing but John. "Do you want to talk about it?"

"Sure." He motioned to Arden and Peter. "Can you guys give us a few minutes?"

"Like glue, remember?" Arden pointed to the same bench Christa had identified earlier. "How about over there?"

"I guess it'll have to do." John walked with Christa and moved her chair in front of him in the center of a pool of warm sunlight.

"This is as far as we're going," Arden told him, stepping in front of them while Peter moved behind and rested against a tree trunk.

"Nothing like a little privacy." John rolled his eyes, then knelt in front of her. "I care about you, Christa Anderson. Very much. If you want to go to Chicago, I'll go with you. We'll get your company started together."

"You want to go with me? But I thought you didn't trust Simple Gifts."

"I don't. But if you're going, I'm going." He drew her into his arms and held her tightly for one timeless moment before his lips brushed over hers, asking a silent question.

Christa couldn't stop her response. She rose into the kiss like a plant seeking the sun. Warm and pliant, his lips covered hers in a caress she'd only dared dream of. She draped her arms around his neck and floated in the magic of his embrace. His strength enveloped her in a featherlight promise of protection. For the first time she realized that accepting and depending on his strength did not make her weak. It bound them together.

Oh, God, don't send him away. Don't take this from me. You can have the company, my dreams, everything. But let me love John.

You couldn't bargain with God. She knew that. His ways weren't hers and no matter how much she wanted it, Christa had a niggling suspicion that when the weekend was over, nothing would be the same. But for now . . .

"You're the most beautiful woman I've ever met."

Giggling, she brushed a hand over his hair. "I'm one of only a few you can remember, silly."

"Compared to you, everyone else is forgettable." He buried his face in her hair. "Why don't you say anything? Am I hurting you?"

"Yes." Her heart ached abominably. She eased away, but not so far that his arms didn't still enclose her. "No, I'm fine. But it . . . it can't work. You're from your world and you'll go back there. I'm leaving here to begin again. We're going different ways."

Christa traced the line of his lips, memorizing the details and tucking them into a tiny hope chest buried inside her heart. For once she was thankful that Arden was close by, his bulky form almost hiding them from view.

"I don't think our paths are the same." Christa shook her head. "What about Sally?" Watching shock fill his eyes, she knew that he'd forgotten the girl and his ties to her. "You see, it's not going to work. And that hurts me."

"It *is* going to work. Faith, Chris. God didn't bring me this far to dump me. He's in control, not us. We'll have to pray." And to her surprise, right there in the middle of Camp Hope with two men nearby, he closed his eyes and began to speak. "God, this is John Riddle—or whatever my name is." He paused, then began again. "Anyway, I know I'm new at this, and I don't know all the right phrases to use or the right way to ask, but Christa and I have some problems and we need help. I love her, and I think she loves me, but the future is all mixed up. So if You could do something to help us, we'd sure appreciate it."

Christa tilted her head forward until she was leaning against his shoulder. "Amen" was the only thing she could add.

———◦◦◦◦———

He was here, so near yet untouchable, always trailed by someone.

The intruder knew his own presence here was ludicrous, but there was no one else. He'd have to clean this mess up himself.

He had until tomorrow noon. After that—

One day—that's all he had left.

Finesse wasn't an option now. Before the plan was ruined he had to grab the man, find what he needed, and get him out of the way. Permanently.

There were too many people around now. But later, much later . . .

———◦◦◦◦———

"Christa's busy with the silent auction. You and I are going to take another stab at finding something on that CD." John led Peter around the corner to the office and froze.

Agent Hiram Deal had a long sharp knife in his hand, and he was forcing open the office door. His body shielded his activity from anyone wandering past the office who chanced to look his way. He disappeared inside, and momentarily Agent Deal emerged with a cell phone clutched in his hand. He moved over by the trampolines and, with assumed nonchalance, dialed.

An agent of the government breaking into an office to retrieve a phone he had only to ask for? It didn't make sense. John motioned Peter closer, making sure they were still hidden behind one of the fall displays the Eversons had left behind. He caught only the last few words of the conversation.

"Everything's in place? You're sure?" A nod. "I'm out today. Guaranteed." Then the agent hung up and ambled off toward the auction.

"Nothing there that would convict anyone. He's FBI; he could claim a reason for breaking in," Peter said. "I'll report that he took the phone though."

"Okay." John entered the office and motioned toward the desk phone. As Peter called to report what he'd seen, John sank into the big chair in Kent's office. John needed a friend to talk to, but Kent and Fred were tied up with a thousand guest details.

Then John remembered the new friend he'd made. He breathed in, closed his eyes, and began to pray. Pouring out all his fears and worries, he marveled as once more the sense of someone listening filled his soul with ease.

"John?"

He opened his eyes and saw Peter staring at him. "The CD. Right." He moved into the main office and pulled out the damaged silver disk. "I don't think I'll find much I haven't seen before, but I'm not ready to give up yet. I'll give it till lunchtime."

"Then what?"

"I've got a list of chores you can help me with."

Peter looked less than thrilled.

"'Like glue' was the order, I think?" John teased, then hunched over the computer. If his answer was here, he'd find it.

⇒•◆•⇐

John and Peter saddled horses for those who wanted to go on an afternoon trail ride. Later they moved risers into place so the guests could sit in comfort while dirt bikers put on a wonderful show. After that the riders invited people to look over their gear and ask questions. Some guests even tried out the bikes and lived to regret it. Kent gave an informal presentation of his ideas for making the camp more usable year-round for all kinds of groups and found lots of support.

By the time Christa offered another clue, the guests were huddled into groups, sipping coffee and sampling Georgia's baking in the Indian summer sun as they tried to solve the mystery.

"It's been a perfect afternoon, don't you think?" Christa rolled up beside John, her face wreathed in smiles. "I can't believe how God is blessing this. If we can get through tonight smoothly, we're in the home stretch."

"Anybody figure it out yet?"

She grinned. "No. Everybody has solved some, but the clues you hid in plain sight have been the hardest for them to find. They'll have a while to work it out; then they can try the hot tubs, play some games, or rest before dinner. Tonight's the big revelation."

"That reminds me, I promised I'd lug that monstrous roast out of the oven for Georgia. I've got to go."

"I'm going to have a shower before dinner, so I guess I'll see you then." Christa frowned. "You will be careful, right?"

"Trust, Christa. Remember?" John tilted up her chin and brushed a kiss across her lips, then straightened to find several interested gazes resting on them.

"Is that a clue?" someone asked.

"Not for you," he shot back, grinning at Christa, who was holding her hand over her smiling lips. "Kent's still talking to Agent Deal," he muttered to Arden. "Can you tell him we'll be back in ten minutes to help move those risers?"

"Sure."

The rest of the afternoon passed in a blur of activity that kept John and Peter moving at full speed. There were many more details to see to, and he had to admit that Peter had changed his attitude and was more than willing to help. By the time the guests had left the hot tubs and he'd gathered up the sopping towels they'd left behind, John's spirits were flagging. Tomorrow loomed, and he was no closer to knowing why October 29 was so important.

"We smell like horses, dust, and sweat. I'm thinking shower. Christa has to say all that preamble before Georgia even serves the meal," John told Peter.

"Okay."

John stepped inside the RV and collected his things. A small card with his name on it lay on top of the table. He flicked it over. One phrase appeared on the back: *Give it back or you die*.

"Peter? You need to take a look at this."

Peter made a call on his cell phone. "Leave it. Someone will check it out," he said as he matched John's pace to the shower house. "You're doing some interesting things out here. My kids have been here a couple of times, but the wife usually brings them. This is the first time I've seen what goes on for myself."

"I'm not sure this weekend is typical, but Camp Hope is used for a lot of different activities." John stepped into the shower. "Apparently they even have snowmobile camps in the winter."

John thought he heard the agent say, "Uh-huh," but the running water made it difficult to hear. He washed quickly, dressed, and stepped out of the cubicle.

Peter wasn't there.

John checked the rest of the room. Nothing. He stood on the step outside and called, "Peter?"

His shadow was nowhere to be seen, though Peter was big, not easily hidden.

Mist crept across the compound, leaving pockets of mysterious shadows. Fear prickled up his spine at the noise behind him.

"Wasn't it you who wanted justice?"

Then the world went black.

Where was he? Christa checked her watch for the sixth time, her nerves fluttering with apprehension. She motioned Arden near. "Have you seen John?"

The man shook his head.

Christa slipped her cell phone from the chair pocket and dialed the number she'd memorized. "Rick? It's Christa. John's missing. Peter also. I haven't seen either for hours. Kent last saw them around four. I know I'm a pain, but something's wrong. I can feel it."

Reassured that reinforcements were already en route, she surveyed the faces around the dining hall. As far as she could tell, all the guests were present and accounted for.

"You're not eating anything." Georgia slid a piece of black forest cake in front of Christa. "Try this."

"It looks wonderful," Christa said but pushed it away. "Save me some, okay?"

"Still haven't seen him?"

"No, and I'm starting to worry." John would not disappear. Not like this. *Oh, God, please help us now. I love John Riddle. You know that. But more than anything I want him to be safe and happy. Please guard him, protect him.*

Christa whispered to Kent that she needed some fresh air, beckoned to Arden, and had progressed to the bottom of the ramp when a hand on her shoulder impeded her movement. She smothered a shriek as she turned around and stared at John's white face and bleeding head. "You're hurt. Sit down." Tears of relief dripped down her cheeks. "Are you all right?" Christa brushed his cheek with her fingers.

"A little worse for wear." He grinned.

"What happened?" Christa scrabbled for control.

"Happened?" John shook his head and winced. His fingers curved around her shoulders. "I met with the blunt end of an object. The guy attacked Peter too, but Pete got in a couple blows of his own, probably saved my life. He's over there by the showers," he told Arden. "He's been shot."

"I'll call for backup." Arden pulled out his radio and related the events. A moment later two men went rushing across the compound toward the showers. "You got lucky," Arden said to John.

"No luck involved. Had to do with faith." He turned to Christa. "That's what has kept us safe, my dearest Christa. Faith. And Peter. He refused to give up." John smiled, then sobered. "I'll explain later. At the moment I'm a little giddy." He leaned forward, allowed her to wipe away some of the blood. "Are they finished with dinner yet?"

"No. They're eating dessert. I called Rick. He should be here shortly."

"Good. Go back inside. Keep the guests there. Arden and I have to do something. I promise I'll come as soon as I can. Don't let anyone leave till I do. Drag the solution to the mystery out for as long as you can."

Christa studied John closely. "You've remembered," she whispered as understanding flooded her heart.

"All of it. Everything."

"I'm glad," she said softly as her heart cracked in two.

"So am I. I promise I'll explain later. But right now I need a few minutes with Arden. Go. Please do this for me."

She didn't want to leave; she wanted to wrap her arms around his neck and cling for as long as she could. "Of course I'll do as you ask."

He helped her turn around, kissed her one last time, then stood back. "Go."

She went, gliding up over the boards, feeling every thump, every crack as piece after piece of her fantasy world collapsed. She loved him, so she couldn't deny him whatever it took to regain his world.

Even if it cost her her dream.

— ⊰•⊱ —

"We're going to collect your answers to our mystery now," Christa announced. "Please fold the papers in two and pass them to the ends of the tables."

Outside, John waited on the doorstep, watching through a crack in the door as the guests turned in their papers.

"Everything look okay?" Arden asked.

"Perfect." He felt a surge of pride at Christa's performance. No one would guess that anything had changed by looking at her face.

"I would like to thank each of you for attending this event. I trust you've had a good time at Camp Hope. We've tried to make it enjoyable as well as offer you a taste of what our camp does. Our goal was to raise awareness of the possibilities that are here and to encourage more people to use the facilities in as many ways as we can handle. You see, we really believe that here at Camp Hope nothing is impossible with God."

John grinned. A heavenly cue if he ever heard one. Finally the element of surprise would work in his favor. He slipped inside. "Please excuse me."

Every eye turned upon him, gaping at his damaged head. He couldn't help that. Duty came first.

He read Kent's shocked expression and knew he was worried for the guests. He smiled reassuringly and tapped his head.

"Got clunked looking for a clue in the wrong place," he grumbled, using the cover of the guests' laughter to stride to the front and whisper, "I wonder if you'd come with me, Kent. I need a few minutes of your time."

Kent nodded, then bent to murmur something to Christa, who sat with her hands knotted in her lap, face white with strain. John longed to hold her while he explained, but there were other things to deal with first.

He walked down an aisle and stopped in front of a table. "Sir? I'd like you to come with me, please."

"I see you're injured, but I have no knowledge of first aid," Agent Deal responded, eyes scanning the room. "I am—"

"Late. Excuse us." John grasped his arm, hauled him out of his chair, and escorted him out of the room and into the center of the compound lit by the lights of several patrol cars. Once the dining-hall door was closed, the pulled blinds obscured any view the guests might have. John let out his pent-up breath.

Already Arden was frisking Deal. "You're an impostor and a liar. You are not an agent of the FBI, and you are not here to help anyone. Officers, would you arrest this man?"

Angie and Rick stepped out of the shadows.

Peter approached, holding out a gun with a silencer. "I believe you dropped this, Mr. Deal."

John felt a surge of relief that Peter was back on his feet and his color looked good.

Rick's eyes blazed with fury while he handcuffed Agent Deal. Angie took great delight in pulling off his huge glasses and the hairpiece he wore.

"Take out those very green contacts and put some different clothes on him and I believe Agent Deal is someone you've met before, Mr. Riddle."

"Yes, I recognize him now."

"I don't." Kent glanced at the others. "Who is he?"

"His code name is Anonymous. He hired our Steven Everson to do his dirty work." John leaned forward until he was almost nose to nose with Deal. "You came to find what he couldn't, didn't you? I know exactly who you really are and what you intended. You will not carry out your plans."

"You can't stop them," the man sneered. "More will come."

"I don't think so. But if they do, we have the means to stop them." From inside, music began playing, a signal that Christa was keeping things going. *Dear Christa.* John returned his focus to the job ahead.

"Where are his so-called agents?" Kent asked.

"There aren't any."

"I should have killed you when I had the chance," Deal snarled.

"But you needed something first, didn't you? Something you were afraid might come to light even if I was dead. Something that would incriminate you." John held up his laptop. "Something like this?"

Deal tried to break free of his captors, but he could not. "You won't stop it in time. There's nothing you can do."

"That's where you're wrong. This is Camp Hope. Nothing is impossible with God." John watched as Angie and Arden escorted a protesting Deal to a nearby police van. "I think that's it, Rick. I need a few minutes with Christa; then I'll go with you. Would you mind getting her, Kent?"

The camp director peered at him, then slowly shook his head.

"I think you should come in and give our guests a brief overview of what's just happened. I'd prefer it if there wasn't a lot of speculation later. Having waited this long to solve the mystery, your story would add something extra."

John looked to Rick. "What do you think?"

"Sure. No details, just a short explanation for the odd activities.

Remember, we don't have a lot of time to stop this murder you've been worried about."

"Right." John followed Kent inside. There was speculation on the faces of the crowd, and some people even looked afraid. Kent was right. If John left now, gossip about what had happened could well ruin Kent's chances to forge ahead with his plans for the camp. He owed the Andersons a great deal. Maybe part of his story would suffice. Then he would leave. Alone.

"I know we're all anxious to solve the mystery, but John has to leave us and before he goes, he'd like to explain." Kent stepped aside.

"Some of you know me as John Riddle. I was brought to Camp Hope by the RCMP for several reasons, the most important of which is that I'd lost my memory. The people in this place took me in, gave me a place to stay, and became my friends. Camp Hope became my refuge." He paused. "Kent probably thought I'd leave after a few days or weeks, but my time here has stretched long past the point of welcome. Yet I've never felt like anyone wanted me to leave, even when I began to suspect that someone was after me and that those people could cause trouble for the camp." He felt Christa's prayers, knew she was silently supporting him. What a wonderful woman.

"So what happened tonight?" a lady called out.

"Tonight I remembered what brought me to Camp Hope. Actually I'm pretty sure God sent me here, but I didn't know that until yesterday when I accepted His Son into my life. Today He gave me back my memories. I'll share what I can." He stepped backward, grasped Christa's hand, and held it as he assembled his thoughts.

"I'm a computer analyst. I live and work in Chicago." He saw Rick glance at his watch and knew he had to hurry. "By mistake or because God is omnipotent, I received information that would disrupt my country's government. When I realized what I'd stumbled onto, I decided to give it to the authorities, but there were some who didn't want that. They threatened me. When I ran, they followed me. The farther I ran, the more they followed. Eventually I arrived at a small town called Love."

He looked at Christa and returned her smile. "I had a CD with information I knew the FBI would need to stop the evil. I hid it in a van—one that had the words *Camp Hope* written on it. I wrote that name on my arm so I wouldn't forget it, then hid myself until the men left. When I thought it was safe, I left my hiding place. The men found me and beat me. I got away but fell down an embankment and hit my head. I woke up with no memory."

"Only a date," Christa whispered so low no one else but John heard.

"That's the gist of it," he concluded. "Now I've got to go help straighten out the mess. I hope you'll remember my story when you think of Camp Hope. You may never know what God will use this place to accomplish, but rest assured that He is at work here. I hope you'll continue to support Camp Hope and its staff. I thank you for allowing me to be part of it."

They began to clap, John's signal to leave. He turned to Christa. "I need to talk to you privately before I go."

Christa followed him out the door. "There's more to it than that, isn't there?" she queried. "Something that will happen tomorrow if you don't help stop it?" She paused outside the door, as if afraid to go any farther. Her eyes widened. "The item! It was a computer, wasn't it? And you've remembered where it is."

"My laptop." He smiled. "Rick has it in his car. I always said you were quick."

"I remembered that phone call. The voice said they had to find the computer."

John watched her eyes flash as he assembled the pieces for her. "The CD was a backup, something I intended to mail to the authorities if something went wrong or if the computer crashed. But it's the laptop that has the actual e-mails. I retrieved it tonight; then I made some phone calls." He grinned. "You know, nothing really is impossible with God. That big boulder by the camp sign hid my computer perfectly. I figured no one would look there and they didn't. The evidence—everything they'll need to stop the killing of an innocent man—is intact."

She glanced at the police car waiting for him.

He curled his fingers around hers. "I'd called the CIA in Chicago that morning. One of their people helped me escape. When I left my office that day, the CIA put a tail on me, but I lost them when I left Chicago."

She nodded but said nothing.

"I have to leave. There are some things I need to do before it's too late." He crouched down. "But I'm coming back. I will come back."

"Don't make any promises, John." Christa frowned. "Is that your name?"

"Sort of. Jonathan." He held her stare. "But to you I would rather be John. I'm just me. The man who loves you, who promised to be there for you, and who intends to keep his promise."

"I won't hold you to it. You have your life back. You have things to do."

"Hold me to it, Christa." He leaned forward, hugged her close, and brushed his lips against her ear. "Because nothing that has happened tonight alters what I said. I love you. And I'm coming back."

"I won't be here. Simple Gifts, remember?"

"We have to leave now, John." Rick's low voice held insistence.

"I'm coming." He kissed Christa with an intensity that had built inside him for months. "Faith, Chris. Remember? Don't give up on me. I'll be back before Christmas. I'll meet you here at Camp Hope, right outside the chapel. I promise."

She brushed her fingertips against his forehead, his brows, down past his lashes to his nose, and then to his lips as if she were memorizing each detail.

He pressed a kiss into her palm, then closed her fingers around it. "I promise."

"Good-bye, John," she whispered, the faintest catch in her voice.

"Not good-bye. Till Christmas."

Christa smiled, but there was no joy in it. He knew her so well that he could read her thoughts. She had faith in God but not in him.

John turned and walked to the car, spent one last moment staring at her, then climbed inside.

Duty. He'd do his duty because for some reason God had entrusted him with that information. But then . . .

Please help her believe.

CHAPTER TWENTY

The snowflakes began their silent descent before Christa awoke and continued to flutter down during the day. When the last of her school friends departed after a hilarious afternoon of sharing, the camp seemed too quiet, too empty.

Abby and her children would arrive on Christmas Day, sometime after lunch, in time for a sleigh ride Fred had promised. Georgia's friend Doug Henderson said he wouldn't miss that. Later they'd all share the huge turkey Georgia was roasting.

Rick and Angie would stop by too, though probably not together. Angie was leaving the force because she'd decided to join the Canadian Security Intelligence Service. For his work with John, Rick had garnered a promotion to sergeant, but still Christa felt sorry for him. Angie would leave before New Year's and she knew exactly how Rick felt.

John remained silent.

In the kitchen Georgia and Kent finished the last of the supper dishes. Needing an escape, Christa rolled her wheelchair outside and down the boardwalk John had created months ago, barely noticing the velvet-robed spruce trees that stood like guardian angels surrounding the camp.

John wasn't coming back.

For the entire month of November the news carried details of a scurrilous plot to systematically get rid of American state senators who refused to do as they were told. No one had guessed the scope of evil planned or imagined the crisscross of ties that bound the Society for Order to government officials who craved power and had no compunction about kidnapping and killing to get it.

One week ago, Christa's plans for her future had died a silent death when she learned that, indeed, Simple Gifts was a front for illegal activities by Kane Connors, alias Agent Deal. His assets seized, Kane Connors had been indicted as an accessory in the kidnapping of Nicolas Petrov and Evan Julian. Simple Gifts now had nothing to offer.

Apparently neither did Christa.

She entered the chapel and blinked away the tears as the pretty little fir tree Georgia had decorated swam into focus.

He wasn't coming back and she knew it.

"I told you I wanted to be completely Yours," she whispered, staring at the cross on the wall. "I know John wasn't Your will for me. I think I always knew. So please heal the hurt. Help me to know what to do next. Show me Your way."

"Christa, it's time to go." Georgia's voice carried through the silent chapel.

The Christmas Eve service. Kent and Georgia would fuss if she didn't go with them, so she'd pin a smile on her face and go along. She wasn't going to ruin this Christmas. Never again would she let her personal pain control her life or anyone else's.

"Coming."

They sang carols all the way to the small, white-steepled church in the nearby community. The service boasted no fancy choir, no musical bells, and no elaborate costumes. But the age-old story of God's love sent to earth as a baby had never touched Christa's heart more deeply.

LOIS RICHER

"Can you imagine the shock in heaven when God sent His Son to a manger? Can you imagine how the angels must have longed to exchange the rough linen for softest silk, to put gold beneath Him instead of straw, to set Him upon a throne instead of in a manger?"

The pastor's voice continued in a whisper. "But God allowed only a star, something He'd created eons before. He let it rise high in that black night and shine brighter than any celestial being. As its rays brushed earth, love beyond the imagining of any human mind flowed to us. How can we ask for a gift greater than that infinite, overwhelming love? May His enduring love bring you much peace this Christmas."

The bulging church swelled with joy as each wished the other Merry Christmas. Christa stuffed down the ache in her heart for the gift she couldn't have. John was gone. God had made His decision.

"Sweetie, Kent and I would like to give you part of your Christmas gift."

Now? Christa failed to decipher the strange look on Georgia's face so she glanced at her brother, with no more success. "Uh . . . okay."

"You have to go outside."

Christa turned, rode down the aisle and out into the snow. A bright blue van sat by the curb, lights on, motor running. "My van came," she whispered. "But I didn't order blue."

"We did."

"Because it's the color of hope. Remember?" Georgia smiled. "We thought maybe you needed a reminder, so we've added one or two."

"Here." Kent handed her a small black box with a big blue stone pasted right in the center. "Press the hope stone."

When Christa pressed it, a door on the van opened and a little platform surrounded by tiny blue lights began to lower to the ground. *Hope.* Tears obliterated her vision.

"We know you've got plans, places to go, jobs to do. Maybe not with Simple Gifts, but God has something in mind. Something He designed especially for you. We wanted you to remember that. Merry

Christmas, Christa." Georgia enveloped her in a soft cloud of fragrance, then stepped back as Kent took his turn.

Hope, the license plate read. She rolled closer, drawn by the glister of blue stones that shimmered and sparkled from inside. "It's filled with hope. I love it. Thank you."

She got herself onto the ramp and pushed the button. The ramp ascended, carrying her up so she could roll right into the van. The interior was blue, the walls studded with tiny blue stones.

Kent opened the passenger door. "Now you have to get in the driver's seat. I'm not exactly sure—"

"I am." Christa was in place a moment later. "Everything is hand operated, just like the one in rehab. I can drive!"

"Okay, then. Drive," Kent ordered with a grin. "We'll follow you home."

He closed the door, followed Georgia into the almost-new camp van they'd bought, then sat waiting for Christa to take off.

There was a big blue stone on the hand control, another on the radio, and yet another on the visor. Christa had a hunch she'd be days finding those stones so lovingly placed throughout her hope van. John would love this.

It took a few minutes to get the hang of things, but soon she was on the road, purring home toward Camp Hope.

Home.

"For as long as You tell me to stay," she said softly.

The big sign stood waiting at the gate: Camp Hope—Where nothing is impossible with God.

She put on her signal and turned into the lane, intending to park by the house. But a glow of light ahead kept her driving under the snow-crusted canopy of evergreen boughs. Through the froth of flakes dancing their way to earth, a pair of candle lanterns protected by hurricane glass and bearing big blue bows were hanging at the very end of the drive. More of Kent and Georgia's doing? She followed the path of lanterns past the swimming pool and into the clearing until she saw him.

John.

He stood in the snow, wearing a big blue overcoat, his bare head dotted with flakes of snow. She braked, unable to take her eyes off him.

He beckoned and she rolled down the window.

"I hoped you'd come," he called.

That low steady tone sent a thrill of delight straight to her heart, but she warned it not to hope too much. He'd only come to say good-bye—forever. He had Sally now.

"Follow the lights," John said.

A procession of blue-ribboned lanterns led to the doors of the chapel.

Christa flicked off the engine, switched to her chair, and was soon on the boardwalk, riding toward him.

"Hello, Christa," he whispered, his navy eyes glowing darker than she remembered.

She couldn't speak, couldn't ask the questions she wanted to. She could only sit there and soak in his beloved face.

"Nothing to say? That's strange. I was certain you'd have a few well-chosen words for me." When he smiled, her heart did little flip-flops. "It's cold out here. Come on; I want to show you something."

She rode beside him and bumped over the threshold of the chapel. Inside he'd built a campfire with an electric bulb, some colored paper, and a few logs.

"I'm not really good with campfires anymore," John explained. "Guess I'm out of practice."

"That doesn't matter."

"What does matter, Chris?" He looked so serious, his forehead pleated in a frown.

"You," she answered without thinking. "Are you all right?"

"Better than all right. I've got my company back."

"Your company?"

"Simple Gifts. It was originally my grandfather's idea." He pulled up a chair and sat beside her. After a moment he gathered one of her hands into his. "He was a very successful businessman who wanted to give back some of what he'd been given. The idea was for the company to pass to my father and then to me. It didn't happen."

"Why not?" The little pretend fire had a heater in it. Christa could feel warm air brushing her ankles, but she wasn't in the least bit chilly, especially not with her hand in his.

"Kane Connors stole it. After my grandfather became ill, my father took over. He died when I was twelve. My mother had two small children to care for so she hired Kane to run Simple Gifts. Before I was old enough to get involved, he'd managed to get her to sign away all her claims to it."

"I'm sorry."

John nodded. "I was consumed by revenge, Chris. I would have done anything to make Connors pay. I lived to get even. Then I started receiving those e-mails." His face hardened. "I had a wireless system set up so Sally could reach me at any time."

Sally again. Christa veered away from that.

"Strange e-mails started arriving. I thought it was a joke at first; then I realized someone in Connors's group had inadvertently pirated my signal. Kane's operations were more deadly than I'd ever imagined. In the e-mails he implicated himself in some high-profile crimes. I finally had more than enough to get rid of him."

He squeezed his eyes closed, then took a deep breath. "I keep forgetting that you probably don't know some of this. Kane wanted to be a senator and more. In fact, he'd made plans to go as far as the White House. He had his people in place, had already begun to carry out his plans. He would have stopped at nothing, including murder. Edicts were issued to clear the way for his triumphant road to become president. But one very powerful, very determined man stood in his way. October 29 was the day the senator of Illinois was to be killed in a drive-by shooting."

She gaped, shocked by his words.

"Kane had connections with many people. Two agreed to appoint him if the seat ever became available. These people—you'd know them as the council—were partners in his scheme to take over almost the entire United States senate within ten years. All to forward their own agenda."

"It sounds dangerous."

"I didn't realize how much. I made up my mind to make him pay. My thirst for revenge was so great, I was even willing to risk Sally. The e-mails were damaging because they told the whole story, and they nailed him as the ringleader. He had to know where I'd sent them. Once he learned that, Kane intended to have me killed. He fabricated a story about me leaving the country to do some research in Korea. That's why no one reported me missing."

His touch sent shivers to her heart.

"I ran and ended up here at Camp Hope. Sally knew what I'd been working on, and she knew Kane hadn't gotten to me because he kept trying to contact her, so she kept quiet too."

"That's not all of it, is it?" Christa whispered.

"Some things are still being investigated. Law-enforcement people were involved in the plot."

"Oh." Christa could have stared at him forever. "And Agent Deal?"

"Kane Connors. He had a fake ID. Everson was his man and when he didn't get what he was supposed to, Kane couldn't take any chances. He knew I'd lost my memory, so he banked on me not recognizing him. If Rick hadn't given us guards, he would have killed me. Instead he helped me remember when he bashed me on the head."

She remained silent, piecing the events together while her mind dwelt on one subject—John was back.

"Do you remember what I promised you?"

"To return before Christmas. You barely made it."

John burst out laughing. "I'm sorry. I had a few loose ends to tie up." The laughter died away as he met her piercing gaze. "I love you, Christa Anderson. I can say that now without any hesitation. I love you more than life. I believe God brought me here to get me off the treadmill of revenge and onto a new road—with you. Will you marry me?"

Christa was a cripple, chained to a wheelchair for the rest of her life. She didn't know how married life would work for her, whether they could have children, what she would do with her life. She didn't know a lot of things. But she did love this man. And she had put her faith in a God who performed miracles.

She took a deep breath. "I'm a paraplegic. That isn't going to change. Are you sure you want to be married to someone who will never walk?"

"I'm sure I want to marry you." He waited. "Don't you believe me?"

"Well, it's been so long and you come from a different life. We're not at all alike. I don't even have a future anymore."

"We'll build one together. I already know you love God. Do you love me?"

"I'm not sure that's enough." She couldn't watch his face anymore. "I'll be a drag on you. You'll have days when you'll wish you could throw me out the window. Or run away. I'm a dependent. I'll always need help."

"Funny, that's exactly what I was thinking." He lifted her out of the wheelchair and sat down with her in his arms. "There are all kinds of dependency. I'm a dependent too. I'll always need someone to keep pointing me back to God for the answers. I'll get frustrated, consumed by my computer. I need someone to tell me to get over myself, to knock me down a peg, to tell me to get a grip. Someone like you," he whispered.

Christa dared not move as his mouth lowered until it touched hers, but then she couldn't wait any longer. She threw her arms around his neck and kissed him back with every bit of tenderness her heart had saved up.

"I love you, John Riddle or Jonathan Whatever-your-name-is."

"Kendrick—" he grinned—"Jonathan James Kendrick."

She leaned back, shocked by his words. "Kendrick Computers!

A household word. Of course you knew a lot about computers." She felt dazed by it.

"Plain old Jon to you, Christa. A man who loves God and loves you and would like an answer to his question, please."

"What question?" She traced the line of his jaw with one fingernail, bemused that he was finally here with her.

He turned his lips into her hand, drew her close again, and told her how much he cared for her.

When she finally pulled away, he was laughing. "I love kissing you, but you're avoiding my question." He drew a small box out of his pocket and opened it. "I'm going to slide this ring on your finger. Then I'm going to kiss you again. After that, you can tell me your answer." He proceeded to do just that.

But there was no need to verbalize her response. He knew.

Ageless moments later, Christa stared at the magnificent ruby surrounded by glittering diamonds. "Oh, my."

"It's your own private campfire to remind you of our special times," he whispered, his voice the tiniest bit unsure. "You did say you'd never forget. Is it okay?"

"I don't need a reminder of you or our time together. You're buried in my heart. But this ring is beautiful, far more than okay."

They embraced, their promise wordless but heartfelt.

She blushed under his gaze. "Come on, let's go tell Georgia and Kent."

After gently depositing her in her chair, he waited till she was ready to leave. Christa threaded her fingers through his, utterly content. "Where will we live?" she mused aloud.

"My business is in Chicago, but we can come back here often. I'd like that. I want to see those changes Kent intends to make around here."

"Maybe I can find someone there who will back His Creations."

"Darling Christa, I own a very large computer company. I can easily fund His Creations. But you may want to put Abby in charge. I think you're going to be too busy."

"Busy doing what?"

"Our wedding. I've decided I want a lot of those same frills you fixed for Kent and Georgia. Your brother tells me he's been swamped with requests to hold another mystery weekend. You'll want to be involved in that, I'm sure. Seems to me you'll be way too busy to have time for crafts. Besides, Abby and her sister need the work and I want you to save some time for me."

"No problem. I'll pencil you in."

"*Pencil* me in? Cheeky." He kissed the tip of her nose. "I'll have you know, I intend to be a very attentive husband, Christa Anderson. I'll take lots of your time. You'll have to pencil in days and days of me."

"Oh, good." She giggled at his leer. After he'd pulled open the door, she rolled inside, her mind busy. "Fund-raising, huh? I guess I could do it."

"Of course you can. But we'll talk about that later." His face wore a strange look she couldn't decipher. "Chris, I want you to meet someone. This is Sally."

"Finally!" Sally laughed, her sparkling eyes dancing with excitement. "I thought you two would never get here. I'm his sister. Did he tell you that?"

"No. I guess he forgot." Christa saw the pride on Jon's face and realized he had no idea about her jealousy. She was glad.

"You've had a lot to discuss," Sally murmured.

"Yes, we have." Christa looked up at the man she loved. "And some things didn't get answered."

"About me? I've been in hiding. Kane tried to kidnap me and blackmail Jon, but I have friends who protected me. I knew my brother would come back sooner or later." She smiled. "He told me about his memories. You're probably wondering why I'm not in a wheelchair."

"Well, kind of. He kept remembering a little girl in a wheelchair."

"I was in one when our parents brought Simple Gifts to the orphanage in Romania. Even then Kane was causing trouble. He'd sold our medicine, scared our doctors away, and left us with only a few nurses and no heat. No one knew if I'd ever walk again, but the Kendricks adopted me anyway." She looped an arm around Jon's waist. "My big brother took very good care of me. Last year he finally talked me into suing Kane Connors to pay for an operation I needed because of his greediness. It's thanks to Jonathan that I'm able to walk."

Christa stared at brother and sister. "I'm happy you're safe."

Sally picked up Christa's hand and examined the ring. "Do you like it? He took forever choosing this design. Said it had to resemble a campfire." She rolled her eyes. "I love him but sometimes my brother is really weird."

"She already knows that, Sal. But thanks anyway." Jon made a face.

Christa laid one hand over his, felt his fingers curl around hers. "Because of your brother, God turned pain into joy. I think he's a miracle—my miracle," she whispered.

Jon preened. "See, now that's more like it."

"I thought it would take a miracle for him to find someone to make him forget his thirst for revenge. He was impossible." Sally smiled.

Jon gazed at Christa, his grin stretching from ear to ear. She knew exactly what he was thinking.

"Nothing is impossible with God," they chanted in unison.

Absolutely nothing, Christa decided later as Georgia and Kent admired her new ring. Their future was totally in His hands.

Where better?

A NOTE FROM THE AUTHOR

Dear Friends,

Thank you for reading Forgotten Justice. I hope the book reminded you of the power and strength of our great God.

When we feel alone or bereft we must remember that God's wristwatch keeps different time. He doesn't work to our schedule, but He always renders justice to those who trust and believe in Him—His justice, His way. My prayer is that your trials will draw you closer to God so you may learn how trustworthy, how reliable He is. God's timetable is right on schedule. All you have to do is wait.

Blessings,

Lois

ABOUT THE AUTHOR

A former human-resources manager for a national chain, Lois now lives in a small Canadian town with her husband and two sons. After delving into the entrepreneurial realm, Lois settled down to full-time writing. It's a job she loves in an environment most would envy. The perks of working in her home office while the birds chirp outside her window, coffee breaks on the patio, and the chance to chat with fans around the world make this a career she wouldn't trade.

This prolific author of twenty inspirational romances for Steeple Hill has also penned a novella for Barbour. *Forgotten Justice* is the sequel to *Dangerous Sanctuary* and the second book in her romantic suspense series called Camp Hope. Lois enjoys making pottery, singing with a local group, and traveling, but her favorite activity is swimming.

You may contact Lois by writing to her in care of Tyndale House Author Relations, P.O. Box 80, Wheaton, IL 60189; or via her Web site at www.loisricher.uni.cc.

Turn the page
for an exciting preview of book 3
in the Camp Hope series

Shadowed Secrets

Available spring 2005

ISBN 0-8423-6438-2

www.heartquest.com

SHADOWED SECRETS
Prologue

16 years ago

"Betsey wants to give you a hug, Mama." Angie lifted her beloved doll and gently placed it beside her mother in the big saggy bed. "Isn't Betsey pretty?" she whispered, careful to keep her voice very quiet.

"She's lovely, dear." Mama's white fingers touched the wrinkled dress at the back, fiddled with the spun gold hair, then settled the doll beside her on the pillow. "Sweetheart, you know I'm very sick, don't you?"

"Uh-huh."

"Remember when we talked about heaven? How God doesn't let anybody in heaven get sick?"

Angie nodded, her mind drawing pictures of the golden streets Mama had talked about.

"I think God is going to take me to heaven pretty soon, honey."

"You mean you're not going to get better?" A tear slipped from Angie's eye and slithered down her cheek. She dashed it away. Daddy said only babies cried. "You won't be my mommy anymore?"

"I'll always be your mommy, Angie. Always. But I'm too sick to look after you. Daddy's going to do that."

"Daddy gets mad at me."

"It's because of his face. The burns hurt him a lot, sweetie. Sometimes they make him say things he doesn't mean, but I know he loves you. He'll look after you."

"Are you sure, Mama?"

"Very sure. Daddy loves you." Her mother closed her eyes, rested for a few minutes.

Mama was always right. But this time Angie wondered if she was too sick to understand. Angie didn't think Daddy loved her. He yelled at her because she couldn't do things, because she didn't know things.

"You're very busy making a house with your blocks, aren't you, sweetheart?"

"Yes, Mama." A very nice house, a happy house where the daddy wasn't mad and the mommy wasn't sick.

"I know it will be lovely. Would it be all right if Betsey kept me company while you finish building that house?"

Angie thought about it. Betsey was her very favorite doll in the whole world. But Mama wouldn't hurt her. Mama had made Betsey for her birthday.

"Okay. Betsey can sleep with you. But don't let Daddy see her. Daddy doesn't like Betsey. He says playing with dollies is for babies."

"I think a doll like Betsey is for anyone who needs a hug now and then. I'd like a hug from both of you." Mama's hand smoothed over Angie's topsy-turvy curls. "Never forget that I love you, Angie. With all my heart. I've prayed that God will show you how much He loves you too. He'll always love you." Mama's voice got quiet and her eyelids closed. "No matter what," she whispered; then her eyelids drooped and she went to sleep.

"Yes, Mama." Angie tiptoed from the room and went back to her blocks. She ate two apples for supper that night and got ready for bed all by herself. She sat beside Mama for a long time, until the house got cold and dark. But Mama didn't wake up. When it was all dark outside Angie heard her daddy drive into the yard.

"Good night, Mama." She leaned over, kissed the pale white cheek, then lifted Betsey from the bed. "I love you."

Her mother's eyelids fluttered. "I love you too, darling. More than anything."

The whisper came so quiet Angie had to lean near to hear it.

"God loves you, Angie. He'll watch over you. You take care of Betsey, my darling. And love Daddy. Good-bye."

The back door opened.

Angie kissed her mama's soft cheek once more, then scurried down the steps and into her own room. After she tucked Betsey into her hiding place she climbed into bed. She closed her eyes and made herself breathe very slowly when Daddy looked inside. She kept breathing slowly long after he left, until her eyes wouldn't stay open anymore.

There was a noise in the night, a bad sound that scared Angie. After a while, she grabbed Betsey and scrambled up the stairs to talk to Mama. But her father was in that room, arguing with someone. He sounded very angry.

Angie didn't like it when Daddy got angry. She hid in the secret place and stayed there until the house was quiet again. After a long time people went downstairs; there was no more arguing. Angie slipped out of the hiding place and crept to her own bedroom. Snuggled up in the big bed, she pulled the pillow over her ears and asked Mama's God to please help.

But God didn't help because in the morning Daddy told her that Mama was gone and she wasn't ever coming back.

WELCOME TO HEARTQUEST

HEART
QUEST.

Visit

www.heartquest.com

and get the inside scoop.

You'll find first chapters,

newsletters, contests,

author interviews, and more!

Must-Reads!

OVER A MILLION BOOKS SOLD!

WILD HEATHER

Olivia Hewes and Randolph Sherbourne
are drawn toward a forbidden love that will
mean betraying both their families.

DANGEROUS SANCTUARY

Kent Anderson is committed to making
Camp Hope a sanctuary for his campers.
But when Georgia MacGregor joins his
staff, her troubled past threatens to
endanger them all.

Visit **www.heartquest.com** today!